P9-EMH-561

UNRAVELLER

FRANCES HARDINGE

AMULET BOOKS
NEW YORK

PUBLISHER'S NOTE: This is a work of fiction. Names, characters, places, and incidents are either the product of the author's imagination or used fictitiously, and any resemblance to actual persons, living or dead, business establishments, events, or locales is entirely coincidental.

Cataloging-in-Publication Data has been applied for and may be obtained from the Library of Congress.

ISBN 978-1-4197-5931-4

Book design by Deena Fleming

Printed and bound in U.S.A.

10 9 8 7 6 5 4 3 2 1

ABRAMS The Art of Books
195 Broadway, New York, NY 10007
abramsbooks.com

To Ulrike, my not-at-all-wicked stepmother,
whose magic takes the form of photography,
origami, lemon marmalade, and kindness

PROLOGUE

IF YOU MUST TRAVEL TO THE COUNTRY OF RADDITH, THEN BE prepared. Bring a mosquito net for the lowlands and a warm coat for the hills or mountains. If you mean to visit the misty marsh-woods known as the Wilds, you will need stout, waterproof boots. (You will also need wits, courage, and luck, but some things cannot be packed.)

When your ship arrives at the great Mizzleport harbor, remember to trade your gold currency for Raddith's ugly steel coins. Don't be offended when the customs folk peer at you through lenses set in hollow stones, or sweep you with iron-fibered brushes. There are reasons for caution where the land meets the sea.

Ignore the hustlers on the docks who will try to sell you anti-curse amulets. You have of course heard that some people in Raddith are able to curse their enemies. It sounded so picturesque when you were reading about it at home, like a fairy tale. As you listen to the peddlers' blood-curdling warnings, however, you may start to feel nervous. You shouldn't really waste money on a so-called protective amulet, but you probably will.

The hustlers may also try to sell you and the other tourists bundled parchments that they claim are maps of the Wilds. (The Wilds cannot truly be mapped. Buy one anyway, just in case.)

As you walk through Mizzleport, you will soon realize that none of the locals wear anti-curse amulets. Your landlord at the inn will gently mock you for buying one. If you ask him how you *should* protect yourself, however, he will shrug and offer no useful suggestions.

You can't defend yourself from a curse, he will tell you. *But don't worry, cursers are rare! Only those consumed by hatred are able to curse. Just make sure nobody hates you while you're here!*

The other locals at the inn will be happy to answer some of your questions. Do cursers really exist? (Yes.) Can curses really set someone on fire, steal their shadow, or turn them into a swarm of bees? (Yes.) Is it true that the power to curse comes from spiders? (No, the Little Brothers are not spiders, however much they look like them.)

What are the Little Brothers, then? Your new friends will tell you, with a certain affection, of the many-legged creatures that live in the cobweb-laden treetops of the Wilds. They are friends to weavers and craftspeople, apparently. They also seek out those consumed by rage or hatred and gift them with a curse. The curse then nestles in the host's soul like an unhatched egg, growing in power, until the curser is ready to unleash it upon an enemy.

Try not to ask the next questions that burn in your mind. *Shouldn't someone do something about this? Why don't you all exterminate these spider-things to stop people becoming cursers?* If you ask this, you will make everyone around you very uncomfortable. *The Little Brothers cannot be swatted like ordinary spiders*, they will tell you. Besides, attempting to harm them would anger the Wilds.

While you are still reeling from everyone's grim and serious tone, the conversation will move on to another subject. (The Wilds are slippery. It is hard to think of them or talk of them for long.)

You will only consider the matter again at the first stop on the route out of Mizzleport. From the raised road, you will at last have a view down to the famous Wilds, which line the Raddith coast. Prepare to be very, very disappointed.

Admit it—the Wilds were one of the reasons you came to Raddith in the first place. You had read stories of these sprawling, misty marsh-woods, veiled with cobweb and dripping with emerald moss. You had heard of the shape-shifting braags, the dagger-toothed marsh horses, the dancing glimmers that lure you into danger, and the pale-handed ladies who offer secrets if you solve their riddles.

Yet here you are, staring down at a meager band of damp, grayish woodland, only a few miles deep. Is that what all the fuss is about? So narrow and dull-looking! How could it possibly hide ancient ruins, secret castles, or mysterious lakes? How could anyone wander lost in the Wilds for years?

If you are rash enough to venture down among the trees, you will discover your error quickly. The innocent appearance of the Wilds is a lie. The marsh-woods are every bit as strange, vast, and perilous as the stories say.

However, it is much more likely that you will lose interest in visiting the Wilds, now that you have seen them. (You only think that you have seen them.) You will believe the evidence of your eyes and mind, which tell you there is nothing worth seeing here. (They are lying.)

Why is everyone so frightened of the Wilds? It is only natural that you should wonder this. *If that's where these curse-bearing spider-creatures come from, why doesn't everyone just get rid of the marsh-woods, once and for all? Surely it wouldn't be that hard?*

No guidebook will tell you this, but the people of Raddith once tried to do exactly that.

Raddith is ruled by Chancery, a government of master merchants who believe in honest dealing, level-headedness and worth you can measure. A hundred years ago, Chancery looked at the Wilds and saw only wasted land. Great dykes were built to subdivide the marshes so that they could be drained more easily. Trees were hacked down, the reeds harvested, and smoke used to clear the spiders.

Then the Wilds struck back.

Huge clouds of mosquitoes surged inland, bringing diseases with them. Upland rivers flooded for no obvious reason. Little Brothers appeared in the highlands en masse, creating cursers and trammeling the streets with great webs. Other things wandered into Mizzleport and left mayhem behind them.

Eventually, Chancery reached an agreement with the Wilds. Their representatives traveled into the very depths of the marsh-woods, where they talked with . . . something. Or somethings. Perhaps a lyre made of bones and stars, perhaps a Little Brother the size of a dinner plate, perhaps a faceless woman with a voice like the yowls of a hundred cats. Accounts vary, but in every version of the story, the Pact was sealed on a boat made of moonlight and spiderweb.

Ever since that time, the Pact has held, and nobody in Raddith is in a hurry to break it.

Knowing none of this, perhaps you will decide that all the stories of the Wilds and the Raddith cursers were invented to entertain tourists. At night, when you see a many-legged shape scuttle across the ceiling of your bedchamber, you will tell yourself that it is a spider, and only a spider.

(It is not.)

Chapter 1

BLAME

FIVE MINUTES INTO THE CONVERSATION, KELLEN WAS GRINNING so widely his face ached. He could see Nettle trying to catch his eye and very slightly shaking her head. She knew what his grin meant, even if this idiot merchant didn't.

I'm going to lose my temper, Kellen thought. *Any minute now*. The inevitability of it was almost calming.

"I didn't hire you to lecture me!" the merchant was saying. "I hired you to *fix the problem*!"

Kellen stood there in the stupid, overdecorated reception hall, letting the flood of words pour over him. The merchant had glossy, angry, frightened eyes. His hair was dyed, but that just made his pale, haggard face look older. Petty, weak, childish. The sort of man who needed chandeliers the size of dinner tables to feel powerful and who made you stand while he sat and ranted at you so that everyone knew who was in charge.

"Are you listening to me?" demanded the merchant.

Kellen's head snapped up, his mind airy and bright with anger.

"The blood's showing again," Kellen pointed out, a little spitefully.

The merchant immediately curled his hands into defensive fists. His gloves were so padded that they looked like clownish silken paws, but even this had not been enough. The blood always found its way through, mysteriously oozing from his palms and fingers until it could not be hidden.

Kellen wore gloves too, for a different reason. He was used to the weight of the iron bands hidden within the cloth. Right now, he was wondering whether that weight would break someone's nose if he punched them in the face.

"They said you knew how to deal with curses!" snapped the merchant. "But you've done nothing, and it's been two weeks!"

Kellen had taken the job against his better judgment. Or rather, he had allowed his rational judgment to outweigh his better instincts. For once there had been a reasonable prospect of a decent payment. Now, however, reasonableness was losing its appeal.

"That's because I was trying to find out who cursed you, and there were *too many suspects*!" Kellen exploded. He could almost feel his leash snap, his temper bounding forward like a big black dog. The aghast silence all around him made him want to laugh.

Oh well. Boring job anyway.

"All the marsh-silk pickers, the carders and dyers, the folks in your felting mills . . . they work themselves to the bone for you, and you pay them spit!" Kellen's voice echoed off the frescoes and ornamental arches. "And the lodgings you rent to them are stinking hellholes, crammed to the eaves with too many families! What did you *think* would happen? I'm surprised they haven't *all* cursed you!"

"How dare you?" Powerful people never said anything original once you stopped showing them the deference they expected. In a state of outrage, they all used the same script.

"Anyway, I *did* work out who cursed you," said Kellen, "and they're already dead. So you don't need to know who they were."

No, the merchant didn't need to know about the sad little note or the body in the river. The dead woman's family didn't need a ladleful of stigma added to their grief. Kellen would have felt differently about the curser if she'd been alive and still dangerous, but she wasn't, so all he felt was pity.

"Dead?" The merchant looked alarmed. "Is that a problem? Can you still lift the curse?"

"Talking to the curser often helps, but all I need to know is the reason for the curse," Kellen said grimly. "And there's no mystery here, is there? *You're* the reason! It doesn't even matter which of your victims cursed you. Because in this case, the problem is *you*.

"*You* made somebody desperate enough to become a curser. You've got blood on your hands. And thanks to the curse, now everyone can see it."

"You're one of those rabble-rousers!" The merchant was recovering from his shock. "Who do you work for! Who paid you to come here and say all of this to me?"

"You did, you idiot!" exploded Kellen. "You hired me to get rid of your curse, and I'm *telling* you how to do it! What did you expect me to do, give you an ointment? You can't cure a curse; you have to unravel it. You have to find the reasons that wove it and work out how to pull the threads loose. And the only way I can see for you to do that . . . is to be sorry.

"You need to understand what you've been doing all this time, and regret it, and change. So you need to spend a month gathering raw marsh silk in the Wilds, or washing the thorns and grit out of sticky fluff until your fingers bleed, so you understand other people's lives. Then you need to find ways of mending the harm you've done and doing penance for anything that can't be fixed. If you do this for long enough, then maybe—"

"Maybe?" The merchant gave an appalled huff of laughter. "You want me to do all this for a 'maybe'? This is ridiculous!"

Kellen had let himself become earnest again. Yes, this whole conversation was ridiculous.

"Fine," he said. "Do what you like. If you pay someone else enough, I'm sure they'll tell you you're blameless and sell you a curse-proof hat. It won't work, but at least they won't be rude."

"Listen to me, you grubby little charlatan!" The merchant leaned forward. "I want my money back, right now!"

"Not a chance!" yelled Kellen. "I did what I was paid for! I've told you how to lift your curse! It's not my fault if you're too stupid to do it!"

The merchant tightened one hand into a fist. There was a *tick-tick-tick* noise as he did so, and the seam across the knuckles of the glove burst open, white eiderdown bulging out through the gap. As more blood seeped scarlet through the exposed feathers, the merchant gave a whimper of panic and clutched his hand to his chest.

"Fetch me more gloves! A cloth! Something!"

Kellen gave an involuntary snort of mirth, and apparently that was the final straw.

"Guards!" shouted the merchant. "Take this fraud into custody!"

Nettle managed to get arrested by the guards as well, by asking politely. She could probably have walked away in the confusion, but instead here she was in Kellen's cell in the local jail, her unspoken opinions filling half the room. Apparently she didn't even trust him to languish in captivity by himself.

Part of him wished that she would just grab him by the collar and yell, *What's wrong with you? Why couldn't you just tell that rich idiot what he wanted to hear? Or maybe just shut up and let him yell at us?*

"You think we should give him back his money, don't you?" he said accusingly. "Well, I'm not doing that! We earned that money!"

"Actually," said Nettle levelly, "we can't. We don't have enough money. They want you to pay for the glove. The one that split."

"What?" Kellen stopped pacing to stare at her. "But . . . that was his fault! You saw him! He clenched his hand and stretched the seams . . ."

"And they're saying one of the tapestries in that room is frayed around the edges," continued Nettle carefully. "They want you to pay for that too."

"I can't believe they're trying to blame that on me!" Kellen was aghast and furious. "That's . . . criminal! That's fraud!"

He looked to Nettle for agreement but didn't get it. Instead, she looked impassive and raised her eyebrows slightly.

Nettle seemed meek and inoffensive if you didn't know her. Her expression was usually rather blank, in an attentive, slightly worried sort of way. She appeared diluted, colorless, as if she were waiting for somebody else to give her an opinion to hold. After more than a year of traveling with her, however, Kellen had learned to read stillness and listen to silence. He had become very good at hearing the things Nettle didn't say.

You lost control again, she wasn't saying. *I told you needed to rein yourself in. When you unravel, so does everything else.*

Kellen's ability to pull apart the threads of a curse came with a mild but annoying side effect. Woven cloth in his vicinity loosened over time and began to unravel. This phenomenon was particularly noticeable when Kellen lost control of his emotions.

"That wasn't me!" he protested. "I didn't unravel anything!"

"You were very angry," Nettle said in a mild, careful tone that Kellen found infuriating. There was something about her "one-of-us-has-to-be-reasonable" air that made him want to be wildly unreasonable. "You've been in a bad mood all day."

This was true enough. He'd had a night of broken sleep and uneasy, half-remembered dreams, and it had left him feeling sour and strung out.

"So what?" Kellen held up his hands in their iron-studded gloves. "I was wearing these!"

Iron damped his unravelling side effect, so there were strands of it in Kellen's boots, hat, and coat lining. The iron-studded gloves muffling his clever, calloused weaver's hands made the biggest difference.

The merchant had demanded to know the reason for these gloves, so Kellen had told him about the side effect. Now it sounded like the man was using this as an excuse to blame every loose thread and pulled seam on Kellen.

"And even if I hadn't been wearing them, it wouldn't happen that quickly, would it?" Kellen pointed out. "I can't just make somebody's clothes fall apart by being angry with them. More's the pity." The truth is, he had been thinking that it would serve the merchant right if his stupid gloves fell off his stupid bloody hands. Thoughts didn't unpick cloth, however.

"Well, we're going to have trouble proving that, aren't we?" Nettle stared calmly at the opposite wall, refusing to meet Kellen's angry gaze.

Nettle was like a belt that rubbed. Familiar, irritating, every little chafe adding to a thousand others. Comforting, necessary. Unavoidable, every twinge of irritation mixed with guilt and a sense of obligation. She might as well have been family.

Her strangeness was something you noticed only when you paid attention to her, and most people didn't. She always held her face and body too still. All her motions were careful and deliberate, as if she were getting used to steering her body, which was in fact the case. Kellen knew that she was fifteen, but strangers found it difficult to guess her age. There was something young-old about her face, a weathered smoothness that spoke of storms survived. He wondered if she would always have that ageless oddness. A young woman with an old woman's careful gravity, and then an old woman with a quiet, fey blaze like a winter sky.

She had Kellen to thank and blame for that. Nettle was his responsibility, and she never let him forget it.

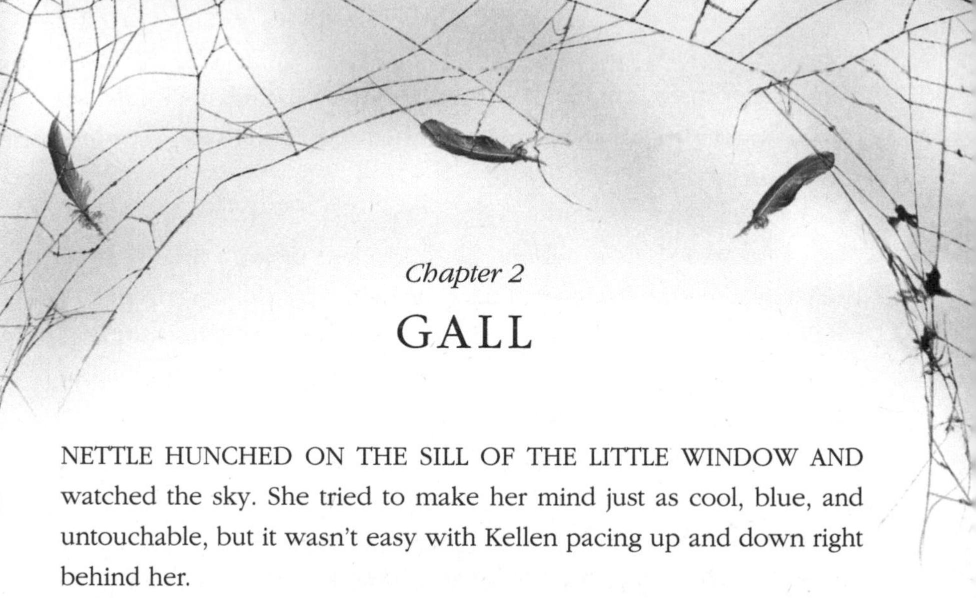

Chapter 2

GALL

NETTLE HUNCHED ON THE SILL OF THE LITTLE WINDOW AND watched the sky. She tried to make her mind just as cool, blue, and untouchable, but it wasn't easy with Kellen pacing up and down right behind her.

"That merchant'll have to get the magistrate to release us, once he's calmed down," he was telling the walls and world for the ninth time. "He still needs me!"

Nettle took a breath and let it cool in her lungs for a second before answering.

"He won't," she said with determined calm. "You humiliated him. He'll convince himself you're a fraud."

"Well . . . he shouldn't!" Kellen glared at Nettle, as if making her back down would somehow change the situation. "All I did was tell him the truth!" He was always like this, raging at the world for not being as it should. His furious innocence was exhausting. Kellen started pacing again, and she knew he was hating her for being right.

The sky was wide and flawless. When Nettle was little, it had just been the roof of her world, a place to store the sun and stars. Since then, she had come to understand the texture of that wild, blue air. She knew its chill strength, its living tremors, the sweet and treacherous way it bore one's weight. Nettle watched the birds and felt her soul reach out, like an amputee wanting to stretch a lost but remembered limb.

I hate being heavy. I hate being here. I hate being right.

As usual, she *was* right. The merchant didn't arrange their release. It was somebody else who came to rescue Kellen and Nettle just a few hours later.

The visitor was six foot tall but, as he ducked through the doorway and straightened, he seemed taller. His dark gray riding coat looked well-made. He could not have been more than thirty, but his complexion was grayish too. There was something quietly forbidding about him, as if a stone lion had found a way to look human.

Nettle felt a tingle in her teeth. This man had a touch of the Wilds, she could sense it—a familiar pang, like the worst kind of homecoming. Then he glanced her way, and she saw that his left eye was covered by an eye-patch of dark red leather. It looked expensive and showy, which only ever meant one thing.

Marsh horseman.

He stood and watched them in silence for a little while. He seemed to be waiting, as if they had asked to see him, not the other way around.

"What?" demanded Kellen at last, getting impatient. Fortunately, the visitor showed no sign of being offended.

"Do you want to get out of here?" he asked. His accent was a lot less refined than his clothes. Mizzleport dockyards, Nettle reckoned.

Kellen opened his mouth, and Nettle cut in quickly before he could say anything sarcastic.

"Yes," she said. "We do."

"Good," said the stranger. There was another pause. Either he was trying to make them nervous, or he didn't consider talking a particularly valuable skill.

"The merchant's had a change of heart then, has he?" asked Kellen, casting a triumphant glance at Nettle.

"Not yet," said the stranger. "But he'll listen if money talks. My name is Gall, and I've been sent to make you an offer."

"Sent by who?" demanded Kellen. Nettle was pretty curious herself. Anybody who could hire a marsh horseman was probably very rich.

Marsh horses were creatures of the Deep Wilds. They could not be bred, trapped, or tamed by humans. It was said that they could be acquired only by trading with the people from the White Boats, at one of the Moonlit Markets held where the Wilds met the sea. The price for such a horse was usually a single, living human eye, of clear vision and beautiful color, willingly given by its owner. Since rich people didn't like giving up their own eye, they would generally pay a fortune to someone poor or desperate enough to surrender one of theirs.

Such an arrangement had consequences, however. The rich buyer might fancy that they owned the marsh horse, but the horse itself always knew whose eye had bought its loyalty. Most marsh-horse owners were philosophical about this unbreakable bond and hired the one-eyed unfortunate to control the horse. Such coachmen or coach-women were generally treated with respect by anyone who knew what was good for them.

"There are questions I won't answer," said the stranger simply. "That's one of them. If that's a problem, I can save us all some time and leave now."

"You can't expect us to—"

"Kellen!" hissed Nettle.

Kellen sighed angrily, then shrugged. After a pause, Gall continued.

"You have a rare talent, boy. Unique, probably. There are plenty of people claiming they can undo curses for money, but they're all liars. You really can. So you should be rich by now. But you're not. You're running from one town to the next on hope and an empty belly."

Nettle exchanged glances with Kellen. The stranger was evidently well-informed. Raddith had no end of con men preying on the desperate by claiming they could cure curses. It had always been hard for a scruffy fifteen-year-old like Kellen to convince people that he wasn't just another charlatan. His attitude also made him a lot of enemies. Word of Kellen's successes were starting to spread at last, but there were also plenty who would swear violently at the mention of his name.

"You need protection," the stranger continued, "and somebody to vouch for you. Someone who can get you rich clients and make people think twice about locking you up."

"A patron, then?" Kellen was clearly annoyed, but he was too honest to deny the truth of the stranger's words. "A mysterious, anonymous patron?"

"If you want to put it that way," said Gall. "We'd tell you which curses to unravel, and we'd see that you were well paid for it. You'd be fed and given somewhere to sleep each night. And trust me, nobody will ignore or underestimate you if you turn up in a carriage with a marsh horse between the shafts."

"*You'd* be coming with us, then," Nettle said sharply. A tame marsh horse never went anywhere without its horseman, and vice versa.

"You'd accept my protection and guidance," Gall said blandly.

"Guidance?" Kellen made it sound like a dirty word, and Nettle didn't blame him. "You mean *orders*."

"Advice," said Gall. "And supervision."

"We don't need to be put on a leash!" snapped Kellen.

"Not everyone would agree," said Gall, and let the silence stretch.

Nettle knew how silences were used, and she had no trouble filling this one. *You make people jumpy, with your strange talent, and the way you pick apart the knots of everyone's secrets. You can't and won't rein in your temper. You cause trouble.*

"Why bother with us at all, then?" asked Nettle. Gall looked at her, and the experience was a little like facing into a damp wind. His one eye was dark gray, like his coat, and almost as lightless.

"My employer needs someone who can unravel curses," he said. "And there's a matter that needs investigating. I think you'll want to hear about it, actually."

"What do you mean?" demanded Kellen.

"You two have put a dozen cursers behind bars, haven't you?" said Gall.

"Sixteen," Kellen corrected him. Unravelling curses nearly always meant identifying the cursers, who were then handed over to the authorities for arrest.

"Do you know what happens to them after that?" asked Gall.

"They get sent to the Red Hospital." Kellen fidgeted uneasily.

"And after that?" pressed Gall. "Do you ever keep track of them? Do you ever visit them in the Hospital?"

"No!" Kellen said sharply, looking unhappy. "I'm the last person they want to see!"

Nettle couldn't blame Kellen for wanting to avoid angry cursers who hated him, but it was also typical of him. He always wanted to put upsetting things behind him so that he could forget about them.

Gall nodded quietly to himself, seeming unsurprised, then reached into his pocket. He drew out a creased and grimy slip of paper and passed it to Kellen. Nettle leaned across to read it over Kellen's shoulder.

A good choice. She has every reason to want revenge against the young unraveller of curses. After all, he's the one who put her behind bars.

There was no signature.

"Where did this come from?" demanded Kellen. "Who wrote it? Who's this 'she' they're talking about?"

"We don't know," said Gall. "The note was found among the belongings of a dead criminal, and we haven't identified the handwriting. But we believe the 'unraveller' they mention is you."

Of course it is, thought Nettle, her blood running cold. "Unravelling" was the way Kellen always talked about his curse-lifting. It was the way he saw things, as a tangle of threads to be pulled apart.

"So what does this mean?" she asked. "Are you saying some criminals are trying to get a curser to take revenge on Kellen? How can she do that if she's a prisoner in the Red Hospital?"

"A good question." The thing that happened to Gall's face was probably a smile. "As far as we can tell, the prisoners there are all secure. They shouldn't have any means of affecting the outside world or harming anyone. But my employer thinks we're missing something. You two have an instinct for cursers, and a knack for prying out secrets. She wants you to take a look round the Red Hospital, to see if everything's as secure as it should be."

"What if we don't take up your offer?" asked Kellen. "What if we say no?"

"I leave," Gall said immediately.

No threats. No dwelling on the desperation of their position. Kellen glanced at Nettle again.

"Let me talk about it with my friend," he said.

After Gall had left the room, Kellen dropped to a crouch with his back to the wall, frowning.

"For all we know, he might have written that note himself," he muttered, clearly rattled. "What do you make of him?"

Cold and weird, thought Nettle, but there was no point in stating the obvious. Pacting with a marsh horse changed you, and never by making you more pink and cheery.

"He doesn't care whether we agree," she said instead. "If we say no, he won't haggle. He'll just go."

"Well, *that's* obvious," said Kellen. "But maybe we should say no anyway."

Nettle said nothing.

"Oh, and you disagree?" asked Kellen.

"I'm not telling you what I think!" said Nettle. "You'll just do the opposite!"

"Then what's the point of even talking to you?" Kellen frowned down at his fists and sighed. "So he's offering us a way out, and we need one. I know that, all right? Is that what you want me to say?"

"No," said Nettle, very quietly.

"What?"

"I don't like him. I don't like this. Any of it."

"But you're the one who wanted to listen to him!" exclaimed Kellen.

Nettle hesitated, trying to find words for her unease. *It smacks of the fen-weed*, her mother would have said. And it *was* like a scent, like the lush, creeping fragrance of salt and sweet rot that told you that you'd taken the wrong turn, that the hungry, unseen bog was just one unwary step away . . .

"It's . . ." She tried again. "The deal looks too tempting. The price looks too *low*. Which means it must be too high—we just don't know it yet."

"So how else do we get out of here? And what about that note?"

Just as Nettle had predicted, Kellen was pivoting to disagree with her. She could see him doing it, even if he couldn't. He was unbelievable.

"If we've got a secret enemy, I want to know," Kellen declared, as if that had always been his argument. "Don't you? And if something crooked is going on at the Red Hospital, shouldn't we find out? If we make a deal with Gall and it goes sour, we can always run away later, can't we?"

Nettle turned away from him, pulling back her temper like a snail withdrawing its horns. She returned her gaze to the sky and tried to let its calm blue pour into her head.

"Do what you like," she told him coolly.

So of course he did.

The black carriage stood outside the town jail, blocking half the street, and nobody objected. Pedestrians kept their distance from the sleek black horse harnessed to it.

The animal was a little too large, a little too beautiful, and glossy as polished leather. It didn't fidget the way other horses did, and its ears didn't flick nervously as Nettle and Kellen approached. The huffs of its breath stirred little clouds of steam before its muzzle, despite the warmth of the day.

It didn't smell like a horse either. It smelled of rain.

Gall went up to it and stroked its mane slowly, gently, and with total concentration. It wasn't like a man calming a beast. Nettle thought of lovers greeting each other, or battle comrades silently clasping hands.

He glanced back at her, and gave a jerk of his head to invite her into the carriage. She climbed up onto one of the seats and set the little bundle of her worldly possessions down beside her.

"Your friend's just being lectured by the magistrate," said Gall, in answer to Nettle's questioning look. "He won't be long."

That's what you think. Nettle suspected the shouting match would probably last for a little while.

"You'll need new clothes if you're traveling with us," she said instead. "Your coat's felted wool, so it's all right. But the cotton shirt . . ." She shook her head. "No trim either. And you'll need buckles and buttons, not laces."

Everything she and Kellen wore was felt, leather, or clotted marsh silk. Woven fabric fell apart around Kellen, not quickly but relentlessly.

"So you're Nettle," Gall said after a pause. "I thought you'd be . . . skinnier. Pointier."

"With a six-inch nose and knees that bend backward?" suggested Nettle. Everyone expected something like that. "Sorry to disappoint you."

"There were four of you, weren't there?" asked the horseman.

"Yes," said Nettle curtly, and added nothing more. If Gall liked the silence game so much, she could play it too.

There had indeed been four of them. Two brothers and two sisters. Cole, Yannick, Iris, and Nettle.

Nettle had been closest to her elder sister, Iris. Sometimes kind, sometimes impatient, Iris had always known Nettle would follow her lead. They formed a united front in quarrels, when Cole was a bossy know-it-all or when Yannick tried to dodge his share of the chores.

Their mother had not been good-natured or fair as the dawn, but after her death she had gained the sweetness of distance, like a blue and hazy hill. Now when Nettle remembered her mother, it was as a warm heart of a peaceful time that she had learned to cherish only after it was over.

It had not been so bad back then, she supposed. Even though she and her family had been living within the marsh-woods of the Wilds.

Their village was in the so-called Shallow Wilds, which were areas of truce. Humankind was allowed to build there . . . and other things could come and go if they chose. Usually they didn't.

It hadn't seemed dangerous back then, just rather dull. Nettle's parents had enough money to own a real house of brick on one of the rocky outcrops, not a wooden stilt-house. There had been a little grove of honey-pears, and a blue boat tethered by the rill. There had been too many siblings, all of them larger and more argumentative than Nettle, and too little to do—no market fairs, no news, no buzzing streets, no surprises.

Then it had all ended. Their mother had perished of a fever and taken their childhood with her.

Another woman had married her father, and Nettle still couldn't think about her clearly. Her own anger and fear frightened her. It blinded her mind, like looking into the sun.

Even though Nettle had only been nine years old, she had started to realize that she was hated. Her stepmother hated her, hated all four of her stepchildren. Nettle didn't know why, nor did she ever find out. Perhaps there never was a reason, except that sometimes these things happened, particularly in the Wilds. Sometimes hate was a wild thing. You might as well expect a wolf to be fair or reasonable.

For two years, they had all lived with her stepmother's warm smiles and hatred. Nobody guessed at the curse growing inside the woman until it was far too late.

One fine morning, the woman had taken all four children out on the boat. And in the middle of a velvet-green marsh lake, jeweled with dragonflies, she had released the curse inside her.

It wasn't pain Nettle had felt as her bones changed inside her. She didn't think it was pain, but now that word had so many meanings in her head she couldn't be sure. It wasn't quite death that she experienced as her mind clenched like a fist and her personality hissed out of its grip like grains of sand between tight fingers.

She didn't remember seeing the others' transformation, though her dreams had painted it since. Iris sprouting dove-white down, Cole's face hardening into a hawk-beak, Yannick's cries of pain becoming a gull-shriek. But she knew what had happened to Iris almost as soon as they changed. Even her heron-mind, cold and narrow as a flint, had remembered that. The bloodied white shape in the undergrowth that fluttered and twitched as an eager hawk-beak tore it apart.

The three years that followed were endless and fleeting as a dream, a relentless, perpetual now where time had no meaning.

Food. Flight. Fear. Coiled-spring instincts spurred her mindlessly, puppeted her body, governed her world.

The only thing that pierced her heron-trance was Yannick.

Sometimes she would look up, and her black, watchful eyes would see another bird soaring high above, and she would *know* him. Some grains of herself would return to her grip. She had lost something, hadn't she? And that gull above her was . . . was . . .

Nettle could still recall the torture of remembering all over again that she wasn't really a bird. *This isn't right. This isn't real. Why can't I think? Why can't I remember? I used to be able to use my brain, and now I can't.*

Then, for a moment, she would know who she was and what had happened to her. She would cling to that knowledge, but it was like trying to keep thoughts straight during a maddening fever. She was dragged away from herself, whirled around, lost. Again and again.

She never saw her hawk-brother or thought about her dove-sister. But her gull always came back to her, and every time he did, Nettle recovered a little of herself for a little time. Just enough.

And then, one day, she was cured.

It *was* pain, recovering her human limbs on that gray day by the green marsh lake. She had fallen over there into the mud, naked and shuddering. She could hear someone near her screaming and screaming. An older boy with wide eyes, clawing at his own face. It was Cole, the long-forgotten Cole. Human again, and realizing at last what his hawk-claws had done to his dove-sister.

High up in the sky she could see a familiar gull circling. *Yannick.* She knew his name now. She reached up a hand toward him wordlessly, begging him not to leave her, entreating him to join her in her new, painfully alert world.

No. She heard his answer as clearly as a voice in her head. The gull tipped on the wind and skimmed away out of sight.

Minutes passed before she noticed another boy standing on the bank, watching Nettle and Cole in flabbergasted horror. He wore thick gloves with metal studs and held four lockets and a ball of twine in his hands.

"What's wrong with him?" He stared at Cole's curled, shrieking form. "Where are the others? There's supposed to be four of you!"

Nettle sat in Gall's carriage waiting for Kellen. Waiting for her savior, and trying as usual to be grateful for her lot.

This is real. This is me, this lumpy body taller than the one I remember from four years ago. This unfamiliar, half-woman thing that bleeds once a month. This face with expressions I've forgotten how to use. Why doesn't this body feel like home? Why is it so exhausting, hobbling along the ground on these soft feet? Why is it a strain being around people and pretending to be one of them?

I used to be able to fly. And now I can't.

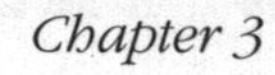

Chapter 3

THE HOSPITAL

IT HAD BEEN A TOUGH WEEK AND A BAD DAY. AND YET, KELLEN admitted to himself, there was a certain satisfaction to riding out of town like a king. People stared at the marsh horse, yanking each other's sleeves and pointing . . . then boggled outright when they saw a familiar, scruffy, adolescent troublemaker waving back at them from the expensive coach.

Maybe Nettle was right. Maybe they were heading to a new captivity. But at least they were doing so in style.

On the outside, the coach was painted a gleaming black, but inside, it was varnished a deep coffee color, with olive-green padded seats and curtains at the windows. It took the potholes of the road with a soft bounce, instead of jarring your bones the way the farmers' wagons did.

And the speed! The marsh horse drank up the miles like water, even on the steep ascents. It overtook wagon and gig, carriage and lone rider, the brightly painted milestones and boundary markers racing past.

Nettle sat huddled on the rear-facing seat, wrapped in one of the warm, soft blankets as if she were cold. She showed interest only when Kellen opened the wicker hamper on the floor, pulled out a rugged, little loaf, and bit into it. The seeds dug into his gums, and the dry crustiness took the moisture from his tongue. It was glorious.

"You wouldn't like it," he said cheerfully but indistinctly. "It's probably poisoned."

Nettle plunged a hand into the hamper and snatched a loaf of her own, then munched it with heartfelt dedication. The hamper also turned out to contain four apples, some rough barley biscuits, and a little round of goat's cheese wrapped in dark purple leaves.

"Well," he said, "at least we know our mysterious patron's got good taste in cheese."

"And we know she's a woman," Nettle said quietly.

"Yeah." Kellen had noticed Gall's use of the word "she" as well. "And she's rich."

"Do you think she's in Chancery?" Nettle asked.

"Maybe," said Kellen.

Raddith wasn't governed by a monarch, nobles, or a parliament like neighboring nations. Instead, it was run by Chancery, a huge, sprawling league of merchants and officials.

The first Chancery had been set up centuries before by the merchants of a market town near the Wilds. Their aim had been to make sure locals could trade without fear. People needed to know that they were buying a horse that wouldn't turn into a bale of hay, apples that wouldn't send them to sleep for a hundred years, and furniture that wouldn't gallop back to its previous owner.

So Chancery had minted steel coins that wouldn't turn to dead leaves with the dawn. They oversaw sales and drew up contracts without treacherous loopholes. They gave inscribed iron necklaces to traders and peddlers who could be trusted. As Chancery took over the town, it became safe and prosperous. Other towns set up their own Chanceries, and eventually these had all joined forces to become a single Chancery governing Raddith.

"She must have influence if she can get us into the Red Hospital without notice," Kellen said thoughtfully. "I doubt most people could just show up and walk in."

"Most people wouldn't want to," murmured Nettle. She was looking paler than usual.

Kellen could have kicked himself. Why hadn't he wondered how Nettle would feel about visiting the Red Hospital? It was full of cursers, exactly the people she had most reason to regard as her enemies.

"You don't have to come in," he said quickly.

"It's all right," she said, without looking at him. Kellen felt a twinge of gratitude. Although he didn't want to admit it, he wasn't looking forward to visiting the Hospital either.

The Red Hospital had been built in a dip between two ridges, because nobody wanted to see it from any of the main roads. Aside from an old turnpike and a scattering of gray stone cottages where the staff lived, there was nothing else for miles but green hillside.

Although Kellen had never seen the Hospital before, he knew it as soon as it swung into view. The straight-backed, many-gabled building was the vivid, dirty red of a congealing wound. Apparently it had been black once, but the outer layer of its iron cladding had been rusted by twenty years of brisk highland rain. It had even bled a reddish stain down the hill.

As the coach descended the winding lane toward it, Kellen felt something tighten around his ribs. He didn't usually mind iron. In fact, his gloves comforted him. Without them, he could feel the tickle of something in his mind waving loose like long hair in a breeze. The iron in his gloves damped and tamed it, whatever it was. However, approaching this much iron was *too much* damping and taming. It felt heavy.

By the time Gall pulled up the coach in front of the building, Kellen's mouth was dry. Some orderlies came out, and Gall climbed down from the carriage and gave them a letter. Kellen could just make out a wax seal in one corner. The orderlies immediately became flustered and very polite, and one ran off back inside.

After a few minutes, a tall, brisk man with blond-gray floppy hair emerged from the building. He looked tired but bounced out to meet them with determined enthusiasm, as if he had never quite worn out his boyhood mannerisms and had decided to keep them.

"Mr. Gall?" He managed a harassed smile. "I'm Dr. Lethenbark. I understand you want to inspect the Hospital and our security measures?"

He looked a little surprised when Kellen and Nettle got out of the carriage as well but accepted Gall's explanation that they were his assistants. Noticing Kellen's apprehensive expression, the doctor gave him a reassuring smile.

"Don't worry!" he said. "It's quite safe in the Hospital. Nobody can cast a curse in this building."

"I know," said Kellen. "But . . . there are some people here who *really* won't be happy to see me." He was starting to feel sick.

"They won't see you at all," said the doctor. "Come with me."

A neat black door with seven locks opened onto a narrow corridor with walls covered in dense, black cloth and a string of little lamps set in the ceiling. At intervals along the walls were a series of palm-sized wooden shutters, about five feet off the ground.

"The walls are soundproofed," murmured the doctor. "If we talk quietly, it won't disturb anybody." He opened one of the little shutters and beckoned Gall over. "It's safe to look. They won't see us."

Kellen opened another little shutter, to reveal a little eyepiece like that of a telescope. When he pressed his eye to it, he found himself looking onto a small, sunlit courtyard.

He could see more than a dozen of the inmates. Some sat reading next to the central fountain. Others strolled along the white gravel paths or chatted in the shadow of ornate steel trees. None of them moved at more than a shuffle, weighed down by the metal plates sewn into their clothes and the chainless metal shackles around their wrists and ankles.

"They're all loose together! And they're outside!" Kellen pulled back from the eyepiece. He hadn't wanted to see miserable captives chained to stakes, but this sight terrified him in a different way. "Couldn't they all escape?"

"The compound's more secure than it looks," answered the doctor. "Besides, those are our 'voluntaries.' None of them *want* to escape. They all asked to be confined here because they're afraid of endangering others."

"They came here of their own free will?" Kellen stared at the inmates again.

"Yes," said the doctor. "It happens now and then. When the symptoms start, and they realize they have a curse egg growing inside them, a few of them decide to resist it. They come to us, and we help them fight it."

A curse as yet uncast was often spoken of as a "curse egg." It was not really an egg, or even a solid thing, but it was something waiting to break open and unleash a curse into the world.

"Does it work?" asked Nettle. "Does the curse egg ever go away?"

She was peering through the shutters, her face tranquil but oddly static. Sometimes she was hard to read. Was she picturing how things might have gone if her stepmother had lived long enough to be arrested? Could she imagine looking through one of these peepholes at the shackled form of the woman who cursed her?

"We're not miracle-workers," the doctor said sadly. "But we can save them from releasing something terrible into the world and having to live with that for the rest of their lives."

"So they stay here forever," said Nettle flatly. "Reading books. What about the curse-egg carriers who didn't hand themselves in? The ones who got spotted and arrested?"

"We're a lot more careful with those," said the doctor, and beckoned them farther down the corridor.

Here the peepholes looked in on smaller cells, where solitary individuals trudged or slumped. The floors were mosaic and the walls were covered in murals, as if the powers that be had tried to soften their bleakness. These inmates wore heavier manacles and iron helms locked into place.

One girl was sobbing in her cell.

"I haven't done anything!" she wailed quietly. "I haven't, I haven't!"

Kellen always felt uncomfortable about the imprisonment of people before they'd actually cursed. But there were telltale signs of a potential curser, if you knew what to look for, so they *could* be identified. Some showed flashes of uncontainable rage or saw things other people couldn't. No, it wasn't fair to lock up an innocent person, but what else could you do? It would be like saying you couldn't take an arrow from a drawn bow because it hadn't hurt anyone yet.

The girl glared up at the door, her face twisting with hatred. For a moment he could almost smell the marsh breeze of the Wilds and sense the misshapen emotions inside her, howling for release. Then she looked away and was just a sobbing girl again. Kellen quietly closed the shutter. No wonder people had found her out.

"Can we move on?" he said, more abruptly than he intended. "We need to see the inmates who were arrested *after* they cursed." Heart banging, he handed the doctor a list with sixteen names on it. "Particularly these ones."

The rest of the Hospital was dedicated to the convicted cursers, those who had cast at least one curse and been caught.

"The people on my list—they're all still here?" asked Kellen.

"Oh, yes." The doctor sounded surprised. "Where else would they be?"

"Inmates get discharged sometimes, don't they?" asked Nettle. "If they've served their time, and they're not a threat?"

"It doesn't happen often," said Dr. Lethenbark. "The hard part is making sure that they're *not* a threat. You know how it is. Once someone has cursed, there's a good chance they'll curse again. Channeling that much hatred, that much power . . . it changes the soul permanently. They're likely to become host to a second curse, then a third, a fourth, and so on."

"But they can't if they're here, right?" Kellen thought of all the cursers he'd helped catch, a montage of faces twisted with hatred.

"No, no," the doctor assured him. "The Little Brothers won't visit anyone here because of all the iron. But that means it's hard to be sure whether our patients would curse again if they left the Hospital. Occasionally, if a patient has seemed tranquil at least five years, we risk sending them to another prison for a trial period, to see if they show symptoms of gaining another curse egg. If they still haven't after a year, they're discharged. But nobody on your list has been here long enough for us to risk sending them away like that."

"How many fail that test?" asked Kellen. "How many become cursers again?"

"Most of them," said the doctor, sounding tired and regretful. "Most of them end up back here."

Skin crawling, Kellen was led to shutter after shutter and peered into cell after cell, seeing face after familiar face.

Some were groggily sedated and sat staring into space with red-rimmed eyes. Others were placidly absorbed in reading, dealing cards, or painting hand-whittled game pieces. Some looked surly and withdrawn, their faces slack with resentment or boredom. All were unkempt and pasty with lack of sun but looked otherwise ordinary.

"You see the problem?" said the doctor. "A lot of the time they can seem so calm, reasonable, and normal. But now and then the mask slips . . ."

"I know you're there!" shouted the woman called Marglass, as Kellen peered into her cell. Hatred poured from her eyes like a black wind. The muscles of her face twitched and puckered like a sack full of rats. Kellen pulled back in panic, really believing for a moment that she could see him.

"Are they ever allowed out?" asked Nettle. "What about visitors, or letters, or contact with the outside world?"

"The patients don't have outings—too risky," answered the doctor. "And nobody comes to visit, I'm afraid, not even their families. We read any letters that arrive for our patients, but they're usually from lawyers. Divorce proceedings, custody of their children, family members taking over their businesses . . ." He sighed.

"So . . . if somebody was writing to one of your patients and encouraging them to get revenge on someone . . ." Kellen asked tentatively.

"Oh, we'd never pass on a letter like that!" Dr. Lethenbark looked shocked. "Ah, here's the last on your list. Jendy Pin."

Kellen peered into a new cell and saw a thin, young woman hunched in a corner, knees drawn to her chin, her ragged dark hair streaming from beneath her helm.

Kellen frowned and turned to stare at his companions.

"What's going on?" he demanded.

"What do you mean?" Gall drew in his brows, looking more alert.

"I remember Jendy!" said Kellen. "She tried to take my eye out with a comb! She's wiry, with a long jaw, and one of her front teeth is broken! That's not Jendy Pin in there!"

Dr. Lethenbark was deeply distressed to hear that one of his inmates was not, in fact, meant to be there at all. He hurried his guests into his cozy, cluttered study where he started making tea for them, then poured hot water into the cups instead of the pot and sat there staring at them blankly.

"Are you *quite* sure it's not her?" he asked. "All the paperwork was in order! She'd been shipped straight up from Mizzleport! I don't understand how this happened! Could they have arrested the wrong person?"

"No, they couldn't!" Kellen told him firmly. "We were there when they took her!"

"Do you still have the paperwork?" asked Gall. "We'd like to see it."

The doctor retrieved a file and handed his visitors a document bearing multiple ink stamps and signatures. The prisoner had apparently been kept in a Chancery cell in Mizzleport, then moved by guard to a prison barge and taken up the canal to Gryte, where the Hospital carriage had picked her up.

"Could the jailers have mixed up their convicts?" asked Nettle. "Maybe the real Jendy Pin was sent to another prison?"

"Unlikely," said Gall. "Arrested cursers are kept in a jail separate from other prisoners."

"I should have listened to her," said the doctor, massaging his temples. "She kept saying that there had been a misunderstanding and that she was a traveling tinker from the lowlands. She said she'd been drugged and kidnapped and had woken up in our Hospital. But lots of the inmates say things like that! And, well, she was quite violent with the orderlies, so I'm afraid we've kept her mostly sedated for the last four months. Poor woman! How could this mix-up possibly happen?"

"It wasn't a mix-up," said Kellen, hearing his own voice wobble. "You can't drug and kidnap somebody by accident. Somebody switched Jendy Pin for the tinker on purpose. And now she's out there somewhere."

Back in the carriage, Kellen and Nettle rode in silence. Kellen's earlier meal sat uneasily in his stomach, and Nettle looked as queasy as he felt.

No enemy was more dangerous than a curser. A curse could cross any distance, penetrate any stronghold, pass through any armor. It could find you wherever you hid, and no bodyguard could defend you from it. The only people truly safe from curses were cursers themselves—cursers could not be cursed. For everyone else, the only defense was to load down any would-be curser with as much iron as possible.

Kellen had made enemies of sixteen cursers but had tried not to let it prey on his mind. After all, they were all safely locked away and unable to strike back at him, or so he'd thought. Now it seemed that one of them had slipped through the cracks and vanished.

Kellen didn't believe in dwelling on the past. Better to crash onward through the world, taking it by surprise, without lingering or looking back. There was nothing behind you worth seeing—only wreckage, regrets, and people who resented you for good or bad reasons.

Even if you didn't dwell on the past, however, sometimes the past dwelled on you. Sometimes it remembered you and came after you for revenge.

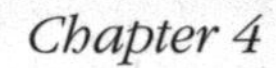

Chapter 4

THE "LITTLE BROTHER"

KELLEN HADN'T ALWAYS BEEN AN UNRAVELLER OF CURSES, barreling from place to place. For the first twelve years of his life, Kellen had even had a home. He could never go back there again, so there was no point thinking about it, but sometimes he did anyway.

Now that he had traveled, Kellen remembered Kyttelswall differently. In his bitter mind's eye, he saw the little hill town for what it was: a shabbily self-satisfied knot of shops and houses, peering over its surrounding wall like a gossip over a fence. A few hundred souls, a town square too small for a ball game, a portcullis rusted into its gate, sloping streets, and too much dust on the wind.

And Kellen had loved it. It had been the center of his world. When he was not helping his father and mother with the loom, or winding thread onto bobbins, he was clambering along the tops of the town's crumbling walls.

He was the best scrambler, the wall-warrior, the king of cats. It was a point of pride to be always a little more in trouble than any of his friends. Not *too* much. Not real trouble. Just enough that Kellen could shrug it off with flair when he met his gang later.

They always gathered to share boasts (and on a few ill-advised occasions, chewing tobacco) in one of the crumbling, unused guard towers. In this lichen-covered aerie, Kellen and his friends could look north toward the upper highlands. They could see other hill towns perched on higher crests, a faint haze of blue hearth smoke smudging the air above each. Beyond these hills loomed the indistinct shapes of mountains, floating like peaked clouds.

To the east, the land descended, hill-hummocked, toward the distant gray-blue of the sea. The clean, bold scars of new roads were pale against the hillside like scratches in dark varnish. A newly carved tunnel in a cliff face gaped a round, surprised, shadowy mouth. Smoke rose from the distant shipyards of Mizzleport on the coast to the northeast.

If Kellen remembered to look, and was in the right mood, he could also see the Wilds.

There was not much to see, mind you, just a long, narrow margin choked with gray-green trees, following the line of the coast. Clouds of birds whirled over it, but tracking their motion made your eyes ache. You never did watch them for long. You blinked and looked away.

Kellen and his friends had once made a game of trying to wrench their minds into seeing the Wilds properly. Under his breath, Kellen chanted all the things that he knew about the Wilds from stories, to counteract the voice in his head telling him that he was staring at something dull.

Marsh horses. Will-o'-the-wisps. White-Handed Ladies. Little Brothers.

It was no good. Even these words became pebbles on his tongue and lost their meaning.

"This is boring," one of Kellen's friends said at last. "Can we do something else?" And of course they had.

That was the way it was with the Wilds.

Kyttelswall had a little too much of three things—wind, cats, and weavers. Of the three, the weavers were the most useful and by far the most trouble.

You could always spot a weaver district. It wasn't just the caged songbirds singing from every house or the *click-a-clack* of handlooms. There was an atmosphere, a swagger, a rough-handed insubordination. This fierce confidence came from the knowledge that they had unseen, many-legged allies.

Under the Pact, the Little Brothers had more freedom in human lands than other creatures of the Wilds. Not only was their curse-making permitted, but they were also allowed to punish the use of any machine that they judged to be a breach of the Pact. In practice, they were even more likely to get involved if the machine threatened the livelihoods of craftspeople and makers. The Little Brothers were protective over all makers, but the weavers were their favorites, perhaps because they too were masters of threads.

Then again, the weavers didn't usually need much help with destroying machinery. Looking back at his early childhood, Kellen's community seemed to be in a semi-perpetual state of exhilarating war. Mostly it was riots about "idiot looms," as Kellen's father called them. Some rich merchant would make the mistake of bringing one of these cumbersome contraptions into town, saying that it would make life easier for the weavers. But the weavers were never fooled. A lumbering machine like that, where all the difficult work was done for you, no strength or skill required? Just another way of squeezing out the real weavers! A way of paying untrained kids a penny or two to man the machine while it spat out cheap cloth, like a cat vomiting up fur balls! The weavers' families would starve, and Raddith would be flooded with cloth with no soul, no artistry! To arms!

There was a jubilation in the anger, because anger was something the weavers were *good* at. The merchant who owned the loom would be dragged out of his house and dunked in the fountain, or would have his behind paddled in the market square. If the weavers got the chance, they broke into his house as well and smashed the offending machine.

Occasionally the Little Brothers got involved on the weavers' behalf. Kellen had never seen one, because they were seldom spotted so far from the Wilds. But you could never be sure that they were not listening nearby, ready to seethe out of the walls.

By the time Kellen was twelve, the battle against the "idiot looms" in Raddith was all but won. Then a new enemy raised its head. Calico! Kellen didn't quite understand why calico was evil, but apparently the weavers in other countries didn't have the sense to riot and stop people using idiot looms. Now those countries had lots of cheap cloth.

They were selling it to Raddith so that the Raddith weavers would all starve, or something like that.

So now Kellen's neighbors weren't smashing machines, they were slashing calico. They were throwing ink and dung at anyone unpatriotic enough to buy and wear it.

Kellen loved times like this. Suddenly mischief and breaking into places were *good* and *brave* and *right*. You and your gang weren't troublemakers anymore; you were soldiers fighting alongside your family, friends, and neighbors. A big, warm, rambunctious "us" against a cold and cowardly "them." *You broke a window? Nice throw, young Kellen-sprat! D'you think you could lob a stone through the high one up there?*

So could Kellen leave the cloth slashing to the adults? Of course not!

It was easy enough to find out which merchants were stocking calico. *Everyone* knew. So one night, Kellen had clambered in through the back window of a merchant's house. That was an evening that he would remember over and over, poring over every detail until they started to become smudged, like a picture handled too many times.

The inside of the storeroom was dark. It was a tall room, moonlight from the slender windows striping the bales and floorboards and gilding the floating motes of silk-dust.

He had taken three hasty steps toward the bales before his instincts halted him. What was that? A sound so faint it might have been the house settling, but stealthy and rhythmic. A hushed, silken *thik-a-thik-a-thik* . . .

The farthest bale was twitching, very slightly. He tiptoed over, curiosity drawing him like an invisible thread tethered to his gut. The sacking around the bale had been torn open, the spring-like pink and green of the exposed calico blazing in a band of moonlight.

On the floorboards below the bale was a mess of brightly colored loose thread. Seated in the middle of it was something the size of a hand. Its busy legs pulled weft loose from warp, so fast that they were a blur. It was shaped like a spider, its body pale and downy, its legs thick and black.

Kellen knew what the creature must be. He knew from descriptions and from the feeling of giddiness that was halfway between terror and the head-whirl of strong cider.

If you ever meet a Little Brother, his father had told him, *treat it with respect. You'll probably be panic-drunk—that's what happens when you meet a thing from the Wilds—but for goodness' sake, keep your head. Don't do anything rash.*

Kellen watched the trembling cloth unravel with a weaver's eyes and knew exactly how much effort had been spent on this fabric. Gathering, spinning, making the thread up into spools, setting up the loom, weaving, printing, then keeping the cloth clean and pressed. Even though he had come to destroy the calico, a part of him felt pain at watching it unravel. But the wrongness of it also mesmerized him. The wicked ease of the undoing was intoxicating, beautiful . . .

His mind felt happy and loose, like a leaf tumbling and dancing in the wind. He fell to his knees beside another bale, used his knife to cut the sacking, and ripped it open. Kellen cut loose a thread and tugged on it. The yank made the cloth bunch up into a grimace. No more of the thread would pull loose.

Then he felt a soft weight on his arm, as the Little Brother clambered to his hand and teased at the thread between his fingers. The cotton thread trembled in his grip, and the next moment Kellen was pulling loose loop after loop, the bright thread flying out of the bale with the gentlest tug. He laughed aloud and surrendered to the wild, destructive joy of it.

Boy and spider raced each other in a frenzy of vandalism, flinging fine arcs of pink-green thread into the air, until everything was webbed with delicate, colorful strands. Bale after bale seemed to explode into a loose mass under their touch, and time unravelled as well, losing its meaning. Afterward, Kellen could only remember how bright and light he felt, how wonderful and easy it was to destroy and destroy, alongside his newest and best friend.

Only when the door banged open did he jerk out of his trance. He stood there, drenched with shock, staring at two equally startled men.

The room was dark, but in a moment they would see the velvety bulk of the spider at his feet . . .

He snatched up the Little Brother and sprinted back toward the window by which he'd entered. The spider was too big to slip away between the floorboards, he had realized, too heavy to scamper nimbly up walls.

"I'll get you out of here!" he whispered to the Little Brother, as he scrambled onto a crate. "I'll see you safe!" It burrowed into the loose fold of his sleeve.

Kellen jumped to grab at the edge of the windowsill . . . then somebody grabbed his ankle. A hard yank tore his grip from the sill.

He scraped his face against the wall as he fell and landed in a painful heap. Somebody kicked him onto his front, then placed a knee on his back. Kellen flailed, swore, kicked, and squirmed, all the while trying not to roll onto his arm, for fear of hurting the Little Brother in his sleeve.

There was shouting, and somebody else ran into the room. Kellen heard a metallic jangle, then his free arm was grabbed. Somebody forced an iron shackle around his forearm and snapped it so tight that it hurt.

The Little Brother screamed.

It was a thin, pale, sickening sound that cut smoothly into the soul, the way a blade slices through skin. Kellen felt a sudden, terrible pain, as if a red-hot needle had been driven into his wrist. The men holding Kellen let go, pressing their hands over their ears. Kellen scrambled up to the window again, half-blind with pain, and tumbled out into the moonlit night.

Kellen sprinted hectically down six streets before he dared stop and tug at the shackle. He slowly wriggled it loose. As it came away, a small torrent of soft, black flakes poured out of his sleeve and pattered onto the street like soot. Scattered among them were a few crumbling, black spider-legs. That was all that remained of the Little Brother.

Doubled up in the street, Kellen sobbed with pain, misery, and remorse.

Everyone knew everyone in Kyttelswall, so of course the men in the warehouse had recognized Kellen. His family gave him an alibi without blinking, however, as did a suspiciously high number of other weavers. His whole neighborhood was ready to ply him with cider and sweetmeats, but Kellen just wanted to hide away.

The Little Brother had trusted him, and it had been killed while in his care. In its last moment, it had bitten him hard, its mandibles leaving a raw, red wound. Kellen had never even heard of a Little Brother dying before. What would this mean?

"It can't have been a Little Brother," his father told him. "They're small—no bigger than hazelnuts. Maybe yours was one of those big crab-spiders from the marshes. Sometimes they sneak into a fruit crate and get brought upland. Just a big, dumb spider. Nothing to lose tears over."

For the first time in his life, Kellen knew his father was wrong. But everyone else agreed and told Kellen not to worry.

Of course, they stopped saying that after the unravelling began.

It started slowly. Kellen's cuffs became frayed, and the seams of his clothes kept splitting. Weaving in his house was suddenly a slow, frustrating business. No matter how many times the thread was unpicked and rewoven, it kept tangling, pulling loose, and refusing to sit tidily in its rows. Soon the nearest neighbors were complaining of similar problems, particularly after Kellen had dropped by to visit.

"There's nothing wrong with the looms," Kellen's uncle said. "So what is it? If we can't weave, we can't eat!"

In another district, it might have taken much longer for anybody to guess who was at the heart of the strangeness. Weavers had a nose for cloth, however, and quickly noticed how ragged and frayed Kellen's clothes had become these days. They also noticed his new restlessness, the way he fidgeted, picked, and pried at everything. The way he squabbled, and picked holes in arguments, and couldn't let anything go.

They were not angry with him. They accepted the truth with nothing but sorrow.

"It's not your fault," said Kellen's mother. She was always the one who handled the difficult conversations. "You're cursed, that's all." She drew in a deep breath, and then slowly released it. Her shoulders slumped sadly, as if she had let go of something heavy but irreplaceable. "And while you stay here, so are we."

I'm not cursed, Kellen could have told her. *I'm not cursed*, he cried out to his family in his head, whenever he remembered that day. *It's something else.* But it wouldn't have made any difference anyway.

The whole neighborhood chipped in, finding things to sell so that they could put coin in Kellen's purse. They all gathered to watch him leave and cheer him on his way. But there was never any question of letting him stay, and Kellen felt that certainty like a stone in his gut.

Nothing could be allowed to threaten the weavers' craft and way of life. Not even one of their own.

Chapter 5

SPIKE

A LITTLE AFTER SUNSET, THE CARRIAGE DREW UP OUTSIDE A small inn. Nettle got out, still feeling sick and shaky. The memory of the Hospital clung to her mind like a bad smell. When she closed her eyes, she saw the cursers, with their iron helms and wintry eyes.

Gall booked three poky little attic rooms, then headed out to the stables with a dead rabbit and came back empty-handed. He ordered the three of them leek pie and partridge broth. It was the best thing Nettle had eaten in months, but she could barely force it down.

After dinner, the trio retreated to the privacy of one of the attic rooms, lit by a cheap, smoky candle that threw black, tremulous shadows on the walls. As soon as the door closed, Kellen dropped into a chair, raking his fingers through his hair.

"None of this makes sense!" he blurted out, looking angry and shaken. "Why would anyone rescue Jendy Pin? She didn't have any friends or family. Nobody liked her!"

Kellen's words were brutal but accurate. Nettle remembered Jendy all too well—a sour-tempered and bitter-tongued bully. One neighbor had made a point of standing up to her, until Jendy's curse turned her into a plague bell. Nobody had shed tears when Jendy was arrested and taken away.

"She couldn't have bribed anyone either," added Nettle. "She didn't have any money." Jendy had been halfway between a fence and a rag-and-bone woman, scratching together a living selling goods of doubtful provenance.

"So what's going on?" demanded Kellen, glaring at Gall. "This is more than just a prison break, isn't it? Is it something to do with that weird note? You know more than you're telling us, don't you? You knew enough to haul us out of jail and drag us to the Red Hospital!"

"You can't expect us to investigate blind!" Nettle said firmly. For once, she agreed with Kellen.

The marsh horseman leaned back in his rickety chair and considered for a moment. He seemed even taller than usual in the cramped, raftered room.

"Yes," Gall said at last. "This is bigger than one prison break. My employer believes . . . that someone is collecting cursers. She noticed that potential cursers were vanishing. Reports would come in of someone acting as if they had a curse egg, but by the time an investigator got there, the suspect had gone. Moved away. Or eloped. Or vanished, and left a suicide note behind. And because it was too early for a warrant, there wouldn't be a hue and cry to find them. Now a convicted curser has vanished from custody. For all we know, this isn't the first time."

"But what's happening to them?" Nettle blurted out. "Are they being rescued? Or kidnapped? Or murdered?"

"There are whispers all over Raddith," answered Gall, "if you know where to listen, of a secret group called Salvation. The rumors say that those carrying curse eggs can run to them and hide. They won't be chained or imprisoned. They won't be blamed or drugged. They'll be protected and helped. We suspect Salvation is real and that someone's creating a hidden league of cursers."

Nettle sank down into a chair. It didn't seem to be a matter of choice. A place where curse-carriers roamed free, uncontrolled and unshackled, despite the rage festering inside them . . .

"What are you saying?" Kellen looked worried. "Some runaway cursers have started rescuing their own kind?" He grimaced. "I can't imagine cursers working together. Wouldn't they end up cursing each other? Oh—but they can't, can they? Cursers can't be cursed."

"We think some of Salvation are cursers," said Gall. "But not all. We suspect there are non-cursers in the league too—armed thugs for dirty work, and spies inside Chancery."

"Inside *Chancery*?" echoed Kellen, sounding appalled.

"That's why we wanted you two to investigate," said Gall. "Because you're *not* Chancery."

"Spies inside Chancery." Kellen was fidgeting and fiddling with his gloves, a sure sign that the mystery had its hooks in his mind. "That must be how they rescued Jendy. She was under guard the whole time, but if one of the guards were crooked . . . We need to know when the switch happened! We need to talk to anybody who saw the prisoner!"

"That was four months ago!" Nettle pointed out. "Nobody's going to remember her!"

"Not many people will have seen her face anyway," said Gall. "Cursers are usually transported in a covered cage. People are squeamish about being seen by an angry curser, even one shackled in iron."

"Wait." Nettle remembered a detail from the paperwork at the Red Hospital. "The prison barge was taking Jendy to Gryte, wasn't it? That's on the Graywater canal."

"Oh!" Kellen's eyebrows rose as he caught her drift. "Yes! We could talk to Spike!"

"We've got a friend who's a brusher and lockkeeper on the Graywater," explained Nettle. "He knows the canal very well." In fact, Spike knew it in ways that most humans never could. "He might know if there's a way of raiding a barge secretly—or a good place to change your cargo without anybody noticing."

"And he checks all the boats that pass his lock," added Kellen. "He might have seen the prisoner."

"Even brushers don't look inside curser cages," objected Gall.

"Spike's . . . different," said Nettle tactfully. "He's very . . . thorough. And determined."

"He's a pain in the neck," said Kellen.

"You *like* Spike," said Nettle.

"Nobody likes Spike," said Kellen.

I know. And that's why you *like him.*

Like Nettle, Spike had once been cursed.

Kellen had unravelled his curse two months after de-heroning Nettle. Back then, Kellen had still been surprised and annoyed by Nettle's persistence in following him around. He clearly hadn't believed that she intended to stick with him indefinitely.

Before being cursed, Spike had been a shipyard inspector in Mizzleport docks, with a long memory for rules and a very short fuse. He had a passionate devotion to the law and tended to get into fights with those who didn't show it the same respect, which ironically meant that he often got arrested for brawling. Given his ferocious obsession with punctuality and hard work, his sudden disappearance was met with surprise and a certain amount of good cheer.

A couple of days later, a dock hand who had lost several fights with Spike suddenly collapsed into a helpless, guilt-ridden torpor. His hollow-eyed babbling made it clear that he had cursed Spike, but it was a lot less clear where his victim had gone.

A year later, Spike's wife heard that there was a boy who could remove curses. Having tracked down Kellen, she hired him to find her husband and unravel his curse. The easy part was working out that the curser had turned Spike into a cedar tree, before chopping him down to dispose of the evidence and selling the timber to the shipyard. The hard part was finding out which boat had been built using Spike's planks, who had bought it, and where it had gone after that.

When Kellen and Nettle did track down the little barge containing Spike's timber, its owner was very resistant to the idea of anyone "rescuing" half its hull. He wasn't sure he believed this story about a cursed man in the timbers, and even if it was true, he'd bought the boat fair and square! He *might* consider selling it . . . but its price was higher now, since he'd done some work on it. So why didn't Kellen run back to Mizzleport and find out how much his employer really wanted these planks?

After that conversation, Kellen ranted and fumed for about an hour. He really *had* believed that the barge owner would drop everything and start tearing apart his own boat to help the tortured curse victim. Kellen started to calm down only when he realized that, in her silent, icy way, Nettle was also utterly furious.

They crept back to the barge just before dawn. Nettle was the lookout while Kellen stood waist-deep in river water, prying out nails. Nettle didn't see the exact moment when the planks wriggled free and shrugged off the last few nails, but suddenly there were loud sounds of splashing and violent swearing. A large, muscular, and entirely naked man was flailing around in the river and grabbing handfuls of riverbank foliage to stop himself from sinking.

Just after the newly disenchanted Spike had clambered up onto the bank, the barge owner ran up, gaped at his tilting boat, and started screaming blue murder. Spike promptly grabbed by him the collar and screamed into his face about "receiving stolen goods."

"My timbers belonged to me!" he had yelled. "You had no right to hold them back from their owner! Thief!" He followed this up by headbutting the man in the face and breaking his nose.

This wasn't the end of his rampage either. Without a word, he marched upstream to the nearest town. During his year as a boat, he had witnessed a host of other rules infringements. A man who had sold the barge owner old nails that kinked painfully in the wood and rusted quickly. A woman who watered down her pitch so that Spike hadn't been waterproofed properly. A lockkeeper who took bribes instead of checking boats thoroughly. Evidently Spike had been fuming about these wrongs for some time and couldn't wait another second to set them straight.

A little taken aback, Kellen and Nettle had watched as the big man charged through the waterfront, picking fights with six people in succession. Anybody who came to calm things down soon found themselves in a yelling match with him. People who tried to agree with him soon found they couldn't.

"I'm starting to see why he got cursed," Kellen muttered, but with a small approving smirk. No doubt he enjoyed watching someone even more impetuous than he was, with some weight to throw behind his punches.

"We need to get him some clothes," Nettle murmured back.

"What for?" Kellen stared at her in disbelief. "We've done our bit.

Let's go back to Mizzleport and get our fee." That remark had triggered their first real, out-loud argument.

"You can't keep doing this!" snapped Nettle. "You can't just . . . transform somebody, then leave them naked and stunned in the mud! You've got a responsibility to him!"

"No, I haven't! He's a grown man!"

"He's stark naked on the waterfront, waving his fists and screaming about rust!" Nettle pointed out. "*Someone* needs to look out for him right now."

"Well, don't look at me! I already saved him!"

"You *started* saving him," Nettle corrected him. "Does he look saved to you?"

"Well, the rest can be somebody else's job," declared Kellen, folding his arms. "He's got a wife, you know!"

As it later turned out, Spike's wife had no intention of taking charge of him either. She had been planning to leave him for another man before the curse, but his disappearance had ruined everything, since she couldn't marry again until he'd been missing for five years. She had hired Kellen to find her husband so that she could divorce him.

When this news was broken to Spike, his anger went out of him, like the air from a crushed sponge. It would come back later, of course, louder than ever, but for a week he was empty and lost and didn't care about anything.

"I'll stay in touch," Nettle had told the big man, and he hadn't argued. "It's going to be hard. And people won't understand." She didn't ask whether there was anything she could do to help. She could tell that he didn't want anyone's help, not yet. He wanted to talk, and he had nothing to say.

So she had sat next to him and given him silence. On the riverbank, they had watched sunlight glimmer on the water and let the hours die softly.

. . . . .

The next morning, Kellen, Nettle, and Gall set off in the carriage, heading for Spike's lock. After half a day's ride, Nettle felt something in her relax and knew that they were drawing close to the lowlands.

The air was different—she could feel it in her lungs. The highlands air was fresher and cleaner but always a little thinner. She grew used to it, of course, but it still left her feeling groggy and out of her element. Here the air was dank, sweet, and full of life. Through the window, she glimpsed flowers she had grown up seeing—great creamy drifts of mayflowers, and voracious creepers with indigo blooms that swaddled whole cottages.

As Kellen shouted directions to Gall, Nettle let the familiarity stroke her senses. It still affected her this way, even though her precious lowlands had killed most of her family, punctured her skin with plumage, and flung her into the sky.

"There!" called Kellen. "Can you get close to that?" On the far side of a meadow, Nettle spotted the telltale line of a high, slope-sided gray dyke.

Gall halted the carriage on a patch of dry mud beside the road. The three of them walked across the meadow to the dyke. It was paved, but lichen and mosses now mottled its grays with greens and yellows. They followed a path beside it for a while, until they found a set of steps cut into the sloped side and climbed up.

The inner wall of the dyke was deeper and steeper. A matching embankment rose thirty feet away, and between them sulked the shadowed waters of the Graywater canal.

A little farther along, a brick bridge arched over the canal. Beneath it ran the black wooden wall of a lock. On the bridge perched a low, wooden building, painted ginger-yellow.

"That's it! That's where he lives!"

I hope he hasn't been fired, thought Nettle, as they drew near the bridge. *I hope he hasn't been arrested for anything. I hope he isn't drinking again.*

Everything seemed tranquil as they approached. When they knocked at the door, it was snatched open by Tonat, Spike's twelve-year-old son. Tonat lived with his mother, except when he didn't. Since the birth of their new baby, his mother and stepfather had become more tolerant of Tonat running off to live with his father for a month at a time.

Tonat stared at Kellen and Nettle for a moment, then his eyebrows rose as he recognized them.

"It's you! You came! How did you know? Have you heard anything?"

Half an hour later, Kellen was sitting on the top of the dyke, kicking his heels and staring down at the coal-gray canal waters. He didn't even look around as Nettle settled next to him.

"How can Spike have disappeared *again*?" he erupted.

"Tonat thinks—"

"I know what Tonat thinks," said Kellen, grumpily.

"He has a point. Spike wouldn't run away from his job—and he definitely wouldn't abandon Tonat. If he'd fallen in the canal, they'd have found the body by now. He *might* have been kidnapped, but . . . that . . . wouldn't be easy. Or quiet." Whenever Spike had been arrested, it had usually involved half a dozen battered people physically sitting on him.

"But what're the odds of the same person being cursed twice?" Kellen groaned, buried his face in his hands, and answered his own question. "Aargh. Pretty high if he keeps punching people in the face."

"I've talked to Gall," said Nettle. "He says we can stay here a couple of days and try to find out what happened to Spike." She hadn't liked asking the marsh horseman for permission, or the feeling that he might say no. "If we don't look for Spike, nobody else will even try, except Tonat."

"But I . . ." Kellen threw a stone into the water with force. "I *did* this already! I fixed him! Why doesn't anything stay fixed?"

And Nettle said nothing. There was no point in telling Kellen, of all people, that nothing was ever, ever, ever fixed.

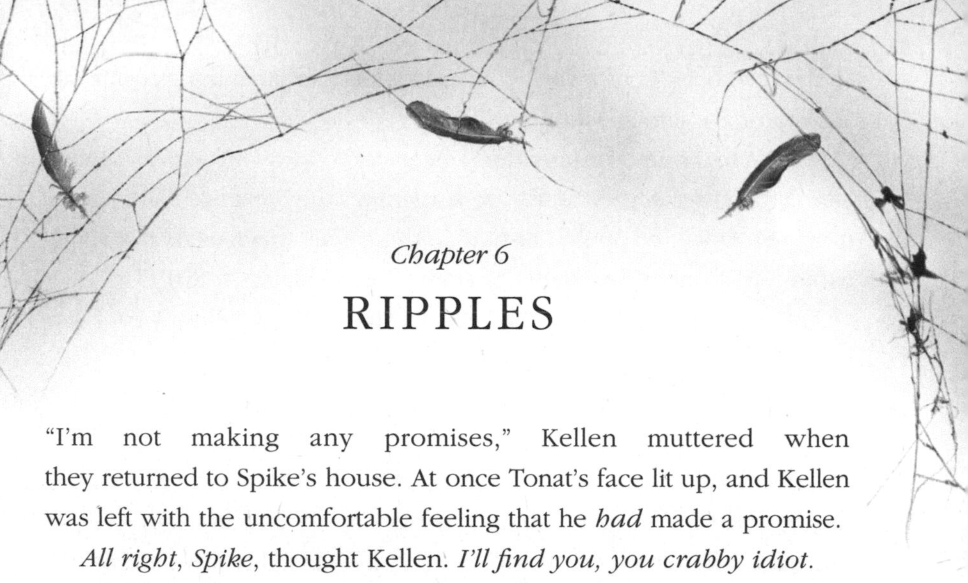

Chapter 6

RIPPLES

"I'm not making any promises," Kellen muttered when they returned to Spike's house. At once Tonat's face lit up, and Kellen was left with the uncomfortable feeling that he *had* made a promise.

All right, Spike, thought Kellen. *I'll find you, you crabby idiot.*

Nettle was right. Nobody else would look for somebody so loud, awkward, and uncompromising. There was a tender place in Kellen's soul, like an unhealed wound. Injustices grated against it and made him grit his teeth. Besides, he liked Tonat. Spike's son was small, quiet-spoken, and shortsighted but had his father's unflinching stubbornness.

"I can show you around," said Tonat.

Spike's sparse little wooden house was meticulously clean, with handmade furniture of wicker and maple and a small potbellied stove. From hooks on the wall hung two cooking pots, fire irons, a long-handled net, and a pair of tough leather gloves.

A finger on one glove had been slightly shortened. When Spike's curse had been removed, his human body had been almost, but not entirely, intact. A few pieces were missing—a finger joint here, a chunk of flesh there. Kellen suspected that these had been lost when the Spike-tree was sawn down in the shipyard. Spike had always been fairly philosophical about this. As he pointed out, at least his human body hadn't reappeared limbless and neatly sliced into planks.

"Do you know how long he's been missing?" asked Kellen.

"At least a week," said Tonat. "That's when I got here. Spike was already gone." Even Tonat always called his father "Spike."

"You've been here a week?" asked Nettle, derailing things as usual. "Do you have enough food?"

"Spike had some oats and dried meat stored away." Tonat shrugged. "And when I see someone fishing, sometimes they give me fish to keep me quiet. Don't tell Spike." Fishing in the canals was illegal, and Spike had made it one of his many missions to enforce this rule.

"Is anything missing?" asked Kellen, trying to get things back on track. "His clothes?"

"Just the ones he usually wears," said Tonat.

"His brushes?"

"Over here." Tonat opened a wooden box. Inside were half a dozen brushes of different sizes, the oiled bristles of which had a faint orange hue. The fine filaments of iron among the other bristles had clearly leaked a little rust despite the oil. "They're all there."

Kellen hesitated, then took off his gloves. He didn't feel any great change as he did so. He never did. Without them, his senses and instincts would start to open, but they always did so gently and imperceptibly, like a flower responding to sunlight.

He picked up one of the brushes. With the handle in his grip, he could almost feel how Spike's hand had warmed and worn the wood.

The room was full of Spike's personality, but it felt interrupted as well. There was a knot here, a place where the calm daily threads had ended in a solid, indecipherable mass. At the moment everything seemed unyielding, but sooner or later he would find something that shifted slightly when he tugged, and pulled loose to reveal, and reveal . . .

Well, it was time to ask the stupid question.

"Do you know if your father had . . . annoyed anybody?"

For a few seconds Tonat just looked at Kellen, eyebrows raised. Then he sighed and began the list.

Tonat had just described his twenty-second suspect when a barge arrived at the lock, traveling from the direction of Mizzleport. Tonat immediately grabbed his father's leather gloves and the smallest iron-fibered brush and ran out.

The barge was an old-fashioned water-trader, tar-slicked and broad-bellied. A middle-aged woman and her two sons poled their boat along with effort, sweating under their kerchiefs.

The canals were the only reliable way of getting goods from the great seaport of Mizzleport into the highlands. Raddith's engineers had outdone themselves in creating the great locks that allowed the canals to zigzag up to the higher ground.

"Ho!" she called when she saw Tonat. "Is he back yet?"

"Not yet!" Tonat scrambled down to the waterside, and Kellen followed.

"You can't stand in for him, boy." She shook her head. "You're too small to work the lock! Me and my boys don't mind doing it ourselves, but not everyone will stand for it! And you don't have the way with those brushes!"

The locks weren't just steps in the canals' climb. Many of them were also checkpoints, to make sure that nothing from the Wilds had stowed away on the boats. Brushers like Spike searched boats and their cargoes, whistling a warning to any supernatural stowaway that might be there and stroking into every nook and crevice with their iron-threaded brushes.

As Tonat leaped aboard and scampered around the cargo, whistling a tune and flicking with his father's brushes, the barge trader tutted and shook her head.

"Poor lad," she murmured. "They should never have given his father the job."

"Hey!" Kellen said sharply, making her jump. "Spike's the best brusher on the Graywater!"

People who recovered from curses were sometimes left with a queasy instinct for things relating to the Wilds. In Spike's case, he could often sense the presence of the Little Brothers and sometimes even their mood and intentions. He didn't enjoy this connection much and had once described it as "like toothache, but talking to me." However, it made him an excellent brusher.

"Yeah, but he's a drunk!" the woman declared. "He's probably at the bottom of a bottle right now—or the bottom of the canal."

Kellen narrowed his eyes. Just for a moment he saw the trader differently, as a loose tangle of threads. Loops of dislike that just needed a tug to pull them free . . .

"He's annoyed you, hasn't he?" he asked impulsively.

"He annoys everyone on the canal!" the woman snapped. "He *is* good and thorough, but that's the problem! He takes ages checking every boat, and if he finds anything wrong—even a cracked lantern—he makes you fill in forms for an hour!"

Tonat had reappeared while they were talking and was listening to the tirade with quiet, owlish fury.

"I don't think you got any Little Brothers in your cargo," he said. "But your ale barrels aren't branded, and you're laden too low. I better get you to fill in some forms."

Kellen might have stayed to watch the ensuing argument, if he hadn't realized that Nettle hadn't come down to join him. It was disquieting, like finding that he was without his shadow.

He found her up on the bridge, looking over the side at the water. She had sunk into a stillness like stone. It was an eerie stillness for which the human body was not designed.

"You'll give yourself backache," he said, and she jerked violently as if he had drenched her with icy water. He didn't look at her as he sat down next to her, knowing that she wouldn't want him to. Instead, he chattered on about his conversation with the barge woman, to give Nettle time to recover. He pretended not to notice her rubbing her eyes with the heels of her hands. When she forgot to blink, her eyes sometimes dried out.

"So the barge captains don't like Spike either," she said at last. "Great. More suspects."

"Do they really have a reason to curse him, though?" wondered Kellen. "All he does is drive them up the wall for a couple of hours each time they bring a boat through the lock."

"What if one of them tried to smuggle something upstream, and Spike got in the way?" suggested Nettle.

"Maybe." Kellen toyed with the tempting ribbon of that theory, before pushing it away. "No. I don't think so. If it was something big, a brusher on another lock would probably find it. And if it was small, you'd carry it up by road and avoid the checks. And besides, that's . . . that's not *personal* enough."

Nettle nodded, looking unsurprised.

"You're right," she said. "Annoyance isn't enough. We're looking for somebody who thinks Spike blighted their life."

That night, Kellen and Nettle slept under blankets next to Spike's pot-bellied stove. Kellen put his gloves on to sleep, for the sake of the furnishings. To nobody's surprise, Gall insisted on staying with the marsh horse.

In the early morning, Kellen wandered across the dew-laden meadow to the carriage, in search of any breakfast that wasn't porridge made with mildewed oats.

Gall was already awake and dressed and in the process of tucking a hunting sling into one of the saddlebags. The marsh horse was eating from a nosebag with a disturbingly loud crunching noise. The ground around the horse was scattered with small feathers.

"Can't it hunt for itself?" asked Kellen, overcome with curiosity.

"It's better if it doesn't," said Gall.

Gall's hair seemed to be slightly damp, and a thin trickle of water was leaking out from beneath his eye-patch like a tear. His clothes looked moist as well, and a very fine mist was rising from them. The marsh horse looked entirely dry except for its mane, which glistened and dripped.

"I have something for you." Gall nodded toward a sodden pile on the grass next to the coach. Kellen crouched and examined them. A jacket, shirt, darned trousers, a worn pair of shoes, a familiar hat . . .

"Those belong to Spike!" exclaimed Kellen.

"There are no new bodies in the canal within a mile of here," said Gall. "You were right, your friend didn't end up in the canal. But apparently his clothes did."

There were so many questions Kellen wanted to ask about the way Gall had spent his night. He had to bite his tongue very hard to stop himself from asking them.

For a moment or two, Tonat looked traumatized by the sight of his father's drenched clothes and the news that they had been dragged out of the canal. Kellen hurried to reassure him.

"No—this doesn't mean he's in the canal! People don't drown, then get undressed! This is *good* news! It means you were right. Somebody cursed him, and . . . well, he probably changed shape like last time, leaving his clothes behind. Then the curser threw them in the river so nobody would know what had happened. Do you see?"

Tonat nodded slowly, still staring at his father's sodden clothes on the floor.

"It's better than good—it's brilliant!" Revelations were falling into place in Kellen's mind. "For all we knew, the curser could have been anybody. Maybe someone sitting at home in Mizzleport, quietly hating your father over breakfast. But if they threw his clothes into the canal, they were *right here*, so we can find them!"

Why wasn't Tonat happy? Didn't he understand?

"Kellen," said Nettle.

And Kellen caught himself and managed to stop smiling. It was hard, though. There was a tug in his mind now, like a current.

He went out again to clear his head. Tiny clouds and dandelion fluff drifted in the wide, blue sky. The canal smelled old and wicked but glittered in the sun. Damselflies hung in the air like needles of ruby and sapphire.

Two black shapes perched on the water's edge, one preening its feathers, the other holding its wings wide to dry. Kellen stared at them as Nettle climbed the bridge beside him.

"Cormorants," he said, and pointed. "Oh—and a heron." The big, gray bird was hunched on the wall of the lock, neck tucked in.

Nettle gave a barely perceptible wince. For some reason, her time as a heron hadn't left her with any affection for them. Instead, she seemed to view them with dislike and distaste.

"We should report finding Spike's clothes," she said, changing the subject. "You're right, it's evidence."

But Kellen's mind was already bounding beyond such things, and he couldn't stop it.

"Yesterday afternoon," he said. "When I found you up here on the bridge."

Nettle's expression closed like a portcullis. She was deeply sensitive about her times of strangeness, and he had broken an unspoken rule by referring to one. But now Kellen could see the bright course of his thought racing ahead of him, and he had to chase it. Her feelings were in the way, but he couldn't stop now, he couldn't.

"You went a bit herony," he said. "Didn't you?"

She didn't look at him, but he could almost feel her receding from him into caverns of ice. Sometimes when she did that, she didn't speak to him for days.

"Do you know what set you off? Please, Nettle! It matters!"

Nettle swallowed and gazed stonily at the water.

"I was watching the ripples," she said quietly. "Fish. The canal's full of fish. Big ones. Fat ones."

Kellen had thought as much.

"I don't think our curser's a barge trader," he said. "Or an old enemy. There's someone else with much more reason to hate Spike. Somebody with a livelihood at stake. Shall we find out who's been giving Tonat those fish?"

Half a mile down the dyke, a few stubborn bushes had managed to sprout on the path. They gave Kellen, Nettle, and Tonat a little cover as they spied upon a lone figure sitting cross-legged on the opposite bank, at the edge of the water.

"That's him," whispered Tonat.

Kellen saw a solitary man patiently watching the place where his fishing line pierced the water. He was probably in his thirties but looked older. His fingers were brownish from cheap snuff. His weather-beaten face was as creased and unremarkable as a pie.

"What do you think?" he asked Nettle.

"I don't know." Nettle sometimes had an instinct for a curser. "Maybe. I don't like his hands."

Kellen stared at the man's hands. The man's thick fingers were patient and methodical, making small gestures and adjustments.

"Why?" asked Kellen.

"They're . . . stealthy."

Kellen wished for a moment that he could see what she did. Cursers often shocked him with their ordinariness. Seething poison in an apple skin. A kraken in a porridge pot.

"If that's him," said Tonat. "Then where's Spike?"

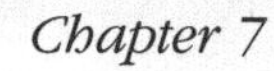

Chapter 7

BLOOD AND WATER

NETTLE WAS ALMOST SURE SHE WAS LOOKING AT A CURSER, though she could not have said why. As with Spike, her erstwhile curse had left her with a sense of the Wilds. In her case, it was like feeling the cold in an old wound, when no normal person had noticed a chill in the air.

"Stealthy," she had said. What had she meant by that?

Holding his thoughts like treasures, so he won't brush the cobwebs off them. Cupping poison in his hands so that he can't spill a drop. Letting a secret cut him off from the world.

She didn't enjoy looking at this man, but at least it kept her mind off the fishing. The last thing she wanted to do was start fixating on the silver ripples that sometimes spread across the surface.

"What do we do now?" asked Tonat.

"Can you unravel the curse yet?" Nettle asked Kellen quietly. "We know the motive. Is that enough?" Every curse was different, and she had long given up trying to understand what Kellen needed and what he didn't.

Kellen chewed his lip, then shook his head.

"I don't have a grip on the curse yet," he said, frowning. "We need to find out what's happened to Spike."

How do you know? Nettle wanted to demand. It was still hard for her to accept that somehow, unfairly, he *did* know some things. The two of them would follow a line of logic step-by-step together, but then they would reach a gap, like a missing plank on a bridge. And Kellen would leap the gap without question, and land on a conclusion, while Nettle remained on the near side, silently shouting, *How do you know?*

"Whatever Spike's become," continued Kellen, "let's hope the curser's kept it."

"Kept it?"

"Yes—for cruelty's sake." Kellen was thinking aloud, and Nettle could have kicked him. He forgot people's feelings when he was like this. "Some cursers want to torment their victim every day. So . . . they turn them into a stool, or a shoe they can grind into the ground when they walk, or a copper kettle they can hang over the fire . . ."

"And sometimes they just turn them into a pebble and leave them there," Nettle said quickly, "and you just have to find the right one."

"Sometimes," agreed Kellen. "But cursers usually have a twisted sense of justice. The punishment fits the so-called crime."

There was a twitch on the man's line. He hauled it in quickly, deftly. Nettle looked away quickly, but it was too late. She had already seen the fish's mottled brown gloss and its acrobatic flip-flop on the shore. She could almost feel and taste it, its cool meat sheathed in shimmer. Some old instinct twanged her like a lute string.

Nettle's gaze fell on Tonat. He was staring at the fish with growing horror, his eyes full of tears.

"Tonat?"

The younger boy turned and ran. He sprinted off along the top of the dyke, then slithered down its landward side in the direction of the fields.

"I'll go!" Nettle told a bemused Kellen and ran after Tonat.

Human legs were better than heron legs in so many ways. Humans could cover ground fast without even thinking about it—or at least most humans could. Nettle had to keep reminding herself how it worked, how to put herself off balance over and over, and catch herself. She loved being *able* to run, but she hated *having* to.

Tonat was taking a headlong course away from the canal, stumbling now and then. Nettle just about managed to keep him in sight until he disappeared into a small copse. By the time she reached the trees, she was out of breath.

The younger boy had climbed an old chestnut tree and was hunched twenty feet above the ground in the crook of a branch. His eyes were clenched shut, as if terrified of looking at something.

"What's wrong?" asked Nettle.

"Fish," snuffled Tonat. And with that word Nettle understood everything.

I'm an idiot. Why didn't I think of it? Why didn't Kellen think of it? He's supposed to be good at this!

"Spike's clothes were in the water," sobbed Tonat. "Maybe *he* went into the water, and his clothes fell off when he turned into a . . . into a . . ." He gulped. "That man gave *me* a fish. And I . . . I *ate* it . . ."

"No," said Nettle. She laid her hand flat against the bark, and pushed, as if she could shove the idea out of the world. But she could feel its *rightness*, the way it fitted the angles of the world. This was the sort of thing that happened.

"I gutted it, and I put it on the fire, and I pulled its bones out . . ." Tonat's voice rose to a whimper.

"No!" snapped Nettle. "Listen to me! It wasn't him! You'd have known!"

Cole didn't recognize Iris, said a voice in her head. *He just saw his dinner and a place for his talons*.

"You'd have known!" Nettle yelled, trying to drown the voice. "Because you love him! You love him *enough*! You *knew* he was cursed, when other people tried to tell you different! You'd have seen through it! You'd have looked at that fish, and you'd have *known*!"

She was shaking. The bark bruised her fingers.

But what if Tonat's right? said the voice in her head. *What will you do then?*

"I'm coming up!" Nettle shouted and kicked off her shoes.

The wind picked up, and the tree gave a creak like a rocking chair. The foliage shook and shimmered, dropping splinters of light into Nettle's eyes as she climbed.

It's true. You know it's true.

"No, I don't!" shouted Nettle aloud, before realizing that Tonat hadn't spoken. She clung to the trunk, face pressed against the rugged bark. Her nose was full of the scent of rot. The windswept foliage swung and thundered around her, with a sound like waves breaking. There was a feeling of rushing vertigo, as if she were falling, falling . . .

And then she heard another sound—harsh, ugly, and wonderful.

She took a great lungful of air and called back to the other sound with all her soul. She felt their cries mingle like instruments uniting in a melody. Something feathered and ungainly broke through the tree canopy. Overwhelmed with relief, Nettle reached out a hand toward the descending shape.

Yannick!

The black-headed gull swooped in, wings wide . . . and smacked into Nettle's face. She lost her grip and fell off the tree.

"Nettle!" Tonat immediately forgot his own torment and started clambering down the trunk.

Not my fault! screeched Yannick, as he fluttered down to land on his winded sister's chest.

You came in like a bullet! Nettle protested, stroking his chocolate-colored head with a fingertip.

You screamed! Yannick said accusingly. *Thought a fox had got you!*

I didn't scream, said Nettle, but there was no lying to Yannick.

"Get away from her!" Tonat was flinging bits of twig at the gull and trying to shoo him away.

"It's fine, Tonat," said Nettle. "This is my brother Yannick."

Nettle sat up, and Yannick took up his usual unsteady perch on her head. It was strange how much she had missed the clammy slither of his webbed feet against her forehead.

If you poo on my head, I'll pull out your tail feathers, she told him.

Tonat stared at the gull, fascinated and uncertain.

"I would *always* know Yannick," said Nettle, slowly getting to her feet. "I'd know him anywhere. I'd know his feathers if I found them on the ground. And *you'd* know Spike."

With Yannick's wing feathers tickling her ears, she could almost believe it was true.

Kellen was clearly relieved to see Nettle and Tonat return. He even let himself look happy to see Yannick.

"So *that's* come back," he said. "Got hungry at last, did he?"

Yes, Yannick told Nettle. *Give me food.*

"We need to stop that man fishing!" hissed Tonat. "And we need to scare away the cormorants! I think Spike's a fish in the canal!"

I could find him, suggested Yannick.

No, answered Nettle. *You'd eat him.*

So would you, said Yannick.

"I don't think he *is* a fish," said Kellen slowly. "I did think so, when I realized why you'd run off. The idea kicked me in the head like a horse, and for a while it seemed so right. It's poetic. This man was going hungry because Spike wouldn't let him fish, so he turns Spike into something he can catch and eat. But . . . I don't think it's cruel enough."

"It would be, if he tricked me into eating Spike!" hissed Tonat.

"No," Kellen said firmly. "That's cruel to *you*. He might do that if he wanted to punish *you*. But letting Spike have a nice cool swim for a while, followed by yanking him out of the water and knocking him on the head? That's too quick. Not enough suffering."

It sounded like enough suffering to Nettle, but she could sense how deeply Kellen wanted to be right. He was invested in saving Spike, so he couldn't let himself imagine a situation where that was impossible. She wanted him to be right too.

A fat ripple broke the surface. The fisherman didn't move, but his face brightened and became more alert. A large fish, Nettle's instincts told her. An older fish, clever with years and sleek with meat . . .

Tonat broke from the cover of the bush and snatched up a fistful of gravel. He hurled them down into the water.

"Hey!" yelled the fisherman as the river surface became a pattern of ripples.

“Stop it!” Tonat shouted hoarsely. “Get out of here!” It wasn’t clear whether he was shouting at the fisherman or the fish. Kellen and Nettle stayed hidden. There was no point in showing themselves as well.

The fisherman glared at the short, furious boy on the opposite bank, and Nettle saw his expression open like a trap door. There was darkness beyond, and things that moved. Then he lowered his gaze, quietly packed up his things, and began walking up away along the path. When his back was turned, Nettle ran out and dragged Tonat back into cover.

“Are you stupid?” she snapped. “Most cursers curse again, remember?”

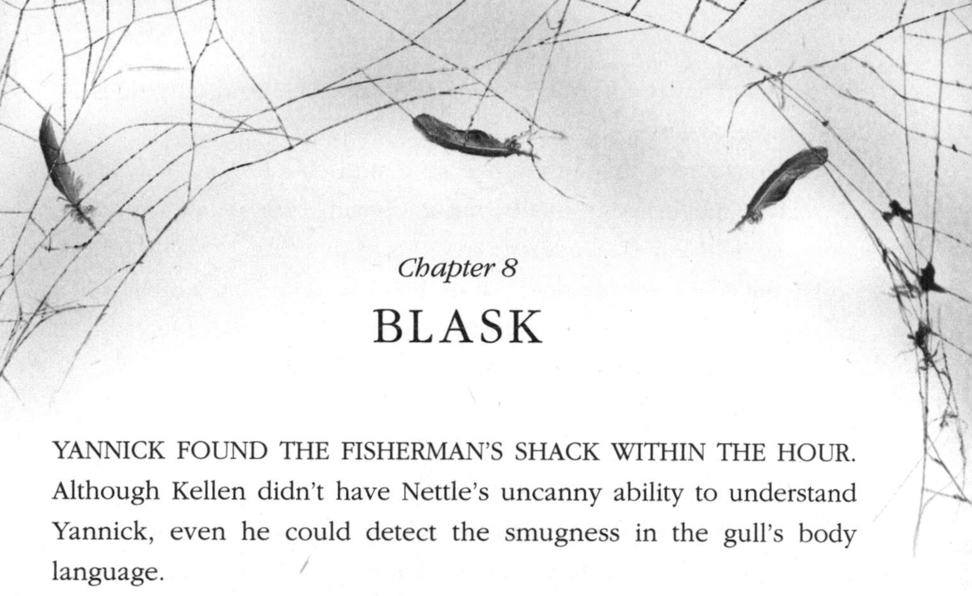

Chapter 8

BLASK

YANNICK FOUND THE FISHERMAN'S SHACK WITHIN THE HOUR. Although Kellen didn't have Nettle's uncanny ability to understand Yannick, even he could detect the smugness in the gull's body language.

The shack was a tumbledown affair. The crumbling stone walls of some long-abandoned farmhouse had been given a crude roof of reed-thatch and a door made of salvaged timbers. The whole edifice was overrun with bindweed.

Tonat agreed to stand lookout. Inside, the shack was surprisingly cluttered and smelled of mold and baked fish. Daylight pierced the darkness through holes in the thatch, illuminating one dingy room with no bed, only a blanket on the floor. Three chairs were huddled next to a table and a large open trunk, brimming with junk and water-blurred papers.

"Look at all this!" whispered Nettle, peering around the room. "Spike could be anything!"

Kellen's senses tingled, and his gloveless fingers flexed. The air felt thick, velvety, and hard to breathe, as if he were inhaling cobweb.

Here. The curse happened here. He could almost see layer after layer of fine silken threads, strung from wall to wall by a thousand obsessive thoughts. He could feel the weight of them tugging on the frame of the world and pulling it subtly out of shape . . .

"Kellen," said Nettle, breaking him out of his reverie. "The furniture doesn't make sense." She pointed to the table and chairs, which were covered in fine carvings of vines and grapes but blotched and blistered by damp. "They're too good for a place like this. And why does he need three chairs?"

Kellen stared at them, then peered into the trunk.

"Maybe they come from a better home with more people," he said. "A home he doesn't have anymore. Look at this."

He pulled a child's bonnet out of the trunk. Then the armband of a Chancery clerk. A woman's scarf. A rusting bridle. Letters, blurred with damp, addressed to *Mr. L. Blask*.

"Souvenirs of happier times," murmured Nettle. "Ghosts of a dead life."

A job, a family, a nice house, a horse . . .

"I think they're reminders that he's been robbed of his happiness," said Kellen. "He can look at them and hurt himself remembering what he lost. And if they get ruined by the damp and weather, then that's just what the world keeps doing to him. Taking away everything he has. He can watch it happen again." He was starting to feel the shape of the curse now, the contours of the curser's mind.

"Does that help us?" asked Nettle.

"Yes," said Kellen with sudden certainty. "It means Spike's not in this box. These are just the memories Blask uses to torture himself." He shut the trunk. "Spike might still be here, though. Look for anything that doesn't fit."

They searched furtively, jumping whenever they heard a rustle from outside.

"What's that?" Nettle was peering upward. Following her gaze, Kellen saw a gleam of metal against one of the blackened timbers holding up the roof thatch.

Both Kellen and Nettle scrambled up onto chairs for a closer look. A picture had been scratched into the dark timber. It was the crude outline of a man with a gap-toothed, shouting face. One of his clumsily etched fingers was shorter than the others.

There was a hook-shaped piece of metal embedded in the picture.

"Is that drawing meant to be Spike?" asked Nettle.

"Yes." Kellen blinked and felt himself starting to grin. "This is the curse-working. This is how Blask cast the curse!" There was usually something—an incantation, a dance, a chant, a sigil, or a bone burned at midnight.

"That's . . . a fish hook, isn't it?" said Nettle in a small voice.

She was right, and just for a moment Kellen's spirits plummeted. For an instant, he doubted all his certainties and began to fear that Tonat had been right after all.

"No," he said, his spirits easing as the light dawned. "No. Spike's not a fish! Look at the hook! It's not in his mouth. It's in his *gut*. I'm an idiot! I watched Blask catch three fish while you and Tonat were gone. *Three* fish! And I *knew* something was odd about it, but I was too busy worrying about whether the fish looked like Spike. Listen—there's no fly on Blask's line, he's using bait. But he never rebaited the hook, Nettle. Not once!" He saw Nettle's eyes widen as she understood.

Kellen reached up and gave the hook an experimental tug. It shifted slightly in the wood. He could see it clearly now—it was the pin trapping a hundred taut threads and pulling the world askew. All he needed to do was yank the hook free. The threads would fly loose, the world would pull back to the way it should be, Spike would return to his rightful form, and . . .

"Aagh!" Kellen pulled his hand away from the hook as if it were hot. "No! Wait-wait-wait! Spike probably has a hook through his vitals right now! If I change him back before the hook's out . . ."

Nettle grimaced, and mouthed a silent "ow." Then she stiffened. Overhead, Kellen realized he could hear the shrill cry of a gull.

"Yannick says the curser's coming back!" Nettle exclaimed.

Kellen's thoughts scattered, then regrouped.

"Get Tonat in here!" he said. "He needs to hide up in the roof and get ready to pull out that hook when we say so! If I'm right, Blask will have Spike with him. Somehow we need to get him back!"

Alone in the shack, Kellen sat on one of the vine-carved chairs, his heart banging. There had not been much time to plan. Outside he could hear the rhythmic rustle of approaching footsteps.

The door opened. The fisherman entered, and stopped dead, staring at Kellen.

Blask looked a lot bigger now that he was blocking the light from the doorway. A scraggy cap with a fringe of fine net to keep the gnats off his neck. Boots so cobbled they were more seam than sole. Wine-stain veins in his nose and cheeks. Brutally ordinary.

He wasn't carrying his fishing rod. As Kellen had hoped, the six-foot-long rod had been left outside.

"What are you doing here?" the fisherman demanded sharply. His accent didn't quite suit his ragamuffin clothes. It smacked of starched collars and doffed hats.

"Hello, Blask," said Kellen promptly. "Debt collectors sent me—told me to see what you still had. Steady!" He leaped up and ducked behind the table as the man made a lunge for him. "Don't get excited!" He was playing a hunch. A move from a nice house to a shack smacked of bankruptcy.

"Those vultures took *everything* from me!" yelled Blask. "What more do they want?"

"They say they never got the full sum from you." There was bound to be someone who still thought they were owed something.

The fisherman threw down his bag and snatched up a heavy cane from beside the wall.

"But what *I'm* thinking," Kellen said quickly, in a complacent, ingratiating tone, "is that maybe I didn't find this place. Tucked away, isn't it? Maybe I just . . . missed it."

Blask hesitated, then slowly put down the cane. It was unnerving how quickly his temper withdrew from sight, like a snake whipping into a crack between rocks. After a moment or two, Blask sat down and nudged a chair in Kellen's direction.

"Maybe you did," he said.

Kellen took the offered chair and sat, trying to keep himself outside easy grabbing range. Beyond the half-open door, he glimpsed a flicker of movement. Nettle, creeping past to grab the rod, he hoped. All Kellen had to do was keep Blask talking.

"I didn't like the job anyway," Kellen said conversationally. "It sounded like you got a raw deal."

"You could say that." Something dark surfaced for a moment in Blask's gaze.

Kellen became aware of further motion outside the open door behind Blask. Nettle's hand appeared in view, brandishing Blask's long fishing rod, the horsehair line wound round the hazel shaft. Her other hand tugged at the loose end of the line.

There was no hook attached. Kellen's heart sank.

If Spike wasn't on the line, where was he? Blask had no pouches at his belt or obvious pockets. Kellen's gaze slid to the bag the fisherman had brought in with him.

"What are you looking at?" demanded Blask.

"Just thought I smelled fish, that's all." Kellen smiled warmly, every inch the affable young blackmailer.

For a second, the curser's eyes flickered with loathing, like black lightning. Then he picked up the bag, laid it on the table, and opened it to show the fish inside.

"Take your pick," he said.

Kellen examined the two bream, a trout, and a couple of small carp and picked one of the bream. Deeper in the bag he could see a folding knife, a ball of spare line . . . and a small, corked pot.

A faint creak sounded from the roof above. Kellen resisted the urge to look up.

"Very generous of you." He wrapped up the fish in his handkerchief. "No, I *definitely* didn't find this place. You're a gentleman."

There was another creak from above, more audible this time. Blask frowned and looked up. There was a sudden rending sound, and chunks of torn thatch tumbled to the floor. Looking up, Kellen could see one of Tonat's legs hanging down through the ruptured roof.

"Hey!" shouted Blask, snatching vainly at Tonat's foot just as it withdrew through the hole.

"Oh, *fudge*," muttered Kellen. He lunged for the bag, snatched up the corked pot, and threw himself at the door.

As he shouldered it open, Blask's strong arm wrapped itself round his neck from behind, yanking him back. Kellen struggled and kicked. The grip tightened.

"Nettle!" he croaked, and threw the pot out through the open door. The little vessel flew a disappointingly short distance, bounced, and lay there on the grass. Then the familiar figure of Nettle darted out, grabbed it, and ran.

Immediately Kellen was hurled aside, his face slamming painfully against the doorjamb. Blask shoved past him and raced after Nettle. Kellen scrambled to his feet and gave chase.

His flying tackle didn't neatly trip Blask in the way he'd hoped. He took a faceful of foot but managed to wrap his arms round the curser's shin. A heavy boot stamped on Kellen's head and arms, but he clung on like a drowner.

"Nettle! Do it now!" Kellen yelled.

Nettle had not run far. She was kneeling on the grass, shaking something out of the uncorked pot into her lap. A fish hook, on which something dark pink writhed and squirmed.

Blask took step after relentless step toward Nettle, dragging Kellen's face through the grass.

With the calm focus of someone threading a needle, Nettle was gently sliding the hook out of the flinching, convulsing worm, taking care that the barb did not tear it. She ignored the curser, even as he drew closer and closer.

"Take your time!" choked Kellen, as another kick made his ear burn and his eyes water.

The hook pulled free, and the worm twisted and coiled in Nettle's palm. As she drew back her hand to fling it away from her, Blask lunged for her and grabbed her wrist. The worm fell out of her hand onto the grass, within easy stamping distance of Blask's feet.

Before anyone could grab it, a winged shape with a dark head swooped in, and the worm disappeared into an eager, hooked beak.

"Yannick!"

Stunned and aghast, Kellen watched the gull wheel away in a nonchalant arc. Then Yannick's beak gaped again, letting the worm fall, its little dark shape making a figure eight in the air.

"Now, Tonat!" Nettle shouted, struggling against Blask's grip. "Pull out the hook!"

Suddenly, there was no worm. Instead, a large naked man hit the grass with an audible *Oof!* and immediately scrambled to his feet, eyes wide with rage and zeal.

After that, the fight didn't take very long at all.

While Nettle tied up the unconscious Blask using fishing line, Tonat fetched the fisherman's bedding blanket and draped it round his father. Now that the fires of rage had burned down, Spike cut a rather dejected figure, sitting damp and goose-pimpled on the grass, his hair sticking up. There was a puncture wound in his right shoulder and another on his belly. Neither seemed to be deep, but they oozed a slow trickle of blood. He was covered in pink and purple bruises.

"A week on that hook," he said. "Feeling it all the way through my innards. And being in that canal water for *hours*. Not able to see anything in the murk—or feel anything, except the cold, and the pain. And sometimes a big, cold fish mouth would clamp down onto me, and try to bite me in two, and I'd think . . . well, that's it for me. But I didn't die."

Cruelty. A quick death as a fish would never have been enough. No, Blask had wanted his enemy to squirm forever in torment and terror. And there was a malicious poetry in getting the fanatically conscientious Spike to help him with his illegal fishing.

Spike sighed and stared at his big hands.

"I never thought I'd go through that again. The first time I was cursed, I told myself I was just unlucky. Wrong place, wrong time. But . . . if lightning strikes twice, you have to wonder if you're wearing a metal hat."

"Blask was a curse waiting to happen," Kellen said quickly. "You were just the last straw, that's all."

"Yeah, but I always am, aren't I?" Spike wiped his face with a corner of the blanket. "I'm just easy to hate."

It wasn't until a little later, after Spike had had a rest and a good meal, that anybody had the heart to talk to him about Jendy Pin's escape.

"A prison barge?" Spike dug a clothbound ledger from beneath his bed. "Give me the date, and I'll check my records." Each entry seemed to have a list of the boats that had passed the lock on that day, followed by all the infractions Spike had spotted during his inspections. "Here we are! *The Temperance* . . . Oh. Yes, I remember that boat coming through!" He closed the ledger grimly.

"Did you see the prisoner?" Kellen asked eagerly.

"I insisted on it," said Spike. "I always do. Most of the guards on the prison barges are used to that. But these guards—I'd never seen them before. And they didn't want me to see the prisoner at all. They tried to bribe me, and not just the usual amounts."

"That sounds crooked as lightning," Kellen muttered.

"Anyway, they had to let me see her in the end." The woman Spike described was young, with no broken front teeth. It sounded a lot like the tinker.

"Spike," Kellen said. "Is there anywhere downstream of here where you could switch a prisoner with a drugged woman and get away with it?"

Spike considered, then gave a bitter snort.

"The third lock from Mizzleport," he said. "When I was a boat, I saw lots of dodgy dealings happening there. That lockkeeper'll turn a blind eye to anything for a handful of coin."

"Thanks, Spike!" Kellen felt his hunter instincts rage into life.

I knew it, I knew some of Jendy's guards had to be accomplices! Now we just need to find out who those prison guards were . . .

Lost in thought, Kellen didn't realize at first that Spike was staring at him pensively.

"Are you all right?" asked the big man.

"What do you mean?" asked Kellen, confused.

"I don't know," admitted Spike. He narrowed his eyes and peered at Kellen with disquieting intensity. "You always look a *bit* weird to me. Sticky. Little-Brother-ish. You give me toothache. But . . . it's a bit worse today."

"I'll put the gloves back on," Kellen said hastily. "That'll damp it down." He always felt uncomfortable knowing that Spike could see his strangeness in a way that he himself could not.

Spike didn't look convinced but watched as Kellen put his iron-studded gloves back on. Then he frowned and reached over to catch hold of Kellen's wrist.

"What happened to that?" Spike tapped the double puncture on the underside of Kellen's wrist.

"That's where the Little Brother bit me, remember? I showed you before."

"No, I mean, why's it like that?" Spike painfully prodded the reddened, inflamed edges of the bite.

"Oh . . . I got arrested." Kellen flushed in angry embarrassment. "They tied me up, so I suppose the rope must have rubbed the bite-mark. It doesn't hurt—it just itches a bit."

"Huh." Spike said nothing more about it but cast occasional glances at Kellen's bite, his face cloudy with uncertainty and concern.

Chapter 9

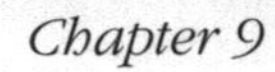

TWO WORLDS

NETTLE'S ARGUMENT WITH YANNICK THE NEXT MORNING HAD the inevitability of gravity. She saw it coming, felt it happening, but couldn't stop herself.

How's Cole? asked Yannick. It was the question she had been dreading.

He's doing well, she said. *Still making progress.* She hoped this would pass, but she couldn't hide anything from Yannick.

You still haven't been back to the sanatorium to see him, have you? Yannick said accusingly. It was true. Nettle had relied on updates from her friend Tansy.

I've been busy, she told him. It was true, and not true, and she knew that Yannick could tell. He knew it wasn't in her nature to be negligent or callous, so he was confused. She couldn't tell him her real reason for staying away from the sanatorium.

I don't get it! Yannick sounded exasperated. *When Cole was raving and trying to kill himself, you were there all the time! And now that he's pulling himself together . . . How long's it been since you saw him? Six months?*

If you care so much, why don't you *go and see him!* snapped Nettle. She had the feeling that Yannick was picking a fight with her.

Oh, now you want to me check up on Cole so you don't have to? Yannick took off from her shoulder in a flurry of wings. *Do you think I'm your trusty animal companion? "Oh good, the bird's back. Let's send it to find a curser's cottage! Let's use it to keep watch!" You didn't even ask me where I'd been!*

Well, where have *you been?* It was a sore point, and Nettle couldn't help letting her bitterness show through. *It's been months! Where were you?*

You don't care! The gull's cries cut the air like metal.

You forgot about me again! Nettle yelled back, giving up on her show of calm as she always did when she argued with Yannick.

Why wouldn't I? The gull's circles grew wider and wider, higher and higher. *You ground-trudgers all look the same.* He spiraled upward until he was a speck, riding the warm air high above.

Nettle watched him, feeling infuriated, bruised, and bereaved. Whenever Yannick pulled away from her, she felt as though a piece of her had been torn loose, like a handful of hair ripped out by the roots. She suspected that Yannick felt the same way whenever there was distance or division between them, but he never *looked* as though he did. There he was, lazily flaunting his wings as if he had forgotten Nettle already, the sky his ballroom.

It had never been like this while they were both birds. As heron and gull, theirs had been a wordless connection of souls, to which they had both clung. That link had helped their bird-minds remember hazily a time when they had not been birds. It had given them back a fragile sense of who they were, so they did not lose themselves completely.

But one day, Nettle had flown down and received her cure, and Yannick had not. He had rejected it, and flown away, and kept his bird-shape. She still did not really know why he had done so.

Now Nettle was human, but the strange bond forged between them during their bird-years persisted. Nettle was Yannick's guy rope, tethering him to human memories, human ways of thinking. When Yannick was away from her, Nettle suspected that he slid back into being bird-like, and she sometimes jealously wondered whether he found that easier than being around her. They still spoke to each other's minds, but their connection was complicated now, briar-tangled with thoughts and memories and crackling with resentment.

.....

Nettle had more or less stifled her bitter mood by the time she rejoined Kellen. He was sitting in the meadow, staring out toward Gall's distant figure. The marsh horseman stood beside the carriage, one hand raised close to his face.

"What's he doing?" asked Nettle.

"I don't know," Kellen stripped the seeds off a grass stem with his gloved hands. "He's been out there for ten minutes, talking to his hand. Is that something marsh horsemen usually do?"

"N-n-no, I don't think so," said Nettle. Gall's jaw was indeed moving slightly, as though he were speaking quietly.

"He's coming back!" whispered Kellen.

Gall strode over to join them.

"I have more information on the prison barge guards who escorted Jendy Pin," he said. "Your friend Spike is right, they hadn't worked on the prison barges before. And shortly afterward, they all handed in their notice."

Nettle was itching to ask how he'd gained the information, but she was fairly sure there was no point in asking.

"Do we know where they are now?" she asked instead.

"We can't trace two of them. The third man turned up in the Shallow Wilds two months ago, in a little hamlet called Havel."

"What was he doing there?" asked Kellen.

"Floating facedown in the marsh." Gall's slate-gray eye gave a dull glimmer that might have been humor. "He'd been drowned. He was only identified by his black jerkin and the scar across his cheek. Nobody knows why he was there. The locals said they'd never seen him before."

"Well, isn't that convenient," muttered Kellen. "Everybody who helped Jendy escape vanished or died." His gaze sharpened as he looked at Gall again. "Who chose those guards to escort Jendy? It's a bit of a coincidence, isn't it, all three of them being crooked? Someone higher up must have picked them for that duty. Who was it?"

"That's not for you to worry about," said Gall. "You've got another job. Get your things ready. We're leaving in half an hour."

"What do you mean?" Nettle didn't like the way the ground seemed to be shifting. "Where are we going?"

"Havel," said Gall curtly. "Where the drowned guard was found."

"Hey!" protested Kellen, his face reddening with outrage. "I want to go to Mizzleport and find out more about those guards! Don't tell us that's not our business! You can't decide that for us!"

Gall looked up at the sky and slowly exhaled. He suddenly had the air of someone who has been displaying great patience against his better judgment and is coming to the end of it. When he looked back at Kellen, his single eye held no warmth at all.

"Yes," he said. "I can. Asking questions in Chancery is a job that needs tact, and you don't have any. That's why you were in jail the day before yesterday. You don't know when to keep your mouth shut. Maybe you should start practicing that now."

Gall hadn't raised his voice, but something about the marsh horseman's stillness sent Nettle's instincts scampering like rabbits. As Kellen drew a deep breath to start yelling, she put a quiet, restraining hand on his arm.

"So what's the job?" she asked quickly. "Are we looking for whoever killed that guard?"

"Yes," said Gall flatly. "And if we're right, that'll lead us to the people who rescued Jendy Pin." He strode back toward the carriage, evidently considering this sufficient answer.

Kellen would probably resent Nettle for defusing things, but she hadn't liked the sudden chill in the air. Arguing with the marsh horseman in a lonely place had suddenly seemed like a bad idea.

When Nettle and Kellen returned to the lockkeeper's hut to say goodbye, Spike was still subdued.

"I'll look after Spike," Tonat told Nettle quietly. "He'll feel better once he's done some paperwork." Nettle wasn't sure that was true. But it would probably help to have his small, determined son there, who saw him as an infuriating hero—rash and impulsive, but brave, honest, and idealistic.

The carriage set off, then stopped at the first small town to drop Blask off with a magistrate. Usually it would have taken Nettle and Kellen ages to persuade the officials that they had a curser in tow. This time, however, Gall showed his papers to the magistrate's man, and all the officials started bowing and scraping.

Blask was blank-eyed with despair as he was led away. Nettle wondered how the fisherman felt, knowing that the curse born from his whole life's bitterness had been pulled apart by a mere boy before his eyes.

Powerful people can wave a piece of paper, and the world dances to their tune. It's the powerless people who need curses. Then we come along and take away the only thing they have left.

As they passed through the occasional village, Nettle noticed the main Chancery building at the heart of each. Foreign visitors always assumed they were temples.

Other countries had legends of miracles, of powerful beings that could walk in dreams or command the lightning. Foreigners wrote of them in gilded scrolls and prayed to them.

The people of Raddith, however, knew perfectly well that such creatures existed. You might even meet them if you were unlucky or foolhardy. But why would you worship them? If on a summer day you met a woman who walked toward you across the surface of a river, lightly as a flower petal, of course you would be polite. But if you told anyone of the encounter later, it would be in an undertone, to warn them away from that part of the river.

You certainly wouldn't build a temple to her. That would be *weird*. It would be like worshipping a violent neighbor or the creeping onset of old age. These were unpleasant facts of life you had to cope with, not something to get excited about.

All the same, there was a Chancery faith—a godless one, but no less devout for that. It was a hardheaded, practical belief that people needed food on the table and, ideally, food that wouldn't suddenly turn to ashes or start singing. It was a merchant faith, a belief in the importance of negotiation, fairness, honesty, and practical good sense.

Although Chancery didn't like to admit it, some of its other core beliefs were similar to those whispered in the heart of the Wilds. *Promises and bargains are sacred, and their exact wording matters. All debts must be paid—paid to the last penny or drop of blood.*

In a sense, Chancery was a child of the Wilds. It was a child rebelling against everything its parent stood for, but it could only have emerged in a country with the Wilds glimmering at its edges.

By the time the sun was lowering toward the horizon, the carriage had descended far enough for a distant view of Mizzleport, the capital of Raddith.

The great seaport was caught in the throat of a mighty estuary dotted with ships. It was always too big for Nettle; she couldn't get a handle on it. She could wrap her head around the big highland towns and boggle at the numbers of people within their walls. But that great sprawl of buildings down below, all those black roofs glittering in the sun like snake scales . . . it was too much.

"That's where we should be going!" Kellen was still bristling after his argument with Gall. He could never let anything go.

"They don't want us getting in their way," said Nettle very quietly. "And . . . maybe Gall doesn't want us finding out too much about his boss either."

At the city's edges, Nettle could see the pale line of the huge, paved barriers that separated Mizzleport from the Wilds that fringed the rest of the coast. They were the pride of Raddith's engineers, higher than a six-story house. They were designed to keep the strangeness out of Mizzleport as far as possible, but also to stop Mizzleport spreading beyond its allotted bounds. It was an agreed boundary, a product of the Pact.

Beyond those barriers, stretching along the coast on either side of Mizzleport, were the marsh-woods of the Wilds, like a long, sodden scarf strung out along the shore.

As the carriage drew closer, the marsh-woods seemed ever more pitiful and disappointing. Just a flat expanse of grayish trees, with occasional water glinting between them, crisscrossed by long dykes that made the whole area seem even more tamed. The villages nestling among the trees were clearly quite close to each other, little neighborly knots of brick and pale thatch among the trees. You could see everything—there were no surprises.

The marsh-woods stretched along the coast to the left and right, as far as the eye could see . . . but the damp band of forest seemed so *narrow*. You could look out across it and see clearly where the trees thinned and yielded to the sea. Not all that far away—three hours' walk at the most.

It's not true. The appearance of the Wilds was a lie. Nettle's knowledge warred with her senses, making her feel seasick.

The carriage turned seaward and raced along a ridge road, aloft on the top of one of the dykes that rose twenty feet above the tree canopy. The marsh-woods spread out below on either side like a gray sea, their foliage misty and indistinct in the poor light. In the distance she could see other ridge roads, running in parallel. These roads were the safest way to cross the Wilds, high above the tree line and partly protected for humans by the Pact.

They were not *completely* safe, however; hence the fact that there were no other horses in sight. Ordinary horses fared badly so close to the Wilds. Some frothed and went frantic with a panic from which they never fully recovered. Others heard the distant hissing calls of their wild marsh-horse brethren and ran headlong into the bogs, where they drowned.

Instead, most of the other traffic on the road was pedal-powered—bicycle rickshaws, cycle sedans, pedal-coaches, and tandems. Even these were less numerous now that evening was drawing in. Despite the protections of the Pact, people preferred not to brave the ridge roads by night.

"We're slowing," observed Kellen. He was visibly bracing himself, like someone expecting to be submerged in icy water. He always hated visiting the marsh-woods. His spirit seemed to rail against their nature.

The coach abandoned the high ridge road and turned left onto a sloping road that descended toward the treetops. The woods rose up to meet them, close enough for Nettle to see the cobwebs that gave the trees their misty grayness. Then the coach plunged into shadow as the woods closed over their heads. Even though Nettle was ready for it, she felt a choking unease, as if she had been swallowed by some dark sea.

It was not simply an onset of darkness. There was a change in that moment that she felt in her bones. A breath that filled her lungs like diamond dust. A moment like awakening and like tumbling into slumber. You never remembered what it was like to enter the Shallow Wilds until you found yourself there again.

While Nettle was reeling, and her eyes still adjusting to the new darkness, the coach slowed further and came to a halt.

"What's going on?" asked Kellen.

"Some sort of barricade." Nettle leaned farther out of the window to peer. "And two sentries."

"Human?"

"I think so."

The Shallow Wilds were zones where neither humanity nor the forces of the Wilds had dominion, according to the Pact. Humans could build and live there but were not permitted to drain the land or cut down too many of the trees. They also had to take their chances with anything else that happened to turn up. Occasionally something did.

"The path ahead is dangerous!" called out one of the sentries, sounding human enough and very nervous. "Can you take another route, sir?"

"No," said Gall, his voice as calm as black ice. The wheels creaked and the carriage rolled slowly forward. The marsh horse's hooves no longer clipped or clopped. They made a damp slapping sound, like a paintbrush hitting a wall. "We are traveling to Havel. We are permitted to pass. Do you want me to show you my credentials?"

"Havel?" exclaimed the younger sentry. "But that's—"

"That's fine!" his older companion interrupted quickly. "Just give us a moment!"

There was a sound of wooden creaking and thumping as the barricade was moved out of the way. Gall had said nothing explicitly threatening, but Nettle hadn't envied the sentries. Flanked by the darkened marsh-woods on either side, with a horse-shaped beast from the Deep Wilds advancing stealthily down the white road toward them, no wonder they had decided to let this coachload of danger find whatever other peril it pleased.

The coach lurched into motion again.

"Gall!" called Kellen. "What was that about? What do they mean, the path's dangerous?"

"Close the windows and fasten them," came the reply. "And Kellen? *You* had better cover your ears."

Nettle slammed the windows shut and bolted them before Kellen could argue. He didn't cover his ears. He was too busy fiddling with the lantern to give them more light.

Gall sounds different in the dark, thought Nettle, her skin crawling. But did he really? Or had she and Kellen just heard him differently when they had the comforting safety of high ground and daylight? *Gall sounds different in the woods.*

The sound of hooves sped up, and soon the coach, which had mastered the highland roads so smoothly, started rattling and jolting. Nettle imagined the road beneath its painted wheels yielding to rock-strewn track. There was a soft *thwack*, then a scrape and swish down one side of the carriage. Some branch raking against the coach's expensive paintwork. Nettle flinched slightly at each faint rustle and bang, feeling as though the trees were closing in.

Then another noise cut through the night like a scythe. A loud, long hiss, like an angry waterfall. The coach lurched into more violent motion, bucking and accelerating.

That sound came from the horse, Nettle realized. *What's wrong with it? Why is it speeding up?*

She wondered whether the mouth that made that hiss still looked like a horse's muzzle, or whether the creature was loosening its own shape, unhooking its joints to flow through the darkness more easily . . .

"Sit on the floor!" Kellen said, suiting action to words. Nettle joined him there, so she wouldn't be thrown out of her seat.

We shouldn't have come, thought Nettle desperately. *What if all of this was a trap? We've come down into the marsh-woods with a total stranger, and nobody else knows where we've gone.*

The carriage gave the worst jolt yet, and Kellen lurched back and banged his head against the carriage wall. He gave a yelp, then laughed aloud, the sound startling in the cramped carriage. His eyes were bright with hilarity and panic. But Nettle was suddenly absurdly grateful for his grin, his idiotic recklessness.

And then another sound came, from the other side of the closed door. It was a sob, an almost human sob.

Kellen turned pale, and his features twisted as if he were in pain. Then he reached up and started tugging the door bolt loose.

"Kellen! What are you doing!" She grabbed at his hands, but he shook her off and scrabbled at the bolt again.

There was another sob. It was a wounded, desperate sound, but something in its desperation chilled Nettle's blood. It needed something too much to leave room for pity or remorse. Kellen flinched as if the sound hurt him, his eyes wide and glazed.

Nettle slapped her hands over his ears.

He elbowed her hard in the ribs and grabbed at her hands. After a second, however, he gave a swallow of effort, and his expression changed to one of intense concentration. He stopped trying to pull her hands away and helped cover his own ears instead.

Behind him, the door rattled, and the bolt shook free from its socket. The door started to open outward. Nettle lunged past Kellen to grab at its handle.

As she tried to yank the door shut, she felt resistance, as if something on the other side were attempting to drag it open. She gave a squawk of panic and hauled on the door with all her strength.

There was a sudden bang from above, as if some weight had landed on the roof. A sharp swish, like a scythe cutting through thick damp grass. Something beyond the door gave a dark, guttural snarl.

The unseen force released the door. Nettle hastily pulled it shut and threw the bolt.

After ten more minutes of gallop, the coach settled into a controlled but bruising jog. The only sounds outside were the swish of leaves against the carriage, the oddly soft plash of hooves, and the hard patter of rain.

Kellen kept his hands over his ears, and Nettle watched him like a hawk. She didn't trust Gall, the marsh horse, or the darkness outside. And apparently right now she couldn't trust Kellen either.

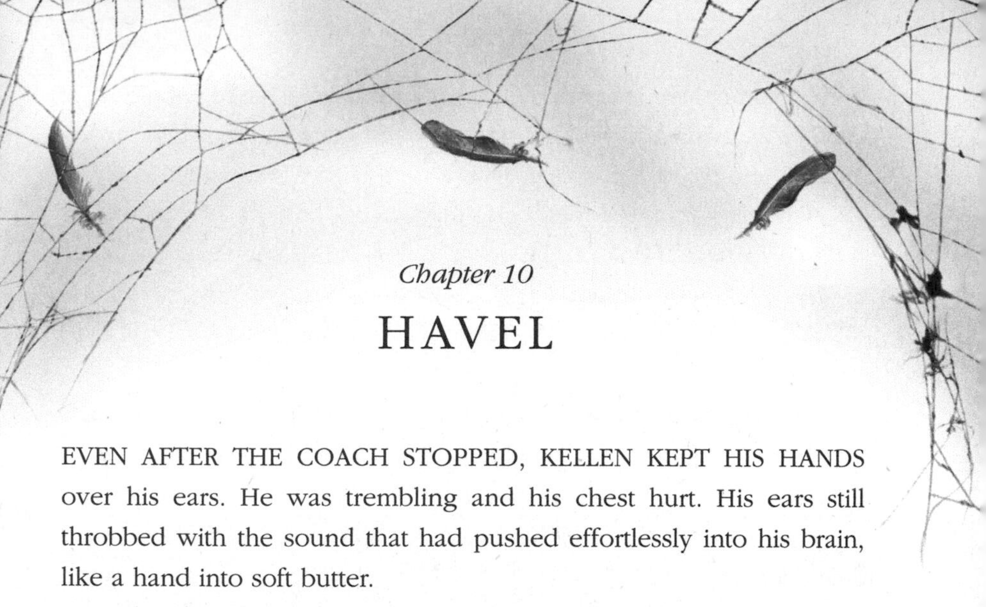

Chapter 10

HAVEL

EVEN AFTER THE COACH STOPPED, KELLEN KEPT HIS HANDS over his ears. He was trembling and his chest hurt. His ears still throbbed with the sound that had pushed effortlessly into his brain, like a hand into soft butter.

Only when Gall opened the coach door with a lantern and mimed to Kellen to uncover his ears did he dare to do so. Groggily, Kellen got out of the carriage and leaned against it, trying not to retch.

The marsh horse was steaming from head to foot, as an ordinary horse might after such a prolonged gallop. It was not panting, however. Its large dark eyes were watchful.

Nearby, Nettle was watching Kellen warily. Gall was talking to a young man in a silk-comber's apron, negotiating for a place to stay.

"If you'll show us the hut, then we'll take care of ourselves," Gall told the stranger, handing him a few coins. "I'm sure you're in a hurry to get inside."

The other man was indeed looking fidgety and nervous. People in Shallow Wilds villages didn't like coming out of their houses after dark unless they had to. Most of the time nothing bad happened if you did, but it was a risk that people got used to not taking.

The light of the lantern gleamed on the wet wood of nearby stilted huts, all dark and silent. Big, shaggy bushes loured between them, and Kellen could smell the damp, lush smells of pinch-bloom, summer sweet, and winking bugloss. The rain had halted now, but everything was still dripping—a faint, persistent, furtive sound.

The young man led them down a path made of white pebbles that rattled slightly underfoot. Their lodgings turned out to be a little stilted hut on the edge of the village, with a rope ladder below the door.

"Will this do?" asked the young man.

"Does it have a bolt on the door?" asked Nettle shakily.

"Yes, lass. Four of them."

"Sounds perfect," croaked Kellen, with feeling.

The hut was basic but dry and started to look more comfortable once Gall had brought in some blankets and food from the carriage. Once their guide had gone, Kellen bolted the door and turned on Gall.

"What was that *thing* sobbing outside and trying to get in? And why didn't you warn us?"

"So you didn't cover your ears," observed Gall.

"No, I didn't! I wanted to know why listening is a bad idea!"

"And now you know," said Gall.

"What was wrong with you back there?" demanded Nettle, fixing Kellen with an accusing look. He had trouble meeting her eye. "Why did you try to open the door?"

"I don't know how to explain!" Kellen didn't really want to remember the experience at all. "There was a lot of . . . pain. And maybe it was somebody else in pain, or maybe it was me. And . . . I had to find them so I could fix it, or . . . something. I don't know! But it was like wanting to jump into a river when you're on fire. I just had to do it!"

"Why just Kellen?" asked Nettle sharply. "I heard the sobbing too, and it didn't affect me."

"The . . . person you heard sobbing targets boys and men," said Gall. "That's why Kellen was the only one affected."

"What about you?" Kellen retorted. "You're a man!"

"I'm immune," said Gall.

"Is that because you're . . ." Nettle gestured at Gall vaguely and trailed off. She probably didn't want to say "weird and maybe not even human anymore" out loud.

"Yes," said Gall, with a trace of his almost smile again. "My pact has its advantages. Anyway, you're safe from her here. She never attacks the village."

"That's nice of her," Kellen said grumpily. He was still feeling sick, shaky, and embarrassed. He hated remembering his limbs acting without his control. "So what the hell *is* she?"

"Have you ever heard of Pale Mallow?" asked Gall.

Kellen hadn't, but Nettle's eyes widened.

"The bog spirit? The beautiful, weeping woman who drags boys and men into the marshes to drown them? This is *her* territory? I've heard stories about her since I was little."

"Great!" muttered Kellen. "Well, what am I supposed to do if the investigation takes us outside the village?"

"Oh, it will," said Gall.

"What?"

"Pale Mallow isn't a bog spirit," explained the horseman. "She isn't a thing of the Wilds, even if she's been acting like one for thirty years. She's human. We even know who she was. A woman called Belthea who once lived in this village. Beautiful, manipulative, and fond of playing her admirers off against each other—everybody seems to agree on that. She made enemies, and one day one of them cursed her. That's when she became the monster she is now. We want you to unravel the curse of Pale Mallow."

Kellen thought of the sob behind the carriage door and had trouble swallowing his mouthful of bread. But one thing Gall had just said made things so much worse.

"Did you say thirty years?" Kellen demanded. "You want me to solve a thirty-year-old curse, while the victim tries to drown me?"

"Why?" asked Nettle sharply. "I thought we were investigating the death of the guard!"

"I said I wanted you to find his killer," Gall corrected her. "There's not much doubt that he was drowned by Pale Mallow. The real question is, why was he here at all? The woods here are dangerous, and

Havel's not on the way to anywhere. So why was he here? I told you, we think someone's collecting cursers. Whoever they are, they must be hiding the cursers some place out of the way. At first my employer thought the camp might be somewhere remote in the highlands, but now she thinks it's probably in the Wilds."

Kellen rubbed at his temples and tried to focus. Yes, you could hide hundreds of secret camps in the Shallow Wilds, and thousands in the Deep Wilds.

"We think this guard was traveling to or from that camp when he ran into Pale Mallow," continued Gall. "Only she knows where he was, and whether he was alone. If cursers are being smuggled through this area, she's the one person who might know. We need to lift her curse so we can talk to her."

At least we have a marsh horse and rider with us, thought Kellen, clutching at straws. *They ought to be a match for Pale Mallow.* Gall was already getting to his feet, however, and heading to the door.

"There's somewhere else I need to be," he said. "I'll pick you up in a few days' time."

Then he departed into the witch-infested night.

Kellen and Nettle slept in their clothes in a nest of blankets, back against back to share warmth. They had slept in worse places with less privacy and no longer had much shyness with each other. There was nothing strange now in the dig of Nettle's sharp shoulder blades, the coldness of her feet, or the way she murmured in her sleep. It was soothing, like the settling noises of one's home at night or the sound of rain.

Far less soothing was the bang of Yannick landing on the hut roof a little before dawn and beginning his morning yodel.

Kellen staggered blearily to the door, flung it open, and stepped out across the threshold before remembering where he was. Fortunately he managed to grab the door frame and stop himself plummeting to the ground below.

"Bloody stilted huts," he muttered. "Nettle, can you—"

Before he could finish the sentence, Yannick had flown past him and collided with Nettle's sleeping form. She sat up, becoming alert with a speed that Kellen always found eerie.

Yannick lurched and squawked, and Nettle rolled her eyes and fetched him a hunk of bread. Then she settled herself cross-legged, her lap full of flapping gull-brother. She took on her heron-like stillness, but with very slight, birdlike twitches of the head and tiny, unreadable shifts in the tension of her face.

She and Yannick were "talking" and, as usual, Kellen felt a pang of irritation. Their rapt, silent converse left him feeling excluded and irrelevant. Nettle translated bits and pieces sometimes, but that was almost worse. He could sense the gaps.

"This is a really lonely village," she said. "Yannick's flown around here before. There's the track back to the ridge road on one side, but on the other side there's nothing. No other villages. Just woods. Havel's a dead end."

"So that's where he's been all these months?" asked Kellen. "Flying round the Shallow Wilds?"

"And the Deep Wilds," said Nettle. "All the way to the sea."

The border where the marsh-woods met the sea was treacherous, shrouded in myth and mystery. That was where the White Boats were said to dock, where the secret markets were held, and where the trees sometimes loosed their roots and drifted like shadows.

"What was he doing out there?" Kellen asked.

There was a long pause.

"Gull things," said Nettle eventually. Once again, Kellen felt as if a door had been politely shut in his face.

He pulled off his gloves and flexed his fingers, feeling a tingle as blood returned to them.

"Come on," he said, more grumpily than the situation deserved. "Let's look around and get this over with."

Kellen and Nettle followed the white path back to the heart of the village, Yannick perched clumsily on his sister's head. Slinking shafts of pale gold sunlight gleamed in the rich green moss that covered the trees, and the morning air was full of birdsong. By daylight, it was easier to see the thirty or so stilted huts that nestled among the trees.

The paths were thronged with villagers. Kellen ducked beneath a newly hung line of washing, then stepped aside to dodge the broom of a man who was sweeping water off the path. The smell of baking bread in the shared brick ovens made him feel hungry.

Up on high ground, a couple of women fed their penned piglets while pretending not to stare at the new arrivals. They were not the only ones furtively peering.

"It's like we're a traveling circus," Kellen muttered. To be fair, they looked a bit like one, with Nettle wearing a gull as a hat.

He felt groggy. Visiting the marsh-woods always gave him a sort of mind-lag as his brain adjusted to their scale.

From above, none of the villages of the marsh-woods had seemed very far apart. And even now, Kellen's brain—his stupid, stubborn brain that should know better—kept expecting to hear dog barks from another village, or perhaps the rattle of cycle sedans from some nearby ridge road. Because surely there must be one not so far away?

But the few noises Kellen could hear were so distant they made the stillness seem more dense. The echoing lament of some bird miles away. A great, papery susurration of leaves when the wind blew. With every passing moment, the quiet of the surrounding marsh-woods was rolling in and overwhelming him.

As they reached the heart of the village, the young man who had leased them the hut hurried to greet them.

"Good morning!" he called. "I'm Armon—we met last night. Can I get you breakfast?" It became clear that Gall had paid for lodgings and meals for the next three days. Armon led them to his family's hut, where his mother served them a breakfast of hot herb bread and coddled eggs on a stone outdoor table.

"So . . . just supposing we wanted to walk back to the ridge road, how safe would we be by daylight?" Kellen asked through a mouthful of bread. Now that they weren't under Gall's watchful, doleful eye, it seemed worth checking their options.

"Oh no!" Armon looked horrified. "Don't do that, not without the carriage! The path's not safe, even in daylight!"

"Then how do you and the other men here get out and about?" asked Kellen. "I mean, you don't spend your whole lives hiding in this village, do you?"

Armon's face fell.

"I wouldn't call it *hiding*," he said. "There's plenty of hard work needs doing in a village, and the bounds are wider than you might think." His defensiveness was answer enough.

"Right," sighed Kellen. "I see." He made eye contact with Nettle and shrugged. "Worth a try," he mouthed.

"It's not so bad," Armon insisted. "Just division of labor. All right, so us menfolk can't help with the foraging, hunting, traveling for trade, and path maintenance. But we can fix up the buildings, spin the silk, look after the animals and chickens, take care of the children, and make sure the rain defenses are kept in shape."

"Couldn't you just block your ears so Pale Mallow can't affect you?" Kellen asked. If he had to face this bog-witch, he needed to know as much possible.

"Then we can't hear her coming," explained Armon, with the patient air of someone who had answered such questions more than once. "Her voice isn't the only thing dangerous about her. She's strong, and sudden, and the sight of her stops you in your tracks."

"She's beautiful?" asked Nettle.

"That's what they say," answered Armon. "Beautiful and frightful. I've never seen her."

"What if you sent out a *big* group?" suggested Kellen. "If everyone's armed, surely she can't take you all on?"

"Chancery have tried that a few times." Armon gave a short, mirthless laugh. "They'd like to rid the woods of her, so sometimes they send teams to capture her. And each time a fog creeps in while they're out in the woods and half the team just . . . vanishes."

"What if I disguised myself—"

"That wouldn't help either. *You'd* know you were a boy, so she would too. If someone knows they're a man or boy, that's what matters. Outside appearances aren't important. It's what's inside that counts—who we are in our *souls*. She can see the truth, even if others wouldn't."

Armon sighed.

"Listen, she doesn't come every time you step outside the boundary stones. I've known people who made it to the ridge road without trouble. One gang of footpads who set up in the forest near here survived a whole week before she killed them all. But she comes often enough that it's not worth the risk."

"So what else have you tried?" asked Kellen. "What *does* work?"

"Not much," Armon answered simply. "Iron and rowan don't affect her—she's not a creature of the Wilds. They're no good against an ordinary human who's been cursed. She's less likely to show up in the middle of the day, particularly if it's bright. She can sink into the marsh without drowning, and she can move quicker than a deer. But she leaves footprints in the mud. We don't *think* she can melt into mist or squeeze through keyholes." He didn't sound completely sure, though, which was less than reassuring.

"Does she ever talk?" asked Nettle. "Has she ever said what *she* wants?"

"No. I've never heard of her using words."

"Before she was cursed, she lived in this village, didn't she?" asked Kellen. "What can you tell us about her? Does anyone here remember her?"

Armon sighed, giving Kellen a concerned glance.

"Don't take this the wrong way," he said, "but you're not the first people Chancery has sent to find out more about Belthea. I know they're still hoping to learn something that will help them catch her. So now and then someone turns up, raking over those old coals and asking all the same questions, and they never find what they're looking for. Then some of them go out into the marsh-woods hunting for Pale Mallow, and we never see them again."

"We're different," said Kellen. "We're too brilliant to drown." He grinned a little wildly, hoping he was right. Armon responded with a doubtful smile.

"All right, I'll take you to Clover," he said. "Visitors usually want to talk to her first."

"Who's Clover?" asked Nettle.

"Belthea's daughter."

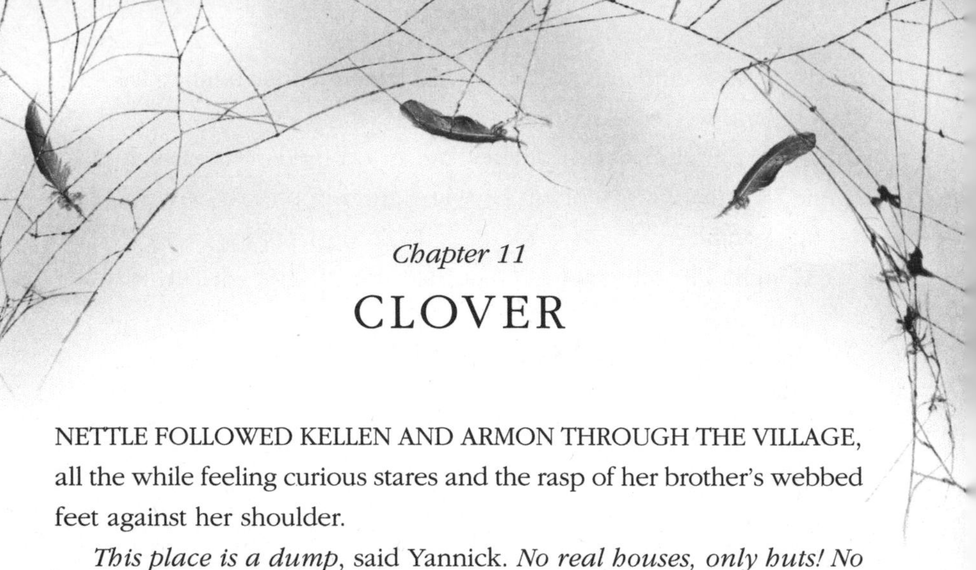

Chapter 11

CLOVER

NETTLE FOLLOWED KELLEN AND ARMON THROUGH THE VILLAGE, all the while feeling curious stares and the rasp of her brother's webbed feet against her shoulder.

This place is a dump, said Yannick. *No real houses, only huts! No barns! No water tank! And all their cooking fires are outside!*

He had a point. Nettle's home village had definitely been bigger and better equipped, with some brick and stone buildings among the stilt huts.

Do you have *to dig your toes in?* she snapped. Yannick's claw-tips were painfully pointed.

You should wear a hat big enough to sit on, her brother replied. *I'm tired, aren't I? I flew all the way, unlike some people.*

You could have ridden in the coach, if you hadn't been sulking, said Nettle, but she put up a hand to stroke one of his feet.

I was already tired when I found you at the canal, Yannick told her suddenly. *Did you even notice that?*

Nobody made you fly all over the Wilds either, said Nettle. She wondered how much of her anxiety he could read. Probably all of it. Whenever Yannick was gone for a long time, she started thinking of ways he might have died. Dead through rat poison. Shot by a farmer. Now she also had to worry about him getting devoured by some unnamed creature of the Deep Wilds.

You don't understand, Yannick told her impatiently. *You lot don't flock. We do. You don't know what it's like to we-think.*

Nettle wasn't sure whether "you lot" meant herons or humans, but it hardly mattered. He was telling her she was a different creature from him, and couldn't understand. He was talking about a "we" that wasn't Yannick-and-Nettle, it was we-the-gulls. Nettle swallowed hard, as if she were forcing down something that wriggled and was full of bones.

We circle, and we drift, and we follow the rest, Yannick went on. *We follow the paths of things.*

What kind of things? asked Nettle.

Boats, answered Yannick. *Ploughs. And sometimes things without names in the woods. I don't know. Things that might be food, or might find food. So the flock drifted out over the Wilds, and I went with it for a while.*

There was more. Nettle could tell. There had to be some other reason why Yannick was so angry.

I found a mate, he said unexpectedly.

It shouldn't have been a shock, but it was. If Yannick had still been human, Nettle reminded herself, he would have been sixteen. What was so strange about him having a girlfriend? Why should the news hurt?

Is she . . . nice? she asked.

Don't be stupid, said Yannick. *She's a gull. Gulls don't walk along the seashore together, talking about their feelings. It's not like that. But one day she became my mate and I needed her. I just did. It didn't matter what she was like. We made a nest in a reed bed. There were eggs. Chicks. Three of them.*

So that's why you were gone so long, snapped Nettle. She could hide her bitterness from anybody else, but not from Yannick. *You made yourself a new family. You didn't need me anymore.*

Nettle shoved Yannick off her shoulder. It was a petty thing to do, and he pecked her ear hard as he reeled away, flapping.

I left them to come to you! he shouted, sounding sad and angry. *I needed them, and I protected them, and only cared about them . . . and then one day I felt a tug inside me, bringing me back to you. And now that I'm with you again . . . my mate and chicks . . . they're just birds. I don't need them. I know the chicks will probably die if I don't go back to help feed them. But I don't need to, so I probably won't.*

I'm not stopping you, said Nettle, knowing that she was. She felt terribly sad, and terribly relieved, and sick at her own selfishness.

Why do you have to be human? Yannick sounded bitter.

Were you happy? Nettle asked.

You know it doesn't work like that, spat Yannick. *I don't think about "being happy" unless I'm with you, and then I never am. Humans are never happy.*

No, agreed Nettle. *We're not.* She didn't look at him. Her eyes hurt. After a while Yannick deigned to land on her shoulder again, and she didn't stop him. They were both still angry. One of Yannick's toes scratched the skin of Nettle's neck.

You're changing too, he told her, harshly. *Each time I come back to you, you've changed a bit more. You're starting to smell different. One day I won't be able to find you because you're not you anymore.*

I suppose I'm growing up, said Nettle.

Is that what you're calling it? asked Yannick.

The question hurt, but Nettle didn't reply.

Belthea's daughter Clover turned out to be a practically dressed middle-aged woman with a thoughtful, kindly face and white streaks in her dark hair. She was a tree-milker and had just come back harvesting sap from weeper trees. She agreed to talk while her cauldron of sap simmered over the fire, spreading a scent of caramel and fresh-cut grass.

"I was fifteen when my mother was cursed," Clover explained. "It was early autumn—the night of the apple festival. I was just old enough to drink the cider." She gave a small smile that quickly faded. "Festivals matter a lot in villages like this."

"They're the only thing that happens," said Nettle, remembering her own early childhood in the Shallow Wilds. The monotony of unmarked time, swallowing your life little by little like a great snake. The festivals were something you could look forward to, dream about so hard that you ached. "We had the plum-blossom festival, the leaf-boat festival, the bramble festival, the mead-making . . ."

"Yes!" Clover's face brightened and became more open. "We have most of those!"

Nettle noticed Clover's large eyes and delicate cheekbones and wondered if she had inherited them from her mother. It sounded like Belthea had always made the most of her looks. Clover's hair was rough-cut and tied back, her hands calloused from tree-climbing and knife-use.

"What happened?" asked Kellen.

Clover sighed.

"I went home from the festival early, before the moon was even up. I needed to make sure that the geese and chickens were shut in, the firewood chopped . . . Lots of things needed to be done. So I didn't see what happened in the end. But while I was there, my mother was everyone's fancy. She danced with six men in a row and went apple-dunking with two others. They had a fight over it—Piller Caddy knocked out Mackin's tooth. Well, it sounds like things went on that way after I left. Everyone got a good skinful of cider, and the dancing moved out to a clearing in the woods. Thick, soft grass, good for dancing in bare feet, you see. They put lights in the trees. My mother was in her green dress that night. It made her look pale, but she liked that. They say she danced, and danced, and danced. And then at one point the moon disappeared behind the clouds, and all the lanterns dimmed. The musicians suddenly found they couldn't play. Their fingers were numb and could only find the wrong strings. Then the moon sailed clear, and my mother . . . wasn't herself anymore. She hurled her dance partner across the clearing so hard he cracked his head against a tree, and she ran off into the woods. She never came back."

"I'm sorry," said Nettle, and meant it.

Clover exhaled and stooped to sniff at her cauldron.

"It was a long time ago, and everyone in the village was very kind. I became everyone's extra daughter. They even built me a new hut so I wouldn't have to live in the one I'd shared with her."

"What about your father?" asked Kellen. "Did he live with you?"

"He died when I was three." Clover gave him a wry look. "I know why you're asking. No, my father wasn't the curser. It was always just my mother and me."

"Do you know who the curser might have been?" Kellen persisted. "Did your mother ever mention anyone that frightened her?"

Clover laughed under her breath.

"Oh, my mother wasn't afraid of anyone! I don't know who it was, but I'll tell you who it wasn't. It wasn't poor Mackin the Spinner, even if the rest of the village thinks it was. He went off to the marshes after my mother was cursed, and never came back, and the rumor went round that he drowned himself because of guilt. But I think he went out there hoping to help her or bring her back. He was *kind*."

"So why did they blame him?" asked Nettle.

"Because he's gone, and it's easier," sighed Clover, staring into the fire. "Nobody wants to believe that they've been living alongside a curser for thirty years. Can you imagine it? Someone that warped. Somebody who could do that horrible thing, and hide it, and still walk around smiling."

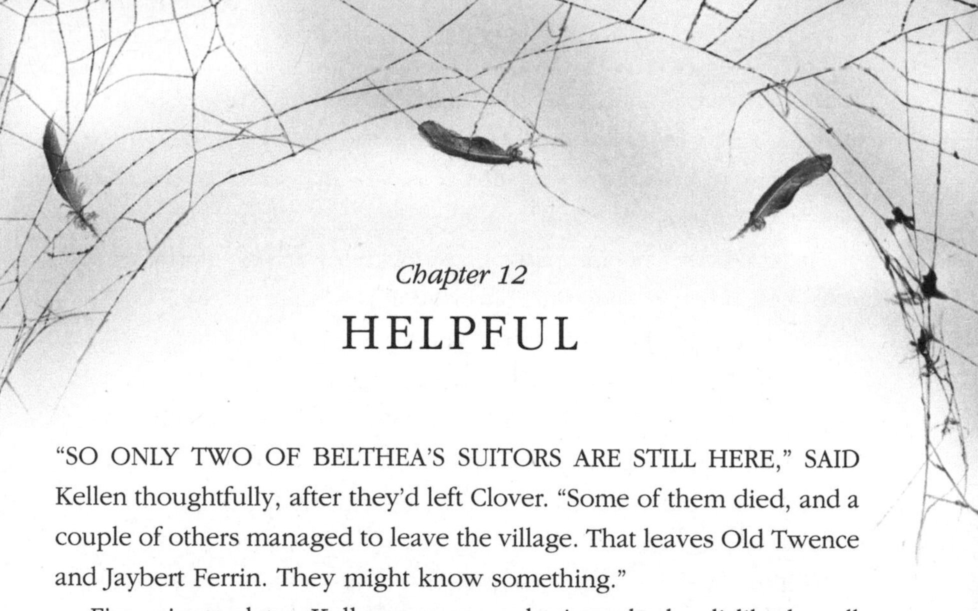

Chapter 12

HELPFUL

"SO ONLY TWO OF BELTHEA'S SUITORS ARE STILL HERE," SAID Kellen thoughtfully, after they'd left Clover. "Some of them died, and a couple of others managed to leave the village. That leaves Old Twence and Jaybert Ferrin. They might know something."

Five minutes later, Kellen was remembering why he disliked small villages. You couldn't just waltz up to somebody in a place like this and casually engage them in conversation. You couldn't blindside them. Everyone knew who you were and why you were there.

By the time they reached Old Twence's hut, he and Jaybert Ferrin were sitting outside waiting for them, with two spare chairs. They had even made tea.

"Well," said Old Twence, with a twinkle in his one good eye, "we thought we'd save you a bit of running around. We knew you'd want to talk to us—the other visitors did—so this way you can do us both at once."

Old Twence was a gregarious man of sixty, whose ready smile showed a good set of teeth. Jaybert looked about ten years younger. He was a tall, shy man with large hands, who said little and fiddled with everything.

Twence did most of the talking, with Jaybert interjecting to agree with his friend now and then. Oh, they had been fierce rivals thirty years ago, but all of that was water under the bridge.

"It was poor Mackin who *really* lost his wits over her," sighed Twence, giving Kellen a meaningful look. Kellen remembered Clover saying that everyone thought Mackin had been the curser.

"So why were you all so obsessed with Belthea?" asked Kellen. It wasn't a polite way of putting it, but he felt contrary and out of sorts. "What was it about her? And don't just tell me she was pretty and wicked. What was she *like*?"

There was an uncomfortable pause, which was only partly annoyance. Kellen had pushed the conversation off the script.

"She had this smile—" began Jaybert.

"She was different, that's all," Twence interrupted. "Graceful, bold, and always dressed like it was a festival. 'Different' was enough to make us think about her, I suppose . . . All's well that ends well, though. We both settled down with good women. Better than we deserve, eh, Jaybert?"

"Nothing's ended well," said Kellen sharply, cutting short Jaybert's obliging guffaw. "Nothing's ended at all. It won't, while there's a woman walking the marshes in torment."

Ah, there it was, a small flash of irritation in Twence's eye. But it faded into placidity almost immediately.

"You're a highlander," Twence said tolerantly. "Highlanders are used to fixing things. But living down here, you learn that there are things you can't mend, however much you want to. If you blow back against the wind, you get dust in your eyes. Death's a step away, so you learn which steps not to take. You keep your chickens penned, and you mark the paths, and you teach your children caution. You live with it."

"Well, I don't!" snapped Kellen. "I don't *live with* things. I don't accept them. I don't give up." He stood up abruptly. "Thanks for the tea."

He walked off, even though he could sense that Twence had more to say. He wasn't going to sit and be served a story, even if it was the one he'd planned to order from the menu.

Nettle followed and fell into step with him. She didn't look at him.

"Don't start," said Kellen, because she had, even though she hadn't. "Yes, I know. They were helpful, and I was rude."

"You *were* rude," said Nettle thoughtfully. "And they didn't get angry. Why not? You're just some loud outsider brat. Why didn't they tell you to mind your manners?"

So perhaps Nettle wasn't picking a fight after all. Her words gave shape to Kellen's own instinctive suspicions, like a string bundling a sheaf of wheat.

"They're giving us what we want on a plate so we won't start looking in cupboards," said Kellen slowly. "Twence was dropping hints that Mackin was the curser, wasn't he? And he didn't like it when Jaybert started answering one of my questions."

"You should carry on being loud and bratty," said Nettle. "Keep everyone's eyes on you. I'll see if I can talk to Jaybert alone."

Armon was happy to show Kellen to the hut where Belthea had lived, on the edge of the village. Grass sprouted from its roof. Its stilts had slumped sideways, leaving the hut resting on a moss-covered boulder. Cobwebs shrouded the hut and hung across the doorway in thick veils, studded with seed husks and dead flower heads.

"Nobody else fancied living here, then?" asked Kellen.

"No," admitted Armon, who seemed reluctant to approach the hut. "We left it for the spiders."

Shallow Wilds villages often had a "sacrifice hut" that was abandoned to the spiders, as a consolation for their webs being cleared out of the other homes and as an offering to any Little Brothers in the area. It was usually a hut that nobody wanted anyway, because it was old, badly built, or seen as "unlucky."

Kellen felt a little trepidation as he approached. There probably weren't any actual Little Brothers in the hut, but it didn't hurt to be careful.

"Knock, knock, Little Brothers," he whispered, as the stories had taught him. "Be kind to a fellow weaver."

He used a stick to push aside the thick swathes of cobweb and entered through the lopsided door. It was difficult to keep his footing on the damp, slanting floorboards, and he had to steady himself against the nearest wall. Amid the web, spider bodies scuttled and fled. Some were dull, hairy, and acorn-sized, others tiny like turquoise beads. Ordinary spiders, not Little Brothers. His pulse slowed a little.

It had probably been a pretty nice hut once. A bed with an actual bedstead, now a collapsed mess of limbs like a fallen foal. Rugs, now seething with wood lice. A tortoiseshell-backed brush. Even a small, blotched hand mirror.

Shoes huddled along the lower edge of the sloping floor. Sturdy clogs for walking the muddy paths, bold blue shoes with inch-high red heels, dainty shoes with rotting ribbons and tarnished copper bells.

It took Kellen a little while to realize what was missing.

"Armon! What happened to Belthea's clothes?"

"What do you mean?"

"Her shoes are here, but no other clothes. Did Clover take them?"

"No!" exclaimed Armon. "She took some things from the house—pots, pans, tools, furniture. But nobody wanted Belthea's personal things, let alone her *clothes*. Maybe a thief from outside the village?"

"A thief would take her shoes," objected Kellen. "And her brush and mirror."

"It can't be anyone local." Armon looked shaken at the idea. "*We* don't go in there."

Kellen noticed some muddy scuffs on the floorboards, besides those left by his own feet. Some were old and dry, but a few looked much fresher.

"Well, somebody does," he said aloud.

Kellen spent the rest of the afternoon talking to people and trying not to lose his temper. Everyone was helpful, and nobody helped.

"She's not really human anymore," said Armon's mother unexpectedly as she made Kellen sandwiches on the table outside her hut. She was a kind-faced, middle-aged woman who seemed as solid and sensible as oak. "Do you really think it would be a kindness, trying to catch and tame her? She's wild now. Let her be."

"Have you heard her crying?" Kellen demanded. "I have." He watched his hostess's worn hands methodically arranging the food. Bread, pickled crayfish, herbs, cheese. "I wouldn't leave my worst enemy the way she is. You must have known Belthea. What did she ever do to you?"

Armon's mother handed him the sandwiches without a word, then climbed the ladder to her hut and shut the door.

Kellen watched her go. He hadn't been angry on Belthea's behalf at first. But now he was.

As the sun set, Kellen took a walk to the very edge of the village, almost shaking with rage. He only started to feel a little better once he was farther out than most local men dared go. He could feel in his gut that this was where he was at home. Walking along danger's boundary line. Pushing his luck.

The birds were so *loud* in the Wilds. Larks, linnets, thrushes, curlews, and shrikes. The moss hung from the trees in swathes, like the cobwebs in Belthea's hut but brilliant green. The leaves, the moss, the lichen all burned emerald in the light of the setting sun.

This is a mistake, his gut told him quite clearly. But he kept walking, even when the white stone path became mossy, muffling his steps.

How quiet the forest was. How loud it was. He was suddenly very aware of his own breathing, the tickle of it passing his lips, the taste of pollen in the air.

There was a rustle behind him.

The sound sent a shock through Kellen, and at the same time it felt inevitable. He spun round, already knowing whose pale face he would see, whose sob he would hear . . .

. . . and took a punch in the jaw.

He fell back onto the path with a surprised yell. Two men were standing over him, scarves wrapped round the lower part of their faces. No Pale Mallow, no mystical threat. Just two wide-eyed, angry men. He felt a flood of relief until he noticed the weapons in their hands. One carried a heavy mallet, the other a sickle.

Kellen rolled over and tried to scramble to his feet, but he was winded and too slow. A weight hit him in the back and pinned him down. A knee at the base of his spine, an elbow forcing his face against the mossy stones of the path.

"You," growled a voice in his ear, "need to know when to leave well enough alone. You're going to stop poking around. You'll wait for your friend to come back with his carriage, and you'll leave, and you won't come back.

"You understand? Are you going to be a good boy now?" There was something shining, close to Kellen's face. It was the blade of the sickle.

Kellen stared at the curved blade and its wicked point and knew that he was going to say no.

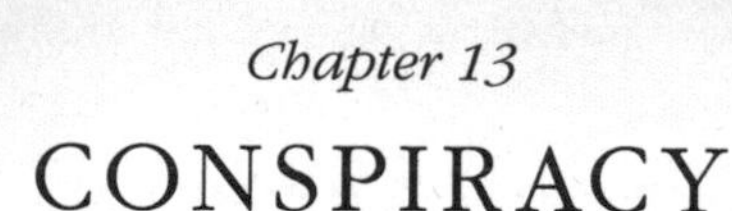

Chapter 13
CONSPIRACY

"SHE HAD THIS SMILE," SAID JAYBERT, THE BUCKET OF CHICKEN-feed hanging forgotten from one of his big hands.

It had taken an hour for Nettle to bring him back to the subject of Belthea. But Nettle was from the Shallow Wilds, and she was the same age as Jaybert's younger daughter. She was quiet, unassuming, and patient and had pushed too gently for him to notice.

"Belthea had a gap between her teeth, just here." Jaybert tapped his own teeth. "And her normal smile—her pretty smile—didn't show it. But sometimes when you were alone with her, she smiled in a way that showed the gap. Like a cat showing its fangs. And you realized that she wasn't kind. And she was letting you see. It made you feel . . . special."

Nettle nodded, trying to understand.

"And then . . . when she let you see how she was—how lazy she was, how mean, how selfish—it didn't feel . . . bad. She'd look at you, and smile that smile, and say 'I don't feel like carrying this up the hill. Can you?' Or she'd say, 'I can't afford that brooch. Can you buy it for me?' And . . . you did. Because her asking meant she was letting you *see* her."

"Didn't she have money of her own?" Nettle asked.

"Oh, she and her daughter made wines and wicker baskets. And they spun silk, like everyone else. But . . . she couldn't bring herself to work much. Not really. She . . . she was a wild thing, like a fox."

You're still in love with her, thought Nettle suddenly.

"So did everyone else give her gifts too?" she couldn't help asking.

"I suppose so." Jaybert's breath caught, as if some old arrowhead beneath the skin had snagged on a nerve. "I suppose she smiled that way at everybody."

A flare of white streaked into view, wings wide. Nettle recognized Yannick's dark brown face, beak agape. His shrill, grating cry made Jaybert drop his bucket.

Nettle heard and understood. And broke into a run.

She ran frantically through the village, then down a path leading into the marsh-woods.

They've got weapons! Yannick was screaming. *Stop, Nettle! Stop! Get help!*

But there was no stopping, and she knew there was no help. Not in this village. Not anywhere, perhaps.

Nettle took a tumble at a corner and fell face-first into cold mud. She felt the shock of the cold, then panic. She had grown up with the dread of tumbling into unmarked marsh, feeling it suck at her limbs and draw her relentlessly down. This wasn't her village, and she didn't know its paths, its unmarked dangers. But she didn't sink. It was only mud.

She struggled backward onto the path, staggered muddily to her feet again, and kept running.

There, ahead of her. Two men were bent over a single figure, kicking at it while it curled defensively, shielding its face, and failing to struggle to its feet. A sickle was raised above the prone figure, as if ready for a chance to strike.

It was Kellen, reaping a harvest of rage and being kicked to a pulp, just as she had always feared.

Nettle collapsed against a birch trunk, winded and exhausted, feeling her muddy fingers slither against the bark. So she was here, but she was skinny and useless and unarmed. Why had she thought she could help? What good could she ever be? She took a deep breath, not knowing what she could do with it.

And screamed.

It was a raw, ragged sound, like bird calls or the howl of the wind. The two men looked up and stared down the path toward her. What did they see? A female figure in the shadow of a birch, shrouded in mud. A gasping, enraged shape, its fingers hooked like claws.

They ran.

Kellen and Nettle took the long route back to their borrowed hut. There, Nettle washed Kellen's bruises and grazes in spite of his objections, then set about changing her clothes under a blanket.

"What's wrong with these people?" shouted Kellen, once he was sure all his teeth would stay in. "Why does nothing in the Wilds ever make sense?"

"Eat something," said Nettle calmly. Kellen never coped well with hunger.

"Well, all we've got is squashed sandwiches, because somebody knelt on me and threatened me with a sickle!"

"That sounds delicious," said Nettle with forced serenity.

While they were eating, Yannick swooped in through the open door, knocked over the lantern, and flapped wildly around the room, nearly getting his wing tip in Kellen's eye.

"Death's teeth!" swore Kellen. "Nettle, can you *do* something about—"

"Yannick saved your life!" Nettle told him curtly as she set the lantern upright again. "He told me what was happening. That's how I got there in time."

I won't ever tell you anything again! screamed Yannick. *Not if you're going to run into danger like that! You could have been killed!*

He was remembering that he was Nettle's older brother. She could feel his sudden ache at being small and unable to protect her. But when he was frightened he also sounded young—younger than her. She let him settle on her lap and fed him squashed crusts.

Now you know how I feel all the time, she told him.

"They probably weren't going to kill me," said Kellen sullenly. "They just wanted to scare me. But . . . tell Yannick I'm glad he was there. I'm glad you both were."

It was almost an apology and almost a thank you. Kellen's entrenched sense of fairness was one of his more bearable qualities.

"But why does anybody want to stop us investigating?" Kellen continued angrily. "Why isn't anybody bothered by a bog-witch haunting the place? Why is everyone still here?"

"Yannick called Havel a dump," admitted Nettle. "And it looked that way to me at first. The buildings are basic, and lots of things are missing. There's no stockade or brick buildings for everyone to retreat to if bandits attack. No barns to keep the animals safe. The food stores aren't made of stone. But they're all *full*. Nobody's hungry. The foraging here seems to be really good."

"Apart from the rampaging bog-witch," added Kellen.

"Apart from the rampaging bog-witch," Nettle conceded.

"Who everyone is happy to leave running around the marshes," finished Kellen. He pushed his knuckles into his temples. "We're not up against one curser this time. This is lots of people—maybe the whole village—trying to stop us investigating. Why? What are they afraid we'll find out?"

Kellen and Nettle talked about keeping watches that night, but didn't. They knew from experience that neither of them coped well with lost sleep.

"If the locals murder us, they murder us," said Kellen. "We might as well die well-rested."

When Nettle woke at dawn, she was alone in the hut. She stretched, her limbs stiff from the cool, early dampness of the air, and felt something tickle her face. She sat up, looked down at the blanket, and sighed.

Peering out through the door, she spotted Kellen, pacing up and down in front of the hut, glassy-eyed and intent.

"Did you forget to put your gloves on last night?" she asked, holding up the blanket, which was fraying badly along one edge.

"No, I didn't!" Kellen curled his gloveless hands defensively. "That can't have been me. Probably mouse-eaten."

Nettle decided there was no point in arguing and clambered down the ladder. The morning mist sucked all color out of the scene, and she could hear the trees dripping with dew.

"How long have you been up?" she asked. A sleep-deprived Kellen was usually more impatient and reckless, and leaped to wilder conclusions, and Nettle didn't think that was likely to improve matters.

"I don't know." Kellen waved a hand dismissively. "An hour or two. Kept waking up from dreams." He sighed, sounding frustrated. "My mind's just . . ." He mimed rapid, whirring circles with one finger.

"We should get breakfast," Nettle said, then jumped as Yannick skimmed down from the gray sky and alighted on the hut roof. A small bread roll was gripped clumsily in his beak.

"Looks like your brother already has," remarked Kellen.

"That's somebody else's breakfast!" Nettle exclaimed, annoyed and alarmed.

"Good," replied Kellen promptly. "Serves them right."

"It's *not* good!" snapped Nettle. Naturally this would be the one time Yannick and Kellen agreed on something. "The villagers already don't like us! We can't give them an excuse to throw us out of here! If my gull starts stealing food—"

I'm not your gull! screamed Yannick. *And it wasn't stealing! I found it on the . . .*

And then he suddenly fell silent and dedicated himself to tearing the roll apart. Nettle sensed the furtive haste with which he abandoned his sentence.

What? she demanded. *What is it?*

I'm not telling you, he said.

You found the bread somewhere, she persisted. *Where was it?*

Yannick shook the roll apart, then spent a maddeningly long time snapping up the fragments. For a while Nettle thought he wasn't going to answer. But she waited, never letting her focus weaken, barely blinking. Gulls were adaptable, but herons were patient.

I couldn't sleep this morning, said Yannick at last. *When I'm with a flock, I sleep when enough other gulls are still and quiet, because that means it's safe. But you two . . . when you're asleep, you keep muttering, and turning over, and* breathing *too loudly. So I got up and flew around, looking for food. And I found some. In a little clearing, a mile or two outside the village. A handkerchief laid out on a rock. Bread. Cheese. Seed cakes. A bowl of something that smelled sweet.*

Where? asked Nettle.

If I tell you, said Yannick, *you'll go wandering out of the village. I'm not making that mistake again.*

"Oh, for crying out loud," muttered Nettle.

"What are you doing?" asked Kellen, as Nettle climbed the ladder to the hut and started clambering up toward the roof.

"Somebody left food out for Belthea," said Nettle. "It was in the marsh-woods, it must have been for her."

"Why would anyone do that?" asked Kellen.

"I don't know, but I need to look at that roll," said Nettle. "Or what's left of it. Yannick! Stop eating it!"

Yannick hopped away from Nettle's reaching hand, a chunk of his prize in his beak, and rebelliously wolfed it down. His motion nudged another large bread fragment, however, so that it tumbled off the roof and landed on the muddy grass below.

"Kellen, can you look at that?" called Nettle. "I think the roll had a line of seeds across the top, but I'm not sure."

"Does it matter?" Kellen picked up the bread chunk.

"Havel has shared ovens," said Nettle, clambering back down the ladder. "We had some back in my village. Everyone had to mark their bread and pies differently, so we could tell whose were whose. Folks cut lines in the top, or added nuts . . ."

". . . or sprinkled seeds." Kellen stared at the chunk of bread, then took an experimental nibble. "Poppy seeds," he said. "Also grit." He spat out a little strand of muddy moss.

Nettle took a deep breath, then let it out slowly.

"Could you both stop eating the clue," she said evenly, "just for a moment?"

"Is it an offering from the village, to persuade Pale Mallow not to attack anyone?" mused Kellen, then answered his own question. "No, it can't be. Nobody would expect that to work."

"Let's head into the village," said Nettle. "Everybody cooks their daily bread first thing in the morning, don't they? Let's see who uses poppy seeds."

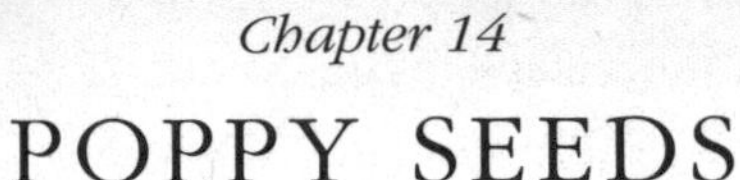

Chapter 14

POPPY SEEDS

THE SUN WAS FULLY RISEN BY THE TIME KELLEN AND NETTLE walked into the center of the village. Yannick was skittish, sometimes riding on Nettle's head, sometimes flitting around.

"We should let them think they've won," Nettle whispered to Kellen. "Try to look like you've been beaten into submission. Act angry and sulky."

"I think I can manage that," Kellen muttered, feeling his bruised jaw.

They found Armon and his mother outside his hut, and Nettle explained that she and Kellen planned to leave as soon as the carriage returned.

"You're sure?" Armon's mother asked brightly, setting down a basket of freshly cooked rolls in front of them. "You're welcome to stay with us as long as you like!" It was the warm, encouraging tone people only ever used when their guests had already promised to depart.

The rolls in the basket had three lines scored in the top but no seeds on the crust. Kellen and Nettle took a couple each and began a casual-looking wander around the village.

Kellen's mind was alight as they walked, sensing the wavering strands of the village. He could almost hear the rumors scurrying from hut to hut like small beasts in the undergrowth. He could feel the storm-tickle of gazes.

They wandered through the village, Kellen apparently sulking, while Nettle made a show of trailing after him and trying to talk him into a better temper. With luck, nobody would realize that their aimless-looking route was actually a quick tour of the brick ovens and campfires.

Kellen kept his eyes open, noticing the bread that was heaved in and out of the oven. Big round loaves, little spirals, and plaits. Rolls scored with crosses, or scattered with nuts, or streaked with berry juice. Nothing like the roll Yannick had found.

He also noticed two men with similar features watching him and Nettle from a distance.

"Those two," he said to Nettle under his breath. "Under the marsh maple."

"Are you sure?" Nettle didn't ask what he meant.

"See the taller one?" murmured Kellen. "The idiot's still got his sickle tucked into his belt."

As Kellen watched, Old Twence turned up and chatted with the two young men in low tones. Kellen could see a familial resemblance between all three.

"His sons?" asked Nettle under her breath.

"Probably," Kellen muttered.

Twence approached Kellen and Nettle, smiling sympathetically.

"Sorry to hear that we'll be losing you," he declared, clapping Kellen on the shoulder.

"Well, I'm not sorry!" Kellen said nastily, and more loudly than necessary. "The sooner I'm out of this swamp pit the better."

"It's too bad of your masters to send you chasing such a cold trail," said Twence sympathetically.

"Yeah," growled Kellen. "I'm not going to find out anything new after thirty years. And I can't unravel a curse if I don't know why it happened."

The other conversations in the clearing hushed. Many of the villagers were staring at Kellen open-mouthed.

"Unravel?" Twence's voice was unsteady. "Do you mean undo? You can lift curses?"

I thought everyone knew! Kellen darted a look at Nettle, who seemed just as surprised as he was. *Oh. Wait. We never actually told them, did we?*

"Well!" said Twence after a tense pause. "Fancy that!" He walked away, casting occasional glances over his shoulder, and began a quiet, urgent conversation with his sons.

"Why do I get the feeling I just made everything much worse?" Kellen whispered to Nettle. The atmosphere had become more tense and troubled. Looking around, he saw fewer smiles.

"Let's beat a retreat," murmured Nettle.

"But we haven't found the poppy seeds yet!" protested Kellen, as Nettle pulled him along by his sleeve.

"No, and that's odd. Just a moment." Nettle took on her sharp, distant, talking-to-gull expression again, her head alongside Yannick's feathered flank. "Listen—I just asked Yannick about the roll, and he says it was fresh. Not stale at all. It must have been left out this morning."

She was right, Kellen realized. The chunk of bread had still been crisp and soft.

"That's why we didn't see anybody cooking rolls with poppy seeds!" said Kellen, catching her drift. "They cooked theirs earlier, before they went out."

Nettle nodded.

"I've been thinking," she said. "I knew there was *something* odd about yesterday morning, but I couldn't work out what it was."

"Well?" asked Kellen.

"When we saw Clover, she'd only just got back from collecting sap, and nobody was surprised. But that means she must get up early. *Really* early." She gave Kellen a meaningful look. "At least an hour before dawn."

"Oh," said Kellen, catching on. Some unanswered questions were trying to form shapes in his mind, like blots on paper that become a picture at a distance.

"These are the Shallow Wilds," said Nettle. "People don't go out in the dark—not unless it's an emergency, or a festival. They definitely don't wander out of their village before the sun's up. But it looks like Clover does. Every morning."

Kellen and Nettle had been waiting outside Clover's hut for quarter of an hour when they saw her come into view, her clothes lichen-stained and her boots muddy. When she saw them, she picked up her stride and hurried over.

"You're leaving?" she asked without preamble, her forehead creased with dismay. Her expression changed as her gaze slid over the bruises on Kellen's face. "What happened?"

"This doesn't seem to be a healthy place for visitors," replied Kellen.

"Is it true you can lift curses?" Clover asked urgently. "Please, you can't just go!"

Her expression was so hopeful and desperate that Kellen decided to take a chance.

"Is there somewhere private we can talk?" he asked. He had the uncomfortable feeling that they were still being watched.

Clover hesitated, looking conflicted.

"My mother's hut," she suggested, a little reluctantly. "Nobody likes going there. Neither do I, to be honest."

Belthea's lopsided hut glistened with the morning dew. Where Kellen's entry had torn the cobwebs, a couple of new webs had already been strung.

"It's such a mess," said Clover, looking at the hut. "I used to dig that patch for vegetables and train beans up those poles. I painted that roof and plucked chickens on that stone over there." She stared at all these traces of her old life with a quiet horror.

The back of Kellen's neck prickled, and he glanced over his shoulder but could see no sign of anyone following them.

"Let's go in," he suggested abruptly.

Clover stared at him in shock.

"I've already looked inside," he said. "And I'm not the only one. Somebody else had been in before me. Come on."

Kellen's instincts were hissing and fizzing as he approached the hut. *Danger, danger*, they called to him, and that very call drew him on.

"Knock, knock, Little Brothers," he whispered, and led the way inside, ducking under the new webs as best he could.

Clover followed him through the doorway, eyes dark and startled in the dim light, her boots sliding on the sloping floor. Nettle slipped in silently behind her.

"You *can't* leave," Clover said. "My mother's been cursed for thirty years! If you don't help her, she might be haunting the marshes forever!"

"Oh, I think I *can* leave." Kellen leaned his back against the grimy wall, feeling tiny shapes scuttle around him. "Yesterday some people kicked me raw, shoved a sickle in my face, and told me to stop snooping around. And everyone's hiding things from us—even you. You have been, from the start." Outside, the trees wavered in the morning wind, juggling shafts of sunlight like knives.

Clover said nothing, but stared and stared at him. She suddenly reminded Kellen of a fawn, holding very still in the hope that a predator will move on.

Kellen impulsively stooped and picked up the pair of Belthea's shoes with bells on.

"Don't . . ." Clover began, then trailed off, just staring at them.

"Did your mother use these for dancing?" Kellen danced them slightly through the air so that the tarnished bells swung. They didn't ring properly, but they made a deadened *chink-a-chink* noise.

"Yes," said Clover very quietly. Her voice was scarcely more than a croak.

Nettle was giving him her *What are you doing?* look, but of course he didn't know. He was chasing his instincts, his mind bright and breezy as a summer wind. He let the shoes dance on through the air. *Chink-a-chink*, to a long-silent jig.

"Why the dresses and not the shoes?" he asked abruptly.

"What?" Clover blinked, and seemed to come out of her trance.

"Why take the dresses and not the shoes? It *was* you that took them, wasn't it? There's old mud prints on the floor, and they look a lot like the ones your boots just made."

Clover glanced over her shoulder, but Nettle was blocking the way.

"Does the rest of the village know you leave food out for her?" Kellen went on. He watched her expression flicker. "They don't know, do they? Do you go out while it's still dark in the hope you'll see her? *Do* you ever see her?"

Clover stared at him searchingly, and then, almost imperceptibly, her shoulders sagged.

"She comes for the food sometimes," she said quietly. "It took a year before she'd approach while I was still there. I brought her dry clothes, but . . . she won't wear them. Only that damn green dress. I didn't bring shoes because her toenails are claws, and she won't let me trim them."

And Kellen should have felt satisfaction at this confession, but the invisible jig was still dancing in his head. *You've missed something*, it said. *There's another step, another peril, something else. Another patch of treacherous bog lurking under the green mantle.* He could feel it singing in his ears.

"I comb her hair," Clover continued numbly. "She lets me do that. Maybe she knows who I am. But she doesn't speak, just growls and sobs."

"Quiet!" Nettle whispered sharply, holding up a hand to halt the conversation. She was staring out of the hut past the cobwebs. "Listen!"

After a few moments they heard a distant shout. A man's voice.

"Clover! Clover, where are you?"

Clover did not answer the call. She pulled away from the door into the shadows, then stayed perfectly still and quiet. Kellen and Nettle also tucked themselves out of sight.

Risking a peep through the doorway, Kellen saw two distant figures on the path leading back into the village. They were of the right build to be Twence's sons, and they were looking this way and that, as if searching for something. At one point, they even glanced across at Belthea's hut but without apparent interest. Evidently they hadn't noticed anyone hiding inside.

The two men exchanged words in low voices, then departed in different directions among the trees, calling for Clover. As their shouts grew fainter, Kellen realized that he could hear other voices calling the same name.

"Why is everyone looking for you, all of a sudden?" whispered Nettle.

"I don't think they are," said Clover. "I think they're looking for the two of you. They must have seen us together. By now, everyone knows you can lift curses. It changes everything." She gave Kellen a worried glance. "You're not just a paid snoop they can scare and send home. You might actually lift the curse if they take their eyes off you. And they just did."

"Are we in danger?" asked Nettle.

"I don't know," said Clover grimly. "Maybe. If the wrong people start panicking."

"But *why*?" Kellen noticed Nettle's wince and continued in a lower voice. "Why don't your neighbors want the curse lifted? What's the big secret everyone's hiding? Is it smuggling? Cannibalism? What?"

"No, it's nothing like that!" Clover was still staring out at the path and the woods. "They're not bad people!"

"Someone here is," Kellen said darkly. "You said it yourself, didn't you? *Somebody who could do that horrible thing, and hide it, and still walk around smiling*."

Clover flinched at the sound of her own words, her brow creased with misery.

"You know who the curser is, don't you?" said Kellen, with sudden conviction. "Why won't you tell us? Are you afraid of them?"

"Yes!" Clover blurted out, her face contorted with anguish. "I'm so frightened it makes me sick! And I hate them—oh, believe me! I really hate them!"

"Then tell me who it is!"

"I can't!" wailed Clover, and gripped fistfuls of her own hair.

"Then you'll never escape them," continued Kellen mercilessly. "You'll live with them here for the rest of your life. And your mother will never escape either. And everyone she kills will be blood on your head—"

"Kellen," said Nettle, softly and suddenly. "Stop." She was staring at Clover with an expression that Kellen couldn't quite read. Her eyes were bright with something that was almost sympathy but not quite. Recognition, perhaps.

"What is it?" Again Kellen had the tantalizing sense that he had missed something.

"Clover knows she can't escape," said Nettle, in a voice that was almost steady. "Wherever she goes, the curser goes. She knows that."

Kellen looked into Clover's dark, haunted eyes and understood. He imagined her striding out in her sensible boots into the marsh-woods, in the predawn half-light, over and over. He imagined her speaking soft words, her calloused hands combing dank, bedraggled hair.

Not out of love or loyalty. Out of guilt.

"How did you know?" asked Clover.

Chapter 15

RED FOOTPRINTS

I said it aloud, thought Nettle, her stomach plummeting dizzily. *Why didn't I keep it to myself?*

She had seen Clover's expression of torment, and understood the reason for it, and had *needed* to stop Kellen talking. But now Clover was looking at her with wild, agonized eyes. Nettle wanted to get away from this woman, leap out through the door, and . . .

And what? Outrun a curse?

"How did you know?" Clover whispered again.

Nettle had to keep the woman calm and keep her talking. For all she knew, Clover might have cursed countless times. She might have a new curse egg swelling in her right now, ready to break loose.

"The apple festival," said Nettle, her mouth dry. "I should have guessed something when you first told us about it. It's a night everyone looks forward to for *months*! Bonfires and games! Songs and apple cakes! You were fifteen, the same age as me—old enough to stay up with the adults after sunset. Old enough to drink the cider, and wear a pretty harvest dress, and join the dance in the clearing under the stars. But you didn't get to do any of that. Your mother sent you home to do all the chores so that *she* could stay out all night, dancing and flirting in her green dress."

"All of this was because of a festival?" asked Kellen, looking appalled.

"No!" Clover protested, agitated. "It wasn't . . . it wasn't only that!"

"It was just the last straw, wasn't it?" Nettle interrupted quickly. She gave Kellen a look full of meaning. *Please don't upset her.*

Clover nodded slowly, looking exhausted and defeated.

"Jaybert said your mother was lazy," Nettle continued. "A wild thing who didn't work, because she didn't like it. But the pair of you didn't starve, so *somebody* must have worked. *Somebody* spun silk and made wines to earn money. *Somebody* looked after this hut, chopped wood, grew vegetables, took care of the geese, cooked, cleaned."

"She said I had to be good for something," croaked Clover.

"I know what it's like to be the good one," said Nettle. "The quiet one everyone forgets about, because they know you'll be good and quiet forever."

"She was different when nobody else was around," Clover said quietly. "We didn't argue, because I didn't know how. But I could be wrong without saying anything."

"What do you mean, wrong?" asked Kellen.

"Oh . . ." Clover waved a vague hand. "Everything I did was wrong. Everything she thought I might be thinking was wrong. Everything was traps, and I always fell right into them and made her angry. She was stronger than she looked too.

"Then some man would drop by, and she'd be all smiles. She'd hug me, and make fun of me, but as if it were a joke between us. Only it never was. She just enjoyed making everyone think I was slow-witted and clumsy and too frightened of the world to survive without her. I started to believe it myself. She didn't like me talking to anyone else, particularly if she wasn't there. But some of the men *did* come by to talk to me—the ones who thought they'd be my new father. They were kind, mostly. And . . . then I had to watch their hearts get broken."

Nettle exchanged glances with Kellen. They had never been in this position before. They had caught cursers, but they had never had one willingly confess, let alone ask for their help in lifting the curse.

"So what happened?" asked Kellen quietly.

"I was coming home through the snow with firewood one day," said Clover, staring at the opposite wall of the tilted hut. "And when I got near home I realized that I had no boots, and my feet were bleeding. Red-smudged footprints in the snow behind me. And I didn't know why. So I followed them back to a clearing, and there were all these red prints, zigzagging everywhere, and between them long, twisting tracks that a snake might leave. Then it all came back to me. I remembered taking off my boots because the tree had told me to so that he could teach me a dance. I remembered the tree drifting to and fro, like a reflection in water, and the sound of its dry roots slithering. And I remembered what the dance meant and what it was for."

A visitation. Cursers sometimes saw and heard things other people didn't. Usually these showed the curser how to cast their curse. A wild thorn bush whispered to them, a mist of midges formed sigils, or a black rabbit met them in a hollow lane and gave them a red book.

"I never meant to use it!" insisted Clover. "But at the apple festival, when I saw my mother turning people against each other, it *hurt*. Mackin and Piller Caddy had a fight over her, and Mackin got his tooth knocked out. I saw him sitting there alone crying. When he saw me he tried to smile, and . . . and it was like a hot knife in my chest. I was supposed to head home, but I . . . I found myself creeping to the clearing instead. I could see the festival dance through the trees. All the lights. The music. It all looked so bright and magical! And there I was in the darkness, my face stinging from the cold. I took my boots off, and . . . and I danced. Something swooped out of me, something huge. I couldn't hold it back. And then the clouds covered the moon . . ."

"And your mother turned into a monster," said Kellen.

"I didn't want that!" exclaimed Clover. "I just wanted everyone to *see her the way she really was*! That was the only thought in my head!"

"I believe you," said Kellen. "The curse worked. Everyone *did* see her the way you did. A beautiful monster, destroying men."

"I tried to bring her back!" protested Clover, and now there were tears in her eyes. "I've tried so many things, so many times! I've confessed to her, I've groveled, I've apologized in every way I could think of! I've brought her favorite food, I've sung her favorite songs, I've told her stories as if she were *my* child. Sometimes just for a moment I think she understands, but . . . it's always so fleeting. I know I can't bring back the people she's killed—that blood will always be on my head. But I just want it all to *stop*! Please! You have to make it stop!"

Nettle was closest to the door, so she was the only one to hear the rustle in the undergrowth outside.

"Hush," she began, but was drowned out by a man's voice, just outside the hut.

"Over here!" came the shout. "I found them! They're in Belthea's hut!"

Nettle lunged toward the door, but one of Twence's sons was already sprinting toward the hut, a pitchfork in his hand, to block off any escape. Other figures were running into view, emerging from the trees or pelting down the path from the village. Most carried scythes, rolling pins, and other makeshift weapons.

"Get behind me!" Clover told Nettle sharply, and pushed forward to block the doorway. She pulled out her long bark-cutting knife and held it in front of her. "Hey!" she yelled at Twence's son. "Keep back! Tell everyone to keep back!"

Everything was upside down. Nettle and Kellen had started the morning with a plan, and it definitely hadn't involved hiding from an enraged mob behind a curser.

It took surprisingly little time for most of the locals to mass outside the hut. Clover's knife and desperate manner made them reluctant to approach, however.

"What are you doing, Clover?" called Old Twence, who had drawn closer than the rest.

"Those two came to help us!" she shouted back. "And I'm not going to let you stop them!"

"Your mother's gone!" replied Twence. "She'll never be who she was, even if they do break the curse. Think of the village, Clover. Think about what you're doing to all of us!"

Nettle could almost hear the *fssst* as the spark of Kellen's fuse touched powder.

"WHAT THE BONE-CRACKING HELL ARE YOU ALL TALKING ABOUT!" he erupted. "WHY DO YOU WANT A BOG-WITCH LIVING NEXT DOOR? WHAT IS WRONG WITH YOU ALL?"

Perhaps it was Nettle's imagination, but it seemed the veils of cobwebs flinched away from him as he yelled. She even thought she felt the mildewed rug squirm for a second under her feet.

"You're not fooling us!" Twence's elder son shouted back. "We all know why you're here! We know why Chancery wants Pale Mallow gone!"

"They want to come here and build their roads!" It was Armon's mother, her face now tight as a fist with resentment and fear. "They want to send in other folks to fill our woods with new villages. Taking our silk and sap and timber, and crowding us out."

"They'll turn us into a trading post!" called another woman. "And they'll set up a Chancery base here, telling us what to do. We know what happens!"

"But their rules won't protect us from the chancers and explorers passing through, will they?" yelled Twence's younger son. "They'll come here with swords and guns. Taking whatever they like. We hear the stories. We know what's happened to other villages!"

"Bandits too!" shouted another man. "How do we keep them away without Pale Mallow? What about thieves and smugglers? Runaway murderers?"

Kellen listened with an expression of incredulity.

"That's why they want to keep Pale Mallow?" he hissed under his breath. "They're using her as a *guard dog*?"

"But they're right!" Nettle whispered back. "All those things really *could* happen with Pale Mallow gone." She hadn't thought about it before, but the villagers' words rang true. "They've got good reason to be frightened."

Now she understood why the village had no defensive stockade or stone buildings to hide inside during times of peril. Havel didn't need them. Pale Mallow was dangerous, but she kept away all the other dangers.

The crowd outside was becoming louder and more militant, fired up by the possible future their words had conjured.

"What are you all planning to do, then?" Kellen shouted at the crowd. "Murder us? In cold blood and broad daylight? Then what? Chop us up and feed us to the pigs?"

"Don't give them ideas!" said Nettle through her teeth.

"What's the plan?" Kellen yelled. "*Is* there a plan?"

To judge by the uneasy mixture of murmurs and glares, no plan for this stage of the proceedings had actually been agreed upon.

"It needn't come to blood, surely?" asked Armon. "We could just tie them up so they can't un-curse anyone, and watch them until their carriage comes to take them away?"

"And let them report back?" yelled someone from the back. There was a frightened and indecisive uproar. The less fierce members of the crowd looked lost and confused, as if wondering how things had reached this stage. The point of no return had slipped past without them noticing. Nettle could feel desperation spreading through the crowd like a fever.

Far above, she could hear the disconsolate, panicky cry of a gull. She knew that if she were outside she would see a winged shape circling above through the gap in the trees. She could feel her brother's impotent sense of urgency.

Yannick, she silently begged him. *Yannick, stay away. Your beak's no use against their knives and pitchforks.*

"If anybody doesn't have the stomach for this, go back to your hut!" shouted Twence. Even he was looking shaky, Nettle noticed, though that didn't make her feel much better. "Clover, you can't hold us all off with that knife!"

"I don't have to!" shouted Clover, loudly enough that the crowd hushed. "I've got a better weapon than that! Thirty years ago, I cursed my mother, Belthea! And if you stop me righting this wrong, Twence, I will curse you where you stand!"

The villagers were shocked into a stillness and silence that lasted a good five seconds.

"Hogwash," said Armon's mother.

"What?" Evidently Clover had not expected this reaction to her great confession.

"You're not the curser," the old woman said with perfect confidence. "Everybody knows who it was."

"It was Mackin, wasn't it?" said Jaybert, frowning. He looked around at his neighbors in bafflement, noticing how many of them were whispering. "What is it? Why are you all looking at me like that?"

"Jaybert," said Twence, kindly enough. "Everyone knows. And nobody blames you."

Jaybert stared at his old friend, and his brows slowly rose. Nettle could sense a penny dropping at the speed of a feather's fall.

"You all thought *I* cursed Belthea!" He looked horrified. "I'd never do that! I loved her more than life!"

"I'm right here, you know, Jaybert!" retorted the blonde woman standing next to him. Nettle guessed that this must be his wife.

"You're bluffing, Clover!" shouted Twence.

Nettle saw the panic in Clover's eye as the crowd surged forward and realized that the woman *had* been bluffing. No curse egg swelling inside her, then. No vortex of darkness waiting to be released. Just a miserable, guilt-ridden woman, tortured by the memory of one terrible curse.

Clover's knife was snatched from her grip. Nettle and Kellen were seized and pulled out of the hut into the daylight. Overhead, Yannick screamed and screamed and screamed.

Somebody twisted Nettle's arm behind her back. Three or four people had grabbed Kellen and pinned him to the side of the hut. Twence's eldest son gripped him by the scruff of his neck. His other hand held the sickle, though it was trembling slightly.

"Listen, all of you!" Kellen shouted. "There's a way everyone can get what they want! Everyone except Chancery, that is, but they're not here, so who cares about them? There's a way to lift the curse, *and* keep Havel small and boring, just the way you like it."

"No, there isn't!" shouted a woman near the front. "We need Pale Mallow!"

"You don't!" said Kellen. "You only need the *idea* of Pale Mallow!"

There were murmurs of confusion from the crowd.

"She's your scarecrow," said Kellen. "People hear the stories and they stay away. There's been enough sightings and deaths—everyone knows she's real. But you don't need the real Pale Mallow anymore. The stories will still keep people away, even if I unravel the curse—*as long as we don't tell anybody I've done it.*"

There was a long pause, and the villagers exchanged glances. Some looked slightly hopeful at the prospect of a non-bloody solution. Others looked darkly doubtful.

"How can we trust you to keep it secret?" asked Twence's eldest son.

"Well, what else are you going to do?" demanded Kellen. "Kill me yourself? Right here, in broad daylight, with all your neighbors watching?"

The tall man went pale.

"Would you use that sickle of yours?" Kellen continued relentlessly. "It's a good sickle. Do you think you'd ever want to use it again after that? Imagine seeing your hands every day and remembering the blood on them. Imagine living here the rest of your life in this village, knowing that everybody knew what you'd done. They'd remember it every time they looked at you—and you'd see it in their eyes. You'd remember my face too. It would be there all the time, like a stain in your eye. Killing me doesn't get rid of me. It means that you *never* get rid of me. Ever."

The tall man's hand trembled on Kellen's collar, then released it as though it were hot.

"You don't want to kill me or my friend," said Kellen, and his voice finally sounded a bit shaky. "None of you do, not really. And you don't have to. So don't."

There was a tense silence.

"I say we let them cure her," said Jaybert's blonde wife unexpectedly.

"But your Jaybert was moony over Belthea!" exclaimed Armon's mother. "He still is!"

"I know that!" declared the blonde woman briskly. "So I'd like a rival I can punch, thank you very much! Not some beautiful demon who never gets old."

Her matter-of-fact tone seemed to bring some of her neighbors back to their senses. There were still murmurs, but Nettle could see weapons being lowered. The dangerous, panicky atmosphere was losing its edge.

Heart thumping, Nettle decided that she rather approved of Mrs. Jaybert.

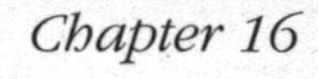

Chapter 16

PALE MALLOW

"YOU'RE SURE YOUR NEIGHBORS WON'T CHANGE THEIR MIND and kill us?" asked Kellen in an undertone, as he followed Clover up the ladder into her hut.

"I don't think so," she said shakily. "As long as nothing else fires them up."

Nettle entered behind them, Yannick on her shoulder. He promptly swooped across the crammed, tidy room and settled on Clover's hammock, where he flapped and flustered, still fidgety with distress.

"Let's not give them time," Nettle said bluntly. "Kellen, do you have a plan?"

Kellen had the *soul* of a plan. He knew what needed to be done, and where, and at what hour. But it wasn't easy to explain properly until it was ordered in his mind, and this made him impatient with questions. He had to remind himself that it wasn't the others' fault that they couldn't see the loose threads of the situation.

"Clover," he said. "Can I see your mother's clothes?"

Nonplussed, Clover unlocked a chest nailed to the wall. She flushed as she carefully took out dresses, cream-colored stockings, linen shifts, gloves, and shawls. Aside from a little fading and mustiness, they had all been preserved with religious care, their colors vivid.

With a weaver's eye, Kellen admired the dresses. They weren't silks or satins, but they were still clearly too fancy for Havel. He reflexively reached out to stroke the fabric of one, but Nettle caught at his wrist.

"Just touching it won't—" he began.

"Don't!" Nettle whispered, looking so earnest and worried that he drew his hand back.

Clover, meanwhile, was staring at the dresses with mute, guilty horror.

"You've never worn any of these, have you?" Kellen said suddenly.

"Of course not!" Clover stared at him appalled. "They're hers! Besides, they wouldn't fit me. My mother was elegant like a deer, and I'm . . . I'm not built the same way."

Nettle picked up a burgundy frock whose fabric had a sleepy, subtle gloss, like oil. She frowned speculatively at it, then at Clover.

"You could get into this one," she said.

"No!" Clover shook her head vigorously. "I can't wear clothes like that. I'd look ridiculous. Like a pig in a silk gaiter!"

"Who told you that?" asked Nettle sharply.

No answer was given, and none was needed. They all knew whose words those had been.

"Put it on," said Kellen.

"I can't!" Clover swallowed. "I stole her life from her! I can't take her clothes as well, that's just . . . wrong!"

Kellen understood. What he was suggesting *was* wrong. It wasn't banned by any law, but it was a little soul-crime, an insult added to a great injustice. And that was exactly why he needed Clover to do it.

"You're still running around trying to be a good daughter," he said. "Nothing's changed, so nothing *can* change. *You* have to change, even if it feels like murder. Tonight it's your turn to wear a fine dress and go out to that dancing glade in the woods."

"You want me to dance that dance again?" Clover looked haunted.

"No," said Kellen. "You need to talk to your mother and tell her the truth."

"I have!" Clover protested in despair. "I confessed everything!"

"No!" said Kellen firmly. "You haven't! You've apologized. That's all you've ever done, Clover—apologize. You haven't told her how you feel. How you've always felt. And if you don't, you'll never forgive her, however hard you try."

Clover looked really frightened now. Kellen wondered if there were feelings she kept under more locks than her mother's clothes.

"You won't be alone," he said. "We'll be there with you."

"Kellen, you can't leave the village," Nettle protested. "Pale Mallow's already come after you once!"

"That's the point," said Kellen, trying to sound more confident than he felt. "We need her to show up! I'm the bait."

Just before sunset, Clover emerged self-consciously from the hut, wearing her mother's burgundy dress. Belthea's bell-shoes chinked as she climbed down the ladder.

"Hmm." Nettle cast an appraising eye over the dress. "It's a little tight across the shoulders because of your arm muscles, but there's plenty of slack in the laces." She looked Clover in the eye. "It fits you."

Clover continued staring down at her burgundy-clad figure as if she thought it might be an optical illusion.

"The sun's setting," said Kellen. "Time to go."

Clover walked through the village in her mother's dress and bell-shoes, with her gray-streaked hair combed loose, Kellen and Nettle at her side. Her neighbors stared but didn't approach. They did not know this dangerous stranger with Clover's face who strode with a wine-colored shimmer and rustle. She might as well have been a beast from the Deep Wilds.

The trio paused near the edge of the village so that Nettle could tie one end of a length of rope securely round Kellen's waist.

"I feel like a dog on a leash," he grumbled.

"If you lose control again and jump in the marsh, we need some way to pull you back," Nettle retorted quietly.

"People have tried rope before," murmured Clover. To judge by her doubtful expression, these experiments hadn't ended well.

Yannick aimed a small, sulky peck at Nettle's ear, then took off from her shoulder to act as lookout. His pale shape was soon lost in the darkening sky.

Kellen blocked his ears with little wads of cloth, then Nettle wrapped a scarf around his head for good measure. Now he could no longer hear the thrum of insects or the steady, stealthy drip-drip of the forest.

As the three of them advanced down the path, the trees closed in around them. Soon the lanterns in their hands were their only source of light. Moss hung in great, green-gray swathes from the branches. Everywhere there was the cold, lush smell of the woods, with its undercurrent of rot, its fierce green freshness, and the scent of a thousand marsh flowers gaping their fat silken petals in the summer dark.

Running into danger was easier than this, thought Kellen. You didn't have time to think or worry. *Walking* into danger was different. You had time to wonder whether this was a mistake, whether it was the last mistake you'd ever make, and whether you still had time to change your mind.

His certainties leaked out of him with every step. By the time the sky was dull lead, and a dozen white moths were whirling around the three lanterns, it was mostly his pride that stopped him turning back.

Over thirty years, the marsh-woods had started to reclaim the clearing. The grass was thigh-high and ridden with giant thistles and sweet-knot. Trees stretched out their boughs over the clearing and tried to touch fingers. There was still a ragged canopy of sky left above, however. A few stars winked through the evening haze, and the moon was a half-closed yellow eye.

The trio hung their lanterns in the trees, then clustered together in the middle of the clearing.

"Time to let her know I'm here," Kellen said. Then he took a deep breath and started to sing.

He didn't often sing. Before his voice had broken, he'd been pretty tuneful, but even the memory of that squeaky competence was now a bit embarrassing. These days, his singing voice was a wayward thing, rough and uneven with lack of practice. Tonight it was also shaky with nerves.

But the song he sang wasn't meant to be pretty. It was a "rough music" weaver song, the sort a mob would sing when they turned up with a fife and cudgels to kick a door down. He imagined his defiant song barging through the glimmering pathways of Pale Mallow's territory, echoing in the dripping glades and rippling the reeds.

He had barely sung four verses when the mist started closing in. *She's coming*, he thought in terror and triumph.

Clover and Nettle both started violently and stared upward toward the sky. Nettle had the fixed, rapt stillness that she always wore when talking to her brother. Looking up, he could just make out the gray-white shape of a high, circling gull. What was Yannick trying to tell them? What had he seen?

Kellen was still staring upward when two hands grabbed his face from behind and yanked him backward off his feet.

His back struck the long, wet grass. Before he could react, he was dragged at speed through the undergrowth by his collar, too choked to yell. Grass and thistle-leaves thrashed his face as they passed. At the edge of the clearing, the rope around his waist brought him up short.

It was only then that he saw the creature gripping him by the collar with her long-clawed hand. He stopped struggling, and his mind went somewhere very cold and far away.

Pale Mallow's eyes were moonlight on dark water, but they were also wounds. He couldn't bear to look at them. He couldn't look away. Her skin was a pale, pearly gray-white, silken as a fish's belly. Her poison-berry mouth was moving, saying something important that he couldn't hear . . .

Her clammy, taloned fingers pried the scarf away from his head. Something small fell out of one of his ears, and he could hear. Pale Mallow's mouth contorted, and he could see the shining paths of tears down her cheeks beneath her unbearable, dark-light eyes. Her sob shuddered through him like an earth tremor.

"Kellen!" someone was screaming. He lay numbly on his back, staring up at the indistinct moon. Was that where the shout came from? It did sound very far away.

He was still being dragged into the shadow of the trees, more slowly now. Pale Mallow's dank green dress clung to her, seemed to grow on her like lichen. Wet black hair trailed across Kellen's face, sodden and matted, with flower petals and dead dragonflies gleaming in it.

Everything was full of pain, but it would end soon, once he was deep in the shadows. There would be peace away from the glare of the moon. There might even be forgiveness.

Someone was pulling on the other end of the rope so that it dug painfully into his waist. They weren't strong enough to win the tug-of-war, though. They couldn't stop him being dragged out of the light.

"No!" wailed the moon. Or perhaps it was not the moon.

The trees above devoured the sky, and the shadow swallowed him. Leaves slapped his face, and brambles raked his clothes. Then he heard the quiet *slish-slosh* of water and felt the shock of cold soaking into his clothes and the loss of solid ground beneath him. He was neck-deep in marsh-water, he realized, his legs sinking below him and tangling in weeds as they kicked. The green surface was already tickling at his chin. An arm around his shoulders drew him downward, relentlessly.

"Kellen!"

A part of his mind heard the cry and tried to shake off its numbness. There were reasons to fight for life, weren't there? Promises. Pride. Some woman he was trying to help—no, two women. A girl who always made him guess what she was thinking. The memory of a loom's hum, and a stubborn pain in his soul like a swallowed barb.

"Where are you?" came the yell.

"Here!" he managed to shout back, just as his face was dragged beneath the surface.

The dark water filled his mouth and nose. It tasted of dead leaves and despair. He would join these dregs now, despite his struggles. The bog would drink out his dreams and thoughts. He would become a part of the marsh, and great blue lilies would sprout where he had sunk. The Wilds always, always won.

But the tug of the rope around his waist was relentless and would not give up.

Unexpectedly, his face broke the surface again, and he spluttered out his lungful of water, gasping for breath. A clawed hand dripping with pondweed moved to cover his face, ready to force him under again.

And then Pale Mallow hesitated.

At the edge of the morass in which Kellen floundered stood two figures hauling on the rope. Nettle's slight figure was visible, but in front of her stood a taller woman, statuesque in a dark red dress, pulling the rope with considerable strength.

"Mother," said Clover, with cold bitterness. "You look ridiculous. Aren't you embarrassed, grabbing at that little boy?"

Pale Mallow did not reply, but she did not move either. Her head was still nestled close to that of Kellen, her cold fingers curled across his face. Her gaze slid over the dress and shoes that had been hers. The low hiss in her throat somehow sounded pained.

"You lied to me," said Clover. "You said I could never wear a dress like this. And yet . . . here I am. And look!" She raised a foot and turned it so that the lantern light caught the bells on her shoe. "Too dainty for me, are they? Oh, your long list of things Clover would never be able to do! I couldn't sing, I couldn't dance, I was an embarrassment when I tried to talk. I had no common sense. I couldn't possibly cope without you, could I?" Clover laughed bitterly, then gasped, as if something had loosened in her lungs. "But I *have* coped without you, for thirty years! And it was easy! It was *better*."

Clover no longer looked sheepish, like someone playing fancy dress in stolen clothes. She seemed to tower in her blood-colored dress.

"I tortured myself about cursing you," she said, shaking with emotion, "but do you know the worst truth of all? I didn't miss you. I hadn't lost a mother because I'd never really had one. You never saw me as your child, did you?" Angry tears glittered in Clover's eyes. "I was just your idiot servant! Somebody to bully, somebody to do everything that you didn't want to do! And I *hate* that I never told any of your admirers what a twisted vixen you are! I *hate* that I laced you into your dresses and cleaned your shoes! All your cruelty, your games—you made *me* part of it! You made everything my fault too! You're not a beautiful temptress. Stop playing your stupid games! You're just a vain, vicious, silly woman who likes to hurt people because it's the only thing you can do! You're pathetic, and useless, and it's about time you grew up!"

Kellen realized that the arms wrapped round his shoulders felt different now. They no longer had the sinuous strength of a serpent's coils. They were frailer and clung to him with the desperation of someone trying not to sink.

The long hair that trailed over his shoulder and face was gray now, and the sobbing in his ear was all too human.

Chapter 17

ADVICE AND SUPERVISION

AS THEY WALKED BACK TO HAVEL, NETTLE NURSED THE ROPE burns on her hands and tried not to throw up. She had seen the marshes close over Kellen's head. But here he was, still in the land of the living, dripping mud and occasionally spitting out pondweed. Beside him, Clover carried her mother with white-faced concentration.

At one point, Kellen fell into step with Nettle.

"Thanks," he muttered gruffly.

"For what?"

"Calling to me back there," he said. "You snapped me out of it." For a moment he looked like he might say something more, but instead he just gave her a damp, crumpled smile.

When they reached Havel, they found the whole village still awake and waiting for their return. Fires were swiftly nursed back into life and dry blankets found for Kellen and Belthea. The children of the village peered at her from the doors of the huts, fearful and fascinated at seeing the local bogeywoman.

The dreaded Pale Mallow was now nothing but a shivering, frail old woman with waist-length bedraggled hair, in the muddied rags of a green dress. Her once-claws were long, broken fingernails. For the moment, it seemed that all she could do was cry.

Clover settled her mother by the fire. Her hands shook as she arranged blankets around the frail shoulders and placed a wooden bowl of hot broth in the frail hands. She said nothing to her mother, her face pale and taut. At the first opportunity, she quietly slipped away in the direction of her own hut.

Nettle waited a while, then followed her. She found Clover sitting on a tree-stump seat outside her hut. She was back in her own clothes, with her hair tied back as usual.

"I'm such a coward," said Clover. "I don't know how to talk to her. After all I've made her suffer—and the things I said in the clearing! What can I say to her?"

Nettle didn't tell her that Belthea would forgive her. She didn't tell her it was all right. Instead, she waited.

"I'll have to find a way to face her, though, won't I?" muttered Clover. "Who else is going to look after her?"

"They'll just have to find someone," said Nettle.

Clover gave a low, bitter laugh.

"No," she said. "No, it has to be me. It won't make up for all the deaths I've caused, but it's the least I can do." Clover sighed deeply. "She needs me."

"She needs someone," said Nettle. "But not you. The last person she needs is you."

"What do you mean?" asked Clover. Her eyes were bright and frightened.

"She's eaten up your whole life," said Nettle. "She made you miserable when you were young. Then you struck back—just once—and ever since, you've been living haunted. Thirty years of running around after her, hating yourself and thinking of nothing else. And now you're going to give up on the rest of your life and spend it looking after her? So she can twist a knife in your guilt every day forever?"

"It's what I deserve, isn't it?" snapped Clover, her expression bleak.

"It doesn't matter what you deserve," Nettle said quietly. "She isn't safe with you."

Clover gasped in a breath, and then couldn't do anything with it. She stared at Nettle, looking winded.

"I wouldn't hurt her again!" Clover managed at last.

"You couldn't stop yourself last time," said Nettle.

"I'm different now! I've never cursed anyone else since that day!"

Nettle believed her—in fact, she had already guessed as much. It was common knowledge that cursers usually cursed again, but she was fairly sure Clover hadn't.

"That's because your mother wasn't around," said Nettle. "And now she is."

"Then . . . I have to go to the Red Hospital, don't I?" Clover blinked back a tear and stared down at her own hands, perhaps imagining them laden with shackles.

The Hospital was where Clover belonged. What else could you do with a curser? Yet Nettle had come to suggest something quite different.

"I think," she said, "you should look through your hut and work out which things you can't live without. Then put as many as you can in a bag and leave Havel forever. Find somewhere else to atone. You hate this place, don't you?"

With that, Nettle got up and left Clover to her thoughts and walked back toward the campfire.

The route took her past the hut on whose roof Yannick was settled, his dark brown head nestling along his back. As she passed, he stopped pretending to be asleep.

Why did you do that? he demanded. *She's a curser!*

And this way she'll never curse again, said Nettle.

How do you know? Yannick's thoughts jabbed at her, beak-sharp. *You wouldn't have done that a year ago. What's got into you?*

Leave me alone! snapped Nettle, and marched away. Yannick's words stayed with her, though, like bruises.

The next morning, the sun rose to find Havel adjusting and rearranging itself. Nearly everyone had conspired to leave Pale Mallow roaming the marshes, and now they were faced with the broken woman they had exiled. Most compensated for their past callousness by offering clothes, blankets, food, or medicine.

Mrs. Jaybert, one of the few who had argued for saving Belthea, showed no sign of actually punching her one-time rival. On the contrary, she had defaulted to the warm, reflexive pragmatism of one used to handling a large family's crises and disasters. She had found Belthea an old dress of good, warm wool and persuaded her to accept a haircut.

Belthea looked small and shrunken as she sat on a bench in the sun. Her cheekbones were still shapely and she had all her teeth, but her face was lined and haggard. There were dark grooves under her eyes, as though tears had worn valleys into her cheeks. Voices and sunlight made her wince and flinch.

"Jaybert's going to build a hut for her next to ours," said Mrs. Jaybert. "That way we can look in on her. We'll say she's a widowed cousin of mine who moved to Havel after she had a brain fever."

"She'll probably have nightmares," said Nettle. She didn't want to discourage Jaybert's wife, but she felt a need to prepare her. "She'll wander and get confused. Don't be surprised if she screams sometimes or tries to eat with her hands."

"That'll frighten the younger children," the blonde woman said thoughtfully, then shook herself. "Well. If they can't learn to be kind, we've wasted our time raising them."

Nettle took a turn sitting with Belthea. The old woman's frail hands had apparently forgotten the trick of using a spoon, and after three attempts she started to cry.

"I can't!" she croaked. "I . . . I can't!"

It was the first time Nettle had heard Belthea speak. She suspected the old woman was not just talking about breakfast.

"You can," she said with the quiet certainty of experience. "It'll just take time."

It would take years, Nettle guessed, and Belthea would never be the same. Would the memory of her victims haunt her? Would she feel drawn to the wild paths during the dark hours? Would she forget to wear shoes or forget that she couldn't sink into the marshes with impunity?

"Let me help you," Nettle said. She gently took the spoon from Belthea's hand and began to feed her scrambled egg.

There was something about Nettle's pool-like serenity and stillness that seemed to calm the old woman. And after a while, croakily and disjointedly, Belthea started to talk to her.

Her memories of being Pale Mallow seemed to be fragmentary and nightmarish. Nettle was gentle and listened patiently.

"I keep seeing all the dead faces," Belthea said at last. "Eyes open, in the dark water . . ." Her own eyes widened, as if she really could see them.

"Do you . . ." Nettle hesitated, unsure whether to risk stirring painful memories. "Do you remember a man with a black jerkin and a scar on his cheek?" That was the way Gall had described the dead prison-barge guard.

"Oh." Belthea's brow furrowed with the strain of memory. "Oh . . . that's the man that was on the other side."

"The other side of what?" asked Nettle gently.

"The . . . the arch." Belthea raised her shaking hands and held them so they formed a pointed arch-shape in the air. "Tree branches . . . like this. I went through . . . and everything was strange. It hurt my eyes. Then I was somewhere else. Reeds. A red tower. A lake. And people—four of them. They didn't see me coming. I grabbed one of them and pulled him back through the arch with me—the man with the scar. And then I . . ."

Her face crumpled, and her eyes filled with tears.

"Do you remember where the arch was?" Nettle changed tack quickly.

Belthea shook her head.

"I saw it again once, I think," she said. "It was full of rocks, and I couldn't get through. And now I can't even remember where it was."

Kellen got up late and seemed surprised to hear about Belthea's new living arrangements.

"Won't Belthea live with Clover?" he asked.

"Haven't you heard?" Mrs. Jaybert's eyebrows rose. "Clover's gone. She left first thing this morning. Knocked on Twence's door to tell him, then walked off with a pack on her back."

Kellen reacted with anger and dismay, just as Nettle had suspected he would. This turn of events wasn't the fairy-tale reunion that he had expected. The villagers, however, were much more philosophical about it.

"It would be hard to live alongside Clover now," Twence said darkly.

There were a thousand conversations that the people of Havel still needed to have. How much should they change their way of life? What new defenses would be needed against thieves and bandits? Everybody was distracted by a hundred new hopes and worries.

Fortunately a feathered lookout was still circling the skies above the village. Yannick swooped down to Nettle with a warning just before noon. Thanks to this, Belthea had been carefully hidden away by the time the black carriage rattled back into Havel, the marsh horse's coat gleaming in the sun.

"Here he comes," breathed Kellen, as Gall's lanky figure approached their lodgings. Even though they'd decided what story to tell him, Nettle felt her stomach flutter with nerves.

"So you're still alive," said Gall by way of greeting. Nettle noticed that the marsh horseman had taken her advice and now wore clothing made from leather, felt, and clotted marsh silk rather than woven cloth. "Let's go inside."

It was dark in the hut. As Gall closed the door behind them, Nettle regretted leaving the daylight.

"So," said Gall. "Any progress on Pale Mallow?"

"Yes," said Kellen hesitantly. "In a way."

"We haven't cured Pale Mallow, but we've got the information we need," Nettle chimed in. "We found someone who had a conversation with Pale Mallow one night, out on the marshes." She swallowed. The story sounded less plausible now that she was facing Gall's unblinking, gray eye.

"A . . . conversation." Gall's tone had all the warmth of a dead snake.

"Yes." Nettle maintained steady eye contact with him. "They'd been putting food out for her, and sometimes she came for it. And talked to them." Before she could lose her nerve, she related Belthea's broken account of the mysterious arch, the unfamiliar place with the red tower, and the fate of the man with the scar. "That must have been the guard from the prison barge."

Gall continued to stare at them, and Nettle couldn't tell if he believed them or not.

"What kind of tower?" he asked. "And where was this arch?" An uncomfortable silence stretched. "Let me talk to your witness."

"You can't do that!" Kellen said quickly. "We promised we wouldn't reveal their identity."

Nettle could almost feel the thin ice beneath their feet fracturing and frosting.

"And this is what you have after two days?" said Gall. "Vague ramblings from some anonymous witness? And no progress with curing Pale Mallow?" The room seemed to get slightly darker around him.

"What do you expect?" demanded Kellen. With horrendous inevitability, he was losing his temper. "You gave us a thirty-year-old case! It's hopeless! I'm not a miracle worker!"

"But you are," said Gall. "Isn't that the whole point of you?" His Mizzleport docks accent was clearer than usual. "You're stalling and playing games."

"And you're not?" shouted Kellen. "You've been dodging our questions ever since we met! We don't even know who we're working for, or why! Unless you start being honest with us, we won't help you anymore."

Until now, everything Gall had done had been leisurely, so Nettle was unprepared for the speed of his lunge. He grabbed Kellen by the collar with one hand and hoisted him off his feet. There was no sign of anger, malice, or effort. It appeared as easy to him as hanging up a hat, and that made things worse. It didn't seem to matter to Gall whether Kellen throttled or not.

"Yes," said Gall, "you will. You will stay here until you've cured Pale Mallow."

"So this is 'advice and supervision,' is it?" choked out Kellen, trying to wrestle Gall's grip off his collar.

"I *am* giving you advice," said Gall, far taller than he had seemed in the light. "And I'll be supervising you while you follow it."

There was a sudden rap at the door. Nettle almost bruised her knuckles leaping to answer it. Gall set Kellen down as the door opened.

Armon was outside, and Nettle was wildly grateful for the interruption.

"Mr. Gall, sir?" he said, looking surprised and baffled. "There's a . . . a visitor to see you."

"A visitor? Here?" Gall looked just as nonplussed. He left the hut and clambered down the ladder.

Nettle stayed behind, to make sure that Kellen could breathe.

"That went well," she said.

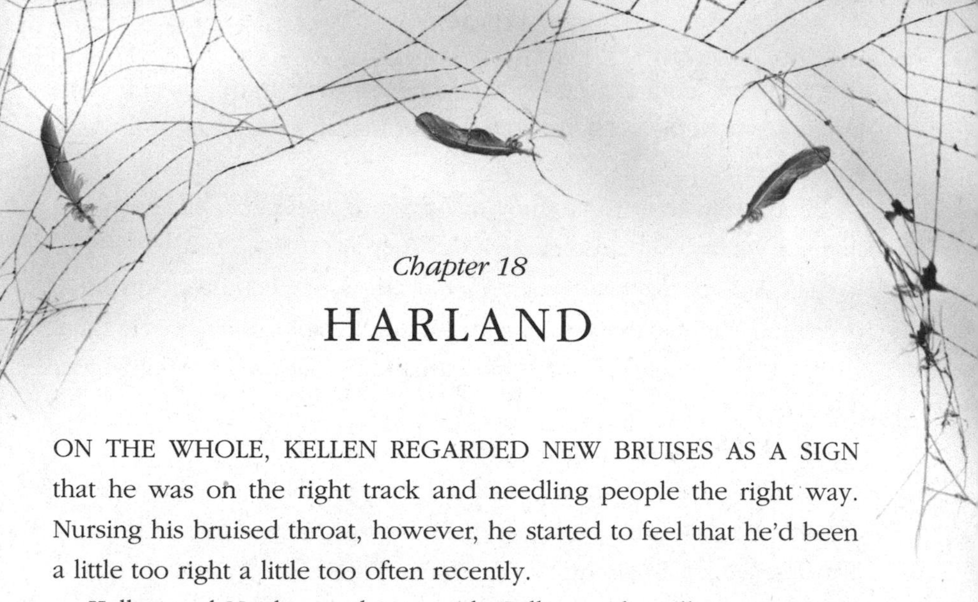

Chapter 18

HARLAND

ON THE WHOLE, KELLEN REGARDED NEW BRUISES AS A SIGN that he was on the right track and needling people the right way. Nursing his bruised throat, however, he started to feel that he'd been a little too right a little too often recently.

Kellen and Nettle caught up with Gall near the village center. As they did so, the marsh horseman halted so abruptly that Kellen nearly walked into the back of him. Gall was staring toward the black carriage and the unfamiliar man standing beside it.

The stranger looked about thirty years old, perhaps a little less. He had rather blunt, freckled features, mousy hair, and kindly, worried-looking eyebrows. His face had seen a lot of sun, his hands a lot of work, and his simple clothes a lot of mud in recent days.

As Kellen was taking stock, the stranger looked up and saw them. Or, rather, he saw Gall—he barely seemed to notice Kellen or Nettle. His face immediately lit up. It wasn't a purely joyful expression, but it was blindingly alive with hope, recognition, and a sort of panic.

"Go back to the hut," Gall told Kellen and Nettle, without taking his eyes off the stranger. He didn't raise his voice, but the feeling of menace was more intense than ever. *Give me a reason to unsheathe my true nature*, said his manner. *Just one little excuse.*

Kellen might have been tempted to give Gall that excuse if Nettle hadn't grabbed his arm and dragged him away.

"Why did you do that?" protested Kellen, shaking her off once they were out of earshot.

"Well, we couldn't eavesdrop on him over there, could we?" pointed out Nettle. Kellen had to admit that this was a fair and reasonable point.

By a roundabout route, they managed to sneak to a hiding place under a willow, just close enough to listen in.

Gall had approached the stranger at the carriage and was towering over him. The marsh horseman seemed taller and more deathly than ever but also strained, as if some dangerous force were trembling at the extent of its leash.

"What are you doing here?" he demanded.

"Looking for you," said the other man quietly. He looked intimidated but didn't drop his gaze from Gall's face. In fact, he stared up at it wide-eyed, as if memorizing every detail.

"How did you even get here, Harland?"

"Nobody was willing to bring me," answered Harland meekly. "Too dangerous, they said. So . . . I walked from the ridge road."

"Walked!" It was the first time Kellen had heard Gall properly raise his voice. "There's a cursed woman roaming these woods, murdering boys and men! It's a miracle you reached here alive!"

It was a miracle of sorts, Kellen reflected. If Belthea's curse hadn't been unravelled the night before, this man Harland would probably have run straight into Pale Mallow. Gall of course didn't know that the woods were now free from her, and presumably neither did Harland.

"I've been trying to find you for a year, Cherrick!" said Harland, and for the first time there was a hint of steel in his mildness. "This was the first time I'd found out where you were *going* to be, and not just where you'd been. I couldn't let the chance go. Whatever the danger."

The marsh horse stirred slightly. It would be natural for a normal horse to shift its hooves now and then, to snuff the air or flinch away from the touch of a fly. But the marsh horse never did any of those things, and so the motion seemed deliberate and unnerving. Gall gave it the very briefest glance, and for the very first time, Kellen thought he looked apprehensive.

"You can't stay here," he told Harland curtly.

"Well." Harland raised his worried-looking eyebrows. "From what you say, I can't actually leave."

Until now, Gall had been maddeningly economical with his words, expressions, and movements. Now he glanced around him at everything but Harland, apparently in search of inspiration or reinforcements.

"Get in the carriage," he said at last. "I'll give you a lift to the ridge road. But then you need to go back to the farm."

"Only if you come with me."

"I can't!" said Gall with sudden venom. "Look at me!" He waved a hand at his own eye-patch, his colorless figure, and the silent, watching horse.

"I am looking at you," said Harland, with only the smallest wobble in his voice. "And I want you to come home."

"It's not my home anymore," said Gall, his voice deadening to its usual tone.

The wind blew, causing the willow strands to swish and hush, drowning out the speakers by the carriage. By the time it had finished doing so, they had walked round behind the coach and their voices were more muffled.

"You know I said we could run away from Gall if things went sour?" whispered Kellen, feeling his bruised throat.

"Better late than never," said Nettle, which Kellen assumed was a down payment on a future delivery of "I told you so."

"Let's get out of here while he's distracted by his . . ." Kellen hesitated, reckoning the odds. "Friend? Brother? Husband?"

"Husband," said Nettle with confidence. She didn't quite eye-roll at Kellen's stupidity, but he couldn't help feeling it was strongly implied.

"I can't believe Gall's first name is Cherrick!" muttered Kellen as they hurried back to the hut. "It's a happy-sounding name. It doesn't suit him at all!"

But perhaps it had once suited him, Kellen reflected. Perhaps it had been a good match for him, in a lost life where his home had not been the road, nor a marsh horse his closest companion.

. . . . .

At the hut, while Kellen packed, Nettle hurriedly scribbled a short note on a scrap of paper.

"We're going to need help," she explained.

"Tansy?" he asked.

"She's closest." Nettle folded the paper up small and popped it into the little wooden tube she kept for the purpose and sealed it with the cork. "And she's smart."

Yannick usually made a big, fluttery fuss about being asked to play messenger pigeon. This time, he let Nettle put the message-tube's ribbon around his neck, then took off into the sky.

A few minutes later, Kellen and Nettle were hurrying along the long lane that led back toward the ridge road, their bags over their shoulders. Soft gold sunlight striped the overgrown lane ahead of them, gleaming green on the thick tufted moss and flickering knife-bright in their eyes. Kellen felt exposed in the open lane, but there was no other choice. If they turned off along one of the smaller paths, they risked falling into a bog or getting lost in the marsh-woods.

Hours passed, and every turning yielded more path, more woods. Nettle kept falling behind, and Kellen's panic gnawed at his patience.

"Can't you . . ." he began, then broke off and slowed his pace to match hers, while he tried to smother his irritation. Nettle couldn't speed up, he knew she couldn't. Her strangeness, and the attention that walking demanded of her, became more obvious when she had to cover ground fast. She wasn't dawdling to annoy him.

To Kellen's highlander ears, the sounds of the forest were foreign and indecipherable. A distant, echoing *knock-knock-knock*. A chuckling, rushing noise that sounded like a brook but changed its pitch sometimes. Long whistles or sharp, guttural coughs that he hoped came from birds.

Even as he was thinking about this, Nettle stopped dead and grabbed his arm.

"Listen!" she hissed. Kellen pricked up his ears but could hear nothing to explain her alarm. No rattle of wheels on stone, no pounding of hooves. Only the same mysterious forest noises . . . but louder now, he realized. The whistles had become a high warning trill. From behind him came restless squawks and chitters, little thunderclaps of birds erupting from the trees, the insectile hum rising in pitch like the voice of a boiling kettle . . .

Nettle grabbed his arm and dragged him into the undergrowth. She plunged into a towering bush covered in speckled yellow-brown flowers, and he ducked in behind her, feeling cobwebs kiss his face. Kellen was almost choked by the smell of the flowers, a rotten-apple scent he could taste on the back of his tongue. The long, dripping leaves obscured his view so that he could see only a small patch of dappled lane.

There was no sound of approach, not even the clatter of a dislodged pebble. Instead, without warning, a sleek, black blur flashed past. The marsh horse was at full gallop, Gall's dark gray figure astride its back. They passed and were gone, silent as a thought.

Kellen quietly blew out his cheeks.

"He didn't see—" he whispered, then broke off as Nettle's grip on his arm tightened. She was still staring out at the lane, tense and alert.

The birds were not settling, he realized. They were still filling the summer air with their warning calls. And then, much closer, he heard another sound—a very soft, breathy hiss.

The marsh horse slid back into view, slowly this time, pawing silently along the lane like a cat. Gall was bent forward, one ear close to its neck, his eye half-closed as if listening. There was no saddle or harness, no reins or bit.

Horse and rider had seen something, sensed something, *known* somehow. They had slowed, turned, and returned.

Cold beads of water slid off leaves and into Kellen's hair. Something tickled and scuttled its way down his neck, but he didn't dare move.

The horse slowly lowered its face to the ground, as if it were about to graze. Instead, it opened its mouth and took a long, deep, hissing breath. For the first time, Kellen saw its lips draw back and a glint of shadow-dappled teeth beneath.

All the tales he had heard about wild marsh horses thundered in his head—all the things they did if they tricked you into riding them or came upon you alone in the marshes. They leaped like cats. Their knife-like teeth scythed through your bones. They ate you from toe to tip in great, tearing bites, leaving only your heart leaking its lifeblood into the bog . . .

Gall straightened and stared in the direction of the bush where Kellen and Nettle hid. The marsh horse moved slowly, silently off the lane and into the undergrowth, entering the denser shadow. Horse and rider were only dimly visible now, except where the scattered, shifting clots of sunlight touched cloth, glossy hide, gleaming eye.

They drew closer, and Kellen wanted to flinch back into the bush, but he held still. Nettle's grip was a vice on his arm.

The horse approached the bush, then passed to one side of it, disappearing from Kellen's view. Another long, hissing inhalation. Then a few soft sounds in the woods behind, so faint that they might have been leaves settling on moss. Only when Nettle loosened her grip on Kellen's arm did he feel sure that Gall and his beast were gone.

Kellen and Nettle struggled out of the bush and back onto the lane, their clothes and faces smeared with cobwebs and heavily scented, dark brown pollen.

"It couldn't smell us because of those flowers," said Nettle, white-faced and shaky.

"Good thinking," said Kellen, as they set off down the track once more.

"It was a gamble," admitted Nettle. "I . . . I wasn't sure that would work."

"Right now we're not inside a horse," Kellen said grimly. "That's good enough for me."

He didn't mention the marsh horse's teeth. He was sure Nettle had seen them too.

. . . . .

The sun had almost set, and Nettle was near tears with exhaustion, when the lane finally began to climb. Ahead, Kellen could make out the dark, solid bulk of the dyke, like a curious raised horizon.

The two guards manning the roadblock were clearly startled when two figures emerged from the woods behind them but made no attempt to stop Kellen and Nettle passing.

"Someone's chasing us!" Nettle confessed abruptly, her face pale and strained. "A man on a marsh horse. Please don't tell him you saw us!"

The guards exchanged glances, doubtless remembering Gall and his horse.

"There's no saying we *did* see you," the older man told her kindly. "You probably crept past us."

Kellen could feel a tension in his chest unknotting itself as they hurried up the lane toward the crest of the dyke. The tree canopy dropped away on either side of them. The wind hit him in the face and chest, like a body-slam from an overexcited dog. Below them, the marsh-woods were stealthily withdrawing themselves, with all their incomprehensible noises, choking scents, and endless, web-filled trees. They were folding themselves small again, making themselves gray and plain.

Kellen and Nettle were out. They were up on the ridge, on a good solid road, with air he could breathe, and no trees to block their view. They could see for miles . . .

. . . and be seen for miles too. They were out but not safe, and the sun was setting.

"We need to catch a lift," said Kellen. "Fast."

"At this time?" said Nettle, nodding toward the setting sun. Right now, everyone on the ridge roads would be hurrying inland as quickly as possible. They were unlikely to stop for mysterious hitchhikers during the last rays of the dying day.

Kellen and Nettle waved their arms at a bicycle rickshaw, then a pedal-cart heaped with reed-bales. Both swerved to avoid them and passed at speed.

"Look!" said Nettle, and pointed at the marsh forest from which they had come. A flurry of birds broke from the darkening trees and took squawking to the skies. Then another flock erupted, much closer. Something was racing toward the dyke, and Kellen guessed that it was fleet and black, with a gray-clad rider.

Desperate plans flashed through Kellen's head. Could he and Nettle clamber down the other side of the dyke and take their chances among the trees?

"Yannick!" said Nettle suddenly, staring up at the sky. Kellen had no idea which of the pale flecks she meant. She tensed, listening to a noiseless voice . . .

. . . then broke into a clumsy, uneven run along the road.

Ahead of her, a vehicle was approaching. It was a cycle sedan, an upright wooden box the height of a man, pedal-powered by two drivers, one in front and another behind. Both drivers were pumping their pedals with furious speed.

As Nettle ran toward it, waving her arms, the sedan slowed and pulled over.

"Nettle and Kellen?" shouted the front pedaler. "Tansy sent us! Are you in trouble?"

"Yes!" shouted Nettle, as she yanked the side door open and scrambled inside the passenger box. Kellen piled in behind her and slammed the door. They collapsed onto the seat, panting for breath. "Please get us out of here!"

There was some squeaking of pedals, and the sedan started moving again.

"There's a man chasing us!" Kellen explained in a hasty whisper. "On a marsh horse!"

A pause.

"I see them," said the front pedaler, in the flat tone of someone trying to stay calm. "They just appeared ahead." He didn't specify how they had "appeared."

Kellen imagined Gall and his beast standing at the road's edge, staring with their three lifeless eyes at the red-gold scene. He thought of the marsh horse drawing in the scent of the air, searching for the smell of its quarry's sweat and blood . . .

For a little age, there was silence.

"We're past them," said the rear driver at last. "And they've gone. I . . . I think they disappeared down the side of the dyke. Are you two all right?"

A minute passed before Kellen and Nettle were sure enough to answer.

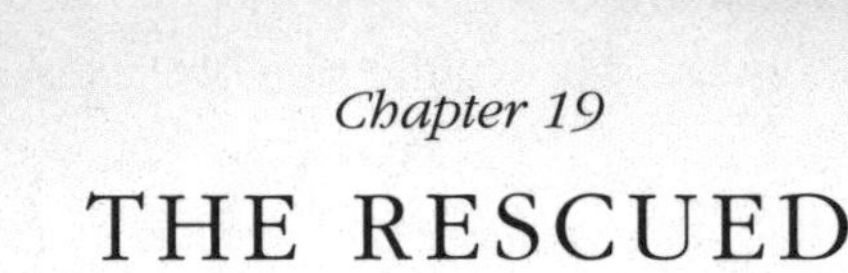

Chapter 19

THE RESCUED

BY THE TIME THE SEDAN REACHED TANSY'S PLACE, NIGHT HAD fallen. The building was perched on a lonely, windy stretch of ridge road, a warm and festive refuge beneath dark racing clouds. Nettle felt a pang of relief at seeing the busy little eating house, with its stained glass lanterns swinging in the wind. At the same time, she felt oddly disconnected from the sight.

It was always a jolt when Nettle left the marsh-woods. She knew that she didn't love them, but each time she adjusted to them, the way a swimmer adapts to their weightlessness in water. Now she felt like she had dragged herself ashore. She was heavy, body and soul.

They didn't enter the main room of the eating house, with its sounds of laughter and accordion music and its smell of roasted meat. Instead, the sedan drivers led the new arrivals up the familiar back stairs to Tansy's private rooms.

Nettle and Kellen were still blinking in the candle-light of the cozy, rug-strewn sitting room when Tansy herself appeared and pulled Nettle into a hug. Nettle didn't like hugs these days. They were too warm and close, a barnyard jostle of big mammals, and made her panicky. But she always made an exception for Tansy and tried not to flinch.

Tansy was twenty-five, and more or less looked it. A single white streak in her dark auburn hair was the only mark of her past ordeal.

"I'm so glad my friends found you!" Tansy's warmth always seemed to fill the room. "What's happened? Are you both all right?"

They were clearly not all right. Nettle's trembling legs unexpectedly gave under her, to her embarrassment. Kellen was a mess of bruises and briar-scratches. Tansy quickly settled them into seats by the fire.

There were a few hard, sharp raps at the smallest window. Tansy promptly opened it and let Yannick in. He meekly stayed on the inside sill, instead of flapping round the room. Even Yannick was unusually well-behaved where Tansy was concerned.

You did it, Nettle told him, almost wanting to cry. *You saved us.*

My favorite "thank you" is bacon, Yannick replied.

Tansy left the room to order food, and a portion of bacon for Yannick. When she returned, however, she was pale with alarm.

"You're being chased by a marsh horseman, aren't you? That's what my friends said. Well . . . one just walked into my main room downstairs. He's asking for you two by name."

Nettle and Kellen both stiffened into panicky alertness.

"How did he find us so quickly?" asked Kellen.

"We can't stay here!" Nettle was exhausted, but there was no point bringing trouble on Tansy. "We'll sneak down the stairs—"

"Neither of you are in any shape to run," Tansy told them firmly. She spent a moment thoughtfully smoothing her hair. "You stay up here," she said. "Bolt the door behind me. I'll go down and talk to him."

"Tansy, he's dangerous!" said Nettle.

"Then I need to keep you safe from him," said Tansy. Her gaze slid to Kellen, and she gave him a small, rueful smile. "It's the least I can do."

Unlike Spike, Tansy had never tempted fate but had been hit by a curse anyway.

Three years before, she had been unwillingly pursued by a doctor with red whiskers and an unfounded belief in his own charm. She had turned him down repeatedly, but had done so smilingly, to avoid offending him. Those smiles had been her undoing. To the doctor's jealously watching singer-wife, the pretty young barmaid seemed to be coyly haggling for more affection, more gifts.

In an evening rose garden, the singer had worked her curse with a bone knife and glue made of tears. She had cut Tansy apart and joined her pieces together anew. At her next performance, she had brought in a great harp of blood-red wood, with gleaming golden strings. Her audience had listened enthralled, but with a feeling nearer anguish than pleasure. They came back to the next recital, though, despite the melancholy the music left in their soul.

It was only by chance that thirteen-year-old Kellen had washed up in Tansy's neighborhood. Since being turned out by his family, he had been drifting from hill town to hill town, earning pennies by running errands, polishing shoes, or cleaning gutters. One evening he was keeping an eye on horses outside the theater when he heard the wailing notes of the harp from within. Unlike everyone else, he understood what they were trying to say.

If Tansy's family hadn't been desperate, they probably wouldn't have listened to the outspoken ragamuffin who turned up at their door. By that point, however, they were willing to try anything to find the missing girl. Kellen helped them steal the harp, the bone knife, and the tear-glue. Then he showed them how the harp should be taken apart and put together again. The bone-frame, the blood-varnish, the gut-strings, the weeping eyes, and living tongue hidden deep inside . . .

It was the first curse Kellen had ever unravelled. It didn't exactly make him famous, but rumors of his achievement slowly began to spread. As for the newly cured Tansy, she had spent several months sickly and weeping, then had rallied with awe-inspiring resolve.

"I can't hide from the world," she had said, before walking back into it.

Tansy's eating house was famous among travelers on the ridge roads and was always busy. Many customers visited out of curiosity to see the "harp-girl," then became regulars because of the food and the hostess's charisma.

At first Tansy had been unable to bear music and had to leave her own establishment every time one of her customers started to sing or play a fiddle. Now she stayed, and smiled, and tapped along to the tune.

"I can't hide from music forever," she always said.

Tansy had a way of smoothing her own hair and her forehead while thinking. At first, Nettle had thought her tanned fingers were seeking reassurance, making sure that her glued seams had not gaped open again. But her face was always thoughtful and calm. There were no seams, no scars. The tear-glue had done its work.

Tansy's eating house had gradually become a useful meeting place for the curse victims Kellen had saved. It was Nettle who made sure they all stayed in contact with each other, with Yannick as reluctant one-bird postal service, but having a base made things much easier. It was also Tansy who had started referring to their little network of erstwhile-cursed as the "Rescued." The name had stuck.

Nettle liked and respected Tansy. She felt more comfortable with the other Rescued, though, for all the wrong reasons.

Nettle sometimes felt as though she were struggling up a dark mountainside. When she looked at Tansy, it was like seeing a distant figure already standing triumphant at the crest, admiring the view. *If she can get there, so can I,* she told herself. It didn't make the path any less steep, however, or the stumbles any less painful. The feeling of hope was mixed with sickening feelings of envy and self-reproach. *There she is. Look at her. Why can't I be like that? Why am I like this?*

Ten minutes after Tansy had headed downstairs, the prearranged knock sounded at the door. Nettle opened it to find Tansy outside, looking flustered and a little puzzled but unharmed.

"That man's gone," she said. "He left in his carriage."

"Thank you for throwing him off the trail!" said Nettle with feeling.

"I don't think I did," said Tansy. "I told him that there hadn't been anybody except my regulars in all night, and he just . . . looked at me in silence, as if he were waiting for me to change my story. Then he said that if I *did* see the pair of you, I should give you a letter."

Tansy handed Kellen a small note, roughly sealed with a blob of wax. He opened it and read it out loud.

"*My employer is willing to meet with you. Come to Clarity Square tomorrow, and ask for Assessor Leona Tharl. If anyone asks why you are there, invent a plausible reason. Destroy this letter after reading it, and discuss the contents with nobody.*"

He looked up from the note, visibly excited.

"Clarity Square! That means she works for Amicable Affairs!"

Officially, Amicable Affairs was just a part of Chancery's wider Negotiation department, a contingent of diplomats and peacemakers who drew up treaties and resolved arguments.

Unofficially, everyone knew that Amicable Affairs was really the large but discreet department in charge of making sure that the Pact was kept and that the Wilds didn't affect the human world more than could be helped. They handled passports and security for those few creatures of the Wilds permitted to visit human territory. They cracked down on the smuggling of eldritch items. Last but not least, they hunted down and arrested cursers and potential cursers.

"*She*?" repeated Tansy. "*Amicable Affairs*? What's going on?"

Over a hot goat's-meat pie and some rosemary tea, Kellen and Nettle gave Tansy a brief account of their recent misadventures, leaving out the successful unravelling of Belthea's curse. Tansy's concern deepened into dismay when she heard about the disappearance of Jendy Pin.

"Someone's rescuing cursers from prison?" Her eyes widened.

"We only know of one," Nettle reassured her quickly. "Your curser's still behind bars, Tansy." She could guess how her friend felt.

We're all children when it comes to our own cursers. They're our bogeymen. They're our nightmares bound in flesh.

"Do you really think there's a secret organization collecting cursers?" asked Tansy.

"There's definitely *some* sort of conspiracy," said Kellen. "Whoever rescued Jendy had contacts in Chancery. Somebody with a high enough rank to make sure that crooked guards were put in charge of the prisoner."

"And if Gall's telling the truth," added Nettle, "somebody's been tipping off potential cursers when they're about to be arrested. You'd probably need spies inside Chancery for that too."

"How far *do* you trust Gall?" Tansy asked.

Nettle and Kellen exchanged glances.

"That's the problem," said Nettle. "Not very far. He's been secretive from the start."

"And then he tried to throttle me," added Kellen bitterly.

"If this Assessor Tharl is in Amicable Affairs," Tansy said thoughtfully, "why is she investigating all of this secretly? Why can't she go through official channels? And why didn't she want you to know who you were working for?"

"Good questions," said Kellen. "We know she must be rich and powerful. So why is she hiding in the shadows?"

"What about that invitation?" Tansy peered at the note in front of Kellen. "Could it be a trap?"

Nettle had been wondering about that too.

"I don't think so," she said slowly. "If we're visiting her office at the Amicable Affairs department, there will be lots of other people there, won't there? Gall and his horse can't spring an ambush on us there without anyone noticing. Maybe it's meant to be neutral ground."

"Anyway, we have to go!" Kellen insisted. "We can't miss the chance of finally getting some answers."

Nettle agreed, with some reluctance.

There seemed to be something else on Tansy's mind, but it was a while before she came to the point.

"Kellen, I got a message from Spike yesterday. He's been worrying about you. Apparently when he saw you, you seemed changed, and he's been thinking about it a lot. Have you been feeling different at all?"

Kellen shook his head.

"So nothing's changed?" Tansy asked delicately. "Nothing odd's been happening lately?"

"No," said Kellen.

"Yes," said Nettle.

Kellen gave her a surprised glance, and Nettle looked away. It was a conversation she'd been putting off.

"Something odd *has* been happening," Nettle said. "Kellen, I know you don't think you damaged that merchant's glove and his tapestry. I know you don't think you frayed that blanket in your sleep either. But I think you're wrong—"

"I had my gloves on!" Kellen expostulated, holding up his gloved hands. "Both times! I didn't do anything!"

"Kellen," began Nettle.

"That merchant just wanted me arrested! Because he was a poisonous old—"

"KELLEN!" snapped Nettle more loudly. "Look at your hands!"

Kellen looked down, then pulled sharply back in his seat, letting go of the tablecloth's edge. He had been fiddling with it, and the fine threads had been pulling apart in his grip. When he moved away his hands, however, the unravelling did not stop. The cloth continued to shiver and palpitate like a living thing for several more seconds, as strands of cotton writhed loose.

"What . . ." Kellen stared at the tablecloth in horror as it finally stilled and settled. "That . . . that's never happened before!"

"Yes, it has!" Nettle told him. "When you lost your temper in Belthea's hut, the cobwebs around you fell apart, and the rug . . . writhed. I felt it under my feet. It's your unravelling, Kellen. I don't know why, but it's started running wild."

Tansy looked thoughtful and concerned.

"Kellen," she asked gently. "Do you remember anything odd happening before all of this started? Did anyone give you anything or shout anything at you? Do you remember feeling strange or seeing anything weird?"

Nettle's skin crawled as she realized what her friend was asking.

"Well . . . I had a weird dream," Kellen admitted reluctantly. "A nightmare, I guess, the night before the merchant had us arrested. I dreamed I was in Kyttelswall, the hill town where I grew up, but it was . . . different. Abandoned, and half-drowned by marshes, all the buildings crumbling and covered in moss. I was wading and scrambling over rubble in the moonlight, because somebody was chasing me. And . . . then I felt their hand on my shoulder, and it was like a spear of ice stabbed through me . . ." He shuddered, then shook himself and laughed.

"Can you remember who it was?" asked Nettle, her chest feeling tight.

"No." Kellen frowned. "It was somebody I knew. But I don't remember who. What does it mean? Why are you both looking at me like that?"

"Not all curses start with a bang," Tansy said quietly. "Some begin small, so small you hardly notice them, then get worse, and worse, and worse.

"I don't think it was an ordinary nightmare, Kellen. I think that was the moment you were cursed."

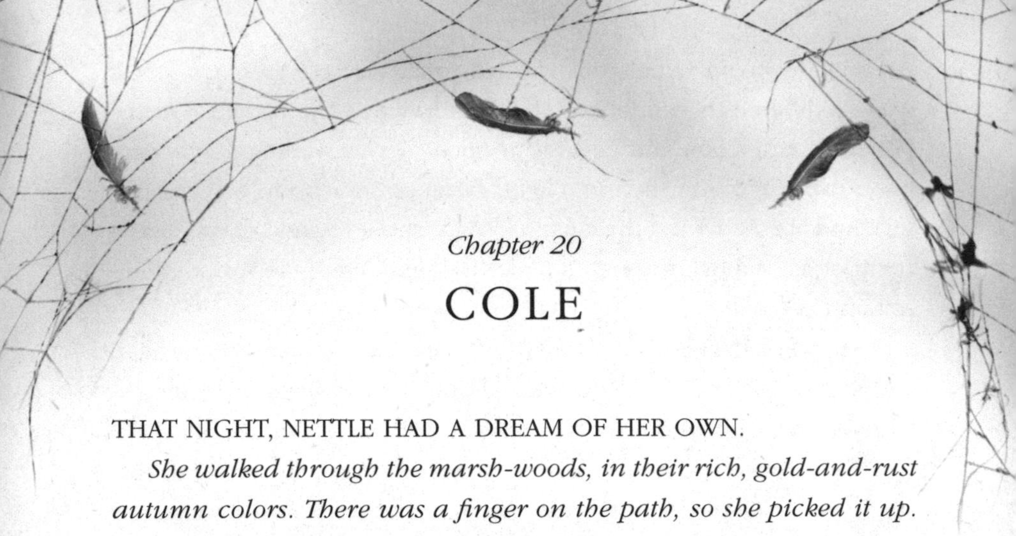

Chapter 20

COLE

THAT NIGHT, NETTLE HAD A DREAM OF HER OWN.

She walked through the marsh-woods, in their rich, gold-and-rust autumn colors. There was a finger on the path, so she picked it up. It was bloodless and cool, like china. She put it in her knitted bag. Farther down the path she saw another, so she walked deeper into the woods and picked that up too.

Ahead twisted the dwindling path, small white shapes gleaming in the shadows. Fingers, toes, an ear, a shard of a broken heart. She picked them up as she went, knowing she needed them all. But the knitted bag was light in her hands, and she realized that it was empty. Everything had fallen out through a big hole in its weave.

In alarm, Nettle turned back to retrace her steps, but where was she? The trees had closed in around her, and the woods were shadowy and pathless. She could see no sign of the pieces she had lost. At her feet quivered a single black feather.

She stooped to pick it up and immediately knew that this had been a mistake. Its fronds smeared her fingers with something slick and dark. The wind rose around her with a long, anguished wail, and the trees began to thrash with violence . . .

A sharp cracking sound jolted Nettle from sleep. She was in absolute darkness, and for a few frantic moments she couldn't remember where she was.

Nettle!

That was Yannick's voice, and Nettle realized that the *crack-crack* she could hear was the sound of his beak against the shutter. She got up from her makeshift bed of rugs and cushions on the floor of Tansy's sitting room and opened the shutter a little. Yannick fluttered in to rest on her head. None of this woke Kellen, who always slept more heavily than Nettle did.

What is it? she asked. The initial response from Yannick was a confusing fluster of exasperation and fury.

You tell me! he said. *I felt it, I came here. What's wrong?*

I had a dream, she told him, but she couldn't get away with that, not with Yannick. She couldn't pass it off as the pangs of leaving the marsh-woods either. She had thought it was just that at first, but now she knew it was something more. Yannick would sense it too.

What else? he asked.

It's just . . . bad sometimes, she said.

Is that all? He seemed uncertain and impatient.

Yes, she told him. *That's "all."* She didn't want to tell him about the invisible bog and the way you sometimes sank in it. You learned the tricks of finding a foothold, and getting a grip on something, and pulling yourself out. And sometimes the tricks didn't work. Some days there was nothing under your feet and you just kept sinking.

She didn't know how far she would sink this time, or when she would find her foothold again. She never did. She didn't want to talk to Yannick about that or the deep fear in her.

Was it Belthea? he asked harshly. *Is that what set you off? She reminded you of Cole, didn't she?*

Leave it alone! she said, because he was right. Belthea's broken, helpless guilt had reminded her of her once-hawk-brother immediately after his cure. It had brought back memories and thoughts that she had been trying to push aside.

I can't, said Yannick, and he sounded genuinely regretful. *We have to talk about him. Is he really getting better? You're going to visit him while you're here, aren't you?*

Nettle found her hands had crept up to cover her ears. It did nothing to shut out Yannick's voice, of course.

Nettle, you need to see him! We need to know if he's . . . changed.

Changed? Nettle didn't like the new gentleness in Yannick's voice. He was supposed to be sarcastic, teasing, or angry. He was only gentle when someone was ill or dead, or when he had bad news.

You remember the things Cole used to say about Kellen, said Yannick. *Back in the bad days, just after Kellen pulled you two out of the sky.*

With a shock, Nettle realized what Yannick was suggesting.

No! Jendy Pin's the one who cursed Kellen—she must be! Cole wouldn't curse anyone. I know he said he hated Kellen, but he was just in pain, and he doesn't talk that way anymore!

Cole had howled himself hoarse the only two times Kellen had tried to visit. Even so, Nettle didn't think Cole had ever resented or blamed Kellen. He just couldn't bear being in a world that held them both.

The sanatorium's less than a mile from here, said Yannick. *It won't take you long to drop in, and see if Cole* feels *like a curser.*

No, said Nettle, teeth clenched.

Well, I can't do it, pointed out Yannick. *I'm a gull!*

You could have done, said Nettle, hating everything. *You could have walked in on two legs and talked to him. If you'd cared enough to be human. But you chose the sky instead of us.*

It wasn't like that! Yannick's thoughts were flustered and ruffled. *I do love flying*, he admitted. *But that's not why I wouldn't take Kellen's cure. I saw you two change back, Nettle. I saw Cole screaming in agony. And I could feel* your *pain. I felt how much it hurt to be human again, and really understand everything that had happened, with no escape from it. I couldn't face it.*

It was more than he had ever explained before, but it made nothing better.

So you left me to deal with it all alone, said Nettle bitterly.

Gray-white wings rasped against her face and flashed out into the dull sliver of night. Nettle sat alone by the window with an empty ache in her mind.

Nettle did not sleep for the rest of the night. When the first trills of dawn chorus began, she gave in, got up, and went downstairs.

To her surprise, she found Tansy already awake in the kitchen, in her outdoor clothes, just removing her boots. Tansy gave her a rueful smile.

"When I can't sleep, I feel better if I get up and keep busy," she said. "I gather kindling, scrub the outside windows . . ." It was reassuring to learn that even the perfect Tansy still suffered sleepless nights sometimes.

"I was thinking . . ." Nettle swallowed and tried to sound casual. "I was thinking of visiting Cole." There she halted, too embarrassed to ask what she wanted to ask.

"Oh." Tansy gave her a shrewd glance, then stooped to fasten her boots again. "Well, I feel like a walk. Why don't I come with you?"

Nettle nodded, almost sick with relief.

How pathetic I am. Like a little child needing someone to hold her hand.

After her curse was lifted, Nettle had found herself in charge of an adult brother in a state of self-destructive collapse and a family home in the Shallow Wilds that she never wanted to see again. She had decided to solve both problems by selling the house to pay for Cole's care.

"Write to Ambassador Ammet," her neighbors advised, and helped her draft a letter.

When you lived in the marsh-woods, it often took a long time to get paperwork processed by Chancery. This wasn't due to negligence or malice. It was a side effect of the way people's minds slid off the Wilds. Chancery clerks were human too, so letters and documents from Shallow Wilds villages lay forgotten on official desks longer than they should. They simply seemed unimportant, to the point of being almost invisible.

Master-Ambassador Shay Ammet had developed a reputation in the Shallow Wilds for being the man you contacted if you wanted to get something done. He spent as much time in the Shallow Wilds as he did inland, so he suffered less from supernaturally induced absentmindedness. He sometimes came to marsh-woods communities to investigate problems himself and understood that not everything could be handled the way it was inland.

In this case, the Ambassador was willing to meet with the orphaned fourteen-year-old who had written to him. Shay Ammet listened as Nettle explained what she wanted and showed him the money from the sale of her home.

"What about you?" was his first question. "Don't you need this money?" He had a long, serious face, large eyes, and an honest jaw. He looked like a headmaster, the sort you wanted to trust and didn't want to disappoint.

"No," Nettle had lied. "I've got a place to stay." At that moment, her greatest fear was that nobody would take in Cole.

"You know that treating your brother may take years?" said Ammet.

"Isn't the money enough?" Nettle asked, trying to mask her panic. "How long can he stay?"

"As long as he needs," Ammet reassured her swiftly. "This is more than enough. In fact . . . if you ever need any for yourself, contact me again and I'll arrange for some to be paid back to you."

Later, Nettle found out that this had been a gentle deception. Shallow Wilds houses weren't worth much by Raddith standards, and she'd naively sold it for much less than the going price. The money she had given Ammet would only have covered six months of care at the sanatorium. However, Ammet had kept his word, and Cole's care continued. Nettle could only assume that the fees were now being paid by Chancery, or by Ammet himself.

.....

The sky was lightening when Tansy and Nettle reached the inland end of the ridge road, where it met the main highway. Set a little back from this junction they could see the sanatorium, a coffee-colored building behind a high wall. The sight of it sent a jolt of mixed emotion through Nettle's frame.

Both of them were wearing face veils to keep off the early morning mosquitoes, but the attendant at the gate recognized Tansy anyway and let them both in. Nettle followed her, feeling both guilty and displaced.

"He's already awake," a nurse told them. She led them through blue-tiled corridors to a conservatory with a view of the small but well-tended garden. In the conservatory sat a single figure in a wicker chair, reading by the morning light.

Cole no longer looked as though something were eating him from the inside, but he was still thin, and his soft hospital clothes hung loosely. The brother Nettle had known was recognizable but stretched into an adult stranger, with a slightly reddened jaw that someone else had presumably shaved.

He's eighteen. Two years older than Yannick. One year older than Iris would have been.

Nettle halted in the doorway. Every muscle in her body seemed to be paralyzed with tension.

Tansy saw the look in her face, then gave her arm a reassuring squeeze and walked into the room. Hidden behind the doorjamb, Nettle watched Tansy sit down opposite Cole and felt worthless as dirt.

That should be me.

Suffering had left deep lines in Cole's face, but he seemed calmer than ever before. He talked quietly, in thoughtful stops and starts. There was no sign of the ferocious anguish that had tossed him around like a cat with a mouse.

He looks like Ma. The thought cut Nettle like a knife. *But does he look like a curser?*

She wasn't sure. Cursers had a whiff of the Wilds, but so did those who had been cursed. She couldn't tell the difference.

Nettle heard Tansy mention Kellen's name and pricked up her ears.

"Kellen?" Cole rubbed his eyes with the heels of his hands, and grimaced. "No, I doubt he'll ever want to see me again after . . . those other times. I'd like to see him some day. But not yet. He pulled me out of the sky into a living hell. I couldn't forgive him for that. But he also rescued me from a living death. When I was a hawk, I couldn't think—I wasn't me at all. Someday, I'll be able to thank him for that. I'll get there."

Cole's eyes were clear and bright in the morning sun, as if he could see his path ahead. Nettle turned on her heel and left silently, unable to bear another moment.

Tansy found Nettle in the garden afterward and linked arms with her.

"You must be exhausted," Tansy said. "You've had a rough few days." She hesitated, as if choosing her words carefully. "If things ever get too much, and you need to get away from it all, you can always come to me—"

"I'm fine!" Nettle interrupted, then felt guilty for snapping. "I wanted to see if Cole looked like a curser," she admitted, staring at her shadow where it marred the flowerbed. "He doesn't, does he?"

"No," said Tansy, giving Nettle's arm a squeeze. "That must have been a relief for you."

Yes, Nettle should have been relieved to see her elder brother so calmly hopeful. Tansy was right; Cole was getting better.

But that was exactly why Nettle could no longer bear to be near him.

Nettle had been praised for visiting Cole during his darkest days. *It must be so hard*, people had said. But it hadn't been hard. Cole's screams had made more sense to her than anyone else's platitudes. When Nettle was with him, it was a relief, as if a confining bandage had been ripped off for a while. In return, she comforted Cole and told him that Iris's death had not been his fault.

It was when Cole slowly began to rally that Nettle struggled. He *had* started to understand that he was not to blame for the death of his dove-sister. Eventually he was even able to talk about difficult subjects, without tumbling into a dark spiral. And when he tried to talk about them with Nettle, she fled and didn't come back.

I'm hateful, she thought.

Nettle had wanted Cole to recover but couldn't bear it when he did. He was learning to forgive himself, but Iris was still dead.

Chapter 21

AMICABLE AFFAIRS

BY THE TIME THE MORNING MISTS WERE THINNING, KELLEN AND Nettle were heading inland, in the cycle sedan belonging to Tansy's friends. In the distance, Kellen could see the long, dark bar of the boundary barrier and knew that Mizzleport lay beyond.

Next to him sat Nettle, sullenly hunched and silent. Whenever they left the marsh-woods, she retreated into some private darkness and wouldn't come out for a day. Kellen tried to curb his irritation. *Do we have to go through this every time?*

All of Kellen's bruises seemed to have swollen overnight, and he ached all over. There was also a weight on his soul that had not been there before.

I'm cursed. Somebody out there hates me with all their heart. The thought filled him with wonder and dismay. He had known that he had enemies, but this was different.

"Could you unravel your own curse?" asked Nettle suddenly, and Kellen realized that she had been thinking about him after all. "We're pretty sure it's Jendy looking for revenge—"

"That's not enough," said Kellen promptly. "Revenge is just a word." He needed a feel for the heart-blood of the curse. "And . . . I don't remember Jendy very well." That was the embarrassing part. "They took her away, and I just forgot about her. I don't have a good sense of her anymore."

The sedan left the ridge road and gray marsh-woods behind and turned onto one of the big paved highways that ran toward Mizzleport. Soon the sedan was surrounded by the squeak, rattle, and rumble of other vehicles as it rattled past white-painted hostelries, wheelwright shacks, and scruffy villages.

Then the big road passed through a great stone arch, and they were in the city.

Here the buildings rose six stories high above the narrow streets. The boundary barriers stopped Mizzleport expanding outward, so everyone had built upward. The bright paintwork gave the buildings a glow despite the shadow—ochre, dark blue, mauve, lemon yellow. Balconies served as lofty shopfronts, flaunting tempting displays of fruit, cloth flowers, and tree syrup.

"My curse could be worse, though, couldn't it?" said Kellen, harnessing his bravado. "Even if I start making everyone's clothes fall off when I walk into the room."

"It *will* be worse," said Nettle, and darted a glance at him. "Kellen, how bad could the unravelling get?"

"How should I know?"

"You say you see threads sometimes when your gloves are off," Nettle persisted. "Where do you see them?"

Kellen didn't much like that train of thought.

"Everywhere," he said. "In the air. Tangled in objects." He swallowed. "And sometimes in people."

An hour later, Kellen and Nettle were aboard one of the little cross-estuary ferries, pressed against the lower deck's rail by the jostle of other passengers. The waters of the estuary were placid and gleamed like metal in the morning sun.

"What did you find out about Clarity Square?" Kellen asked quietly, trying to ignore the butterflies in his stomach.

"It's where Amicable Affairs diplomats have offices," answered Nettle, "and where they handle special passports for Wilds creatures. Bookbearers, mostly."

The other passengers were all absorbed in the view, chattering excitedly in a range of different languages. The penny ferry allowed foreign visitors staying in Mizzleport's so-called Whitestone Quarter to take a boat tour across the estuary, stopping at some of the grandest buildings so that they could feel they had seen Raddith.

Mizzleport presented a bold and dramatic face to the water. Along the waterfront were the cannon-topped forts that protected the estuary, the customs house that looked like a little castle, and the three great trading halls in their streaky gray-blue stone. It was all a great show for the foreigners, of course. Chancery didn't usually bother with huge, pompous buildings where smaller, more practical ones would do. Foreigners, however, expected that kind of thing and didn't respect your city unless it had them.

"There it is," murmured a foreign woman behind Kellen, pointing at a little island ahead, with a solitary sculpture at the top of a tall square base. It was a metal mosquito the height of three men. Foreigners were always fascinated with it, and indeed it was intended as a message for them.

Centuries before, when an enemy navy had blockaded Mizzleport, some unknown local had cursed the foreign admiral. The curse turned him into a huge mosquito, which was immediately smashed by his terrified men, after which his armada fled in confusion.

You can invade us by land or sea, the sculpture told foreigners, *but if you do, even the mightiest of you will not be safe from the weakest of us. You can armor yourself in iron or steel, great monarch, and ring yourself with guards, and hide behind the greatest army in the world. None of it will protect you.*

The ferry docked near the customs house. There were impatient mutters while the brushers and officials examined the vessel with maddening thoroughness, making sure that nothing supernatural was clinging to the hull or the anchor rope. The passengers were also quickly brushed and checked as each stepped off the gangplank. Some foreigners protested, but others were clearly delighted by the novelty.

"Clarity Square's somewhere behind the Hall of Exceptions," murmured Nettle.

The pair followed the crowds along the promenade, down a shady walkway, and into the great hall's public chamber.

It was too big for comfort or sense, with hundreds of voices echoing and jumbling beneath its great vaulted roof. At desks along the walls, Chancery officials sold numbered tickets, stamped documents, and answered questions. In the center stood a man-high hag stone, a hunk of rock with a smooth, natural hole in its center. Now and then, someone passed money or objects through the hole, to make sure they were what they appeared.

"There!" Nettle grabbed Kellen's arm and pointed. A figure was making its way through the crowd, which reflexively parted for it, sensing its strangeness. It was about six foot tall, and Kellen's brain insisted that it was a person, in the same way that it insisted that the Wilds were really dull woods. The creature was shaped like someone in a loose robe, but somehow one couldn't look straight at its face. It carried a book, or at least there was a book where its hands ought to be.

"A Bookbearer," said Kellen, under his breath. "Didn't you say Clarity Square deals with them? Let's follow it!"

Kellen and Nettle followed the Bookbearer across the hall, dodging the crowds, and through an arch in the opposite wall. The figure ahead moved at walking pace but too smoothly. There was a slight roll in its motion, but it was like the gentle rock of a moored boat. A pretense to cheat the eye, Kellen suspected.

Beyond the arch, a shady, walled promenade led to a courtyard the size of a small market square. Clean-scrubbed blue stone buildings faced each other across the cobbles as if holding a meeting. Some of the doors had people queueing patiently outside them, many of them holding bundles of papers or packaged goods. To one side, several Bookbearers gazed at a lily pond with entranced attention.

"This must be Clarity Square," Kellen said under his breath.

"Look out!" Nettle whispered urgently.

Kellen realized that their Bookbearer had turned and was gliding steadily toward them.

The Bookbearer halted in front of Kellen, who tried to see it and only partly succeeded. The robe was possibly gray, or maybe the color of roses after twilight has leached their color. When he looked into its face, he felt as though he were staring down one of the old, shadowy hollow ways, the ditch-low footpaths walled in by trees and roofed with shivering green.

It didn't say anything, but he felt its mind brush inquisitively against his, with a tickling sensation like feathers. It had noticed them following. It believed that they must need it for something. It wanted to help.

"Don't say anything," muttered Nettle through her teeth.

Like all things of the Wilds, the Bookbearers were mysterious, but it seemed that their purpose, or perhaps their wish, was to witness contracts and bargains. If you recruited their help, they would listen carefully, selflessly, and without judgment. The words of the agreement would appear in their book, and everyone involved would be bound to it forever. Nobody could break an agreement that a Bookbearer had witnessed, and terrible things would happen to anyone who tried.

This strange power of theirs was the reason why a select few were allowed in Mizzleport. Usually people were happy with a paper contract backed up the force of law, but just now and then they wanted to make sure that a bargain *couldn't* be broken. This was particularly important when it came to peace treaties with foreigners, who sometimes didn't see bargains as sacred.

"Kellen," murmured Nettle, in a warning tone.

Nettle was right, of course. It *was* dangerous talking to Bookbearers. If they took a chance remark as a promise, they might add it to their book and bind you to it forever. The wrong word might pull your entire future out of shape. Yet Kellen was suddenly tempted. He knew what was happening to him, and why he was suddenly gripped by a nervous high. *Panic-drunk*: the frightened giddiness of encountering something from the Wilds. It made you reckless, it made you unlike yourself, you had to rein it in, and yet, and yet . . .

"What's in it for you?" he asked the Bookbearer aloud, feeling himself smiling as he stared into that faceless face. "Why do you want to help so much?"

"Hey!" came a shout. A Chancery clerk was running over.

Kellen started violently. Sounds and sunlight returned to him with a rush, and he realized how they had faded while he was looking at the Bookbearer.

"You can't talk to the Bookbearers!" snapped the clerk. "Anybody who wants one to witness a contract has to get proper approval and paperwork. Join the queue like everyone else." He gestured toward a long line of people snaking from one of the doors. "Some of these people have been waiting for hours!"

"Yes, we have!" called a man halfway up the queue. "Why's everything so slow today?" There was a chorus of agreement from those around him.

"We're not here for a Bookbearer," Nettle told the clerk quickly. "We're supposed to meet Assessor Leona Tharl. She's expecting us."

"The Assessor's very busy today and can't see anyone!" Looking inexplicably harassed, the clerk hurried away.

He had just disappeared into the office when Kellen felt a gentle tap on his shoulder.

"Excuse me." A familiar freckled man in laborer's clothes was standing behind them, looking self-conscious and out of place. "Are you friends of Cherrick?"

The last time Kellen had seen this man, he had been in Havel, entreating Gall to come home. It was Harland.

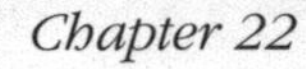

Chapter 22

THE BOOKBEARER

KELLEN WASN'T SURE KNOW HOW TO REACT, LET ALONE HOW to answer Harland's question. If Harland was here, did that mean Gall was too? Kellen tried not to glance around for any marsh horses he might have missed.

"I saw you with him in that village—in the Shallow Wilds," explained Harland, then looked sheepish. "Sorry, you probably don't remember me."

"You're his husband, aren't you?" asked Kellen, taking the plunge. Harland's face brightened. It looked like Nettle was correct.

"That's right! Do you know where he is?"

"He's not with you?" That was a relief anyway.

"No." Harland's face fell. "Back in Havel, he . . . he wouldn't talk to me properly unless I got in the carriage. Then he drove me back to Mizzleport and turfed me out on the edge of town." Harland obviously wasn't very good at hiding his feelings. Seeing his stunned, hurt expression felt like eavesdropping.

"We don't know him very well," Nettle said apologetically. "We only worked with him a couple of times. We're here to see Assessor Tharl."

"You too?" Harland blinked and rallied himself. "Do you know what's going on? These queues are hardly moving, and the clerks are running around in a panic. Everyone's trying to hide it, but I think something's wrong."

"Why are *you* here?" asked Nettle.

"I . . ." Harland looked down at a letter in his calloused hands. "I wanted to ask Assessor Tharl about releasing Cherrick from his contract."

"Release?" asked Kellen. "Doesn't he want to work for her?"

Harland looked embarrassed and conflicted.

"A year ago, Cherrick . . . found himself in some trouble. He was a bit wild when he was younger, but everything had been peaceful for years. Then some men he used to know turned up at our farm to cause trouble. There was a fight, and a man died. Cherrick has a bit of a temper."

There was plenty Kellen could have said about that, but a look from Nettle silenced him.

"It was an accident really," said Harland. "And Cherrick didn't start the fight. But it was his blow that knocked the man through the window. The magistrate agreed it wasn't murder—he said Cherrick wouldn't hang if he could pay a life's worth in gold to the dead man's family." Harland sighed, and shrugged sadly. "I'd have paid. I'd have sold the farm. I told Cherrick so. But he kept saying he didn't want that. The next thing I knew, someone else had paid the life-gild, and Cherrick was gone. So I started searching for him."

"So Leona Tharl paid the life-gild," concluded Kellen, "in exchange for him pacting with a marsh horse and working for her."

"Yes, that's what he told me yesterday," said Harland. "I asked him how I could buy his freedom. I mean, I could spare an eye if I had to. But apparently my eyes aren't worth anything to anyone." He gave a sad little grimace and tapped at one of his eyelids. "Shortsighted," he explained. "He just kept saying I was better off without him and should go home. But I can't give up on him." Harland fiddled with his letter, looking disconsolate but determined. "Maybe Assessor Tharl will listen to me. It's worth a try."

"I don't like this," said Kellen, after Harland had left to talk one of the clerks into delivering his letter. "Something *is* wrong, and there's no sign of Assessor Tharl. Let's get out of here."

"Kellen," said Nettle, in the cool, calm warning voice he had learned to recognize. Only then did he sense something behind him, like the tingle of winter sunshine on his back.

He looked over his shoulder, and found a Bookbearer silently approaching. He couldn't tell whether it was the same one as before. Nettle pulled him out of its way and it drifted past them.

It didn't visibly make any motions toward him. And yet, once it had passed, there was a brown paper note in Kellen's hand. He unfolded it and read.

> *You have been noticed by your enemies, and you are in danger. Leave quickly. Follow the Bookbearer. It will lead you to safety, and answers.*

Kellen wordlessly handed Nettle the note and looked around for the Bookbearer. It had already vanished from sight.

"Did you see where it went?" he asked.

"Through there." She pointed to a small, open door, not the archway that led back to the main hall.

Beyond the door, they found themselves in a narrow corridor with high, unshuttered windows. They were just in time to see the Bookbearer disappearing around the next corner ahead of them.

"This could be a trap," murmured Nettle, as they set off in pursuit.

"I know," Kellen whispered back. But what was the alternative? Give up on the Bookbearer, and the promise of answers? What if he and Nettle really were in danger and this was someone's attempt to show them to safety?

The corridor led to a narrow, book-lined room, then a tapestry-lined meeting room, then another corridor, then a courtyard. Now and then, they glimpsed the Bookbearer gliding silently ahead of them, then disappearing around the next corner or through the next door.

Every so often, Kellen heard the faint sound of footsteps in the corridor behind them. Perhaps it was some clerk hurrying to put a contract in the files, but as he and Nettle hastened on, the footsteps quietly hurried after them.

At last a door opened unexpectedly onto an empty road. Kellen blinked in the sudden sunlight. The Bookbearer waited at a turning just long enough to make sure they had noticed it, before drifting into an alley.

It led them through a maze of narrow alleys. Above, the blue sky still blazed, but its warmth didn't reach down into the shadowy streets.

"Where is this?" asked Nettle. "Where are all the people?"

It appeared to be an old warehouse district, waiting to be torn down. The buildings were empty and had been stripped of their woodwork, windowpanes, and everything else useful. A stray cat picked its way through one of the abandoned buildings.

Ahead, Kellen glimpsed the glint of water. The alley turned a corner and became a stone towpath that ran alongside a narrow, lightless canal with high, green-stained banks. Small, black wharfs jutted from the bank.

At the far end of the towpath, in the shadow of a great stone arch, the Bookbearer stood and waited. To Kellen's eyes, blinded by the contrast of sun and shade, it was even harder to see now, a shape carved out of fog.

"There's too much wrong with this," Nettle whispered. "Even if they have a special passport, Bookbearers aren't supposed to leave Chancery premises without a guard. None of this is right."

The off-gray figure under the arch began to move forward. It was still gliding, but no longer in the same gently rolling way as before. There was something pale held in front of it, but Kellen suddenly felt sure it was not a book.

"You're right," he whispered. "Run!"

The pair of them turned tail and prepared to sprint back the way they had come, but another two figures had appeared in the alley. These looked far more human, despite their ghostly-looking face veils, and both seemed to be carrying long knives in either hand. Kellen considered bolting into one of the abandoned buildings, but already he could see other figures moving in the shadowy interiors.

"We're surrounded!" exclaimed Nettle.

Kellen looked over his shoulder at the canal, wondering in desperation if they could jump into it. He was still staring at it when a nightmare broke the surface and erupted into the air.

The huge, sleek black shape leaped impossibly high, water cascading off its flanks. It landed on the towpath, crouched low like a cat, and made a husky, cavernous noise, like lost children wailing in the depths of a cave. On its back Gall straightened, water pouring from his gray clothes and seeping from beneath his eye-patch.

Kellen was still staring, heart rattling like a pea in a whistle, when the marsh horse attacked. He saw its jaw hinge open impossibly wide, and then a shutter seemed to slam in his mind as it refused to see what he was seeing. He could hear screams from the men in the alley. He saw something fly out and hit a wall, leaving a red smudge. It looked like a severed arm.

The thing in the gray robe flung something at Gall's head, but he knocked it out of the air with his riding crop. Then the marsh horse pounced on the indistinct creature, which dodged and shimmered backward. The robed shape melted into mist that fled away up the towpath, zigzagging and dwindling like a deflating balloon. The last wisp disappeared into a crack between paving stones.

The other veiled figures in the abandoned buildings melted back into the shadows or fled in panic down the narrow alleys. At last all was silent, except for the gulls, the muffled sounds of the city, and the sound of water dripping from the marsh horse and its rider.

"You killed a Bookbearer," said Nettle, in a small, shaky voice.

"No," said Gall. "It isn't dead. And that wasn't a Bookbearer."

The object the marsh horseman had struck to the ground with his crop was a little cage fashioned from small, white bones.

"Change of plan," declared Gall. "All hell's broken loose. Come with me."

Kellen looked at the blood on the marsh horse's muzzle and for once decided not to argue.

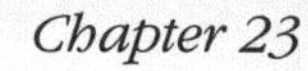

Chapter 23

A VOICE IN THE DARK

"HE'S TALKING TO HIS HAND AGAIN," WHISPERED NETTLE.

Gall was walking ahead of them, one hand lifted to his mouth. It was hard to see him distinctly because of the clouds of steam that rose from his clothes and from his horse's mane and flanks. The water that drenched them was shimmering away into mist.

"I think his hand's talking back," said Kellen suddenly.

Nettle listened intently and caught the faint murmur of another voice.

"You're right," she whispered.

"Alive and unharmed," Gall was telling his hand. "Yes, we followed the stink of marsh pollen."

Ruefully, Nettle remembered the bush where she and Kellen had hidden in the Shallow Wilds. She should have guessed that the pollen scent would still be clinging to their clothes. Perhaps that had helped Gall track them to Tansy's place too.

The marsh horse finished licking the blood off its muzzle with its long, tapering black tongue. By the time their group reached streets with other pedestrians, horse and rider looked as presentable as two such creatures could.

If we ran away now and tried to lose them in the crowds, would they track us down again? wondered Nettle.

Her eye strayed to the leather bag in Gall's other hand, which contained the bone-cage thrown by the false Bookbearer. It seemed there were even more sinister things abroad than Cherrick Gall and his man-eating horse.

.....

Gall led them into a smart terrace of new houses, their brightly colored paint gleaming, their black tiled roofs immaculate, fine mesh shielding every window from insects. Some even had mock-stables for their pedal-coaches. The marsh horseman approached the side door of a slim, mauve house and let them in with a key.

Within, everything was a lot less sedate. A footman with a drawn pistol was posted just inside the door. Two servants in the sitting room seemed to be packing papers and books into trunks with frantic haste. Gall paused to have a murmured conversation with them, then handed one of them the bag full of bone-cage.

Gall led Nettle and Kellen up two narrow flights of wooden stairs, then halted outside a door. He pulled something small out of his pocket and held it close to his mouth.

"We're outside your room," he said. "Can we come in?"

This time, there could be no mistake. The object answered in a female voice, clearly enough for Nettle to overhear.

"Yes, of course you can come in," it said a little testily. "I'm not in a state of undress!" A small pause. "Well. I suppose I am, technically. Never mind. Bring them in."

The room beyond the door was lit by only a single oil lamp, its flame set so low that it was a tiny blue, quivering ghost. By its very dim light, Nettle could just make out the square bulk of a four-poster bed, the silhouette of a toilet table, and a big wardrobe chest against the wall. It was someone's private chamber, but there was no sign of its owner.

Nettle's instincts prickled uneasily. She could smell scented powder, potpourri, and beeswax ointments, but there was a whiff of something else that made the hairs rise on her skin. A touch of the Wilds.

"Close the door behind you," said the female voice. "Quickly!" Gall obeyed. "You had better put the cameo down by the lamp where they can see it."

Carefully, the marsh horseman laid a small object next to the lamp on the dresser. Nettle could see that it was indeed an old-fashioned cameo, perfectly round and about two inches across. Its tiny picture showed a woman in profile. She was not young, but her hair was still dark. Her face had hard lines and a watchful, amused gaze. The brush used to paint her image must have been eyelash fine.

As Nettle was staring at the cameo, the image of the woman turned to gaze back at her.

"I am Leona Tharl," said the tiny face. "I'm glad Gall found you before anything terrible happened."

"It *did* happen," said Kellen grimly. "Just not to us."

"Oh, Gall!" chided the cameo. "Really? Again?"

"I did say there would be some cleanup required," the marsh horseman remarked with stony calm.

Nettle caught a faint, whispery sound from above that made her tense. She scanned the ceiling and caught a hint of shadowy motion that flitted in her peripheral vision, wheeled, skimmed back, and vanished into shadow.

"There's something in this room," she said quietly. "Something dark. Flying around."

"Yes," said the woman-cameo, sounding embarrassed and agitated. "Yes . . . I'm afraid there is. That . . . well, that would be me."

The small, dark shape wheeled and flickered across the ceiling, then came to a halt on a picture frame. Nettle could just see its brown, furry body dangling from the frame, its wings folded like tiny umbrellas, its ears twitching.

"You're a bat?" she asked.

"Not usually," the Leona-cameo assured her. "I've only been a bat since about four o'clock this morning. I did intend to meet you at Clarity Square. I wasn't expecting this . . . inconvenience."

"You've been cursed?" Kellen stared up at the small, winged shape.

"Yes," said Leona, her voice not entirely steady, "and I'm *really* hoping you can do something about it."

"How can you talk?" Nettle blurted out. She could remember how her mind had narrowed when she was a heron, how her faint fleeting memories had slipped from her grasp over and over. "Why are you able to think?"

"Believe me, this is *not* easy," said the cameo with feeling. "And I'm not at all sure I can keep it up. It's lucky that I happened to own this cameo. I commissioned it from an artificer on one of the White Boats, as a way to keep in touch with Gall. I operate it through thought alone, so I can still use it to communicate. But keeping my head clear is . . . getting harder."

"Do you know who cursed you, and why?" asked Kellen. Nettle could sense his sympathies shifting. He had walked in with a grievance, but now there was a cursed woman clinging upside down from a picture frame.

"Only in the most general terms," said Leona. "Gall, you've told them about Salvation, haven't you?"

"A little," said Nettle.

"They're a league of criminals collecting cursers," said Leona bluntly, "in order to use them as weapons. At least, that's what I believe. Everybody who tries to investigate them disappears or becomes cursed. I've been on their trail for a year, secretly gathering evidence and trying to sabotage their operations. They must have found out who was working against them, and set one of their pet cursers on me."

"But that's not how curses work!" exclaimed Kellen. "You can't just pick whatever target's convenient and fire a curse like a gun!"

"Oh good," Leona said tartly. "Then I must be imagining being a bat. I daresay I'll feel better after a little lie-down."

"There's no need—" began Kellen.

"I know, forgive me, I'm having a very bad day." The bat fluttered, then folded its wings again. "I'm sure you're right—I'm sure that curses don't usually work that way. But I promise you, this conspiracy *does* target its enemies with curses. And . . . well, look at me!"

"I can't unravel the curse if that's all we know," said Kellen. "I need some idea what was going through the curser's mind."

"I see," Leona said faintly. "That's . . . unfortunate. I was hoping you'd be the ace up our sleeve. A way of curing those cursed by Salvation. And I can't afford to be taken out of the fight right now—their agents are making a move against all my operations . . ."

The cameo's mouth broke off and grimaced. Then it made a chattering sound, followed by some high chirrups. Above, the bat was wheeling duskily around the ceiling, nearly colliding with the walls.

"Assessor!" growled Gall urgently. "Assessor, can you hear me!"

The cameo gave a series of rapid clicks, and then the bat landed on the curtain rails and hung fluttering from its feet, dark against the pale drapery. It seemed to be eating something.

"Apologies," the cameo said faintly. "A moth. It sounded . . . distractingly delicious, and I lost control . . ." Her laugh sounded a little like a sob. "Oh, that does not bode well for the evening."

Leona's shaky focus made it hard for her to talk for long, so Gall filled in some of the gaps.

In the early morning, the cameo had summoned Gall to Leona's house so that he could prevent her well-meaning servants shooing their mistress out of a window. Since then, Gall had been running around trying to deal with crises.

"Now Leona's out of action, the Salvation agents haven't let the grass grow under their feet," he said grimly. "A secret base of hers has been raided and ransacked. Three of the allies that she trusted most in Amicable Affairs have gone missing. All that was left behind was their clothes, lying on their office chairs as if their owners had evaporated. And I only just stopped the Assessor's files being carried out of her office to be 'treated for paper-sprites.' Salvation's probably looking for the evidence she's been gathering on them."

"If she's got some proof of Salvation's crimes, why don't we give it to someone in charge?" asked Kellen.

Nettle noticed Kellen's use of "we." Apparently "we" now included Leona and Gall.

"Chancery *are* the people in charge," interjected the cameo. "And we don't know which of our colleagues we can trust!"

"We don't know who the leader of Salvation is," elaborated Gall.

"That's what the Assessor's been trying to find out all this time. We think it's someone high up in Amicable Affairs, and we don't know who. We don't want to take our findings to the wrong person."

"And once I come forward with my testimony, it'll be obvious I'm a bat," Leona added. "Then somebody else will be asked to take over my department. For all I know, a Salvation agent may be waiting in the wings to do just that."

From downstairs came a panicky cry and the sound of commotion, followed by a thunder of feet running upstairs. Gall tensed beside the door and only slightly relaxed when one of Leona's servants burst into the room.

"Assessor!" The old man addressed his remarks to the cameo, eyes glazed with alarm. "It ate him! That bone thing ate Gerden!"

"Careful, you fool!" Gall closed the door that the servant had left wide open. "Windows and doors *shut*! The Assessor is trying not to fly away!"

"Calm down, man, and tell us what happened!" Leona insisted.

"The cage of bone," gasped the servant. "Gerden was taking it out of the bag to put it in an iron-studded box for safety, and he vanished!"

"Idiots!" growled Gall. "I told you not to touch it!" He himself had carefully nudged it into the bag using his riding crop.

The marsh horseman rushed from the room with the servant in tow. Kellen and Nettle hurriedly followed, closing the door behind them to stop their bat-hostess from going astray.

In the kitchen, Nettle and Kellen found Gall and several servants staring at the bone-cage, which lay on the kitchen table, protruding from the leather bag. The cage was simple and square-cornered, the yellow-white bone fragments glued together by something tar-like and lashed with what looked like dark wire or sinew. Dirty, disheveled birds' wings hung slackly from the sides.

"What does it look like?" Leona's cameo asked impatiently. Since the bat had been left in her bed chamber, she couldn't see the cage herself.

"Disgusting," said Kellen, leaning dangerously close to peer.

Nettle stared at it as well. The bars of the cage were made up of small bones, the uppermost tapering into what looked like long, discolored claws . . .

"Finger bones," she said aloud. "Those are fingers. And other hand bones."

"What are these?" asked Kellen, nudging a heap of clothes sprawled over one chair.

"Those are Gerden's," said the frightened old servant. "They fell to the floor when he vanished."

"Oh." Kellen's eyes gleamed with revelation. "That's what happened to those other friends of Leona, isn't it? Their clothes were found but they weren't! Maybe the fake Bookbearer attacked them with its cage before it came after us."

"We need to know what that creature is," said Leona. "Gall—do you have any ideas?"

"No," said the marsh horseman. "It smelled of mildew and smoke. And she didn't like it at all."

It took a moment for Nettle to realize whom he meant by "she." Somehow it hadn't occurred to her to think of the marsh horse as anything but an "it."

As the others argued and theorized, Nettle looked at the finger bones. In her head, old tales coalesced into a theory.

I know what it is, she thought suddenly.

From under her lashes, she glanced around the room. Everyone was peering at the cage and theorizing but still aiming wide of the mark.

Should I tell them? Do I really want *to help them? We're acting like we're all friends and allies, but are we? How many people in this room will turn out to be enemies?*

Her gaze fell upon Gerden's crumpled clothes. They were too pitiful to ignore. She had to say something.

"Has anyone heard of a Dancing Star?" she asked aloud, and felt self-conscious when the room hushed. "It's called that because its lantern makes a bobbing light."

"So it's a will-o'-the-wisp?" asked the old servant.

"No," said Nettle and Leona simultaneously.

For some reason, highlanders found it hard to understand that there were many different kinds of eerie bobbing lights that you might encounter in the marsh-woods. The prankets were mostly harmless, the Jinny-of-the-lanterns would try to lure you to your death, and the moonticks wanted to settle in your ear so that they could drink the color from your dreams. The Dancing Stars were different again.

"According to the stories," continued Nettle, "Dancing Stars use their lanterns to search for something in the marshes. Nobody knows what. But their lanterns don't burn oil, they burn souls. So the Dancing Star detaches its hands and leaves them among the roots of a tree—the sort of roots that are good for climbing or mooring your boat. When somebody gets too close, the hands catch their soul and trap it. When that happens, the person vanishes. All that's left behind is their clothes. Eventually the Dancing Star comes back, reattaches its hands, and puts the soul in its lantern."

Everyone's gaze turned back to the grisly cage on the table.

"It might be two hands," Kellen said, looking sickened, "if they had extra joints. And long, brown claws."

"If our people are trapped in that cage," asked Leona, "can we get them out?"

"I don't know," admitted Nettle.

"Where's its lantern?" asked Kellen. "And why are its hands glued into a cage like that?"

"I don't know that either," said Nettle. "It's weird. And if it *is* a Dancing Star, it shouldn't be here! They stick to lonely parts of the Deep Wilds. They don't even go near villages, let alone a city."

"Maybe somebody else found its hands," suggested Gall, "and made them into a cage. Plenty of uses for a weapon that makes your enemies vanish. The Moonlit Market—the one where the Wilds meets the sea—had lots of wares like that. Things made from bits of people and other creatures, not all of them dead." For a moment, his expression was bleakly distant.

Nettle remembered that Gall had seen one of these markets first-hand. She wondered what actually happened when you gave your eye for a marsh horse. How was the eye taken out? Was it still alive somewhere? Could Gall still see through it?

"So maybe somebody *did* buy the cage at the Moonlit Market," said Kellen. He had the happy, eager look he always had when fragments were slotting together in his head. "What if the Dancing Star agreed to work for them because it was the only way to get the cage back? Maybe that's why it's in Mizzleport. Somebody brought it here."

"Smuggling in such a dangerous creature would be highly illegal," said Leona, starting to sound excited. "If we found out who it was, we could have them arrested!"

"I don't know about you," Kellen said slowly, "but if I were the leader of a sinister conspiracy, and I had the chance to recruit a murderous Deep Wilds monster, I wouldn't want it obeying anybody but me. We don't know who runs Salvation, but maybe the Dancing Star does. If we could find some way to catch it—"

He was interrupted by a sharp rapping noise that made everyone jump. Someone was knocking loudly on Assessor Tharl's front door.

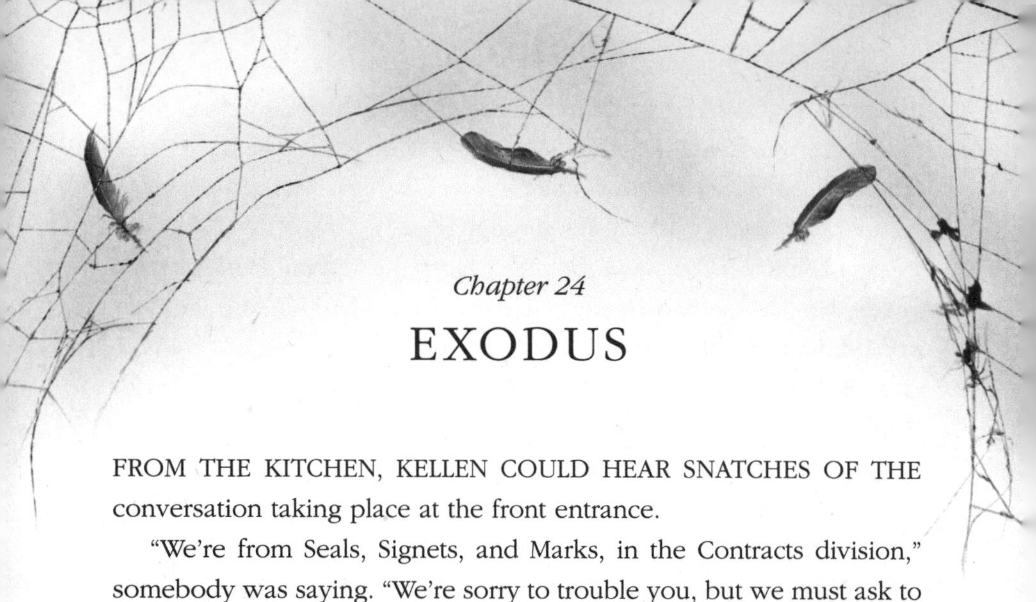

Chapter 24

EXODUS

FROM THE KITCHEN, KELLEN COULD HEAR SNATCHES OF THE conversation taking place at the front entrance.

"We're from Seals, Signets, and Marks, in the Contracts division," somebody was saying. "We're sorry to trouble you, but we must ask to have a quick word with your mistress."

"The Assessor isn't well enough for visitors, I'm afraid," the maid could be heard explaining.

"We won't be a moment," insisted the visitor. "It's just that a dozen documents were issued today with her seal but no signature. That wouldn't usually be a problem, except that we're hearing rumors that this is happening without her consent or knowledge—that someone is taking advantage of her illness. In fact, some people were even suggesting that she's been kidnapped. I don't like to intrude on an invalid, but a two-minute conversation would clear this up."

Kellen swore quietly. As a bat, Leona could do many things, but she couldn't sign a document. Or bluff her way through a two-minute conversation, for that matter.

"What now, Assessor?" asked Gall.

The cameo opened its mouth and gave a thin, nervous *skreek* followed by a series of rapid clicks. Gall's expression creased into something that looked slightly like panic.

"Do you think those people are from Salvation?" asked Kellen. Leona's fear of an all-pervasive conspiracy was rubbing off on him.

"I don't know," answered Gall. "But we can't let them near the

Assessor. Any one of them might be an enemy agent." He looked up at the nearby servants, who were waiting uncertainly for orders.

"Stall!" he told them. "Stall them as long as you can!"

It took several precious minutes to catch the bat, even with three people, a butterfly net, and a large lace tablecloth. Even Leona's patches of lucidity didn't help.

"I do apologize!" the cameo told them, as the bat's fleet, dark shape dodged between their clutches yet again. She sounded panicky and embarrassed. "I really am trying to be caught, but . . . it's hard to master one's instincts!"

Kellen wondered whether she was talking about her instincts as a bat or her own elusive tendencies. If Salvation had spent a year trying to work out the identity of their frustrating, shadowy opponent, perhaps that was why one of them had turned her into a bat.

At last Gall's net managed to swipe the tiny shape out of the air, leaving it tangled in the fine mesh. Leona's cameo gave a few panicky chirrups of terror, then fell silent.

Gall, Kellen, and Nettle were hurried into the basement by Leona's elderly steward. They passed through a door with four bolts, along a vaulted underground passage, and up a ladder into a wood-turning workshop. The wood-turners gave them a discreet nod as they emerged but said nothing. They didn't comment on the iron-studded wooden box carried by Kellen or the fluttering sounds issuing from the cloth-covered birdcage in Nettle's hand.

In the alley outside, the carriage was waiting. The marsh horse stood quietly, crystal streams of rainwater falling from its mane, but Kellen couldn't forget seeing its muzzle red with blood. Gall climbed up to take the driver's seat while Kellen and Nettle scrambled into the coach. They were barely seated before it lurched into motion.

"What now?" asked Nettle, her voice muffled by the thunder of rain on the roof. "Where are we going?"

"We need to keep on the move," Gall called down, "keep the Assessor safe—"

"We can't ride around forever!" exclaimed Kellen. "Leona's losing her grip! Soon she'll just be a very safe bat, and Salvation will take over her department and destroy all her files, and everything she's done will be for nothing."

"I think you're upsetting her," said Nettle, frowning at the chittering birdcage.

"We need to catch the Dancing Star!" said Kellen. His mind quailed at the memory of the gray-robed figure, but there was no help for it. "It's our best chance to find out who's running Salvation—and prove it. And we've got something it wants." He knocked on the iron-studded box, which contained the bone-cage.

"Maybe, but if we find it, how do we catch it?" asked Nettle. "How do we stop it turning into smoke and disappearing down a crack, the way it did at the canal?"

This was an annoyingly good point.

"Assessor!" Kellen leaned over, with his face close to the birdcage. "I know it's hard, but we really need you to focus! Do you know where we can get equipment to catch a creature from the Wilds?"

There was a series of chitters, and then a few scattered syllables. Leona was trying to speak.

"Songhill . . . Ask Songhill." Each word from Leona was obviously an exertion of will, and these words were followed only by tiny keening squeaks.

"Songhill?" asked Kellen. "Who's Songhill?"

"I've heard of him," said Gall, with an unusual hint of respect in his voice. "Warden Songhill. He used to be a shadecatcher, trapping stray barghests and shadow-calves that washed up in the city harbor during storms. He'll know how to capture a dangerous creature like this one."

"Where do we find him?" asked Kellen.

"He works for Perilous Contrivances now," said Gall. "So we're going to need a boat."

.....

The rain was easing by the time the carriage pulled to a halt in a dark alley full of the sound of the sea. On either side, warehouses dripped in the gloom.

"Come on." Gall clambered down from the coach.

Nettle and Kellen got out and followed Gall out of the mouth of the alley. Beyond lay a small, sheltered dock full of small fishing vessels and rowing boats. Only a few lumpers, brushers, and Chancery officials were braving the drizzle, their face veils damp and clinging.

Looking out across the dingy-gray sea, Kellen could glimpse the solitary island that he had seen that very morning, with the large, steel mosquito sculpture at its peak.

"And Perilous Contrivances really have a base out there?" he asked, shielding his eyes from the rain.

"Nobody wants them on shore," said Gall.

Kellen knew of the Department for Perilous Contrivances, Engines, Facsimiles, and Automata. Its job was to test out new or foreign inventions, to see whether they could be used safely in Raddith. In this case, "safely" meant "without annoying the Little Brothers." The web-sprites had very strong opinions about which machines or inventions were acceptable in Raddith, and their reasoning was usually mysterious. Unfortunately, the only way to find out if they objected to something was to try using it, and see whether one ended up neck-deep in irate spiders.

"Here's some money to hire a boat." Gall dropped some coins in Kellen's hand. "And you can show this to Songhill, so he knows you're from Assessor Tharl." He passed Nettle a document with a Chancery seal, and then, a little reluctantly, placed Leona's cameo in her hand as well.

"Aren't you coming with us?" she asked.

"I need to hide the carriage," he said. "It's too recognizable, and so am I. I'll catch you up." Without another word he stalked back into the alley.

"How is he going to catch up with us if we're in a boat?" Kellen whispered to Nettle. The damp evening air offered no suggestions.

. . . . .

Nettle and Kellen took it in turns to row the little boat. The iron-studded box and the covered bat-cage were tucked under the canvas at the stern, out of the rain. The estuary mouth was sheltered, so the waves were small. The rain had left the water churned and silty, and here and there the breakers chased little fleeces of scummy froth.

Kellen had taken his gloves off to row. They made it too hard to grip the oar, and he didn't want them getting rusty from seawater.

"I hope Leona's right to trust Warden Songhill," he said, heaving on the oars. "If he turns out to be an enemy, we'll be stranded with nowhere to run."

Nettle didn't answer for a few moments. She was looking at him in a doubtful, calculating way, as if deciding whether to say something.

"What?" he asked, losing patience.

Nettle glanced toward the bat-cage, which was still chittering and squeaking, then carefully wrapped Leona's cameo in her handkerchief and put in her pocket.

"How much do we trust Leona and Gall?" she asked very quietly.

"What?" The question took Kellen by surprise. It made him feel derailed and a little annoyed.

"Everything's happened so fast, we've been swept up into helping them." In the dimming light, Nettle looked pale and earnest. "But we've just met Leona, and we've only known Gall a few days. Until two hours ago, we didn't trust them. And you were right, what Leona was saying about her curse sounded weird. Maybe we shouldn't believe everything she says."

"She's definitely not malingering, though, is she?" Kellen pointed out.

"No, but maybe she did something to make someone hate her," said Nettle. "We don't know, do we? We've only heard one side of the story. And we don't know anything about Salvation, except what she and Gall have told us. What if it's not what they say it is? What if it's . . ." She trailed off, as if she didn't know how to finish the sentence.

"Salvation tried to kill us!" pointed out Kellen.

"We don't know if that's what they were trying to do," said Nettle. "We don't even know if those people at the canal *were* Salvation."

"But there's people getting cursed and disappearing! And if Salvation are the ones hiding Jendy Pin, then they're behind my curse too."

As soon as the words were out, Kellen realized that he hadn't really thought this through before. What if Leona was right, and Salvation *did* have a way to aim curses at anyone who might cause problems for them? Perhaps the curse that had landed on Kellen wasn't the result of a deep, personal hatred after all. His spirit lightened at the thought.

"We don't know . . ." Nettle began, then sighed. She suddenly looked disappointed and exhausted. "Fine," she said quietly, closing the conversation like a book. "Never mind."

Kellen continued rowing. Evidently things were not fine, but he was too irritated to ask why. Somehow he was left feeling as if he had failed a test.

As the island drew closer, Kellen could now see that the steel mosquito's square base was a building, with shuttered windows and a zigzag set of stone steps leading from the waterline to its door.

"I think someone's seen us coming," said Nettle quietly. "And . . . they don't look friendly."

A man was standing on the steps with an umbrella in one hand and a lit lantern in the other. The latter was held threateningly close to the match-cord of a small cannon, which pointed toward the boat.

"Who are you?" he shouted. "I'm not due a delivery today!"

"We need to see Warden Songhill!" Kellen called back. "We've been sent by Assessor Tharl!"

"The Warden's not here!" the stranger shouted back. "And he's not Warden anymore either. Go away!"

While the visitors were absorbing this shock, the rowing boat rocked slightly from side to side. Looking out to his right, Kellen saw an arrowhead of turbulent water race past, as if something large beneath the surface was speeding toward the island.

The marsh horse and rider broke the surface in a wild, impossible leap, and seemed to hang in the air with the spray, before landing in a crouch on the rocks at the base of the island. Both poured seawater, their shapes shrouded and transfigured by lank, dark weed. The lantern light gleamed on the horse's wet hide, the angles of its joints and sinews looking crooked and wrong.

The stranger stood frozen to the spot as the marsh horse spidered its way up the rocks toward him, hooves splaying oddly to grip the slick, barnacled surface. Gall straightened in the saddle and shook out his steaming coat.

"I'd move that lantern away from the cannon," he called out. "Accidents happen."

The stranger allowed the boat to dock and its occupants to disembark, but with a very bad grace. Every now and then, he gave Gall and his horse fearful, resentful looks.

It was hard to guess his age. His face and head were shaven, and his eyebrows were patchy with scars. His forehead and neck were covered with what looked like either pimples or insect bites. Under his thick, woolen cape, he seemed to be wearing a tight-necked doublet covered in small iron studs.

"You'd better come in," he said, with the same tone he might have used for ordering his last meal.

Kellen had been expecting the room they entered to be full of vast, diabolical mechanisms of foreign origin, glinting with iron and spitting sparks. He was disappointed to discover instead a dull-looking office, with narrow desks, hanging oil lamps, and huge, inky ledgers.

Every wall was covered in locked drawers of different sizes, each with their own label. *Antagonian oyster-sheller*, read one label. *Owl-scarer*, said another.

"What's happened to the Warden?" Gall asked.

"He agreed to help your Assessor Tharl, that's what happened!" snapped their host. "And now he's been framed for smuggling prankets as exotic pets! They arrested him this morning!"

Another of Leona's allies had been taken out of action. Kellen doubted that this was coincidence.

"Listen," Kellen said urgently. "We're sorry to hear about the Warden, but we need your help—"

"Oh, no!" interrupted the shaven-headed man, his eyes wild with alarm. "No, no, no! I've seen what happens to people who help your Assessor Tharl with her secret war. Tell her to ask someone else!"

"Um . . . she can't really do that," said Nettle. She unwrapped the cameo and held it up for the stranger to see, then pulled the cloth off the bat-cage. He stared from one to the other in incomprehension.

"Is . . . that . . . Creskin?" the cameo croaked blearily.

Creskin's jaw dropped. He stooped to peer at the small, dark shape that hung upside down in the cage, swiveling its delicate ears. Then he gave a muffled choking noise and broke down into helpless peals of laughter.

"They got you too!" he croaked. "Your little furry face!" He wiped his eyes and looked more serious. "It's over, then. Salvation's won."

"Not yet!" insisted Kellen. "Listen—there's a creature we need to capture. If we can, then maybe we can find out who the leader of Salvation is and get them arrested! Maybe we could even get your Warden out of prison. But we need your help. Is there anything here we could borrow to trap a creature from the Wilds? A really dangerous one?"

Creskin sighed bitterly.

"All right," he said. "I'll show you everything we have. But you're not going to like it."

At the top of a short flight of stairs, Creskin opened a door onto a bare, brick room. Doors studded with tiny panes of green glass looked out on a small balcony. Aside from a warm hearth, the only other object in the room was a person-sized cage made up of narrow iron bars, the gaps between them filled with fine iron mesh.

"This is the room where I test devices," said Creskin. "If a few hundred Little Brothers turn up, I hide inside the iron cage." He glanced at his guests. "That cage can keep out Little Brothers, so maybe you can imprison your Dancing Star in it. If you can get it inside, which I doubt."

"We've got bait," said Kellen.

"If you say so," said Creskin. "*I* say nothing from the Wilds is going to walk into a cage of iron unless it has no other choice."

"So what about other ways of catching it, then?" asked Kellen, remembering that Warden Songhill had been a shadecatcher. "What else have you got?"

"Nothing!" exclaimed Creskin bitterly. "We *had* some traps. A beautiful rowan-wood orrery-mesmerizer. A sickle-weed net woven by tree-women, and half a dozen puzzle bottles. But Amicable Affairs requisitioned them all from us. They said we didn't really need them, we were only facing Little Brothers—"

"You must have something else!" Kellen's heart sank.

"I have this doublet to stop Little Brothers getting inside my clothes," said Creskin, "and some goggles to protect my eyes. That's it."

While everyone was reeling from this revelation, Gall suddenly stiffened, as if he had heard something. He paced quickly over to the balcony doors and opened them, staring out to sea.

"Something's coming," he said.

"What?" Creskin edged past him and stepped out onto the balcony. "Where?" He tugged a spyglass out of his pocket and crammed it to his eye, then gave a sharp intake of breath.

"What is it?" asked Kellen, following him out onto the balcony. Peering into the gloom, all he could make out were a few distant smudges against the dull gray of the sea.

"Four boats coming from the bay," said Creskin hoarsely. "And . . . something else. Something pale, moving just ahead of them across the water . . ."

Kellen looked for a way to break the bad news gently and settled for breaking it quickly.

"That's probably the creature I was talking about," he said, feeling his chest tighten. "It's . . . a soul-sucking fog monster from the Wilds. And I guess it's brought friends."

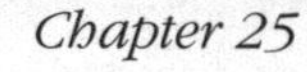

Chapter 25

DANCING STAR

"YOU LED THEM HERE?" SHOUTED CRESKIN, LOOKING ANGRY and panicky.

Nettle couldn't blame him. He was probably right. Perhaps the carriage had been seen near the dock, perhaps she and Kellen had been recognized in the boat, or perhaps the Dancing Star had sensed the location of its hands. Whatever the case, it was probably their fault.

"How can we hold them off?" asked Kellen. "Can we use your cannons?"

"They're not loaded," said Creskin. "And even if they were, they wouldn't fire on a wet day like this. I just use them to bluff, that's all."

Nettle gave Kellen a panicky glance. The situation was sounding more desperate by the moment.

"Well . . . what about all those inventions downstairs?" asked Kellen. "Will they help against the people in the boats?"

"Only if we want to peel pineapples at our attackers," said Creskin dourly. "Or crochet them a sock."

"THIS PLACE IS A JOKE!" exploded Kellen. "I knew it was a mistake to come here!"

There was a slithering sound as Creskin's woolen cape began to writhe and unravel. He gave a yelp, pulled it off his shoulders, and threw it away.

"What was that?" he gasped.

"Sorry!" Kellen's face contorted with panic and misery. "Sorry, sorry, sorry! But . . . we don't have any weapons. We don't have anything. And those boats will be here in five minutes!"

"Not if I can help it," Gall said grimly. He turned and strode back toward the stairs.

"They're getting closer," murmured Nettle.

Despite the deepening gloom, she could see the boats more clearly now, the occupants working the oars, a wraithlike gray shape gliding above the water ahead of them . . .

. . . and then an arrow-shaped crease in the surface heading right for them.

A moment later, chaos broke out in the little armada.

"They're down to three boats!" declared Creskin, staring through his spyglass. "The fourth is belly up with people clinging to it. Three people. Wait, now I can only see two—aaagh!" He lowered his spyglass abruptly, looking sick.

Kellen eagerly snatched the telescope from Creskin's trembling hand and pressed it to his own eye.

"I can't see Gall or the horse," he reported. "They must be swimming around under the boats. And . . . I can see a couple of men standing up in the boats, holding long things like lances, and looking down over the side . . ."

Nettle didn't like the sound of that.

"What's the Dancing Star doing?" she asked.

"Nothing," said Kellen. "It's just hovering there."

Nettle took her turn with the telescope. Immediately her view was almost filled by the boats, hazy with mist and the dusk. She could just make out the figures of their crew, watchfully tensed, twitching their heads this way and that to watch for an attack. As she watched, one man pointed, and another stabbed his lance down into the water, then shook his head.

For a second, a black equine head broke through the crest of a wave, eyes foam-white and jaw agape. Before the men in the boats could react, something gray and indistinct darted into view. It lunged at the black head, which promptly vanished beneath the waves. The gray shape remained, a vaporous outline of a figure, rippling slowly and strangely in the dim light.

"I saw Gall's horse just then," said Nettle, "and the Dancing Star attacked it. I think it's protecting those men so they can keep rowing. Gall's slowing them down, but he hasn't stopped them."

"That's bad," murmured Kellen. "We can't catch the Dancing Star if we're battling three boatloads of murderers at the same time!" Then his face cleared and became bright with excited concentration. Nettle recognized the look in his eye and apprehensively dropped her gaze to his hands. Sure enough, he still hadn't put his gloves back on.

"What are you doing?" she asked, as Kellen picked up the iron-studded box and moved it into Creskin's metal cage.

"We need to catch the Dancing Star alone, don't we?" said Kellen, as he opened the box and shook the bone-cage out onto the floor. "So we need it to get here before the boats do."

He strode to the hearth, pulled a red-tipped poker from the embers, then marched back to the cage. Before anybody could stop him, he plunged the red-hot point into the bony mass. There was a stink of burning, and the bone-cage jumped and shuddered horribly, like a thing in pain. A few tiny threads of sinew glowed like wicks and crumbled.

"Kellen!" gasped Nettle.

"We can't stop the boats," said Kellen, his face keen and animated, "so I've given the Dancing Star a reason to get here faster!" He looked at Nettle and Creskin's horrified faces. "What?"

Undulating like the smoke from a dead candle, the Dancing Star sped toward the island, outpacing the boats easily. Nettle watched it from the balcony and felt her heart plummet. It sprang between wave-tips in leap after impossible leap, its mist-robes billowing raggedly as it did so.

Creskin swore violently and armed himself with an ash shovel. He glared at his guests with furious, conflicted annoyance.

"Why did she have to send children?" he muttered under his breath, before apparently coming to a decision. "Look—this is *my* base, *my* job. I'll find a way to shut your monster in the cage. You two just . . . take the bat-lady and find somewhere to hide, will you?"

Kellen reflexively snatched up the bat-cage but made no move to flee.

"We can't leave you to face it alone!" he said.

"Just hurry!" shouted Creskin.

It was too late. Nettle leaped back just in time as the balcony doors were suddenly flung open. They hit the wall with so much force that their panes frosted, and one hinge broke, leaving a door dangling slantwise. Nettle and Kellen flattened themselves against the wall, holding their breath.

The Dancing Star glided from the balcony into the room. It still bore the appearance of a figure in a hooded robe, but now the cloth was smokily indistinct and moved sinuously like a sea-thing. The creature raised sleeves full of darkness, in which Nettle could just make out dull gleams of bone-yellow, the handless stubs of wrists.

It moved slowly toward the iron cage and Creskin, who seemed to be rooted to the spot with panic. The Dancing Star tilted its head to one side, then the other, considering.

But it did not advance into the cage. Instead, it slowly turned its cowled head toward Creskin.

That is mine, it said, in a voice like the crackling of embers and the scream of green branches in flames. *Fetch it for me. I will pull out your soul if you do not.*

It drew closer to Creskin, who flinched away from it, backing up against the wall.

"All right!" he squeaked. "This isn't my fight anyway! Let me pass by, and I'll . . . I'll get it for you."

"What?" exclaimed Kellen. "You can't!"

Nettle watched aghast as Creskin slipped past the writhing gray shape and stepped into the iron cage. He halted next to the bone-cage, swallowed, and turned to face the Dancing Star.

"On second thoughts," he said shakily. "Maybe I'll pound these bones to dust with this ash shovel." As he raised his shovel threateningly above the box, he cast a brief, meaningful glance toward Nettle.

Realization hit her like a brick. Creskin had never intended to surrender the bone-cage. He was goading the Dancing Star into entering the cage so that Kellen and Nettle could shut them in together.

But you'll die! she thought. *I can't do that!*

The Dancing Star rose up like a gray wave about to break, and for a moment it seemed it would crash down upon Creskin. Then it halted and drew back.

You have my hands, it said. *I have your friends.*

And it turned to face Kellen and Nettle.

"Stop!" shouted Creskin as it began to glide toward them. "They have no part in this!"

Kellen grabbed Nettle's arm, and they fled out onto the balcony. The evening wind hit them like a boisterous dog and nearly bowled them over. The very air was rough and alive with the roar of the sea.

"Up!" yelled Kellen, and started to climb the wall, finding toeholds in the weathered brickwork. "The mosquito!"

Nettle saw at once what he meant. The huge sculpture of a mosquito perched on top of the building was made of steel. If they could climb up onto that, the Dancing Star might not follow. The wall was ice-cold and clammy under her fingers as she began to climb.

Below, she heard a rage-filled, anguished hiss, like rain on a bonfire.

"Leave them alone, or I'll do it again!" shouted Creskin.

Looking down, however, she saw the Dancing Star glide out onto the balcony and tip back its faceless head to look up.

"Hurry!" Kellen shouted from farther up the wall. Even carrying the bat-cage, he was racing ahead of her. Nettle could have yelled back, but that would have meant un-gritting her teeth and losing her concentration. It was all very well for Kellen, but not everyone had spent their early years clambering over town roofs like a cat.

Nettle's foot slithered in a crevice and slipped out of it. She gave a yelp as her cheek slammed against the wall, and her fingers seared with the strain of keeping their grip. Her unsupported foot scraped desperately against the brick, then found a slender purchase.

She gasped for breath and opened her eyes again, only to find that the Dancing Star had risen up beside her.

Nettle could feel its stare from within the shadow of its cowl. Within the depths of that darkness, she thought she saw a cold light burning—one tarnish-colored, cruel, solitary light.

It reached one handless sleeve toward her, then halted the motion without touching her. A shudder went through it.

Your soul smells of the marshes, it said, and there was a terrible yearning in its voice.

It wasn't quite true that Nettle felt pity. She felt cold. Miserably, bitterly cold. But the coldness was not hers alone. She noticed how ragged and wraithlike the thing's robes were and remembered that it was injured. She suddenly imagined, or rather felt, what it would be like to be ripped from the silence of the Deep Wilds and plunged into Mizzleport. The hard cobbles, the smells, the incessant rattle and hubbub, the sky served up in ragged strips above the tall, narrow streets . . .

No, it was not pity. It was recognition, as if in a deserted place she had heard a distorted, eerie echo of her own voice.

"I hate the city," she hissed suddenly, with savagery that was not a pretense. "It's like a scab."

The creature made a surprised rustling noise, then a sound like a sigh.

Voices everywhere, it said. *Like . . . dirt. Hard corners. Yellow lights.*

"Too much," said Nettle with feeling. "Too much of everything. It hurts."

Too many hearts beating, said the Dancing Star. *Like thunder. It deafens.*

"Too many *people*," said Nettle fiercely. "All their thoughts and glances jumping on and off me, like fleas."

"Hey!" Kellen shouted from somewhere above. "Get away from her!" A stone plummeted downward, narrowly missing the head of the Dancing Star.

It paid no attention. It was slowly reaching for her again, the ribbons of its smoke-robe flickering like gray flame. She sensed its cold, simple want, its desire to reach out and claim the soul that smelled of its home. She would wink out, and her clothes would flutter down to the damp rocks . . .

But Nettle did not flinch back. She looked into the quivering light in the cowled abyss, and saw.

She saw a boat made of fire, surrounded by a raging darkness. Rigging flared red as it burned through and fell away, and great glowing-edged holes spread through the sails. A jungle-wild tree line was charging toward her, white trunks breasting the waves. And then the boat was crashing in among the woods, splintering boughs and igniting timbers, amid the outraged howl of a thousand winds . . .

"Nettle!" shouted Kellen, shocking her back to reality. The rain, the cold, the monster floating inches away . . .

"Don't touch me!" she gasped, remembering how to draw breath. "If you do, I can't talk to you anymore! You'll be all alone again. Alone in that city of stones and bricks and yellow lights!"

The creature stared at her, and into her, but drew no closer.

"It's all right, Kellen!" shouted Nettle. It wasn't; it was anything but all right. But it was something else, and she didn't know how to explain it to him. "Just . . . stay up there! Please! And . . . Master Creskin? Please don't hurt the bones anymore!"

She could just make out Creskin's concerned voice calling out questions, but she couldn't afford to listen. For once, she was following her instincts.

"Where's your lantern now?" Nettle asked the Dancing Star, trying not to let her voice tremble. "You should be marsh-walking under a hunting moon. You should be watching the tidewaters climb the tree trunks and sink again, until the twists of their roots are bare. You should be smelling the flowers of Grief-Comes-Smiling and hearing the crickets sharpening their wings. And . . . and there's something you need to find, isn't there?"

The creature made the hissing, rustling noise again, and this time it seemed like a noise of pain. It flung back its head and dragged its arm stump through its mist-robe, leaving new rents in it. Nettle suddenly thought of a caged bird pulling out its own feathers from misery and despair.

"Your masters will never let you go home," she said ruthlessly. "You'll never see the lilies breathe out pollen clouds as the winds blow. You'll never feel the green mantle ripple under your feet. Never. Unless you let us help you."

Cannot, cannot, cannot, came the anguished answer. *Bound in blood on a contract of skin . . .*

"What if you *couldn't* obey your masters?" said Nettle. "If you were trapped, you couldn't, could you? That wouldn't be breaking the contract. It wouldn't be your fault. Then we'd have time to find a way to release you from your bond, so you could go home."

The Dancing Star did not answer. It rippled with unreadable emotions, slipping in and out of translucency.

"We'd let you have your hands back," said Nettle, "while you were prisoner."

The creature gave a long bonfire-hiss of longing.

"Let's go back down," said Nettle quietly, hoping the hair-slender connection between them held. "Back to that room. Back to the cage."

She started to climb down, looking only at the wall and her numb, blue fingers as she did so. Her neck prickled all the while under the gaze of the monster by her side.

Chapter 26

ENDING THE SHADOW WAR

"HOW DID YOUR FRIEND GET THE DANCING STAR TO STEP INTO the cage like that?" Creskin asked Kellen in a hushed voice as they hurried downstairs to the office.

"I don't know," admitted Kellen. "She just . . . talked to it." He didn't really understand himself what had happened. He'd only heard fragments of the conversation below him, and he could tell Nettle didn't want to talk about it. He had left her kneeling shakily next to the iron cage, still engaged in quiet conversation with the creature within.

"Now—what can we do about those boats?" Creskin muttered. He flung open drawer after drawer, pulling out strange devices. One cumbersome contraption had a fearsome curling blade on the front and huge, mounted springs.

"Wait! I thought you didn't have any weapons?" exclaimed Kellen.

"This is a weed-puller," muttered Creskin. He pointed to the other equally alarming devices on the table. "Air-powered seed-cannon. Medicinal head-massager. That thing with all the spines reads the weather, apparently. But your friends in the boats don't know that."

"Huh." Kellen stared appreciatively at the deceptive armory. "They don't know your cannons aren't loaded either. Nobody actually *sees* cannon balls flying, do they? Do you have anything that makes smoke and goes bang, even in the wet?"

Two minutes later, Kellen discovered the pure, rapturous joy of making something explode.

A small clockwork firework box under a bag of flour. A scramble to get behind cover. A *tick, tick, tick*, then the hard *clack* of a flint . . .

The bang that followed shocked his ears, thumped him in the breastbone, and somehow also made a satisfying *fwup* noise like a big mouth sucking in air. The bag disintegrated, sending up a man-high cloud of flour like a plume of smoke.

"That," shouted Creskin from behind the overturned table he was using as a shield, "was a warning shot! We have three more cannons, and as you can see, *our* gunpowder fears no rain! Next time we'll put a hole through one of your boats!"

Everyone in the three remaining boats had thrown themselves flat in response to the detonation. Eventually one or two people gingerly sat up again, to peer at the island. The boats were now less than twenty yards from the island, but they had not fared well since the Dancing Star's departure. One was perilously low in the water, despite desperate bailing.

"We are an official delegation from Amicable Affairs sent to apprehend criminals!" shouted a man in the rearmost boat. Kellen assumed that he must be the leader. "You have attacked us without cause and are all under arrest! Lay down your weapons!"

"You're sure they're *not* a real delegation?" whispered Creskin, looking a little unnerved.

"They turned up with an illegal Dancing Star and marsh-horse-stabbing weapons." Kellen wrinkled his nose. "Pretty sure."

The boats had crept closer, the foremost now a mere five yards from the shore.

"We don't believe you!" shouted Creskin to the boats. "Don't come any closer! Turn your boats around and leave!"

"You don't have the numbers to make that kind of demand!" called the leader.

"And you," announced Creskin, "don't have a Flambodian Spring-Mounted Lung-Scrambler!" He raised his head above the table and poked the weed-puller over the top edge. There were cries of alarm, and a crossbow bolt thudded into the wood of the tabletop.

Kellen took advantage of the distraction to sprint out, hurl a small, open box into the nearest boat, then dart for cover once again. The box landed between the thwarts with a rattle, then emitted a faint, tinkling string of notes.

"What . . ." One man stooped to stare at it, then leaped back, desperately slapping at his arms and legs. "Aagh! Get them off me!" Everyone else in the boat fell into similar convulsions, trying to brush tiny shapes off their faces and clothes. Kellen could just make out more many-legged specks leaping from the shore with preternatural ease to land on the boat.

"Musical box," said Creskin. "Little Brothers *hate* them."

"Ooh!" Kellen drew in his breath through his teeth. "That man's trying to stamp on the Little Brothers! That's not a good idea, is it?"

There was a loud scream.

"No," said Creskin with a wince. "It really isn't."

"This is your last chance to surrender!" the leader shouted hoarsely. "Do it now, and allowances can still be made! Otherwise . . ."

At that point there was a long, muffled bugle note from the direction of the harbor.

"Did you hear that?" called Creskin. "The harbor guard must have heard my cannon fire. That horn blast was a question. If I don't reply on my bugle, they'll know I'm in trouble, and they'll send the boats out. Their boats are a lot faster than yours." He took a deep breath, visibly steadying himself. "Your move."

Someone in the be-spidered boat managed to kick the musical box into the water with a melodic *splong*, and the infestation of Little Brothers started to wane. The leader stared toward the island, white-faced with rage.

If they come for us, they'll overrun us in seconds, thought Kellen, his heart beating in his ears.

For a moment, Kellen thought the enemy leader was going to order a full assault. Then the man's eyes flitted across the cannons, the alleged Lung-Scrambler, the table-shield that might hide countless horrors, and his spider-bitten comrades. The water suddenly swirled dangerously, making the boats rock, and several of his allies stabbed vainly at the waves with their lances. The leaking boat tipped dangerously, her gunwale nearly dipping beneath the surface.

"Pull back!" the spokesman commanded sharply. There was a splash and clack of oars as his comrades obeyed. "Quickly!"

The three boats rowed away into the darkness. The leaking vessel was the last to disappear, its occupants struggling to keep her afloat. Kellen hardly breathed until the sound of rowing faded.

His pulse was just returning to normal when a marsh horse and rider suddenly lurched out of the water onto the nearby rocks. As before, there was something wrong and unhorse-like in the way the animal's limbs bent, but this time it also moved lopsidedly. One of its legs gave under it, and it sank to the rocks with a long hiss.

Kellen ran over. He could see a round, dark wound in one of the horse's haunches. Gall was crouched beside her, tenderly cupping his hand over the injury.

"Did they hurt her?" called Kellen. "What do we—"

As Kellen drew close, Gall twisted round and hissed at him, like a cat. His face was water-bleached and twisted with some emotion Kellen didn't recognize.

Kellen recoiled and fell backward. His mind spun off its spindle, as it sometimes did when he ran up against something pure Wilds without warning. He felt loose and untethered, as if he might laugh out loud, or dance into the sea . . .

Creskin grabbed Kellen under the arms and dragged him away.

"I'll fetch meat from the store for her!" Creskin shouted to Gall. "I'll be quick!" He turned his attention to Kellen. "You're just panic-drunk. Snap out of it!"

Kellen shook himself and glanced back at Gall, who was once again hunched protectively beside his monstrous horse.

"While I'm gone," said Creskin, "stay away from that man. His horse needs to eat flesh to heal, so right now that's all we look like to him."

.....

The sleek-sailed boats of the harbor guard arrived a short time later. Their captain was understandably curious about the explosion that half the bay had heard, the fragments of blood-stained clothing washing up against the rocks of the island, and the wounded marsh horse.

His mood was not improved when he was told a confusing and unlikely tale of conspiracy and was asked to believe that a small caged bat was actually a high-ranking Chancery official. However, his manner changed once he was shown an undeniably real illegal Dancing Star hovering ominously in an iron cage. After talking with it for ten minutes, he emerged looking pale and in desperate need of a drink.

"I'll need to tell the harbormaster," he said. "He won't thank me for this. If that creature's telling the truth, this is an emergency . . . You say there's more evidence of this conspiracy?"

Kellen glanced at the caged bat.

"I know somebody who's spent a year collecting it," he said.

The boat journey back from the island was much swifter and more comfortable than the outward trip in the rowing boat. This was, however, the start of a very long night.

Kellen and Nettle spent ten minutes in the harbormaster's office explaining the events of the night, the disappearance of Jendy Pin, and everything they had been told about Salvation by Leona. Over the next few hours, they had to explain the same thing again and again to a series of increasingly important-looking people, some with their official robes disheveled because they had only just been roused from bed.

Runners were sent to Leona's office in Clarity Square to protect her files from Salvation. They arrived too late. The files, and the evidence they contained, were gone.

"Did she have any copies?" asked one of the important people. Nobody knew the answer, of course, except Leona.

It took a long time to coax some sense out of her. Eventually somebody had the idea of feeding her so that she would be less distracted by the whine of insects. This involved the rather undignified process of wrapping the Assessor in a tea towel with her head peeping out and feeding her milk from a baby bottle, but it had some effect.

In an interval of coherence, Leona revealed that she *had* kept copies of all important documents in her own house. She had briefed her servants, in an emergency, to smuggle her papers out through the secret passage, then stash them in a number of secret hiding places—hat boxes, barrows, barges, and one mobile puppet theater.

Once the servants were located and the paperwork gathered, the assembled luminaries pored over it, exclaiming in alarm. They were shocked to discover how many potential cursers had been spirited away from beneath Chancery's noses, and even more shocked to realize how many of the conspiracy members were working in Amicable Affairs.

There was a lot of shouting, demanding of records and files, arguing about who could be trusted, and piecing things together by comparing documents. This was probably fascinating if you cared about that sort of thing, but it left Kellen increasingly bored, confused, and annoyed.

"We need to act quickly—tonight!" declared someone who was apparently the head of the entire Contracts division. "Arrest those we have proof against, and see if any of them incriminate their allies under questioning!"

Arrest warrants were hastily drawn up. There was a big debate before the last was signed.

"Are we sure about *him*?" asked one of the shorter, balder officials. "He's one of Chancery's guiding lights! Is your Dancing Star sure he's the one who bound it with a contract?"

The last question was directed to Nettle. The Dancing Star seemed unwilling to talk except at her prompting, so now most people seemed to regard her as its keeper.

"Yes," said Nettle for the nineteenth time. "It was Shay Ammet." For some reason, these words seemed to depress her.

"Are you all right?" Kellen asked Nettle later, when they had the chance to talk quietly.

"I'm fine," she said quietly. "It's just . . . I met Shay Ammet once. He's the one who helped find Cole a place at the sanatorium. And I think he might have been covering some of the fees."

Kellen could see why this might have upset her.

"We'll find someone else to pay them," he said quickly. "Leona, maybe, once she's cured."

But Nettle continued frowning down at her hands.

"I thought he was kind," she said, in a flat, disappointed tone.

On the other side of the room, the arrest warrant for Shay Ammet was being signed.

"I need someone to keep talking to me," said Leona, who had been revived again by a spoonful of minced earthworm. "I can't keep my head straight for long . . . but I . . . I want to know if they were all caught."

It was the early hours, and still the lamps burned in the harbormaster's office; still people paced and waited for word. Kellen was groggy with tiredness but also too nervous and jangled to sleep. Nettle was nodding in a nearby chair. Colors glared and everything seemed a little unreal.

Kellen talked and talked to Leona until word came. And when word came, it was almost good.

Nearly all the Salvation suspects in Amicable Affairs had been arrested. The sole exception was Shay Ammet, who had disappeared from his home. On his desk had been discovered a single pale blue rose, with an attached card that read: *To L. T., with respect*.

Leona listened to this report with bleak calm.

"Running away like that is a confession of guilt," she said, after the messenger had gone. "It'll convince the waverers, but . . . I wish we'd caught him."

"What do you think the rose means?" asked Kellen.

"It could be a threat, or a salute, or a farewell," replied Leona. "Who knows? I've met Shay Ammet—he thinks he's a gentleman." She laughed under her breath. "I'll probably get it tested for poison, just in case."

"So do you think he's the leader of Salvation?" asked Kellen.

"He was always one of my prime suspects," said Leona. "Yes, I think the big fish has slipped from the net."

Everyone else in the room seemed to be treating the latest report as news of success. There was a lot of back-slapping and hand-shaking.

"We haven't won, have we?" Kellen asked quietly. "We've driven Ammet out of Amicable Affairs, but he's still out there. He's still got an army of cursers. And we're still cursed and running out of time. Nothing's over."

"Oh, no, indeed," agreed Leona. "Ammet and I have thrown down our masks, that's all. No more long duels of feints and puppet mastery, no more stealthy moves and countermoves. I've stepped into the light and spread my cards on the table. I'm sure his next move will be just as decisive.

"Only the shadow war has ended, Kellen. The real war is about to start."

Chapter 27

THE SCREAMING CLOUD

FOR TWO DAYS FOLLOWING THE CONFRONTATION AT THE island, Nettle and Kellen were left in a strange and uncertain limbo. They were allowed to stay in two of Leona Tharl's guest rooms and found themselves being looked after by the Assessor's servants. Nettle found it hard to sleep in the comfortable bed and was afraid of breaking the bone china cups.

She waited on tenterhooks until she received word from the sanatorium. Thankfully, it turned out that Cole's care had been paid for by a Chancery grant, not Ammet himself. Ammet's disappearance would not leave Cole homeless.

The fight against Salvation had been passed on to the proper authorities, and Kellen and Nettle were no longer included in the planning. Neither, for that matter, was Leona. As predicted, Chancery had handed her department over to somebody else for the moment. There was no question of leaving a bat in a position of responsibility.

Now and then, some important Chancery clerk with an impressive moustache or complicated title would turn up to ask Kellen questions about curses. Kellen always emerged from these conversations fuming.

"They keep talking as though Salvation is done for, now that it's on the run," he told Nettle. "All they care about is rooting out its last agents in Chancery! I keep telling them that they need to hurry up and hunt down the secret base."

Nettle couldn't blame him for being upset. Unless Salvation was found, he had no chance of finding out more about his own curse, let alone lifting it. Nettle had been keeping a worried eye on Kellen, and it hadn't escaped her attention that some of Leona's furnishings were starting to look a little frayed. She was also concerned about Leona, who seldom spoke now and was moving more sluggishly than before. Both were on borrowed time.

"We know their base is in the Wilds," Kellen muttered to himself, frowning. "And what was it Belthea told you? She went through an arch and turned up somewhere else, and that's where she found the man with the scar?"

"That's right." Nettle cast her mind back. "A place with reeds, a lake, and a red tower." So much had happened, she had almost forgotten Belthea's strange testimony.

"Let's ask the Rescued," said Kellen unexpectedly. He didn't usually like asking for their help, but these were apparently special circumstances. "Some of them have friends who travel the Wilds. Maybe someone will recognize the description."

Nettle could think of one more individual she might ask about Salvation's base, and it was not long before the chance arose.

The following morning, Nettle was brought back to the harbormaster's office to negotiate with the Dancing Star, whose iron cage had been carefully brought to shore.

"It wants the bone-cage taken apart," she told the nervous onlookers. "Then it's willing to release the people trapped inside."

A plate-mail-clad Amicable Affairs master-craftsman was called in. Carefully he took the cage apart with long-handled tools while the Dancing Star watched, sometimes flitting and fidgeting like an expectant parent, sometimes rustling words of advice or caution, which the craftsman diligently obeyed.

When the final wire was pulled loose, suddenly there were four naked, terrified people sprawled on the floor. Clothes and brandy were found for them, and they were sent home to their frantic loved ones.

The box of finger bones was pushed into the iron cage, and the Dancing Star reached out eager, misty sleeves. Wrist bones like misshapen marbles leaped out and nestled against the arm-stub, followed by finger bones large and small. Joint found joint, long digits stretched and flexed. The Dancing Star turned its hands this way and that, examining its pointed claws, and gave a long, gratified rustle.

I shouldn't feel so relieved that it has its hands, thought Nettle. *I shouldn't want it sent back to the Deep Wilds. It'll only start stealing souls and burning them again.* She couldn't help the tug of fearful sympathy, however. The creature could not be blamed for its nature, any more than a snake could be blamed for its fangs.

"So Shay Ammet bought the bone-cage at the Moonlit Market?" she asked.

Yes, came the answer. *I could sense where my hands were, so I followed him as he traveled back through the woods. When he noticed me, he made a bargain with me.*

"When you followed him, what route did you take?" Nettle felt a tickle of uneasy excitement. "Do you know where Salvation's base is?"

I cannot say, answered the Dancing Star.

"You can't say?" asked Nettle. "Is that because you don't know, or because of your contract?"

The Dancing Star was swaying from side to side, with a leisurely motion like a boat rocking at rest. Nonetheless, Nettle sensed a hungry eagerness, barely suppressed.

I cannot say, it repeated. *Perhaps . . . I could lead you there.*

"It keeps saying things like that," murmured the guard on watch. "Whatever it thinks will make us open the cage."

"Perhaps" wasn't a promise. "Perhaps" was bait. Nettle took a step back from the cage.

On the third night, the thunder broke and Salvation struck back.

Two of the three powerful dignitaries who had signed the warrant for Ammet's arrest were cursed overnight. One became an artfully fashioned doll of folded paper, who had to be kept away from drafts and flames. The second heard deafening laughter wherever she went.

The other signatory was the Master Pactwright of the Contracts division. He was not cursed, but his daughter was. She dissolved into mist before his eyes and floated skyward to form a tiny cloud in the shape of a screaming face.

Staring out of the window at the early morning sky, Nettle could just make out a small, faint pattern in the clouds that looked like eyes and a gaping mouth.

"It *is* her!" declared the Master Pactwright, pacing up and down in Leona's parlor. "You can't see her face so well when the other clouds roll over her. She's . . . she's drowning in them."

During the late-night emergency meeting, he had seemed soldierly and dependable. Now he was pale-faced with haunted eyes.

"It should have been me," he said. "Why her? She's nine years old!"

"It's to frighten everyone out of acting against Salvation," answered Gall, who had reappeared that morning. The disturbing bleached pallor the sea had given him was still fading, but his horse now appeared fully healed. "Even those willing to risk their own lives think twice when their loved ones are on the line."

Kellen blanched, and Nettle wondered if he was thinking of his own distant family.

Yannick, Yannick, Yannick, thought Nettle, *please be safe! Why haven't you been back to see me? Please be sulking, please don't be hurt or captured. I'm sorry I snapped at you . . .*

The Master Pactwright turned away and paced, cupping a fist in his hand as if he were thinking of punching the wall. His gaze kept moving restlessly around the room, as if he couldn't bring himself to look at Kellen or Nettle.

"I need your help," he said bluntly. "You can unravel curses, can't you? I can show you her room and the place where she melted into mist."

Kellen was staring up at the distant cloud with quiet horror and anger.

"I can't make any promises," he said. "If it's a curse from Salvation, I probably can't lift it yet. But I'll have a look."

.....

As the black carriage rattled through the streets, Nettle peered out of the window at the tiny distant cloud and tried not to imagine what it would be like to feel yourself dissolve into icy vapor. Was the cursed girl staring down at the dark sprawl of the city, sick with vertigo and buffeted by the winds? Did it hurt when birds flew through her?

Yannick, where are you?

The Master Pactwright answered questions about his daughter flatly, without looking at them. No, she didn't have any enemies, and he couldn't think of anybody who might be jealous of her. She was a good girl. Timid but clever. Fond of poetry and dogs.

The carriage drew up outside a slender, four-story house painted a bright lettuce-green with yellow shutters and balconies. Gall opened the door to let them all out.

"I'll keep watch out here," the marsh horseman said quietly. Like Nettle, he seemed to be grimly braced for the next dose of trouble.

"It was here," said the Head of Contracts, in his wood-paneled hallway. "She came down from her bedroom in her nightdress. She was shaking—she said she'd had a terrible dream. I tried to put my arms around her . . . and she . . ." There were tears in his eyes.

Above on the landing, a red-haired woman in a smart gown gave them a troubled look, then withdrew swiftly into one of the rooms. Nettle wondered if that was the cloud-girl's mother.

"Can we see your daughter's room?" asked Kellen.

They passed a footman who stepped aside, staring firmly at their shoes. A maid hurried away down the landing.

The little girl's bedroom was small but lovingly covered in colorful rugs, tapestries of picnic scenes, and tiny paintings of dogs. To Nettle's surprise, the Master Pactwright left the room, abandoning them to their investigation. As Kellen pulled off his gloves and began to examine the books by her bedside, Nettle stood fidgeting uncertainly.

"Kellen," she said.

"What?" Kellen was absorbed in looking around the room, his face set in a frown. His ungloved hands made small involuntary twitches, restlessly searching for something to seize upon.

"Nobody here wants to look us in the eye, did you notice that?" Nettle didn't like the prickly atmosphere. "Some of them ran away."

"Maybe they blame us," said Kellen, peering at a cross-stitch of a pony. "We annoyed Salvation, didn't we?"

"Maybe." Nettle's gut said otherwise.

As Kellen continued to search, she could see his frustration coming to the boil.

"Oh, hagnight!" he swore at last. "I was hoping that she'd been cursed by someone she knew after all. But she sounds really normal and harmless. She wasn't in anyone's way. So it probably *was* Salvation, which means I don't know where to start! I don't understand this kind of hate. How could anyone hate some little kid who never did them any harm? She's nine years old!"

I was eleven when I was cursed, thought Nettle. *Wasn't I harmless?*

The thought was stupid, unfair, and selfish. She hated herself for thinking about herself while some poor girl was screaming in the sky. At the same time, the thought made her feel very alone.

And then her brain, which had been sieving the noises of the city in search of a single voice, finally heard it. There it was, like the gleam of a coin among dead leaves.

Nettle gave an involuntary gasp of joy and ran to the balcony.

She shielded her eyes and gazed at the eddying seabirds above, overwhelmed with hope and need. Was it wishful thinking that made one black-headed gull look familiar? No, it wasn't her imagination, the bird was circling downward toward her . . .

"Yannick!" she called aloud, and even gave a squeal of laughter as the gull landed with a flourish on the rail of the balcony.

Where've you been? he demanded. *I went back to Tansy's place and you were gone!*

Sorry, answered Nettle. *I just . . . thought you'd find us. You always do when you want to.*

When you shut me out, I can't! snapped Yannick, his white-rimmed eyes earnest and angry. *I only found you when you started tugging at me again.*

Nettle wasn't sure whether she understood, or whether she should argue, but she was just too happy to see his chocolate-dipped head again.

I've got so much to tell you! she said.

No, listen to me first! insisted Yannick. *That man Gall, the one chasing you? He and his horse were right outside this house until just now.*

No, it's fine! she assured him. *We're working with him now. The curser conspiracy is real, and . . . What did you say? What do you mean, "until just now"?*

Nettle peered down into the street. Yannick was right. Gall, the black carriage, and the marsh horse were gone.

Nettle stepped back into the bedroom, leaving Yannick on his rail.

"Kellen," she said. "Gall's gone. Wasn't he supposed to wait for us?"

Kellen's eyebrows rose in confusion. Behind him, the Master Pactwright stepped into the room, looking deathly pale as if he were bracing himself for something.

"I need to know the truth," the man said. "Can you save my daughter?"

"I don't know yet!" said Kellen. "I've only been here half an hour. But . . . it's going to be hard unless I know more about the curser."

"Then I'm sorry," said the Master Pactwright. He turned and gave two sharp raps on the wall.

In response to this signal, four men entered the room. They moved with wary menace and carried rope and two large sacks. One discreetly held a blackjack flush against his forearm, with the ease of practice.

"Hey!" yelled Kellen. "What's going on?"

"Don't be afraid," said the Master Pactwright. "They want you alive."

Nettle bolted for the balcony but was grabbed before she could reach the door. A firm hand muffled her scream. Just before the balcony shutters were slammed shut, she saw Yannick's startled shape taking to the air.

As Nettle was pinned to the floor and her wrists bound behind her, she could hear Kellen struggling and fighting.

"We were trying to help you!" she shouted.

"I have no choice," said the Master Pactwright. "Salvation say they will lift their curse on my daughter if I hand you over to them. I'm sorry; I wish there was another way."

"That's not how it works!" Someone was trying force a gag into Nettle's mouth, but she bucked and twisted to keep her mouth free. "They're lying to you! They couldn't lift their own curse if they wanted—"

She got no further because somebody grabbed her by the hair and slammed her head against the floor. It wasn't hard enough to knock her out, but it sent blinding pain through her temple and a shoal of stars across her vision. She gave a yelp of pain, her eyes filling with tears, and before she could recover, the gag was forced into her mouth.

There was a muffled howl of rage from Kellen. Twisting her head to look at him, she could see him glaring at her attacker in mute fury, a sackcloth gag between his own teeth.

We were your only hope, Master Pactwright! Nettle would have yelled if she could. *Your daughter's only hope! You idiot!* Her forehead burned, and she could feel something tickling against her cheek. *Blood*, she thought. *Probably blood. I'm bleeding*. She closed her eyes tight for a moment against the storm-roar of her frustration and the sickening pain in her head and fought for calm.

But there was no calm. Everyone around her was shouting. There were other noises too, and the soft sensation against her face was more insistent now, too insistent to be the trickle of blood.

The men in the room were yelling in confusion and alarm. The rug beneath her face was stirring and seething, tickling her skin like a tide of ants. The cord that bound her wrist was twitching and writhing like a snake.

From all sides of the room she could hear the stealthy whisper of soft threads unravelling.

Chapter 28

FURY

FOR KELLEN, IT DIDN'T FEEL LIKE LOSING CONTROL. IT FELT LIKE breaking through.

It was as though he'd spent his whole life bashing himself like a fly against the dull, smoky glass of other people's stupidity. Their pathetic ignorance, their selfish blindness, their smugness, their cowardice. He was bruised and battered from the long, futile battle.

Now he struck the glass like a bullet and felt it shatter. Everything in his path, he suddenly felt, would splinter before his anger.

The gag in his mouth was shivering itself apart, its dry threads writhing against his tongue. Whoever was holding him screamed in terror and pain and let go of him. The cords binding Kellen's wrists spasmed and came loose.

He stood, spitting out a wad of loose threads, and felt his mouth fix in a grin of rage. At his feet, the cords were twitching like baby eels as their fibers frayed. All around the room, tapestries were twitching themselves apart, the little girl's cross-stitch tugging loose its stitches with a *snick-snick-snick*.

A few feet away, Nettle sat up, pulling the wriggling rope from her own wrists. The bloodied smudge on her forehead was more fuel for Kellen's furnace of anger.

"You tried to tie us up," Kellen said. It seemed very funny all of a sudden. "You tried to tie *me* up!"

The man who had grappled him was backed against a wall, gripping his own hand and gasping in horror and pain. There was something wrong with his fingers, Kellen realized belatedly. A quiver of pale feathery motion at his fingertips as the skin unknitted itself, a trickle of blood from knuckle to wrist . . .

"Make it stop!" shouted the Master Pactwright.

Kellen couldn't. He couldn't do anything but stare, as the man began to scream . . .

"Kellen!" Nettle flung open the balcony doors and beckoned urgently. He sprinted after her, out onto the balcony.

If in doubt, do something so stupid your enemies won't want to do the same.

He threw one leg over the rail, then the other, his rage still filling him with giddy white lightning. The drop from the balcony to the street jarred every bone in his body. There was a thud and a gasp of pain as Nettle landed beside him.

They broke into a limping, desperate run. Behind them were cries of *Stop!* and *Thief!* Others took up the cry. Of course they did. Hadn't two young ne'er-do-wells just jumped from the window of a respectable house?

As Kellen passed, a tasseled canopy collapsed onto the stall beneath it. Flags came apart in the wind like multicolored dandelion clocks. A wicker chair crackled and toppled sideways. He could hear people on either side giving gasps and squawks of alarm. Were their clothes unravelling, or their skin?

"Your gloves!" panted Nettle.

But Kellen didn't have his gloves anymore. He had put them down in the cursed girl's chamber and never picked them up again.

A rope hauling a large chest up to a high window suddenly snapped. There were screams as the chest hit the cobbles and smashed, scattering wooden shrapnel and broken glass.

Kellen's mind and veins were still full of white fire, but now panic was mixed in with the rage. He kept thinking of his would-be captor, clutching his bloodied hand. What if that happened whenever he touched anyone? Somebody blundered close to Kellen, and he flinched away and took off down an empty-looking alley, hearing Nettle a few paces behind him. Was she keeping up? And was she far enough behind to be safe?

At the end of the alley, he ran out and found himself on the estuary waterfront, where goods were being loaded onto the quays. As he sprinted down a pier toward the water, he saw the rope of a crane bristle and snap, dropping a pallet of bricks. On nearby boats, mooring ropes lashed like cats' tails. Rigging unwound itself, dropping heavy sails onto unsuspecting heads. Sailors ducked as booms swung unexpectedly across the deck.

"Kellen!" called Nettle behind him, but he couldn't stop or let her get close. He kept running to the end of the pier, tugged off his boots, and jumped into the water. As the icy water soaked the felt of his clothes, he swam out a dozen yards, then splashed around, treading water.

The waterfront was a frieze of staring faces. Those boats that could move away from Kellen did so. Nettle was still on the quay, pointing at him, explaining presumably. The slap of water against his ears stopped him hearing what anybody was saying.

I can't stay afloat like this forever, he thought. *But at least out here I won't hurt anyone*. The wild energy of his anger had abandoned him. He felt cold and sick, his limbs heavy with waterlogged cloth.

Eventually some Amicable Affairs shadecatchers showed up to deal with him, as if Kellen were some shadow-calf from the Wilds washed into the harbor by a stray current. Only when he agreed to put on iron shackles was he allowed out of the water.

Kellen was taken to the local jail in a pedal-carriage, accompanied by two Chancery officials who sat opposite him and watched him like hawks. Nettle didn't ride with them, so he fidgeted in silence, worrying about her. How bad was her forehead injury? Had his unravelling done her any harm?

He was led down to a solitary underground cell and left in an iron cage, still manacled. Only then did the truth hit him.

This is a curser cell. They've locked me up like a curser.

He reached for his sense of outrage and couldn't find it. At the moment, all he could think about was a screaming man's hand unravelling.

Over the next two days, the guards brought Kellen food, water, and a few books. There were no visitors. For once, Nettle had failed to get herself imprisoned with him. Perhaps everyone was afraid that he would reduce her to a pile of loose threads. Perhaps they were right to worry.

At one point, he heard a muted conversation on the other side of the cell door. He recognized the voices of two Chancery officials who had visited Leona's house.

"I know he's not a curser, but where else could we put him? Assessor Tharl should have warned us that the boy was a menace! It's lucky that no lives were lost. We can't have someone like that running around loose!"

"It would be different if he was *useful*," agreed a second voice. "But they say he can't lift the curses cast by Salvation. Are we sure he can remove curses at all? So many charlatans make that kind of claim . . ."

"Well, he'll no longer be our problem once he's in the Red Hospital . . ."

Kellen closed his eyes tightly and tried to fight down a surge of panic. He remembered the Hospital's gray-faced, torpid inmates in their helms and shackles. Now Kellen would join the others he had sent there, to trudge and weep and rave in a windowless room and maybe never see the sky again.

In the middle of the night, Kellen was woken by the sound of bolts being drawn. He blinked up at the doorway, where Gall stood silhouetted. In one hand, the marsh horseman held an iron helm with a built-in muzzle and a collar on a chain. Kellen promptly scuffled backward until his back was against the wall.

The marsh horseman raised a finger to his lips.

"Put this on!" he whispered.

Kellen told Gall what he could do with his helmet, in anatomical detail.

"I've told them I'm here to take you to the Red Hospital," said Gall quietly. "If you're not wearing that helm when we walk out of here, they'll get suspicious. We need to get you and Nettle out of Mizzleport. As quickly as possible."

Kellen walked out of the jail at the end of Gall's chain, his heart banging. The heavy helm and muzzle blocked out his peripheral vision, so he couldn't see whether people were watching.

He barely dared believe it when the jail door opened onto the warm summer night, and he saw the black carriage waiting outside. For once, he was genuinely glad to see it.

Gall made a show of pushing Kellen into the carriage, where Nettle was waiting for him, her eyes bright with suspense and her gull-brother on her lap. She startled Kellen by leaning across to give him a brief, awkward hug. She never usually hugged anyone by choice.

"I was afraid we'd be too late!" she said.

Her forehead had a big bruise and a small blackened cut, but it didn't look as though any of her skin had been frayed from her flesh.

"You're all right!" he blurted out, feeling almost sick with relief. "I didn't . . . I didn't hurt you . . ."

Nettle shook her head.

As the carriage rolled smoothly and swiftly down the intermittently lit streets, Kellen removed the helm and unfastened his shackles. Nettle produced his familiar, iron-studded gloves, and he felt an unexpected pang of affection for them as he put them on. Beyond the coach windows, the dark houses rose like the sides of a ravine.

"We're getting you out of Mizzleport," said Nettle. She opened the carriage window just wide enough for Yannick to fly out. Kellen noticed a message capsule on the gull's leg. "A message for the Rescued, to let them know you're safe," she explained, and gave a wry little smile. "Some of them were talking about storming the jail."

Kellen gave a surprised laugh. Even this news couldn't raise his spirits, however.

"They were going to send me to the Red Hospital," he said, his throat feeling tight.

"I doubt that," Nettle said darkly. "Haven't you heard about this?" She handed Kellen a piece of paper, crudely printed. "Lots of powerful people in Chancery received it last night."

Kellen skimmed down the page.

By now you will be aware that I am a part of the group known as Salvation. Some of you who have known me a long time will feel shocked and betrayed. It is true, I have acted in the shadows and in defiance of the law, but I saw no other option. It was the only way to help those of my countrymen who have always been persecuted in Raddith and locked away even when they had committed no wrongdoing.

We would have been content with discreetly rescuing these victims, if we had not found ourselves under attack. I regret that violence has occurred. I also regret the suffering that the three recent curses will cause, but there was no other way to impress upon you all that pursuit of us must cease.

My friends are not unreasonable, in spite of everything they have suffered. All they want is to be left alone. Even though I too have been chased from my home, I am still willing to negotiate.

Knight-Clerk and Master-Ambassador Shay Ammet

"Cheeky grotbag!" exclaimed Kellen, feeling a welcome rush of anger. "I can't believe Ammet's trying to cut a deal after everything he's done. Nobody's going to listen to that!"

"Chancery *are* listening, Kellen!" Nettle said earnestly. "I overheard two department heads talking the last time I was in the harbormaster's office. Those three curses the other night scared people badly. Nobody wants their loved ones turned into clouds. So some of the Chancery leaders have already opened negotiations with Ammet."

Kellen swallowed hard to stop himself swearing. Then again, why was he surprised? This was Chancery. They had made a bargain with the Wilds themselves. Of course some were already wondering if they could come to an agreement with Salvation.

"What was the point of everything we did, then?" he asked. "What was the point of Leona collecting all that evidence, and getting batted, if Salvation's going to get everything they want? What *are* they asking for anyway?"

"I don't know all of it," said Nettle. "But they've made Chancery promise not to try to find them while negotiations are going on. And . . . they're asking for you to be handed over to them. As a goodwill gesture."

"What?" Kellen's skin turned cold. "Me? Why does Salvation want me?"

Belatedly, he recalled the words of the Master Pactwright as he'd handed them over to the Salvation thugs. *Don't be afraid. They want you alive.* Then Kellen remembered the ambush by the canal. Had Salvation been hoping to carry him away in the Dancing Star's bone-cage?

"We don't know," said Nettle. "But we had to get you out of that cell before anybody decided to use you as a bargaining chip."

"So what happens now?" asked Kellen, his mind reeling. "Are we fugitives from the law?"

"Yes," admitted Nettle, looking deeply uneasy. "We are. Gall got you out of jail just now using forged documents sealed with Leona's signet ring. And I . . ."

She trailed off and pulled a wooden bottle out of her bag. It was covered in carvings and studded with bronze nails, pieces of ivory, and shards of crystal. The ornate stopper was glued into place with black wax.

"Is that a puzzle bottle?" asked Kellen. They were old-fashioned capture devices, and a bit unreliable, but still highly prized. He'd only seen pictures of them before.

"Since we were going on the run anyway," said Nettle, rather shakily, "I guessed we'd want as much information as possible. So I stole the Dancing Star."

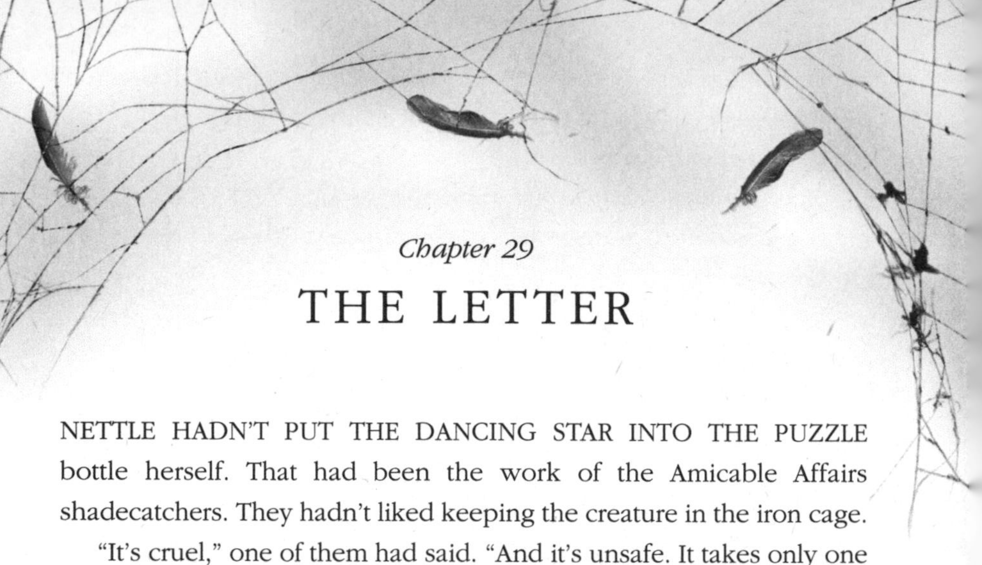

Chapter 29

THE LETTER

NETTLE HADN'T PUT THE DANCING STAR INTO THE PUZZLE bottle herself. That had been the work of the Amicable Affairs shadecatchers. They hadn't liked keeping the creature in the iron cage.

"It's cruel," one of them had said. "And it's unsafe. It takes only one person to fall for its tricks and open the cage. We'll bottle it now and take it away."

Using long-handled tongs, the clerks had poked the unstoppered bottle into the cage. The creature had made an eerie, shrill, breathy sound, then clawed at the air as its vaporous essence was sucked into the bottle. The clerks had hastily thrust in the stopper, sealed it with hot wax, wrapped it in muslin, and put it in an iron box.

While they were busy, Nettle had crept away to find her brother.

Yannick had been scornful of Nettle's heist plan until she bribed him with cake. As it turned out, a squawking, uncoordinated gull crashing from room to room, knocking over vases and candles, made an excellent distraction. The clerks from Amicable Affairs probably still didn't know that the cloth-wrapped object in their iron box was nothing but a candleholder.

By the time Nettle had finished her story, Kellen was snorting with astonished laughter and looked a lot more like his usual self. Much as Nettle often wanted to slap him, she hadn't liked seeing him so deflated, haunted, and un-Kellen-ish.

"I wish I could have seen that!" he exclaimed in delighted awe.

He leaned over to peer at the bottle, with its glistening nails. "Can the Dancing Star hear us?"

"Not unless I twist that." Nettle nervously tapped a spiral seashell fastened near the bottle's base.

"How far do you trust it?" asked Kellen.

"About an inch," said Nettle, turning the bottle carefully in her hands. "And I think there are some things it *can't* tell us, because Ammet's forbidden it. But it doesn't like him much, so we might persuade it to drop some hints."

Nettle glanced up and realized that Kellen was regarding her with concern.

"Are you sure you're all right?" he asked. "You look a bit pale."

"I . . ." Nettle gave a shaky little sigh. "I'm supposed to be the cautious one, aren't I? The voice of reason. And now . . ." She held up the bottle. "Thief and fugitive."

It was the truth, but only a part of the truth. She tried to stop her hands shaking.

I don't know what I'm doing. I don't know where this goes. I've hurled myself down this course and now I can only see darkness ahead.

I feel like I've stepped off the edge of a cliff.

As the carriage wove through the dark warren of the city's streets, Nettle watched the brooding houses race by, the lanterns outside flickering under the fine, powdery rain. It was a warm, muggy night without stars or moon—a good night for mosquitoes and knife-men. The streets were quiet, and the coach's wheels splashed through the puddles with a sound like thin glass breaking.

Slowly the fist-tight streets loosened their grip, and buildings grew sparser, as they left the city. Gall took the carriage down narrow, winding roads and farm tracks and eventually into woods. At first this was ordinary woodland. The trees' jerkins of moss were light and patchy, the foliage cobweb-free, the ground rough but solid under the wheels.

Nettle fell asleep and missed the moment when they passed into the marsh-woods. She woke hours later when the carriage was bumping over soft ground and coming to a halt. She noticed at once the change in the taste of the air. She felt more alive, more aware of smells, sounds, and the pain in her head. Next to her, Kellen was blinking himself awake.

She clambered groggily out of the carriage, her back damp with sweat. The pearl-gray, predawn light showed her trees ghostly with dew-studded webs. The mossy ground sucked gently at her boots. The early birds scattered their crystal shards of sound.

"We're in the Shallow Wilds," Gall called down. "A quiet part. Unlikely to get company."

As Nettle was stretching her stiff limbs, a familiar shape swooped down through the trees and landed clumsily on the carriage roof.

Yannick! Nettle was relieved to see her brother. *Did you deliver the note?*

Yeah, yeah, said the gull. *Bird-post successful.* His thoughts felt tired and grumpy. *Did you tell Kellen the latest?*

Not yet. Nettle knew what he meant and felt her shoulders tense up. *I haven't had time.*

You've got time now, haven't you? Yannick pointed out. Nettle knew that he sensed her reluctance and was puzzled by it.

Feeling her brother's beady eyes on her, Nettle cleared her throat.

"Listen," she said aloud. "Hapness thinks he might have discovered something."

Hapness was a member of the Rescued. For years he had been forced to hide in a cellar, until Kellen unravelled the curse that made him burn like paper if sunlight touched him. These days, he made a living carving little wooden toys and knew a lot of traveling peddlers as a consequence.

"One of his peddler friends recognized the description that Belthea gave us," Nettle continued. "The red tower, the reeds, the lake. He goes there to trade sometimes, and . . ." She hesitated.

"And what?" asked Kellen impatiently.

"And this peddler says the villagers always buy more than you'd expect. Not big things like clothes or tools, but little luxuries—pipe tobacco, paper, sherry, moustache wax, gout medicine, newspapers."

Understanding dawned across Kellen's face.

"Little luxuries," he repeated. "If you went into hiding in a hurry, you wouldn't take luxuries with you, would you? But later you'd miss them, if you were used to them, so you'd want to buy them if you got the chance . . ." He grinned excitedly. "We've found them, haven't we? Salvation's base must be near that village!"

"We don't know that for certain," objected Nettle, but Gall was already striding to the carriage with new urgency in his step.

He came back with a parchment, which he unfolded and held under Nettle's gaze. At first she could make no sense of it, with its chaotic swirls of color, cryptic inscriptions, sigils, and tiny pictures. Then she noticed that along one edge was a strip of blue decorated with waves and boats. If that was the sea, then the rest must be . . .

"Is that a map of the marsh-woods?" Nettle asked, the hairs rising on the back of her neck. She had known that such things existed but had never seen one.

"*Wailing green*," Kellen murmured, reading the scrawled words over her shoulder. "*Hammer-tongues . . . Over-under.*"

"Now, where's this village?" asked Gall. "What's its name?"

"It doesn't have a name," said Nettle. "But it's far into the Deep Wilds, right among the reed beds. You can reach it only by boat. The red stilted tower is where the villagers store their winter food to keep it dry. The lake is butterfly-shaped . . ."

As she talked, Nettle felt increasingly nauseous. She felt as if every word were sealing their fate and binding them to a course that led toward Salvation. It was too late to turn back now, though, wasn't it? Too late to hide the news that Yannick had brought her.

Neither Gall nor Kellen seemed to notice anything odd about Nettle's manner. They were too busy poring over the map.

"What about that one?" Kellen tapped at a tiny, butterfly-shaped blotch of blue on the map, his eyes bright and fierce. "That must be the lake! Look, it's surrounded by reeds!"

"It's a splat," said Nettle harshly. "We can't go to Chancery with a splat and some hearsay. They won't believe us. We don't have any proof."

"Maybe we can *find* proof." A small, wild smile was starting to creep across Kellen's face. "Let's go there." He tapped the map again. "Let's find Salvation ourselves."

"That's insane!" said Nettle, but at the same time there was a dream-like sense of inevitability. Hadn't she known that Kellen would suggest something like this?

"Is it?" asked Kellen. "Look, Chancery have promised not to go looking for Salvation. But we haven't. So we find Salvation. And then we send a friendly gull to let Chancery know where we are and what we've found."

Hey! objected Yannick. *I don't take orders from you!*

"It'll still just be our word—" began Nettle.

"It doesn't matter!" interrupted Kellen. "That's the beauty of it! Chancery will *have* to send troops after us, because they need to capture *me*! I'm their bargaining chip!"

It was a terrible plan, but not quite terrible enough for Nettle to dismiss it out of hand. It had its own flawed, reckless logic, like all Kellen's plans.

"No," said Gall.

"What do you mean, no?" demanded Kellen.

"Salvation wants to capture you, so you're not going anywhere near them," said Gall. "And neither is Nettle. I'll hunt them down, but I'll leave you both somewhere safe first."

"Hey!" Kellen flushed with anger. "You need us!"

"Your curse is a liability, and so are you!" snapped the marsh horseman, sounding unusually agitated. "If you could control yourself, we wouldn't be on the run right now."

"I lost control because we were being attacked!" yelled Kellen. "And where were you when that happened? You were supposed to be outside the house! Where did you go?"

Nettle flinched as Kellen's yell echoed through the woods, startling birds, but he had a point. Why *had* Gall vanished at the very moment when they needed his protection?

The marsh horseman spent a few moments staring at the ground, teeth clenched.

"I *was* waiting outside," he said. "But I was handed a note. I had to check . . ." He took a deep breath, as if intending to finish the sentence. Then he shook his head and started to walk away between the trees.

"Hey!" called Kellen. "Where are you going?"

"To hunt," said Gall over his shoulder. "Meat for the horse. Don't worry, it'll guard you till I'm back."

"You're never honest with us!" Kellen bellowed after Gall. "How can we trust you?" There was no response, only the click and drip of water finding its secret ways down leaves and bark channels. The forest had swallowed the marsh horseman as if he were part of it, which in a sense he was.

Gall came back nearly an hour later with a dead rabbit. He threw it to the horse, which snapped it out of the air with a flash of long, gleaming teeth. No more nosebags. No more pretense.

"All right," Gall said abruptly. He pulled out a narrow slip of paper and handed it to Kellen. Nettle peered over Kellen's shoulder and read.

Please for the sake of pity at least speak with me. I would not trouble you if I had any other choice. I am staying at the house with the lamp on Button Road. Harland Melbrook.

"It's his handwriting," said Gall. "So I went to Button Road, to find out what was wrong. I thought you were safe in the Master Pactwright's house. But Harland wasn't there. He hadn't been at those lodgings for two days."

"But this note . . ." Nettle dared a glance at Gall. "If he was writing to you, isn't it odd that he signed his full name?"

"Yes, it was odd!" Gall ground one heel against the moss. "But I thought if someone made Harland write it, he might have penned it strangely to let me know that it was a trap. I thought it was a trap for me, not you two."

"So that's why you're trying to tuck us somewhere safe?" asked Kellen. "Because you didn't protect us before? Well, that won't work. If you leave us behind, we'll run off and start looking for Salvation anyway. You just won't be there to protect us."

It was hard to tell with Gall, but it looked as if Kellen's words had penetrated.

"This isn't a note," said Nettle suddenly. "It's the bottom part of a letter cut off from the rest. You can see the scissor cuts."

"Wait!" exclaimed Kellen. "When we saw Harland at Clarity Square, he had a letter with him, didn't he? He said that he was hoping to talk the Assessor into releasing Gall from his contract. What if he handed it in and a Salvation agent got hold of it? Look—this might be the bottom part of that letter!"

Gall took the note back and stared at it for a long time.

"So Harland got no answer to his letter," he said quietly. "Maybe that's why he gave up and went home." He went back to the horse, and began combing the leaves out of its mane. "It's a good thing," he said quietly. "The farm can't cope without him."

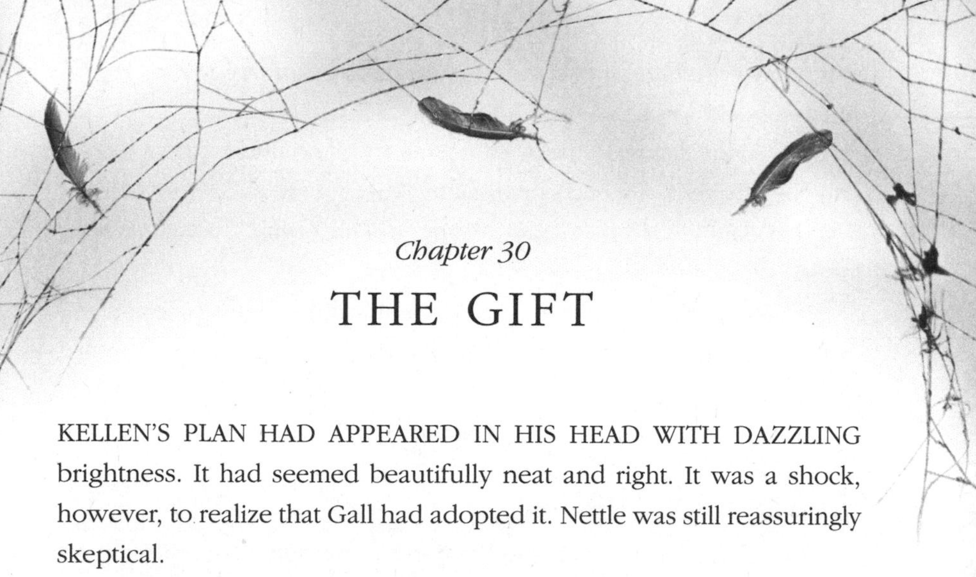

Chapter 30

THE GIFT

KELLEN'S PLAN HAD APPEARED IN HIS HEAD WITH DAZZLING brightness. It had seemed beautifully neat and right. It was a shock, however, to realize that Gall had adopted it. Nettle was still reassuringly skeptical.

"I still think it looks like a splat," she muttered, examining the Wilds map.

"Look," said Kellen, knowing he was beating a dead horse. "Is there any chance your brother could save us all some time and fly over to the lake to see if there's a red tower—"

The gull gave vent to a frenzy of infuriated squawks.

"He could do that," Nettle said coolly. "He could fly into the heart of the Deep Wilds by himself, far from me. And he might even remember why he was there and come back. Or he might join a flock and only think of us again in the spring. It's bad enough that you want him to fly back from the Deep Wilds to Chancery with a message!"

"All right, all right!" Kellen gave up.

Meanwhile, the marsh horseman was rummaging through a trunk inside the coach, his face drawn and intent.

"What are you looking for?" asked Kellen.

"A gift," growled Gall, frowning at the bottle in his hands. "Honey wine," he muttered. "Let's hope that's good enough."

Kellen understood his meaning. You didn't always need a gift in the Deep Wilds, but it was bad to be caught without one.

Humans could enter the Deep Wilds, but there were rules, or at least an etiquette, of lethal importance. *Don't carry iron. Don't harm the trees or break the soil without their permission. And bring a gift, in case you're asked for one.*

Even if you followed these rules, there was no guarantee of safety, only slightly reduced odds of disaster. There were still plenty of pitfalls that could leave you dead, insane, or stuck with a badger's head instead of your own.

As this was passing through Kellen's mind, his gaze fell upon the carriage again. Most of it was wooden, but there were also metal bolts, steel struts, springs beneath the box . . .

"Wait!" he said. "The carriage has iron in it! We can't take it into the Deep Wilds!" It would be about as safe and welcome as bringing a lit candle into a gunpowder factory.

"No, we can't," said Gall. "We'll need to abandon it at the boundary and continue on foot." He squinted up at the sun, glittering through the dense canopy of leaves. "Get back in the carriage," he said. "If we ride hard, we can be out of the Shallow Wilds by nightfall."

Kellen looked down at his gloves and realized that he wouldn't be able to take them into the Deep Wilds either.

I should be glad that we're following my plan, he told himself. *This is what I wanted.*

But he didn't like the wet sunlight, which gave everything a glossy-eyed glare. He didn't like the stealthy morning mists, the ghost of the night's dew. And he didn't like the thought of abandoning the carriage and walking gloveless into the Deep Wilds. He could almost feel it waiting silently for him, like an open mouth, ready to swallow him whole.

For the rest of the day, the carriage jolted along the twisting, overgrown path between the trees. At first it made brisk progress, its wheels slicing through the bracken. As the hours crawled by, however, the mud became thicker and the undergrowth wilder. Yannick came and went, sometimes flying up through the trees.

"I thought your brother didn't like scouting ahead?" Kellen asked at one point.

"He says it's not so bad if it's just above the trees, and he's not going far," explained Nettle. She looked nervous and fidgety, however, until Yannick returned.

By dusk, the carriage was starting to struggle. At one point, Gall had to stop so that the passengers could get out and pull out the briars and ivy that had collected in the spokes. Bats occasionally flitted past at head-height, avoiding the great, pale web-canopies above.

While Kellen and Nettle were wrestling the briars, Yannick swooped down to land on his sister's shoulder. Nettle conversed silently with him, looking concerned.

"There's smoke a mile ahead," she said. "Campfires, Yannick thinks."

Gall grimaced.

"We should go round, then," he said. "There's a fork in the path ahead."

Kellen peered past the carriage and could just about see that Gall was right. On the left, there seemed to be a narrow mossy track peeling away from the main path.

Somewhere far ahead, there was a faint sound like a stick snapping underfoot.

"Get in," whispered Gall. In the twilight, his eye-patch looked like an abyss in his face.

Nettle and Kellen clambered quickly and quietly back into the carriage, which shuddered carefully back into motion. As they turned onto the mossy track, there were worrying scrapes from tree branches against the sides of the carriage. Soon, however, the track widened out, and the going became much easier than it had been on the main path. The carriage sped up, the moss muffling the noise of the wheels.

Mile followed mile followed mile. They couldn't find the old path again, but it didn't matter. This one was taking them on a better, more direct route.

There was a tiny warning voice in the back of Kellen's head. *Beware convenience*, it said. *Beware the peddler who knows exactly what you want to buy, the thing you find in your pocket just when you need it, the gold coin out on the thin ice. And beware the path that you don't notice at first, even though you should have done.*

He was too tired to listen to that voice. His eyes closed, and sleep settled on his mind like dark ash.

Kellen was woken by a sickening lurch that flung him from his seat. In the darkness, he heard Nettle yell. There was no time to understand what was happening, why the carriage was hurtling down some unseen hill, why the marsh horse was giving a deafening hiss that somehow reeked of fear . . .

Then everything tipped sideways, and Kellen was flung about like a rag doll, bouncing off wall after wall until the darkness took pity on him.

"Are you bleeding?" the kind voice asked again.

Kellen blinked, the daylight flooding his mind and washing the sense out of it. He was sitting on the ground, a warm hand supporting his back. Around him were scattered flinders of wood, some still with paint on them. On the other side of the clearing, the remains of the carriage lay on its back like a dead creature, its shafts shattered, one wheel missing.

"My friends . . ." he said.

"They're fine." The stranger wore good, simple, huntsman's clothes, and boots with cleft toes for tree-climbing. "They're over there, and there."

Kellen glanced across the grassy glade and could see Nettle being helped out of the wreckage by another figure, also dressed in hard-wearing clothes, patched with strips of fur. Gall stood at a distance, striped by the shadows of birch trunks.

"You're lucky we found you," continued the stranger. "Don't touch the leaves on your face. They'll bring the swelling down."

There was indeed a damp, clammy sensation against Kellen's forehead. Despite the instruction, he couldn't help brushing his fingertips against the poultice. It fell to his feet and withered to a feathery mass of skeleton leaves.

"Sorry," he said, trying to think. Why did the daylight have to be so bright? "We need to fix the carriage. Can you help me find the wheel?"

"It's over there," said the stranger, pointing. "But it won't do you any good."

Kellen tried to look in the direction of the pointing finger but couldn't focus. There were two blurred fingers, three, nine, all pointing in different directions. *You need to take off your gloves*, buzzed a voice in his ear, or perhaps his mind. *Then you'll see.* He did so, and at once spotted the stray wheel, wedged among the roots of a tree. The roots had grown into the wood of the wheel, which was now sprouting sprigs and leaves of its own.

"You have a gift," the stranger said pleasantly.

Kellen opened his mouth to say that he was tired of his gift and that it was more of a curse really, and he wasn't sure it had been "given" to him on purpose at all. But then he realized that he had misunderstood. His companion's words had been a question, not a statement.

"You have a gift?" said the stranger again, warmly, expectantly.

A gift, Kellen thought hazily. *That's right. We did have plans to bring one, didn't we? I can't remember why. But these people deserve something after all their help.*

"Yes," said Kellen, feeling in the jumbled pockets of his memory. "Yes, of course."

"Oh, yes! I see you did bring one!" The stranger was staring at something on the ground. "A fine present!"

Lying on the grass was a carved wooden bottle, studded with nails and shards of ivory. It looked familiar, but Kellen couldn't remember what it was.

It's ugly, though, isn't it? If these people want it, why don't I let them take it?

Kellen opened his mouth to offer the bottle, then hesitated, as memories danced over his mind. A cowled figure. The bottle gripped tightly in Nettle's pale hand. The bottle was . . . important, wasn't it? Why had he believed he could give it away? That thought no longer felt like his own.

He looked up at his new friend, who smiled back. Its eyes were as rugged and red as peach stones.

Nothing had changed, but Kellen felt a sudden squirming in his stomach, as if he had kicked over an old log and seen a hundred pulpy and chitinous things scrabbling over its rotten underbelly. Everything was still bright and fair, but his gut suddenly remembered that it should be night.

Where was Nettle? There! Standing next to a figure that was trying to feed her something glass-clear and wriggling, a pink, pulsing heart visible through its flesh. When Nettle saw Kellen watching, she gave him a furious glare, as if he had walked in on her without knocking, and stalked away on her heron-legs. The other figure followed, its lean face swaying at the top of its black swan-neck.

There was Gall in the shadow of the trees, dancing with a figure that wore a coat similar to his own. Its head was that of a horse.

Where is our gift? whispered the air, the trees, the insect whines, ever more insistent. *Our gift, our gift, our gift, our gift* . . .

"I can't give you the bottle!" yelped Kellen, hearing his voice shrill with panic. "It's not mine!" He knew that gifts had been brought, but he couldn't remember what they were, or where. "You . . . you can have the carriage!"

"But it's *broken*," said the stranger, its voice hardening.

Kellen heard the whispers turn to hisses, felt the sunlight become cold. Too late he knew that this was the point where the fairy tale turned bad. The test failed, the insult given, a fatal wrong step around which fractures spread and spread without remedy until the ground gave way . . .

"But the thing in the bottle's broken too!" he yelled, desperate. "You wouldn't want it! Look in the carriage, there's . . . there's cloth-covered seats! And velvet curtains! And . . . and . . . bread, and . . . you can take it all!"

There was a change in the wind, like an intake of breath. He shielded his face with his hands, but no blow descended. Peering through his fingers, he realized that he was no longer the center of attention.

The overturned carriage rocked on its roof as half a dozen figures leaped on it and began pulling it apart. The remaining wheels bounced away like living things, the curtains were yanked free and flew skyward, the walls came away like the front of a doll's house. A flock of wooden bolts sped away with birdlike grace. Chassis and shaft, splinter and spar were whisked away. With a dull tinkle, a few fragments of metal fell into a heap on the moss.

The stranger pulled an unlit candle out of a pocket. The wick began to glow, as it sucked the daylight out of the clearing.

"Hey!" Kellen leaped up and grabbed the stranger's shoulder. It was already too dark to see his companion's face. "Where are my friends? What have you done with them?"

To his surprise, he felt his fingers bite easily into the creature's shoulder. It was like gripping a loose ball of wool, and a moment later he felt threads tumbling over his fingers and wrist.

"Aaaah!" shrieked the dark figure. "Look what you did to me! Look what you did!" The shadowy shape ran from Kellen screaming, its candle-flame bobbing away among the trees and vanishing. The screams grew fainter and fainter with distance, then melted into musical laughter before fading away completely.

Kellen stood alone in the dark and cold, feeling threads tangled round his hand. He was suddenly aware of his own bruises and the whirr of the crickets like sarcastic applause. It was as though he had just woken from a dream. Already he could feel his recollection of it blurring and fading.

What had just happened? Where was the carriage? Where were the others? Why was there a sticky patch on his forehead that smelled of honey?

"I hate the Wilds," Kellen muttered under his breath.

It took a while for Kellen, Nettle, and Gall to find each other. There was no sign of Yannick, and for a while Nettle would not stop searching, scanning the moonlit, web-laden trees for any sign of him.

"He's not here," she said at last, in a small voice.

"Hadn't he flown ahead to scout?" asked Kellen. Nobody could quite remember.

"The carriage has gone too," said Gall, "except for the metal parts. And there's no sign of the luggage that was inside."

"I think we . . ." It was hard for Kellen to recall the bright sunlight dream that had dazzled his mind. "We . . . gave the carriage away? Or took it apart?"

"Did we trade it for something?" asked Nettle uncertainly. "They wanted us to eat . . . but . . . but we didn't . . ." Some unvoiced thought made her look pale and a little sick.

"We must have entered the Deep Wilds without realizing it," said Gall. "Our entry with iron was . . . not appreciated." There was a horseshoe-shaped bruise on one of his hands that looked a bit like a bite-mark. "But we live." His horse was motionless as an ebony statue, but for a moment the moonlight seemed to catch a frightened crescent of white in its eye.

"So . . ." Nettle peered at the dark threads wrapped around Kellen's hands.

One long strand stretched away from the loops in Kellen's fist and twisted off among the trees. After exchanging a glance with Nettle, Kellen started to follow it, winding in the thread as he went.

An hour later, the loops of thread were heavy enough to weigh down his arm, and the sky was light enough for him to see that the thread was red. The ground was growing softer as they advanced, and after one rash step, Kellen had to be pulled out of an unexpected bog, his left leg mud-caked from the knee downward.

"Stay here." Gall mounted his horse, which stepped out into the bog. It sank until the marsh water was halfway up its flanks and near the top of its rider's boots. Then the beast glided away as easily as a swan, leaving a dark tear in the green mantle behind it. Aloft on its back, Gall ran his finger along the red thread as he followed it.

An hour later, just as Kellen and Nettle were starting to become panicky, horse and rider returned, Gall drawing a small boat along behind him. The end of the red thread was tied to a ring on its prow.

The boat was slender and white-painted, big enough for two people. The inside was scattered with stray feathers and glossy cherry pips that looked as though they had just been spat. Two paddles lay across its thwarts, the handles carved in the shape of fox's heads.

"It could be a trap," said Nettle, as Kellen knew she would. "Once we're out in the middle of the marshes it turns into frogspawn or snaps shut like a clam. Somebody's idea of a joke."

"I think it is a joke," Kellen said uncertainly. His memory held the after-echo of mocking laughter, though he couldn't remember why. "But I think it might be a gift too."

"There's no other way onward," said Gall, and these words were also inevitable. "The way ahead is marsh, and the horse won't let you two on her back."

The boat rocked as Kellen and Nettle reluctantly clambered aboard. When they drew their paddles through the water, it made a silvery sound like a chuckle.

Chapter 31

THE REEDS

NETTLE SHOOK TANGLED WEED FROM HER PADDLE AND BLINKED the early sun out of her eyes.

The morning marsh mist was tinted honey-gold by the morning light, giving everything a sweet and dreamlike look. The trees that emerged from the green-mantled marsh water seemed gauzy and unreal. Dew still gleamed pearl-bright on the coiled fronds of the ferns and emerald moss that sprouted from miniature islands.

Ahead of the boat rode Gall, his horse still half-submerged, neither man nor beast blinking as the sunlight dappled their faces.

"We're lost, aren't we?" Kellen said helpfully.

"We can hold a course using the sun's position," said Gall without looking round. "Sooner or later we'll see something on my map."

"At least we still have that," murmured Kellen.

A quick inventory had shown them that many things were missing. Their steel coins were gone, leaving them with only some small change in brass. Kellen's gloves were missing. Thankfully, there were provisions in the saddlebag, and they still had the puzzle bottle containing the Dancing Star.

"If we do find the village, what then?" asked Nettle, trying to keep herself rooted in the practical. "Do we risk talking to them? What if they're all on Salvation's side?"

"Probably not," Gall said thoughtfully. "If the village were in league with Ammet, he'd have found out his people were trading with them for luxuries. And if he knew that, he'd put a stop to it. He's too careful to risk giving away Salvation's location like that."

“Then someone else is sneaking out of Salvation to trade with the village, behind Ammet’s back?” Kellen raised his eyebrows, considering. “Nice little black market, probably doing well out of it.”

After discussion, it was decided that Nettle and Kellen would risk entering the village to make inquiries. They looked normal enough to pass for peddlers, whereas Gall and his horse did not. The marsh horse and rider would also be better suited to exploring the surrounding area.

“All right,” Gall agreed, reluctantly. “But you need to keep a low profile. Kellen—don’t do *anything* that might give away who you are. Don’t lose your temper. Don’t handle anything woven. And don’t lift any curses.”

“It’ll be fine!” said Kellen. “Salvation think Chancery have me under lock and key! They won’t be expecting us to turn up on their doorstep! And if we run into trouble, we can always send Yannick to get you . . .” He trailed off, then gave Nettle a wary glance. “Nettle, do you think your brother’s coming back soon?”

“I don’t know!” she snapped, her anxiety returning with full force.

“I’m sure Yannick’s all right,” said Kellen quickly. “He’s probably off somewhere doing . . . gull things.”

Gull things. With a jolt Nettle remembered that Yannick’s nest was in the Deep Wilds.

That’s it, isn’t it? When he flew into the Deep Wilds he forgot about me. I knew it might happen. He forgot he was a boy, and remembered he was a gull, and flew back to his mate and chicks. Of course he did.

The thought should have been comforting, but it made Nettle feel even more dejected and alone.

By midafternoon, Kellen’s and Nettle’s hands were blistered. They were in tidal marsh-woods now. Nettle could tell this by the narrow, blackened tide-marks on the moss of the tree trunks and the slight tang of salt in the air. The farther they went, the higher the tide-marks were above the surface of the water.

At dusk, they tethered the boat to an overhanging branch. In the belly of the little vessel, Nettle and Kellen slept back to back, despite the heat of the night. The contact was reassuring. Gall offered to keep watch.

It was an uneasy night.

Nettle dreamed that the sun was blazing through the tree canopy so that the shivering leaves gleamed like green glass, delicately dusked by the fine, choking mesh of a hundred cobwebs. Nettle could see a silhouetted gull struggling in the webs, wings twitching and thrashing, narrow head jerking helplessly. She tried to shout Yannick's name but could make no sound.

She woke when the boat wobbled violently. A savage hiss sounded, dangerously close, followed by a squelching, rending sound. After a moment, the marsh horse raised its jet-black head near the boat, its mouth dripping.

"We dealt with it," said Gall flatly, his face floating in the darkness like the moon. "Go back to sleep."

Halfway through the next day, as the rain set in, they found a landmark, or at least a "marsh-mark." Two tall trees rising from the water had entwined intricately to form a great arch.

The marsh horse pulled its head back slightly, like a cat smelling something bad.

"An arch!" said Kellen. "Like the one that Belthea described!" He was staring up at it with a mesmerized half-smile.

"There's a shape like this on the map," said Gall, squinting at the parchment. "It's labelled . . . 'Throat.' "

"Let's take a closer look," suggested Kellen.

"Are you joking?" said Nettle, appalled. "You want to get close to 'Throat'?"

"I won't go inside it, all right?" Kellen was already propelling the boat forward, his face alive with fierce curiosity. Nettle recognized the feverish brightness in his eye, the reckless desire to invite calamity. Of course, he had been without his gloves for over a day. Why hadn't she expected this? "I just want to see if it—"

Nettle never did find out how that sentence would have ended. The water beneath them suddenly heaved, and the arch gave a noise like a sepulchral gasp. Water was abruptly and forcefully sucked into the arch, carrying the boat with it.

As the pearl-pale boat was dragged between the two trees, just for a moment Nettle felt a bitter gust of wind hit her face. Ahead, she saw a beach covered with white driftwood, and the charred ribs of long-wrecked ships, picked over by big, blind crab-spiders. She saw this, but also the marsh-woods, as if the two different scenes were paintings on glass, held one in front of the other.

Then the boat was yanked back through the arch, and she was fully in the marsh-woods again, gasping as she remembered how to breathe and think. Gall was gripping the mooring rope, and she guessed that he had hauled them back by main force.

"Did you see that!" Kellen was ecstatic. "That was another place! Those arches—they're in two places at once! Just then, *we* were in two places at once!"

"If you ever do that again," growled the marsh horseman, "little pieces of *you* will be in a lot of different places."

The downpour grew heavier as the day went on. It was deafening and many-voiced, rumbling against mossy wood, pattering against leaves, splashing into the marsh.

Yannick, Yannick, where are you? Nettle felt achingly alone.

Halfway up a tree, in a great, shaggy nest of tangled sticks and moss, a heron watched them paddle past.

Herons still made Nettle's skin crawl. She didn't like the way they coiled in their necks to stand hunchback. She didn't like their dagger-beaks and November-sky plumage. She didn't like the slow, stealthy movements of their legs, or their pale, merciless little eyes. She followed the bird with her eyes as it heaved itself into flight, great wings beating the air with a *wump-wump-wump*, its bulk heavy with swallowed fish and small-boned prey.

Nettle realized that Kellen was staring at her.

"I hate them, that's all," she said. He knew how she felt about herons, so she hoped he would leave the subject alone. But he was still frowning at her in confusion.

"Hate what?" he said. "What were you glaring at?"

Nettle's heart turned to ice. She glanced over her shoulder, to see if she could catch another glimpse of the heron. Even in the dim light she could see that the wide-winged shape was still there, but now it hung implausibly in the air, beating slow and silent wings. The shape was no longer gray either. It was black.

"It's nothing." Nettle turned her cold face forward into the rain and kept paddling.

As the light began to fade, the trees yielded to reeds, and these reeds gradually thickened to become a forest, their feathery tops a full eight feet above the water. The going was hard until Gall and his horse found a watery channel where the reeds had been pushed aside, just wide enough to admit a boat.

The little convoy entered the channel, flanked on each side by the high, rustling walls of the reeds. The channel wove through the reed-forest, sometimes meeting junctions with other channels, like converging roadways. The water beneath their boat gently rose and fell, like the chest of a creature lost in sleep.

Nettle liked the reed-forest even less than the marsh-woods. There was no way to see anything coming, nowhere to run, and the rain drowned out most other sounds. They were blind, deaf, and helpless.

"This is ridiculous!" Kellen shouted over the rain. "It's a maze!" There was no sun to navigate by now.

"People must use these channels," said Nettle. "Look!" Nestling among the reeds was a long, slender pole painted white and blue as a waymark, a flag rippling at its tip.

"It doesn't tell us where to go, though, does it?" said Kellen, then brightened. "Wait! We can ask the Dancing Star!"

"We do need to find shelter for you two quickly," said Gall, looking at his bedraggled companions and the water sloshing in the base of the boat. "Somewhere safe, so I can leave you and go hunting. I need meat for the horse. It's . . . becoming urgent."

Nettle didn't want to imagine what would happen if a marsh horse were left hungry for too long. Reluctantly, she took the puzzle bottle out of her pocket and carefully twisted the spiral seashell.

"Can you hear me?" she asked. At first there was no response, but when she held the bottle to her ear she heard a long, rustling sigh.

We are in the Deep Wilds. The crackling voice of the Dancing Star tickled against her ear. Its tone wasn't exactly happy, but it sounded more vigorous than before.

"Can you sense where we are?" asked Nettle.

Are you alone? asked the voice, its tone changing slightly.

"My friends are here too." Nettle glanced at her companions. "We think there's a village nearby. Can you tell us how to find it?"

There was a long pause, during which crackling noises came and went like sea-sounds in Nettle's ear.

Head windward, the Dancing Star said, then fell silent and would not speak again.

The little convoy followed the wind as best they could through the maze of channels. Dusk had settled in by the time they heard the first dog bark, and they knew that they must be drawing closer to somewhere inhabited. At last their channel opened up, and they found themselves gazing out across a reed-fringed lake.

"Look!" whispered Kellen, and pointed. "Just like the peddler said!"

At the water's edge was a small wooden tower, its gabled roof jutting up into the sky. It had been built on the remains of a dead tree, the broken spars of which still curled up around its base like gnarled fingers. Twilight was draining color from the world, but Nettle thought the tower's paint might be red.

Beside the tower stood a stilted hut, linked to the tower by a wooden walkway. A rope ladder ran down to a floating raft-quay, where a small boat and a canoe were tethered. Two raggle-taggle piebald dogs burst out onto the walkway, and a torrent of barking shattered the stillness.

As the door of the hut opened, releasing a blaze of lamplight, Gall and his horse sank beneath the marsh water with eerie speed. In an instant they were gone, leaving only swirling ripples and a stream of bubbles.

An old man stepped out of the hut holding a lamp. He looked frightened but determined.

"Good evening!" called Kellen, the orange lamplight falling on his rain-slicked and slightly manic face. "Sorry to bother you, but we really need some shelter!"

The room at the base of the tower was dry and well-swept and contained a table, two reed-wicker chairs, and two mattresses stuffed with dry moss.

The old man provided Nettle and Kellen with woolen blankets, a jug of small beer, and a basket of bread and dried fruit. He was about Kellen's height, with a face scarred by pranket burns and hands calloused from reed-weaving.

"Most people call me Uncle," he told them, and Nettle couldn't blame him. Giving your real name to strangers in the Deep Wilds was asking for trouble, particularly during the hours of darkness. Nettle was very aware of how she and Kellen must appear. Two children in a pearl-pale boat of strange design, arriving just as twilight was ebbing into night . . .

"It's all right!" said Kellen, who had evidently realized the same thing. "We're not creatures of the Wilds! We're human! We're not going to shapeshift into giant weasels and eat your children!"

Stop. Talking. Nettle gave Kellen a firm nudge with her foot.

"Guests are guests," their host assured them quickly. "Our village offers hospitality to all."

In the Shallow Wilds, you kept your doors shut after dark, to stop strangeness getting in. In the Deep Wilds, you offered the strangeness shelter and dinner, to stop it getting annoyed.

.....

Sometime after Nettle and Kellen had curled up in their blankets, still in their clothes, the rain stopped. Kellen was already asleep, and not for the first time Nettle envied the way he could lie down and simply go out like a candle. She lay awake, listening to the creak of the hut's stilts, the gentle lap of water and the gravelling of crickets in the humid night.

There was another sound in the darkness, she realized, a soft rustling hiss. For a panicky moment she thought of snakes, then realized that the sound was coming from the bottle in her pocket. She had forgotten to twist the seashell back to its original position.

You are awake, said the voice in the bottle. *Your breathing betrays you.*

Nettle carefully took out the bottle and held it to her ear.

"What do you want?" she whispered.

You wish to know of Salvation, said the Dancing Star.

"Yes." Nettle stared up into darkness.

Are you alone? came the question. *Will anyone hear us?*

In the shadows of the hut, Nettle could barely see Kellen, but she could hear his faint snore nearby. She didn't know how loudly she could speak without waking him.

"Just a moment," she hissed. She got up, opened the door, and slipped through it. Outside, the dimly moonlit scene was so still it might have been a drawing in charcoal and chalk.

I can lead you to Salvation, rustled the creature in the bottle. *You, and only you. Do you understand?*

Nettle swallowed and raised the bottle to her mouth to answer. Before she could do so, however, another voice made her jump.

"What are you doing?"

Down below, she saw Gall's pale face looking up at her, and the black silhouette of the marsh horse. The horse was stirrup-deep in the marsh water, and Gall's clothes and hair were drenched once again. She had heard no whisper of reeds to warn of their approach. Perhaps they had risen from beneath the water, as swiftly and silently as they had sunk into it before.

"Why are you here?" Nettle's voice came out sounding shrill and furtive.

"I wanted to keep an eye on you," said Gall. Once again he let the double meaning hang. "Going somewhere?"

"I thought I heard a noise, so I came out to look," Nettle heard herself say. She hadn't planned to lie, but Gall's drowned-ghost stare had knocked her off balance. Nettle didn't want to tell Gall what the Dancing Star had said. If the creature heard her betray its confidence, it might never talk to her again. She would be shutting a door that she might need.

"What did you expect to see?" said the marsh horseman. "You've been looking over your shoulder all day. What are you afraid of?"

"We're in the Deep Wilds!" said Nettle, feeling her face flush with warmth. "I'm afraid of everything!"

Including you, she thought.

Nettle couldn't see Gall clearly. He was a mosaic of moonlit fragments—a pale face punctured by the eye-patch, stirrup glints, stars in the horse's deep eyes. Menace hung in the air like the smell of snow.

"I've been wanting to ask something," she said. "Kellen still thinks that once we find Salvation, we'll lure Chancery here. Is that what *you* intend to do? Or do you have other plans for those cursers if we find them?"

"It depends," said Gall, his voice tombstone cold. "I'll do whatever I need to. Why do you care?"

Nettle's spine tingled as a drop of perspiration traced its way down. Marsh horsemen went feral sometimes. They lost themselves to kinship with the horse, sloughed their last shreds of humanity like dead skin, ran bloodily amok, and then rode off to live in the marshes.

He shouldn't be here, Nettle thought suddenly. *It's becoming too natural for him. He's losing track of himself, the way Yannick does sometimes.*

"Can you warn me when you're about to start killing?" she said icily. "I don't want to be around when you forget how to stop." She stepped back into the hut and closed the door.

Sometime later she furtively opened it again, to see whether Gall was still watching the tower. She could see the marsh horseman down below, but he didn't seem to notice her. His attention was fixed on something in his hand—a limp, pale rag that drooped across his fingers. His expression was stark, blank, and a little lost.

The object was the right size and shape to be a letter fragment, sodden with marsh water. As she crept back to bed, Nettle imagined Harland's carefully penned name blurring like a distant memory, the pale fibers turning to pulp.

Being human was hard. It took practice. If you spent too much time being something else, it was difficult to find your way back. Perhaps Gall was running out of reasons to try.

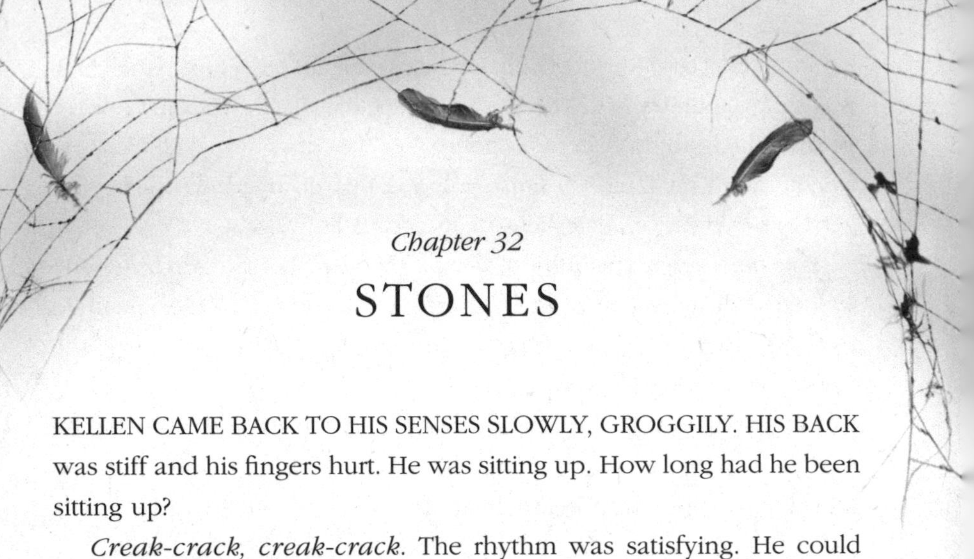

Chapter 32

STONES

KELLEN CAME BACK TO HIS SENSES SLOWLY, GROGGILY. HIS BACK was stiff and his fingers hurt. He was sitting up. How long had he been sitting up?

Creak-crack, creak-crack. The rhythm was satisfying. He could feel himself slipping into a happy trance again.

Behind him, he heard a rustle as Nettle turned over on her mattress. Then there was a muffled gasp.

"Kellen, what are you doing?" she hissed. "Stop that!"

"In a moment," he told her sleepily. *Creak-creak, crack.* "I've nearly finished . . ."

Nettle stamped over to the door and threw it open. By the morning light from the doorway, Kellen saw what he was doing.

One of the woven reed chairs was now nothing but a wooden frame and a heap of stiff stems, every strand removed and unknotted. Kellen's bleeding fingers were busy pulling apart the last reeds from the other chair. It took an effort of will to stop.

He looked over his shoulder and could see that his blanket was now a mass of loose woolen threads.

"I . . . I can't . . ." He didn't know what he wanted to say. "I don't even remember . . ."

"We can't let anyone see this!" said Nettle, hastily gathering up the wool as if that would somehow help. "If the locals find out that you unravel things . . . if anyone works out who you are—"

Kellen watched numbly as Nettle tidied, and flinched away every time she came close. He was terrified by the thought that he might see her unravel at his touch, bleed, and scream.

Once Kellen followed Nettle out onto the walkway, however, he was quickly distracted from such morbid thoughts. The two dogs from the night before ran out to bark at them again, dancing forward and back but keeping their distance. The evening before, Kellen had thought the dogs were black-and-white. Now he saw that their darker patches were a deep, earthy red, like dried blood.

A whistle called the dogs back to Uncle, who was standing at the door of his hut. He seemed slightly surprised to find his guests still there after sunrise. Perhaps he had expected them to fly away during the night in a chariot drawn by bats.

"So what brings you worthies to our withered lily of a village?" he asked. Deep Wilds folk often talked like poets without noticing, and on another day, Kellen might have found it amusing.

"We got lost!" said Nettle quickly, covering for Kellen's numb silence. "We were lucky to find this place. Since we're here, though, we thought we'd ask around, find out if there's anything we should bring you and your neighbors the next time we come by."

"You're deep in the Wilds," said Uncle mildly. "Deep enough for talking trees and Maids-a-Weeping. Not many come this far without a reason . . . and I doubt all the trade we can offer is worth a second journey."

Kellen could almost hear the unasked question. What were two young peg-sellers doing so deep in the Wilds, in a boat clearly too fine and strange for them?

"The truth is," Kellen said, "we're supposed to do a little business at the sea's edge, if you know what I mean. For someone in Mizzleport. If we prove ourselves, they'll send us again."

For the first time, Uncle looked as though he might believe them. A rich merchant with expensive tastes might send a small group to buy wonders at the Moonlit Market from the people in the White Boats. The old man frowned deeply, looking concerned.

"You're not the first I've met bent on visiting the Moonlit Market," he said, "but you're the youngest. Why don't you both stay for a few days, then go home instead? Don't break your mothers' hearts by becoming a winter's tale."

Kellen and Nettle paddled their pale boat out onto the butterfly-shaped lake, dodging the lily pads and the matted tangles of broken reeds and flotsam.

"Do you think this is the whole village?" murmured Kellen. Across the lake, he could see several great trees rising from the water, crusted tide-marks darkening their trunks. Each had one or more reed-thatched huts perched in it like shabby wooden birds.

"I doubt it," Nettle answered quietly. "They can only put up huts in places where they won't sink. Trees. Rocks. Water shallow enough for stilts. The village might spread out for miles."

Nettle was looking even paler and more withdrawn than usual, Kellen realized. There were dark circles under her eyes as if she'd slept badly.

"Are you all right?" he asked.

"Kellen," she said slowly. "I talked to Gall last night. I . . . I'm not sure it's a good idea, all of us being in the Deep Wilds together."

"What do you mean?"

"Well, everyone has . . . anchors, don't they?" Nettle didn't look Kellen in the eye and seemed to be choosing her words carefully. "Things that stop them drifting loose and . . . and crashing into rocks. And when there aren't any anchors anymore . . ."

Just for a moment, Kellen looked at Nettle as an Unraveller and could almost see stray threads that he might pull. Secrets that might be teased out, stories to unwind. But she was knotted so very tightly, and he knew she wouldn't thank him for prying.

"So what do you want me to do about it?" he said instead, a bit irritably. "We're here for a reason, aren't we? If we don't find Salvation, we can't help Chancery catch them. And we need the cursers to be arrested, so I can talk to them so that *maybe* I can unravel their curses!"

Including mine, he thought, remembering the mess of dismantled chair.

Nettle took a deep breath as if to say something else, then shook her head, looking frustrated.

"Forget it," she muttered, then nodded toward the distant huts. "Everyone's looking at us."

People were coming out onto their walkways to stare at the new arrivals, with the quiet shamelessness of woodland creatures seeing something new and possibly dangerous. Dogs were barking from quays and wooden walkways. Most were black-and-white, but a few were red-and-white like Uncle's.

When Kellen and Nettle paddled over to the first tree-hut, a young woman tethered her tame fishing cormorant to the rail and hurried to bring them leathery little seed biscuits. Shortly afterward, four men stopped gathering driftwood with long-handled nets and poled their raft over to join the conversation.

Talking to Deep Wilds folk always made Kellen fidgety. They spoke slowly and ignored the little, commonplace spiders that scuttled everywhere, even over their clothes and faces.

They're like sleepwalkers, thought Kellen, but that wasn't right either. In some ways, Deep Wilds people were more alert than anyone else, instincts spread wide to catch every tremor. They were like deer or songbirds, accustomed and attuned to perpetual danger, continual fear.

Deep Wilds folk always picked their way through sentences like travelers edging through treacherous marshland. *Don't say the wrong word, in case a listening owl-knight steals your eyes to wear as jewelry*. Even their chores were little rites, performed with care. *Sweep your front step this way and not that so that the fox-faced women prowl past your door and not through it*. It made Kellen feel that he was surrounded by invisible traps he might step into at any moment. It made him hungry for the highlands where you could swear at a stump you stubbed your toe on, or sling your boots on a table, or take fruit from a crab apple tree without some hidden doom descending on you.

But what would happen if I broke all the rules? Kellen could feel himself starting to grin a little.

"So what do people need around here?" Nettle was asking.

The locals exchanged glances.

"You won't do a lot of business in our village, I'm afraid," said the woman with the cormorant. "We don't use coin at the moment." She hadn't volunteered her name. Neither had her friends.

"We *used* to buy from peddlers," admitted one of the men. "But that was when we had our hag stone. Please don't take this unkindly, but without it we don't know gem from giblet."

"You had a real clear-sight hag stone?" asked Nettle.

A hag stone was a flint with a natural hole through its center, worn by water or weather. They were much sought after for their ability to reveal trickery from the Wilds. Chancery owned some so large that one could pass coins and other small items through the hole to make sure they were real. A clear-sight hag stone allowed you to see the true forms of things by looking through the hole.

"A beautiful one," said the woman, with wistful pride. "We could look through it at strangers' goods and coin and make sure they weren't glamoured leaves or enchanted wasps."

"But it's gone," one of the wood-gatherers intoned sadly. "Nobody's fault, and no help for it. Poor girl!"

"*He'll* tell you about it," said another one of the wood-gatherers, nodding toward a boat twenty feet away. "It's all he talks about now."

The other boat was so ramshackle that it looked like a beaver's dam with a hull. Its single occupant was a young man with dark red hair, who was gesturing with his barge pole to get their attention.

As Kellen and Nettle paddled over to the beaver-dam boat, Kellen realized that the red-haired stranger was only about sixteen or seventeen. His face was narrow and clever, with scooped-looking cheeks.

"I wanted to talk to you!" he declared. "I'm Dog."

Kellen was so startled by the name that for a moment he didn't notice the phrasing. *I'm Dog*. Not *They call me Dog*, or *You can call me Dog*.

"Wait a minute!" he blurted out. "Is that your real name?"

Dog winced a little and managed to turn it into a smile.

"You've seen the red dogs?" He nodded toward the homesteads on the bank. "Sometimes a bitch gets big-bellied when none of our dogs have been near her." He looked out at the rustling, gray-blond reed-forest. "Then we know something from out there has come visiting and mated with her. When her pups pop out, they're always red as wine." He gave a shrug that said, *It happens*.

"But what's that got to do with you?" asked Kellen.

"I'm the same way," said Dog, looking uncomfortable. "Born red-headed, with no likeness to my kith and kin. So they called me Dog, because they said I had more in common with those pups."

"But how—"

Nettle's kick caught Kellen neatly in the shin. He was fairly sure that if he continued the sentence she'd do it again. Evidently this was one of those subjects you didn't ask about.

"It doesn't matter," Dog said impatiently. "Is it true you're heading to the Moonlit Market? You need to take me with you!"

"What? Why?" Kellen was taken aback.

"I need to find a cure for someone who's turning to stone!" said Dog. "The people in the White Boats will know! I need to talk to them—"

"Slow down!" interrupted Kellen. "Turning to stone?"

"A woman from our village took our hag stone with her on a trip into the reed-forest." Dog looked uncomfortable suddenly and scratched at his red hair. "She . . . she says she swallowed it. Ever since then, she keeps swallowing pebbles, and she gets grayer and stonier with every rock she eats. If I don't do something, soon she'll be a statue! I don't have much to trade at the market, but I'll give anything I have for a cure."

"Well, maybe it won't come to that." A suspicion was already forming in Kellen's mind. "Does she have any enemies?"

"No!" Dog flushed angrily as if Kellen's words were an insult. "Everybody loves her!"

Well, some people clearly do, thought Kellen.

"Can you take us there?" he asked. "I'd like to have a look at her."

"I can give you directions," said Dog, looking a little sullen, "but I shouldn't go there with you. Her husband doesn't like me."

I can't imagine why, thought Kellen.

"You think she's been cursed, don't you?" said Nettle quietly, as they paddled away.

"Let's hope so," muttered Kellen. "If she is, maybe we can do something about it." Even gripping the paddle, he could feel his fingers tingling. Excitement buzzed in his chest like a swarm of golden bees.

"I'm not saying we shouldn't help her," said Nettle carefully. "But . . . you remember what Gall said about keeping a low profile? If you unravel her curse, and word gets out—"

"We have to take the risk!" said Kellen. "Listen, I think she's the person we're looking for! Didn't you hear what Dog said? This woman went into the reed-forest and took the village's hag stone with her. Why would she need it?"

"The locals use it for trade." Nettle always caught on fast. "So she was heading into the reed-forest, all by herself, to trade with somebody . . ."

Kellen nodded.

"If this is a curse, we need to break it," he said. "I think this woman's the one in contact with Salvation. Which means she'll know where to find them."

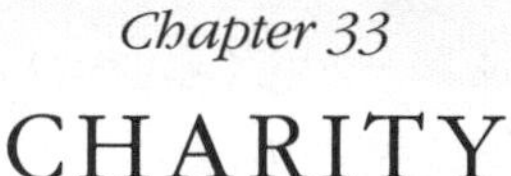

Chapter 33
CHARITY

ANOTHER STALK LASHED NETTLE'S FACE AS SHE AND KELLEN paddled along the narrow watery channels through the reed-forest. On either side rose the dense, high reeds, close enough to touch, throbbing with insects and shivering with the wind.

Dog's directions had been given with the brusque confidence of someone who never had to direct strangers. *Take that channel as far as the strangle-lilies, then turn right, and you'll see the trickle that ducks under a maple bough. When you reach the dancing dolls, you're close.*

"This can't be right!" muttered Kellen, as they grabbed handfuls of reeds and hauled their boat along through a channel so narrow it barely seemed navigable.

Then, quite suddenly, a loud *clatter-clatter-clack* erupted above their heads, like someone rattling a bag of wooden spoons.

"What's that?" Kellen pointed. Attached to one of the sturdier reeds was a small wooden figure, limbs dangling loose, a cord trailing from its body down into the water. Kellen's paddle had hooked on the cord, making the wooden shape rattle.

"Dancing doll," said Nettle, remembering Dog's words.

"I think it's some kind of early warning system," said Kellen. "Look!" Farther down the channel, more dolls dangled from posts nestling among the reeds. Each trailed a cord into the water and across the channel. Any passing boat would set the dolls clattering.

Not long after this, the channel reached a patch of open water. A small house of good timber stood on a dozen stilts. The thatch of its roof was fresh, lush, and squirrel-tail gray. There was a flat-bottomed boat tied to the floating quay, a sharp-tipped barge pole resting along its length. Nettle couldn't help noticing that the boat was tethered multiple times, as if someone feared it might wriggle loose of its moorings and make its escape.

A man stood warily in the doorway, waiting for them. He was tall and dark-haired, with just a little gray creeping into his beard.

"Hello!" Kellen's smile was probably meant to be reassuring. "We heard your wife was turning to stone! Can we see her?" All day his mood had been teetering and tipping like a spinning top, and now he had an air of dazed hilarity.

"We're going to the Moonlit Market!" Nettle added quickly, before the stranger could take offense at Kellen's manner. "If we know what's wrong with her, we can look for antidotes while we're there."

"To tell the truth," said the tall man, in a softer voice than Nettle had expected, "I'm willing to try anything."

There were only two rooms within the house. One was a little workshop hung with bronze tools. The other was a living space draped with soft marsh-silk rugs and hangings. The wick of a brightly painted clay lamp flickered under its cloudy glass dome.

By its light, Nettle could see a single figure, slumped forward but struggling to rise from its deer-hide chair, arms trembling under its weight. It was lumpish and thick-limbed under its long, loose blue gown, but Nettle could just about see that it was female.

"Oh, no," said the bearded man very gently. "No, dearling. Please." He laid a tender hand on one bulging arm, and the shape collapsed back into the chair.

The afflicted woman's skin was gray, pitted, and covered in pale rosettes of lichen. In the hollows beneath her brows, living eyes looked out, framed by calcified lashes. Her mouth was a deep crevice from which miserable, creaking moans escaped. Only the long, fair hair that fell from her scalp showed that she was young.

"She keeps wanting to go out and find rocks, even now," explained her husband, tucking a rug back in place around his wife. "If she finds one and eats it, then *this* gets worse."

The husband said that his guests could call him the Carpenter, and his wife Charity.

"She's always charitable," he said fondly, stroking one gray, ravaged hand. "She gives everyone the benefit of the doubt, until there's no doubt left."

"Hmph," said Kellen, eyes bright. "You look like you have somebody in mind when you say that."

The Carpenter gave his wife a quick, concerned look and patted her hand.

"You'll notice that we live away from our neighbors," he said. "We used to live on the lake, but there was some trouble. My wife is kind and friendly to everyone, and there was one person who saw more in that than there was. He kept after her till he frightened her. In the end, we moved out here."

Nettle imagined all the work that must have taken, abandoning the great sturdy trees at the lake's edge and having to plunge long stilts down through deep water into the mud.

"Was it Dog?" Kellen asked bluntly.

The stone woman's eyes widened and she emitted a small, pitiful bleat.

"This is upsetting her," her husband said. "Let's talk in the other room."

In his workshop, the Carpenter sighed and ran his hands through his hair.

"Yes," he admitted, "I did mean Dog. Do you know where he got his name?"

"He's named after the red dogs," said Nettle promptly. "The ones with Wilds blood in them, and hair the same color as his."

"Nobody else here has hair that color," said the Carpenter. "Not his mother, nor the man he called father. He's a Wild seed, and everyone knows. It happens with dogs, and sometimes it happens with people too—though his mother never admitted it."

Out of the corner of her eye, Nettle saw Kellen's eyes widen as the penny dropped.

"This deep in the Wilds," the Carpenter went on, "someone like Dog is born now and then. Someone with a face like a knife who can smell storms coming and whose heart works differently. They don't love, but they fix themselves on someone, the way a fox fixes on a hare, or the tide fixes on the moon."

"And he 'fixed' on your wife?" asked Kellen.

"He'd lie on our roof at night sometimes, crooning to her," said the Carpenter. "He'd bring her gifts from the forest. Strange things. Dead things. Flowers made of bone, and eggs the color of emeralds. So we moved out here."

"But what's to stop Dog following her here?" asked Kellen. "He does, doesn't he? That's why you hang up the dancing dolls, so you can hear him coming. Why don't you just get a dog to keep watch?"

"We had one." The Carpenter frowned. "My wife loved it. One night it went missing, and she wouldn't get another in case it happened again."

"What about your wife's little trips into the reed-forest?" asked Kellen suddenly, eyes shining in the lamplight. "Does she ever run into Dog when she's out there alone?" He had the fierce, curious smile he always wore when he was veering off the road into thorny terrain.

"What are you saying?" The Carpenter scowled, his voice dropping in pitch.

And this is why Kellen gets kicked in the head, thought Nettle, gritting her teeth.

"Oh, I'm not saying she'd meet him on purpose!" Kellen said, holding up his hands innocently. "But she *did* always go alone, didn't she, to sell goods to somebody? Did you ever know who she *was* meeting?"

"Of course I know. We have no secrets from each other." The Carpenter didn't raise his voice but spoke with quiet, wintry force. "A group of unfortunates, that's all, hiding in the forest and trying to survive. Highlanders, lost without the things they know. She just wanted to help them. I told you, she's charitable!"

Nettle tried not to react, digging her nails into her palms. *A group of unfortunates. Highlanders.* It had to be Salvation. The nest of cursers really was somewhere nearby, in the whispering, shivering reed-forest.

"Did she ever tell you where they were?" asked Nettle, feeling her heart bang.

The Carpenter shook his head.

"That woman's under a curse," said Kellen, when they were paddling back to the lake. "I'm sure of it."

"You think someone in Salvation did it, don't you?" asked Nettle.

"I don't know," mused Kellen. "Salvation sometimes curse people who are a threat to them. "'Charity' might have found out too much about them. But . . ."

"But they were meeting her alone," finished Nettle. "They could have just murdered her and hidden her body in the bog."

"Yeah," agreed Kellen. "Much easier. Salvation don't have a reason to curse her. Of course, cursers don't always need a *good* reason. They're gobbled up with blind hatred—sometime it flies out and hits the nearest target."

Nettle winced but said nothing.

"If it isn't Salvation," Kellen went on, "then it has to be someone in the village. But who?"

The wind rose, and the reeds gossiped drily. In the distance, Nettle heard the breath-in-bottle note of a bittern booming. *Whom?* it seemed to ask, in its resounding, hollow voice. *Whom?*

Just for a moment, Nettle thought she heard other notes in the wind's voice, other words . . .

"Let's get back to the lake," she muttered. "You could start to imagine things out here."

. . . . .

Back at the butterfly lake, people softened a little when Kellen mentioned wanting to help the Carpenter's wife. The young woman and her husband seemed to be universally loved.

"She's a sunbeam, and he built most of the huts in this village," Uncle told them. "Such a shame. He'd walk through fire for her."

When Nettle asked locals about Dog, it became clear that everyone assumed he was some Wilds creature's offspring.

"He's a Wild seed, all right," said an old woman who sat polishing a horn knife with a smoothing stone in slow, careful swipes. "It's not his fault, and he makes himself useful. We need timber for the huts and boats, and he finds it."

"How?" asked Nettle. She knew that it was forbidden to damage a tree in the Deep Wilds without permission.

"The woods tell him where to find trees felled by storms. And sometimes they even give him leave to use his axe. He has a way with them."

"So . . . he's a help here, not a danger?" asked Nettle, trying to digest this information.

The old woman hesitated, then gave a noncommittal little shrug.

"You don't throw away a knife just because it can cut you," she said, looking down at her own newly sharpened blade. "You handle it the right way, that's all."

"But the Carpenter and his wife were afraid of him?" pressed Nettle.

"Oh, that girl never knew when to be afraid," the old woman answered with a smile. "She'd clean the fangs of a snake if it said it had toothache."

Nettle's attention was attracted by the sound of a loud splash behind her. She suddenly realized that Kellen's boots and most of his clothes were lying in a heap on the quay. Kellen himself had jumped into the water, to the delight of some small children who were playing in the water, sleek and fearless as otters.

"Your friend should be careful of the weeds," remarked the old woman. "And the leeches."

Kellen had pulled himself up onto the lowest bough of a big tree and was chatting animatedly with the younger children in the water below him. As Nettle watched, one little girl pointed upward, and to Nettle's dismay Kellen began to climb, still wearing nothing but his wet undergarments.

"There were very good reasons for that," Kellen assured Nettle when he finally hauled himself back up onto the walkway.

"What *were* you doing up that tree?" she asked.

"Making a mark to show how high I'd climbed." Kellen was shivering a little but grinning like a maniac. "All the kids have made marks like that. And do you know who has climbed highest? The girl everyone's calling Charity. Her mark's right up there, on the upper fork."

Nettle peered upward and spotted the place he meant. But that would mean climbing until the trunk was a span wide and swaying, and the boughs barely strong enough to hold your weight . . .

"Everyone tells us that she's kind and too trusting," said Kellen. "But she's more than that, isn't she? She's friendly, bold, and *reckless*. She's the sort of person who goes off alone into the reed-forest to meet with suspicious fugitives because she feels sorry for them."

"Not the sort of person who usually runs away," said Nettle.

"Exactly," said Kellen. "And yet she moved out to that lonely hut. Weird, isn't it?" He pushed his wet, spiky hair out of his face. "Another odd thing—Charity's still getting worse. She shouldn't be, should she?"

"No," said Nettle. "She can't even stand, so how is she finding new pebbles to eat?"

Kellen's eyes were bright and speculative.

"Nettle," he said slowly. "Was there anyone you met today who gave you a bad gut feeling?"

Nettle sighed.

"Yes," she admitted. "There's no good reason—I thought maybe I was imagining things—"

"Me too," said Kellen.

“If we’re right, what do we do?” said Nettle. She was fairly sure that they were talking about the same person. “Do you think you can lift the curse?”

“Maybe, if I can talk to Charity alone.” Kellen knitted his brows. “No,” he murmured, sounding more certain. “I need *her* to talk to *me*.”

“You think the Carpenter would trust us alone with his wife?” asked Nettle.

“Of course he won’t,” said Kellen. “But we need to find a way, and soon. I don’t think she’s got much time left.”

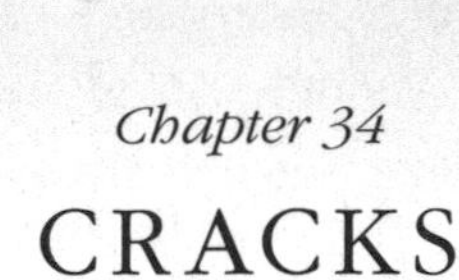

Chapter 34

CRACKS

JUST BEFORE SUNSET, AS THE INSECTS WERE CHANGING THEIR tune, Kellen and Nettle were hunched in their little boat, concealed in the thick of the reeds. They were not far from the Carpenter's house but had not ventured close enough to trigger any of the dancing dolls.

"He can't stay in the house forever!" muttered Kellen, feeling restive.

"Shhh!" Nettle held up a hand.

There were sounds of motion coming from the direction of the stilted house. The thud of a closing door. The creak of wooden planks bearing weight. The swish and splash of disturbed water. The *clatter-clack* of a wooden doll dancing, then another.

Through the tangled mesh of reed stems, Kellen could just make out the Carpenter standing in his long canoe and driving it forward with his punting pole.

Kellen and Nettle stayed motionless for a couple of minutes after the faint sounds of rustling and paddle-splashes faded. Then they wrestled their boat out of its hiding place and headed down the channel toward the stilted house. As they reached each doll, Kellen carefully cut its cord so that no clatter would call the Carpenter back.

They moored quickly against the floating quay, then climbed the ladder to the stilted hut.

"We probably don't have long," muttered Nettle. "I'll keep watch."

That's the wonder of Nettle, Kellen thought, feeling a surge of respect. *She'll nitpick every plan to pieces beforehand, but once you're neck-deep in it, she's cool as dew.*

The main door to the hut wouldn't open, so Kellen levered open a window shutter and used his knife to slit the grimy, insect-proof gauze beyond it. He slithered through the window, landing with a faint thud on the wooden floorboards. There was a faint, snuffling moan from across the unlit room. By the pinkish light from the window, he could just make out the misshapen bulk of the cursed woman, still in her chair.

"Don't be scared!" he said, quickly putting away the knife. "I'm here to help!"

The cursed woman watched his approach with frightened eyes.

"I was here earlier, remember?" said Kellen. "This was the only way I could talk to you properly. Can you whisper? Even a little bit?"

The gray jaw trembled. A faint, creaking breath. No words.

It had been a lot to hope for. If she could get the words out, that would change everything, he was sure of it. But it could never be easy to cough everything up, after all this time. Stones and words, words and stones, all swallowed down one by one until she was granite-heavy and helpless.

"It's all right," he whispered, hoping he was right. "You just listen."

Kellen crouched down next to her, his mouth close to the lumpy gray oval that was her ear. He took a deep breath and trusted his instincts.

"*I know*," he said.

There was a little catch in her breath, and the bright, still-human eyes turned toward him, shimmering.

"I know you couldn't tell anybody about him. They wouldn't believe it. The village needs him, so everyone sees what they want to see. They *like* him. Maybe you tried not to believe it either and told yourself you were imagining things. But you weren't. It isn't love. It's obsession. He's fixed on you, that's all. The way a fox fixes on a hare. The way the tide fixes on the moon. The way a creeper strangles a tree. You never wanted to leave the village, did you? You never wanted to live stranded in this lonely hut, away from your friends and family. You agreed to it because you were scared. *But not of Dog*."

The woman in the chair gave a faint sob, and a single tear ran down her stone cheek. As it trickled, there was a faint cracking sound, and a fine black fracture appeared in the stony surface of her cheek.

Yes! thought Kellen. *That's it!* It was only a tiny fissure in the curse, but it was a start. Charity was still locked into silence by the stone, but hearing the truth she could not speak was having an effect.

"Everyone likes the Carpenter," Kellen whispered. "The kind, reliable Carpenter. So you couldn't tell anyone when he started to scare you. But you don't need to tell me. *I know.* You were always too wild for him, too warm and bold and free. He couldn't bear it. You were supposed to be *his*. He didn't like you being friends with everyone, or going places without him, or loving your dog as much as you did. When your dog went missing, did you wonder? Did you know?"

She gave a shudder like a silent sob, then a wheezing, retching sound. A tiny pebble tumbled from her mouth and landed softly in her lap.

"He wanted to cut you off from everyone else," Kellen continued. "Everyone you might go to for help. But he couldn't keep you caged . . . until you started turning to stone. Suddenly he had an excuse to watch you every moment and keep you here all the time. You got worse while you were in his care. Was he really protecting you? Or was he feeding you stones?"

She coughed, and a fine gravel spilled from her mouth. Her jaw began to move more freely. Her next sob sounded almost human.

"You can't keep the truth inside anymore," Kellen whispered. "You have to tell it to me." He had brought her as far as he could with his own words. The last leap had to be hers. "You know what he is, don't you?"

The stone woman took a deep, shaky breath. Her hands clenched with effort, crumbs of stone breaking away from the knuckles.

"Ckkkhhh . . ." she began, then wheezed in another breath. Cracks appeared at the corners of her eyes and mouth, as if a mask were breaking. "Cuursserr."

She choked, tears streaming from her eyes. A hollow rattle sounded in her chest, then she doubled up, coughing up stone after stone.

With Kellen's help, Charity managed to stand. Some chunks of her stone carapace fell away, but much of it still clung to her.

"We need to get you out of here," he whispered.

The door was easier to unbolt from the inside, but getting Charity to the boat was no simple matter. Both Kellen and Nettle were needed to support her through the door. Helping her down the ladder was slow and nerve-racking, the two of them standing below her and guiding her heavy, cumbersome feet onto each rung.

The floating quay tilted ominously when she touched down, and when she stepped into the boat, it sank dangerously low in the water. After Nettle stepped in as well, it came close to shipping water.

Kellen swore, and stooped to take off his boots.

"What are you doing?" asked Nettle.

"We can't all go in the boat!" said Kellen, pulling off his shirt. "Look at it! I'll have to hang off the back."

Charity stiffened. Not far away they heard the faint, stealthy swish of a paddle through water.

"Quick!" mouthed Nettle.

Kellen hastily dropped his boots and clothes into the boat and lowered himself off the quay into the water. It was much colder than it had seemed at midday.

There was no hope of escaping by the channel they'd used before. That would lead them straight into the path of the Carpenter. Instead, Nettle hastily paddled down another watery avenue, trusting to luck.

Kellen clung to the back of the boat and kicked along, as quietly as he could. He tried not to think of leeches or marsh fever. He tried not to remember tales of fish-eyed, water-breathing children whose grip was like winter.

Behind them, they heard the sounds of doors flinging back on their hinges, feet running across wooden boards.

"Where are you?" The Carpenter sounded desperate and frightened. "Whoever you are, please bring her back! It's not safe to take her in a boat!"

The plea might have tugged at Kellen's conscience, if he hadn't seen Charity flinch at the sound of her husband's voice.

He's like a fair fruit eaten hollow by wasps, thought Kellen. *There's no heart in there, only poison and buzzing.*

Sunset clouds were dulling to the west, and dusk was breathing gray-violet unease into the reed-forest. Nettle paddled slowly and carefully, face set in a continual wince. Every sound they made, each drip or dull thud against driftwood, sounded painfully loud.

Kellen was just starting to hope that they had managed to escape when a grouse bulleted from the undergrowth and into the sky, the patter of its wings startling as a pistol shot. Charity flinched, one heavy, stone-caked arm hitting the gunwale with a loud bang.

Everyone froze.

He must have heard that, thought Kellen. Was that a distant splash and scrape? Yes, there was no mistaking it now, the faint *husssshh* of torn water and the creak of wooden boards under foot, coming from the channel behind them. The Carpenter was coming.

"Get the boat into the reeds!" hissed Kellen. "I'll distract him!"

Nettle's eyes widened and she furiously shook her head, but Kellen didn't stay to argue. He pushed away from the back of the boat, flinging one arm over a piece of driftwood to keep himself afloat. With his free hand, he grabbed handfuls of reeds and dragged himself in among the rustling stems. He spat out pondweed, stems jabbing at his face.

When he dared look over his shoulder, the pearl-pale boat and its occupants were no longer visible. Nettle must have driven the boat in among the reeds. He barely had time for relief before the Carpenter slid into view, standing on his flat-bottomed boat.

From Kellen's water-level view, the bearded man looked enormously tall, a water-striding giant silhouetted against the sky, the sharp-tipped barge pole gripped like a spear.

I need to lead him away from the others, thought Kellen. He began to scrabble his way deeper into the reeds, making no effort to be quiet.

A little frog clinging to a reed stem fell clammily onto his face, then into the water.

"Stay where you are." The Carpenter's voice was still quiet and reasonable.

Kellen did not stop. Suddenly a wicked spear of darkness slammed through the reeds just to the left. "I said, stop!" It took Kellen a moment to realize that the Carpenter had stabbed his sharp-tipped pole into the reeds, a foot from Kellen's head.

Kellen froze, his grip on the driftwood becoming slippery. *Did he miss me on purpose, or was he trying to stab me?*

The next thrust was much closer. Kellen gave an involuntary yelp of panic as he deflected the jab with his forearm.

"Don't!" shouted an unfamiliar female voice. Kellen could only assume it was Charity. "I'll come home! Just . . . don't hurt anyone!"

"I'm protecting you, dearling," the Carpenter told her, still glaring down at Kellen with twilight-filled eyes. "It's all I've ever done." He raised his pole again, ready to stab.

Then the man stiffened and took on a thoughtful look, as if he had had a change of heart. It took a moment before Kellen noticed something sharp sticking out of the man's chest. It was a wooden point, with darkness spreading from it through his shirt. It retracted abruptly, and the Carpenter fell over sideways, out of Kellen's field of vision.

Kellen remained where he was, gasping and shivering, one arm gripping his driftwood float. He heard stealthy stem-crackles and faint splashes, as if something large were moving away through the reeds, and then silence.

When at last Kellen and the others dared emerge from hiding, they found the Carpenter floating dead beside his flat-bottomed boat, next to the abandoned pole. There was no sign of the person or creature that had killed him.

Charity's real name was Linnet.

She wept quietly on the way back, but kept brushing the tears away with an air of impatience. Every time she did so, more stone crumbled, showing the pink flesh beneath, as if the tears themselves were loosening the rock.

"Don't pick at it," Nettle told Linnet firmly. "You'll take the skin off. Treat it like scabs; it'll fall off when it's ready."

When Linnet fell into an exhausted doze, the other two talked quietly.

"Did you see who killed the Carpenter?" asked Nettle.

"No," said Kellen. "Too many reeds in the way. Did you?"

"Not very well," said Nettle. "It happened too fast. A figure lunged out of the reeds and stabbed the Carpenter, then pulled back among the stems. I couldn't see who it was." She frowned. "You'd need to be very strong to drive a pole right through someone, wouldn't you?"

"You can't always tell who might be strong," said Kellen. "Particularly round here." He was fairly sure that the two of them suspected the same person, but it seemed neither were willing to say so aloud. Adrift in this shivering, whispering gray sea, anyone or anything might be listening.

"He must have been hiding in the reeds, spying on the house," Nettle said. "We never told him we suspected a curse, but he must have worked it out when we asked if she had enemies. And when he guessed who the curser was . . ."

I suppose I should be grateful to him for saving my life, thought Kellen, but his stomach felt cold.

Would Dog be there on the butterfly lake tomorrow, ready to smile his long smile at Linnet and his other neighbors? Would anyone notice whether the tip of his punting pole was darker and redder than before? If they did, would anybody say anything or do anything? Or would the fate of the Carpenter, and the sins of the Carpenter, become just more open secrets settling into the village's silence, like dead leaves sinking to the marsh bed?

Perhaps not everything the Carpenter had said was untrue. Perhaps Dog would come at night to lie on Linnet's roof and croon to her and leave little gifts on her windowsill—dead things, strange things, and eggs the color of emerald. If he did, Kellen suspected that people would shake their heads over it but accept it. He was their Wild seed after all. Their tree-talker, their firewood-finder. A knife that could cut you but wouldn't, as long as you handled him right.

"She's got terrible taste in men," Kellen said aloud.

"It might not be her fault," said Nettle. "Maybe terrible men just have taste in her."

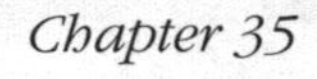

Chapter 35

SHATTERING

BY THE TIME THEY GOT BACK TO LINNET'S HOUSE, KELLEN WAS shivering badly. Linnet found dry clothes for Kellen to wear while his own dried. He felt weird putting on the Carpenter's garments, but by then he was too cold to argue. He discovered fat leeches on his legs and ankles, and when he pulled them off, the wounds oozed.

I need more plans that don't leave me neck-deep in marsh, he thought.

While Nettle made them all soup in the little ember-kettle, Kellen asked Linnet about the highlanders she met with in the reed-forest. At first she didn't want to talk about it.

"It'll wait till tomorrow, won't it?" asked Nettle. "She's had a long day!" This was presumably her tactful way of saying, *She's still half-statue, and her homicidal husband just died.*

"No, it can't wait!" exclaimed Kellen. "We're running out of time!" *I'm running out of time*, was what he really meant. The Carpenter's clothes were made of woven cloth, and already he could feel a few loose threads starting to pull free from the cuffs and tickle his wrists. "Linnet, you know what those highlanders are, don't you?"

Linnet's honest face took an expression both furtive and mulish. *Yes*, thought Kellen. *She knows.*

"They're not bad people!" she said defensively. "Just unhappy and unlucky. They won't do any harm if you leave them be."

"They're cursers!" said Kellen. "It's their nature to do harm! They can't even help it. Listen to me!" He hadn't planned to tell Linnet all about Salvation, but now he did. He told her about his own curse and the Leona-bat. When he described the nine-year-old cloud-girl, Linnet turned pale and finally relented.

"I'll tell you where I met with them," she said at last. "But . . . believe me, they're not all bad. Maybe some of them did what you say, but the ones I met just seemed frightened."

Kellen remembered the words of one of Linnet's neighbors. *That girl never knew when to be afraid. She'd clean the fangs of a snake if it said it had toothache.*

After the soup, Linnet went to bed. Kellen and Nettle kept an eye on her for a while, to make sure the weight of her remaining carapace wasn't suffocating her in her sleep.

"She shouldn't be alone tonight," said Nettle. Kellen noticed that she looked pale and anxious but wasn't too surprised. Nettle often seemed tense and concerned after an unravelling, just when he was starting to relax.

"Yeah," he said. "Besides, it's night already. I don't fancy paddling back to the storage tower in the dark."

Nettle nodded silently, frowning into space.

Kellen found some more blankets and laid them on the floor near Linnet's bed so that he and Nettle would be close at hand if the cursed woman called out or had trouble breathing. Then he looked over his shoulder to speak to Nettle and realized she wasn't there. She wasn't in the Carpenter's workshop either.

Opening the main door, he looked down and spotted her standing on the moonlit wharf. Her head was bowed, and she was hugging herself tightly, as if cold. She didn't seem to notice him calling her name or the creak of the rope ladder as he clambered down to join her. Only when his feet hit the wood of the wharf did she give a start, glancing at him over her shoulder.

"Didn't you hear me calling you?" he asked.

"No." She frowned down at the marsh water. "Sorry. The wind . . ."

"What wind?" A faint breeze stirred the reeds, but not loudly enough to drown out a voice. He decided not to make an argument out of it, however. "What are you doing down here?"

Nettle didn't answer but raised her head to look at him with dark, troubled eyes. She took a deep breath, as if steeling herself, and he knew that something was badly wrong.

"Kellen," she said in a small, tight voice.

"What is it?" His imagination scampered anxiously through possibilities. Was she injured or ill? What had he missed?

"What are you planning to do?" she asked. "Are you going to tell Gall what Linnet told us? Are you going to give him the directions?"

"Why wouldn't I?" asked Kellen, baffled.

"Do you really think he's going to stick to your plan?" asked Nettle. "Yannick's missing! Right now we *can't* send a message to Chancery. Do you think Gall's going to sit around waiting for Yannick to find us? I don't. I think he'll change the plan."

"Change it how?" Kellen hadn't even considered the possibility.

"I don't know," said Nettle darkly. "But he didn't want us along, did he? What was he planning to do if he found Salvation by himself? Kidnap Ammet, maybe? Or just run amok and kill as many cursers as he could before they killed him?"

"That's insane!"

"Haven't you been paying attention?" said Nettle bitterly. "Gall's changing! I tried to tell you before. He's going feral!"

Kellen hesitated, trying to think. Perhaps Nettle was right. Perhaps the marsh horseman had become grayer and more deathly as they went deeper into the Wilds.

Everyone has anchors, Nettle had said before. Perhaps Harland had been Gall's anchor, and later Leona. Now Gall had lost both of them. He still had his marsh horse, but Kellen didn't think it was a stabilizing influence.

"All right, we'll keep an eye on him," he said. "But we *have* to tell him, Nettle! We'll need his help! Do you really want to go looking for Salvation without his protection?"

"Kellen." Nettle closed her eyes tight and took a deep breath. "I don't want to go looking for Salvation at all!"

Her words took the wind out of Kellen's sails. He couldn't make sense of them.

"What—"

"We shouldn't have come—let's just go back inland, Kellen! We can tell Chancery as much as we know and leave it at that! That way, nobody needs to die!"

"And let Salvation win?" Kellen couldn't believe it. "If we don't do something, Ammet will make his deal with Chancery—"

"So what?" exploded Nettle, with startling force. "Would that be so bad? What if a deal was possible?"

"Don't you remember what Salvation's asking for?" yelled Kellen, forgetting all about keeping his voice down. "They want Chancery to hand me over!"

"But Chancery doesn't have you, so they can't hand you over!" Nettle sounded desperate and wretched. "Salvation will have to settle for something else!"

"They're not going to 'settle' for anything, ever!" interrupted Kellen. "They've got cursers! They'll just hold Raddith to ransom over and over again!"

"How do we know?" shouted Nettle. It was jarring and strange to hear her voice raised. "What do we really know about Salvation? We've been taking Leona Tharl's word for everything! What if there's another side to the story?"

Kellen couldn't believe what Nettle was saying. Aside from Nettle's usual doubts and quibbles, it had felt like they were marching to the same tune. He couldn't work out how they'd fallen out of step, or when.

"They curse people!" he pointed out.

"Yes," said Nettle. "But curses can be lifted. They haven't killed anyone."

"We don't know that!" said Kellen. "And we know they've tried!"

"Do we?" asked Nettle. "They've turned up armed to ambush us, but it's always Gall who starts the bloodshed, isn't it? They've always tried to capture us alive. What if they really haven't killed *anyone*? What if they're just trying to defend themselves? What if Chancery can make peace with them before anyone else gets hurt?"

"Of course they can't!" Kellen raked his fingers through the weed-stiffened tangles of his hair. "Look—even if a deal was struck, what do you think would happen then? You think that army of cursers would just sit there happily in the reed-forest, not cursing anybody? That won't happen! You know what cursers are like as well as I do! Better than I do!"

Kellen saw Nettle flinch and felt bad. She didn't like being reminded of her time as a heron, but he'd come too far to stop.

"Once somebody has a curse egg in them, they curse!" he continued. "They always curse! And they nearly always keep cursing!"

"What if that's not true?" asked Nettle, and Kellen was thrown off balance again.

"Of course it's true! Everyone knows—"

"Everyone could be wrong!" insisted Nettle. "We only know about the cursers that get caught! Of course *they* stay angry enough to curse again. We lock them away for years in windowless rooms in chains and iron helmets! But what if there are lots like Clover, who only curse once and never get caught? Or people with curse eggs who don't want to curse. Linnet said—"

"What does it matter?" Kellen waved his arms. "We can't just leave them running loose! If they're not stopped—"

"Stopped?" said Nettle, in a small, quiet voice.

"I don't know!" Kellen kicked at the planks of the wharf with a thump. "Yes! Stopped!"

"Then I suppose Gall's way of 'stopping' people would do, wouldn't it?" said Nettle in the same cool way. "Much less trouble than dragging them to the Red Hospital. But do we really want to be a part of that?"

It was too much, that quiet, accusing tone and Nettle's refusal to look him in the eye.

"Where the hell did this come from?" he yelled. "What's got into you? You've been acting weird since . . ."

Suddenly he didn't know how to finish the sentence. Since they came to the Wilds? No . . . earlier. Mizzleport? Earlier than that? He wasn't sure. He'd thought that he'd learned to understand all Nettle's silences, but had he been mistranslating some of them for ages? Could she have been silently screaming something that he'd never heard? This was stupid! Why did he have be a mind reader anyway?

"Why didn't you say anything before?" he exploded. "Why are you like this? Why don't you ever, ever, EVER just . . . talk to me properly?"

"I want you to understand," said Nettle, in the same tight little voice. "If you tell Gall where to find Salvation, there's no going back. Something will happen. Maybe he'll get killed or captured. You too, if you go with him. Or maybe Gall and his horse will run amok and start murdering people. Bloodshed in the Deep Wilds, Kellen—it always *means* something, and usually something bad. Whatever happens, there won't be any making peace with Salvation afterward. No bargains, ever. Only war and the bloody path. Is that what you want?"

Kellen listened, open-mouthed. All he really heard was Nettle saying "you" instead of "we."

"Aren't you coming?" he blurted out. The possibility hadn't even occurred to him. That wasn't the way things worked. He and Nettle bickered, and they tugged the plan to and fro like two terriers with a slipper, and sometimes he pulled harder and sometimes she did. But after that they always plunged into the mission together, side by side. Neither let the other go into danger alone.

Nettle gritted her teeth and still wouldn't look at him.

"No," she said.

All his arguments wilted before the frosty finality of that one small word.

"Fine," he said, but nothing was fine. What he felt, but couldn't say, was that he had counted on her. The nuisance who followed him everywhere had become someone he trusted more than anyone. He had known—or believed—that she had joined the hunt for Salvation because she wanted to help him lift his curse. It had bothered him, and had made him feel guilty, stressed, and grateful.

But apparently his fate wasn't that important after all. He didn't have the right to be upset about that, but he was.

He turned and climbed up the ladder, leaving Nettle staring out at the shivering of the moonlit reeds.

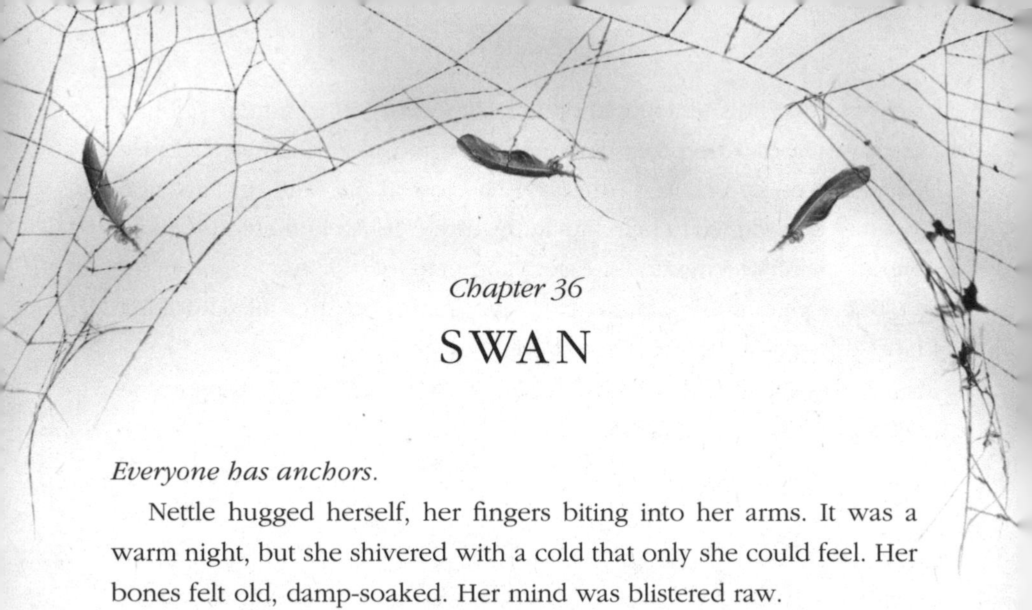

Chapter 36

SWAN

Everyone has anchors.

Nettle hugged herself, her fingers biting into her arms. It was a warm night, but she shivered with a cold that only she could feel. Her bones felt old, damp-soaked. Her mind was blistered raw.

She could see that the water was unruffled, the reeds and leaves barely trembling in the night air. And yet, in her ears and mind, the wind still howled.

Kellen hadn't heard it. He hadn't felt the wood of the wharf furtively squirming under their feet. The moon he saw didn't weep secretive silvery tears down the black fabric of the sky. She couldn't tell him about any of it, and he couldn't hear, in that other world with a normal moon.

Everyone has anchors. But the ropes break one by one. You feel the whiplash in your heart. You know you'll be adrift when the storm comes. And sometimes you have to loose the last anchor yourself.

There was a rising note in the wind that wailed as though it had a throat and a breaking heart. There were words in that wail, drawn out and distorted out of shape.

From the depths of the reed-forest, Nettle could hear a thrashing, crackling sound. Looking out across the gray sea of the reeds, she saw a distant turbulence, where the feathery tips were twitching and parting, as if a big creature were forcing its way through the reeds.

Nettle's chest tightened. She knew exactly what was approaching. She could picture it in her mind's eye with nightmare vividness.

It's coming, she thought, with a despair that was almost like relief. *I always knew it would come back. I couldn't stop it in the end.*

Nettle dropped to her knees and tugged at the mooring rope of the pearl-pale boat with shaking hands. The knots were stubborn, and loosened resentfully, the bristles biting her fingers. As she stepped aboard the boat, it bobbed unsteadily under her feet, like a beast nervously sensing a change in routine.

Kneeling at the prow, Nettle snatched up the paddle and struck out, carving the water fiercely with stroke after stroke. She could hear the words called by the wind-voice now.

Take it, it cried, in a tone of maddened anguish. *Take it, take it, take it . . .*

Fleeing was hopeless. Nettle knew that. All the same, she gritted her teeth and paddled. Cold water coursed down her arms, drenching her sleeves. Amid the reeds hung the Carpenter's dolls, and it seemed to her that some of them had faces. Then she was in new channels, walled in by quivering, gray reeds. She could navigate only by memory of the directions she'd been given and by the weeping moon above in the bright black sky.

Even when the nameless village was left far behind, and Nettle's breath was coming in little sobs, she didn't dare slow. Still she heard crashing and rending behind her, and sometimes a sound like the beating of wings.

Blind with tiredness and the moon, she didn't notice the trap until it was too late. She did not see the two low boats that had lurked like logs among the reeds to the left and right. Even when figures rose up in them and grabbed at the sides of her boat, she was slow to react. She had not been ready for them, so they seemed unlikely and unreal.

"No!" She realized too late that her flight had been halted. The paddle was snatched from her hand. "No!"

In panic, she twisted in her seat to stare back the way she had come.

Behind her she could see the rushes thrashing in turmoil, as something large struggled through them. Something black, something taller than a man, with wings spread wide.

Nettle screamed as a vast, black swan crashed into view, its wings half-furled, its neck moving snake-like, seekingly. Its black feathers were sticky and bedraggled. The moon glinted on the human eyes set in its head.

It saw Nettle and came for her, with the lopsided frenzy of a wounded thing, leaving dark red stains on the broken reeds.

With two pallid, child-like arms, the Swan held something out toward her—a veined, squirming thing with a drooping head and bulging, pink-skinned eyes.

Take it, the Swan insisted, eyes glossy and maddened with despair.

Nettle screamed and thrashed as one of the men grappled her. It took her several moments to realize that he was trying to talk to her. It was hard to hear him, with her ears full of the wind and the cries of the Swan.

But then she remembered where she was, and why. So she closed her eyes, clenched her teeth, and forced herself to listen.

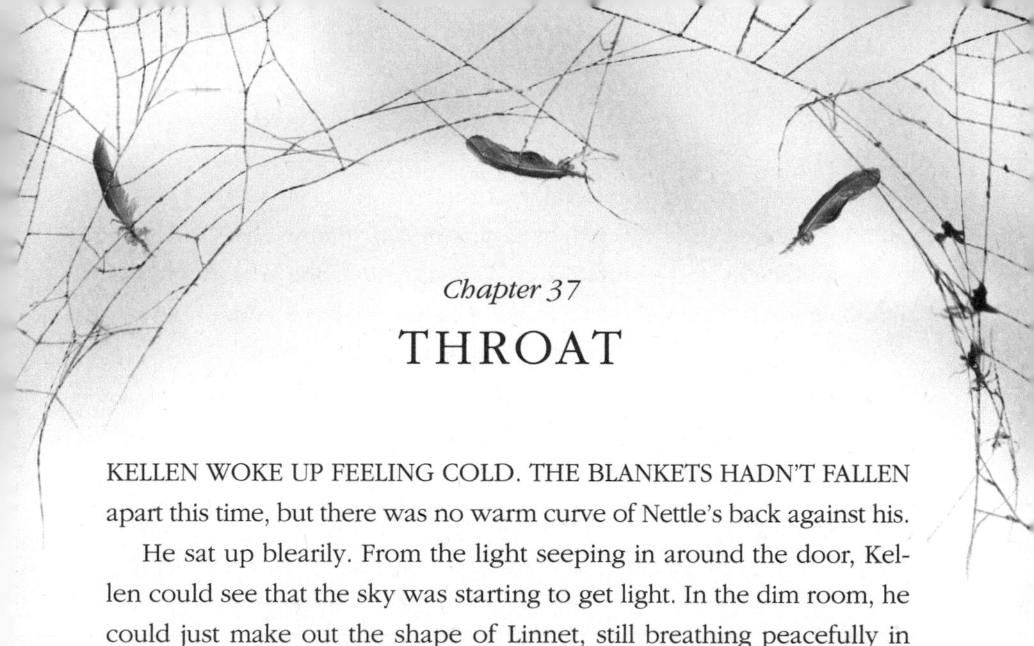

Chapter 37
THROAT

KELLEN WOKE UP FEELING COLD. THE BLANKETS HADN'T FALLEN apart this time, but there was no warm curve of Nettle's back against his.

He sat up blearily. From the light seeping in around the door, Kellen could see that the sky was starting to get light. In the dim room, he could just make out the shape of Linnet, still breathing peacefully in her bed. Loose fragments of stone littered the bedclothes around her.

There was no sign of Nettle. With a sinking of the spirits, Kellen remembered their argument.

She'll be sleeping in the workshop, he told himself. *We'll talk everything through once it's morning. We were just tired and strung out; that's why we ended up yelling. It'll be all right.* His mind would not lie quiet, however, so he tiptoed groggily to the door to look for Nettle.

He searched in vain. The poker-faced puzzle that always followed him like his shadow was nowhere to be found.

Kellen was sitting on the wharf, staring at the place where the pearl-pale boat had been moored, when Gall and his horse arrived. One moment Kellen was alone, the next he looked up and saw horse and rider looming over him. Dank weed trailed in the horse's mane and across the shoulders of its rider. It didn't look as though Gall had shaved.

"You weren't at the storage tower," Gall said, in a flat tone that somehow implied an accusation. "We only found you because we could smell your blood in the water."

The thought made Kellen feel a bit sick and even less keen on leech bites, but he was even more upset to learn that Nettle hadn't returned to the tower.

"Nettle's gone," he said.

"Gone?"

Kellen gave an angry, miserable shrug.

"She's jumped ship!" he said, bitterly. "She's abandoned us." The reality was sinking in, and it hurt. "We had an argument. She kept saying we should all give up and go back and tell Chancery what we'd found out." He flung a stone into the water. "She must be heading back inland."

Kellen gave a bare-bones account of the quarrel, and of course it was impossible to do this without mentioning his conversation with Linnet.

"This woman told you where she met her contact from Salvation?" Gall leaned forward in the saddle. "Tell me!" Seeing his ominous intentness, Kellen couldn't help remembering Nettle's warning that Gall was changing and going feral.

"We're just going to spy on Salvation, aren't we?" Kellen blurted out.

"It's best if I go alone," Gall replied. "I'll tell you what I find when I get back."

"Oh no you don't!" declared Kellen. "I'll give you the directions, but only as we go, so don't get any ideas about leaving me behind! There's room for two on that horse of yours, isn't there?"

If I'm there, I can stop Gall doing anything drastic, Kellen told himself. He hoped it was true.

Gall seemed to wrestle with this for a few seconds, then sighed.

"It's not safe to leave you here," he conceded. "By morning, the whole village will know that you lifted that woman's curse. If Salvation have spies here, they'll work out who you are. My horse won't let you on her back. But I'm sure that woman you saved can lend you a boat."

When Kellen woke Linnet, she agreed to lend her boat with a readiness that made Kellen feel guilty.

"I can't use it yet anyway," she pointed out, glancing at her stone-cased arms and legs.

Dawn was still only a pale thought in the sky when Kellen paddled after the marsh horse and rider through the mist-filled village. Here and there Kellen glimpsed the gray outlines of tree houses, their rope ladders pulled up, their boats moored and empty.

Kellen took a channel leading north, as Linnet had instructed. She had told him which marks to look for on the waymark poles and which turnings to take. Beside him glided the marsh horse, occasionally turning its long head at sounds he could not hear, to stare at things he could not see.

When the dawn came, Gall's clothes steamed their way to dryness, making him look as though he were on fire. The mud retreated too, flaking and peeling away from the clotted marsh silk. The wet weeds in the horse's mane crisped, browned, and fell away.

Now that he saw Gall by daylight, it was easier for Kellen to notice other changes. The marsh horseman's hair seemed to have grown an inch over the last two nights. His fingernails were moss-stained and appeared to be longer and more pointed than before.

"Gall," said Kellen after a while, wanting to hear a living voice. "Did you come this way when you were scouting?"

"I think so," said Gall, sounding less certain than Kellen expected.

"Did you get lost?"

Gall's brow puckered, and he hesitated, as if the question required serious thought.

"Not exactly," he said, sounding a little embarrassed. "We . . . ventured too far seaward and took a while finding our way back."

"Seaward?" Kellen was baffled.

"Yes." Gall's frown deepened. "We kept wanting to go seaward." He shook himself almost imperceptibly. "It's fine, as long as I pay attention."

Kellen shifted uneasily. Something had been drawing Gall and his horse seaward, deeper into the Wilds. How long had this been going on? By the sounds of it, the strange force was calling them still.

It was brilliant midmorning when they glimpsed a small, shimmering patch of open water ahead. From it rose a wide, dead tree, its bark shaggy with gray and yellow moss, its tortured branches overrun with white-flowered creepers. The tree had a great cleft down the middle, almost to the waterline. Some human or inhuman hand had filled the gap with rocks, stacking and mortaring them to form a strange wall.

"Linnet said she met her customers at a dead tree with a wall inside it," Kellen whispered. "That must be it."

"Why would anyone build . . ." Gall halted himself. "No point asking such questions in the Wilds."

Kellen *did* have a theory, though. Seeing the way the great tree's branches curved inward to form an arch above it, he had a hunch that this was the other end of Belthea's mysterious arch. Perhaps Salvation had bricked it up rather than risk murderous bog-witches coming through to kill more of their men.

"I don't see anyone there now," Gall said quietly.

"No, but Linnet says her customers sometimes leave her notes between the stones of the wall," explained Kellen.

"Notes?" Gall's eyes narrowed. "That might give my horse a scent to follow."

They paddled closer, ripples skimming silkily ahead of them. Despite the brilliant daylight, there was a heavy, unnerving atmosphere that reminded Kellen of the other Throat they had encountered in the Wilds. Sunbeams were heavy on his lashes, like gold coins.

When they were yards from the tree, a little warning voice started clamoring at the back of Kellen's head.

"Hang on," he said suddenly, as he glimpsed something quivering in the depths. He leaned over the side of the boat and reached down into the water. His fingers brushed against threads rough as horse-hair . . .

. . . a moment before the net lifted beneath boat, boy, horse, and man.

The marsh horse gave a deafening hiss as it found its hooves flailing in the mesh. It lunged and lashed, one great hoof nearly tipping over Kellen's boat.

There were shouts now on all sides, as brown-clad men and women rose from their hiding places among the reeds and behind the tree. It was they who had raised the net, and now they hauled on ropes to tighten it around the struggling marsh horse and rider. Gall was trying to pull out his knife, hampered by the panicked flailing of his beast. As Kellen watched, it rolled in the water, only succeeding in submerging its rider and tangling itself further.

"Kellen!" Gall's face appeared above water briefly. "Get out of here!"

Dive into the water! Kellen's instincts told him. *Swim for the reeds and hide in them!*

Before he could move, though, he heard a dull, velvety thud. Gall snarled silently, a slender shaft of wood sticking out of his chest. The horse gave a scream like rending steel. Only then did Kellen notice that some of the attackers held bows, all of them trained on Gall.

Every thought of running away dropped out of Kellen's head.

He reached over the side and grabbed the net in both hands. *Come on!* he shouted silently to his spider-bite and his curse. *Be a gift, just this once!* He gave a less than valiant croaking cry as he let his rage and anguish flow out through his gloveless hands.

Nothing happened. Nothing . . .

And then the thick cord in Kellen's grip bristled and lashed like an angry boa. He held on and saw some of the brown-clad figures tugged off balance as the ropes in their hands went feral. The rope bristled as its fine strands burst free. The knots of the net loosened.

The horse's screams were deeper and hungrier now, with a predatory, growling undercurrent. It surfaced and shrugged off the quivering, disintegrating strands of rope, its nostrils flared. The human screams became shriller and more panicky.

Gall slid off the back of his horse as it rose up and reared, gleaming and dripping. Then it gaped its terrible, thousand-toothed mouth and lunged.

Kellen sat frozen in his boat, unable to stop watching. Everything seemed to happen very quickly and very slowly. He saw every glistening droplet flung by the horse's mane as it twisted in the air. He saw a body topple, suddenly headless. He saw the white flowers of the creeper now spotted with scarlet. He saw the ambush party try to escape, saw some of them dragged back screaming. He saw dark red spread in the water under the heartless, innocent blue sky.

"Gall!" He paddled over to the marsh horseman, who was flailing in the water, face contorted with pain. As Kellen had guessed, the shaft in his chest was an arrow.

Another arrow skimmed over Kellen's head and hit the tree trunk.

"Careful!" called someone. "Don't hit the boy!"

Gall grabbed his horse's harness with one hand and seized Kellen's collar fiercely with the other.

"Hold your breath," he said through his teeth.

Kellen had only time to take half a breath before the marsh horse surged away and plunged beneath the surface, its trailing rein dragging Gall after it. Kellen was yanked out of his boat by Gall's grip on his collar and into the marsh.

Cold water covered his face and went up his nose. His vision filled with yellow-green, swirling mud and murky stems. He clenched his eyes shut, feeling plants whiplash his face and arms as he was dragged on and down, on and down, half-choked by the grip on his collar.

They drown you and eat you, he remembered. *That's what marsh horses do*. His lungs turned to poison, and he knew that soon he would breathe marsh water, then breathe nothing at all evermore. He struggled against Gall's hand on his collar, digging his nails into the knuckles, but it had a grip like iron.

Unexpectedly, he lurched upward and his face broke the surface for a second, long enough for a coughed mouthful of flotsam and a hastily taken breath. Then the horse plunged again, pulling Gall and Kellen with it.

For what seemed an age, Kellen was hauled in the wake of the horse through the dim-bright, cloud-jewel, watery world, submerged too long between each breath, yet still just about breathing.

At last he felt air on his face, and gasped and gasped, as he was dragged painfully over something that prickled and jabbed. Gall's grip on his collar slackened, then released him, and at last Kellen could breathe properly. He coughed and retched, throwing up marsh water and spitting out leaves. Then he found the strength to look up.

He was lying on a shore of bones. No, it was driftwood, twisted and bleached weirdly white. It was heaped across a little island that rose up from the marsh, a few tall trees at its center. Their black tresses wept willowlike into the water, where more driftwood swayed and rolled.

In the shadow of the nearest tree stood the marsh horse. Nobody could mistake it for a real animal now. Its black shape was all wrong, a nightmare mockery of a horse, full of scimitar-curves, waterfall twists, torrent muscle. Nostrils wide, long teeth slightly bared, it sniffed at its motionless rider and the arrow sticking out of his chest.

"Gall?" Kellen's throat was rough from marsh water. "Are you all right?" He scrambled toward the marsh horseman but then froze as the marsh horse lifted its head and tensed. He felt its gaze fix on him and burn. "Gall!" he called urgently. "Tell your horse I'm a friend!"

For a few moments, there was no response. Then Gall swallowed with obvious effort and opened his one eye. The horse nuzzled his hand and relaxed enough to let Kellen draw close.

"What do I do?" Kellen stared down at the arrow. It was sticking into the left side of Gall's chest. *Isn't that where his heart is? Or doesn't he have one?* "Do I pull it out, or . . . or break the shaft?" He knew soldiers did that sometimes.

"Don't touch it," said Gall, very faintly. "It's rowan. If I get rowan splinters in my blood . . ." He didn't need to finish the sentence.

"Can we strap you to the back of the horse?" asked Kellen, clutching at straws. "We need to get you back to the village. Someone there might be able to help!"

Gall was already shaking his head.

"The village is no good. Salvation knew we were coming. The net, the rowan arrows—they were ready for *us*. They must know that we were at the village. They'll look for us there next."

Kellen sat back on his heels, thunderstruck.

"Nettle!" he exclaimed. "What if they followed her from the village? What if they catch her?"

"They won't need to," said Gall. "She went looking for them. It's obvious now."

"What are you talking about?" Once again, Kellen could feel the ground shifting under his feet. There was no solid earth anymore, only marsh.

"She crept off to join her own kind," said the marsh horseman. "Don't you understand yet? Don't you know what she is? She's run off to join Salvation."

Chapter 38

SEAWARD

"DON'T BE STUPID!" KELLEN'S BREATH ROARED IN HIS EARS. HE was drenched, nauseous, and in no mood for jokes.

"Nettle's a curser," said Gall, "or she will be soon. I wasn't sure, but I am now."

"No." Kellen's mouth turned dry. "She's not! Of course she's not!"

"I didn't guess at first," said Gall. Speaking seemed to cost him some effort. "She's clever. She's careful. But the rage showed through now and then. And haven't you noticed—sometimes she stares like she's seeing something we can't?"

Yes, yes, of course Kellen had noticed Nettle being jumpy, glaring at nothing, or twitching at sounds he hadn't heard. But that was just how she was! Always maddeningly cautious and watchful, with a hawk-eye for the problems and dangers Kellen wouldn't see coming. It was Nettle being Nettle!

Wasn't it?

"I think the Dancing Star knew," Gall continued. "It looked into her soul and saw something like itself. Didn't you ever wonder why it liked her? And did you know she was talking to it secretly outside the tower the night before last?"

"That's . . ." Kellen didn't even know what he wanted to say. "This is stupid! She hates cursers! She's been fighting Salvation with us, every step! We'd never have got here without her!"

Gall furrowed his brow and seemed to think about this.

"Yes," he said. "Maybe she wasn't Salvation's agent at the start. I don't know when she turned to their side. But she must have done."

"Nettle wouldn't betray us!" yelled Kellen.

"Then who did?" demanded Gall, his one eye fierce. "Who else knew where we were going? Only Linnet, and she couldn't have warned anybody even if she'd wanted to. She was covered in stone, and you were sleeping in her room. Nettle follows you everywhere. But all of a sudden she sneaks off into the night, and the next morning Salvation are ready for us."

"No!" yelled Kellen. "Nettle has funny patches! She has ups and downs! That's all!"

"Or she has cursed again and again," Gall continued relentlessly. "Somebody cursed *you*. Maybe it wasn't Jendy Pin."

"Shut up!"

Kellen realized that he was shaking, his ungloved fingers hooked and twitching. He shuffled hastily away from Gall on his knees, worrying that a chance touch might set the horseman unravelling.

Gall closed his one eye and said nothing for a few moments—just long enough for Kellen to worry that he had passed out or died.

"Listen," said the marsh horseman at last. "We need to get you somewhere safe while I'm still alive, and then you need to get away from the horse as fast as you can. Once I'm dead, it won't be pact-bound, and you'll be food."

"Hey!" snapped Kellen, his anger and alarm finding a new direction. "I'm not following a plan where you die!"

Gall made the small grimace that was his approximation of a smile.

"Those plans are the only sort we have left," he said.

Kellen got up and stamped around, wondering why he felt so upset. He hadn't ever liked the marsh horseman, had he? But at some point, Gall had stopped being the enemy. He had thrown himself between Kellen and hostile swords often enough to become a comrade. And somehow, over time, Kellen had become a little better at decoding Gall—his stubbornly morose reserve, his uncontrolled temper, his glimmers of dark humor. It was too late to think of him as just a monster.

"Oh, shut up!" snapped Kellen, hearing his voice become squeaky and hoarse. "Those aren't the only plans! I can . . . pull your arrow out!

Maybe you'll start healing once you don't have rowan sticking in your chest. Or maybe you'll die and your horse will eat me—but at least we'll have tried!"

"That's a really terrible idea," said Gall, but Kellen thought he saw a flicker of exhausted amusement.

"Then we'll look for help together!" shouted Kellen. "We'll head inland and find a village, or a homestead, or something. We'll get somebody to treat you. I'm not leaving you behind, and you can't make me!"

There was a pause, then the marsh horseman made a noise that was halfway between a sigh and a snarl.

"I'll need help getting back on my horse," he said.

Even with the horse lying flat on its belly, it took time and effort to get Gall back astride his steed. On Gall's instructions, Kellen used rope to bind him into place, tying his feet into the stirrups and the reins around his hands.

The marsh horse bared its teeth when Kellen tried to mount as well. In the end, Gall smeared some of his own blood onto Kellen's forehead, and this finally persuaded it to let him sit on its back. Kellen sat behind Gall, so he wouldn't jog the arrow shaft.

"When you were unconscious, I even thought it might eat you," Kellen admitted.

"If I died," Gall said affectionately, "she would mourn, perhaps for centuries. But . . . she probably would eat me, yes."

The horse edged carefully down the driftwood shore, its hooves splaying so that their webbing showed. To Kellen's relief, when the horse took to the water, it sank only to the fetlocks and began a slow, splashing walk that accelerated into a trot. The motion was surprisingly smooth, like the rolling of a boat or the rocking of a cradle.

The horse's feet pounded spray that chilled Kellen's face and fractured into rainbows as the sun caught it. The trot became a canter, then a gallop. Trees raced past like pack predators. Kellen hung on to Gall's back, gripping handfuls of the marsh-silk coat.

Gall's wrong about Nettle, thought Kellen. But it was no good. The marsh horseman's words laid siege to his mind.

For a while, Kellen had sensed a secret shadow over Nettle. He had told himself that her dips of mood were just her nature. Nettle, always tense, always wound tight as a clock spring. Nettle, who flinched and receded into somewhere dark inside herself whenever cursers were mentioned. Because she hated them so much. That was it, wasn't it?

She can't be a curser! he thought suddenly. *The other Rescued would know. They'd sense it!*

His spirits rose at the thought, then plummeted just as quickly. Would they notice? Cursers carried a scent of the Wilds, but so did those who had recovered from a curse. Even if Nettle's soul smelled of the Wilds, the other Rescued wouldn't have suspected a thing.

Other memories crowded into his head. Nettle hearing of Salvation for the first time and sinking into a chair, white-faced with emotion. Nettle asking Kellen why he trusted Leona, telling him that perhaps the Assessor was lying about Salvation, perhaps there were other sides to the story . . .

Then Nettle in their last argument, talking in a strangled little voice and refusing to look at him. Almost begging him not to go in search of Salvation. Trying to convince him that it wasn't too late to strike a deal with Ammet. Worrying about the cursers that Gall might kill . . .

You know what cursers are like as well as I do! he had yelled back at her. *Better than I do!*

And she had winced as though her soul were wounded.

Overhead, the sun made a heroic but ill-advised charge against a black army of clouds. Its enemies overwhelmed it, and the brilliant morning sunshine went out, leaving the marshes in a dour false twilight.

The trees that flashed past were denser and stranger now, with wild roots rising out of the water like the scribbles of giant children. Kellen saw a dead seal draped over a branch, crows pecking at its face. He quailed at the thought of the wave or storm that could have thrown the poor animal that high.

Wait. A wave? A seal?

"Where are we?" he called out suddenly.

There was no reply. Kellen felt a prickle of anxiety run up his spine.

"We're still riding toward the sun!" he shouted. He'd been too miserable and distracted to notice before. "This isn't the way back inland! Where are we going?"

Still no response. Gall did not turn his head or react at all.

Is he still conscious? Kellen wondered in panic. *Is he still alive?* Gall was tied onto the horse, he remembered. Was Kellen clinging on to a dead man, on the back of a marsh horse no longer tamed?

"Gall!" he screamed, and thumped the man's back. "Can't you hear me?"

But the marsh horseman said nothing, and the horse did not slow. Instead, it galloped ever faster below the darkening sky, following the instinct that led it seaward.

Kellen yelled himself hoarse. The wind stung his cheeks, and his clothes never dried, always soaked anew by spray. He became numb with cold, drugged by doubts and exhausted by strangeness, until he lost track of time.

When Kellen came to himself, true twilight had descended. The marsh horse's gallop had slowed to a trot. The water had a sea-like swell, gently rising and falling between the tall, cobweb-laden trees with a slow, sighing *hush* and *haa*.

The horse slowed to a walk, then halted. It drew in its breath in a long, un-horselike sniff, and then twitched its head. Kellen was surprised to feel it trembling slightly.

"What is it?" he whispered, then felt stupid. Was he expecting the horse to reply? "Gall?" he croaked, his voice sounding very small in the gray-white, sea-voiced hush. The marsh horseman did not respond.

Leaning sideways to peer past Gall, Kellen tried to work out what was frightening the horse.

Before him, the gray-silver water heaved as if breathing. Beyond the dark stripes of tree trunks, Kellen glimpsed something huge, shapeless, and white . . .

At first glance, his numb, exhausted mind told him it was a castle. A shambolic mound of a castle, fifty feet tall, all its angles crumbled to softness.

Then he blinked and saw that it was no castle of bricks and mortar. It was an ungainly, improbable heap of flotsam and fragments, timbers and trees, leavings and lost things, all muffled and disguised by a hundred layers of snow-white spider-silk. The dark openings he had taken for windows were just shadowy holes in the cobweb. The crenellations were the ribs of a broken boat, shrouded in white web. The pennants and flags were just trailing lengths of loose, gauzy gossamer, swaying in the breeze. The whole ghostly island drifted and shifted with the swell of the water, rising and falling.

Yet Kellen's heart still banged at the sight of it, and the horse beneath him quivered and would not go on. The white, all-smothering cobweb seemed to have a muted, pearly glow, like the moon through fog.

In his gut, Kellen knew that he had been right the first time. It *was* a castle.

There were stories of castles unexpectedly discovered in the Deep Wilds, and few of these ended well. Where else could they go for help, though?

"Look, you brought us here!" Kellen told the horse through chattering teeth, hoping it could understand. "I don't like it much either, but what else can we do? Your master's dying!"

After a pause and another couple of head twitches, the marsh horse began walking slowly toward the web-castle. As they approached, the ghostly island occasionally seemed to glitter. Kellen realized that the whole edifice was seething with motion.

Small gray bodies, eyelash-fine legs, and tiny eyes glittering like crushed glass. Scuttling along crevices, skimming across wide, white expanses of web. Like spiders, but not spiders.

Little Brothers.

Around the edges of the great mound floated a loose skirt of oddments, bound together with white web so that they seemed snow-touched. The marsh horse stepped nervously out of the water onto this raft of fragments, which dipped and bobbed under its feet. With each step, sticky strands clung to its hooves.

Set in the side of the huge, white castle-mound was a door. Its dark red paint was ravaged and bleached, but it was surprisingly clear of web, its brass doorknob glossy like an invitation.

Aching with stiffness and cold, Kellen slithered down from the horse and nearly fell sprawling. Looking up at Gall, he could see that the tall man's one eye was closed and his face bluish-pale. The arrow still stuck out of his chest, the fletching now damp with spray. He still seemed to be breathing, however.

"I'll get help!" Kellen whispered. Weak with cold, he stumbled over to the door, feeling sticky webs sucking at his feet. He placed his hand on the doorknob and paused.

"Knock, knock, Little Brothers," he called out, as the stories had taught him. "Be kind to a fellow weaver."

Then Kellen took a deep breath and opened the door to the web-castle.

Chapter 39

CASTLE OF SILK

BEYOND THE DOOR, THE LIGHT WAS DIM. THE PALE, WEB-smothered floor was uneven and treacherous underfoot and clung stickily to Kellen's boots. His view ahead was obscured by dozens of great, hanging curtains of web, beyond which he could see only shadow. High above him, faint white and blue lights glimmered and winked.

"Hello?" he called out. "We need help! There's a wounded man outside!"

Little bumps raced beneath the surface of the floor, the fine threads rising and falling. Against the shadowed whiteness of the hanging web draperies, he could see motes of gray-dark scuttle-freeze, scuttle-freeze.

"I know you can hear me!" he yelled, too tired, cold, and battered to play games.

A stealthy draft from the doorway behind him set the webs trembling, like pale ghosts quivering with laughter or terror. One gossamer veil billowed and enveloped Kellen's face. Reflexively, he clawed it off, and then stared in shock as the mess of white web on his fingers frizzled and came apart. With sudden misgivings, he looked up at the great web his hand had brushed. It was quivering like a thing in pain and rapidly dwindling, its sticky threads unknitting.

"Wait!" He snatched at it stupidly, helplessly. "I didn't mean . . ."

Kellen's gesture brushed another veil, which also began to unravel. A messy, gray clot of it fell down next to his feet. Where it landed, the web of the floor also began to flinch and come away. As the fine white threads released their hold, Kellen felt the floor beneath his feet loosen and shift dangerously.

Perhaps the whole castle was held together by the webs. If it unravelled completely, would all the flotsam collapse into the water, taking Kellen with it?

There was the faintest of silken sounds from all around him, and the Little Brothers seethed from the shadows.

Kellen felt them run up the backs of his legs and into his clothes. Tiny feet tickled against the skin of his back, his neck, his hands, his scalp. A fine gauze of threads settled hazily across his view like a veil.

"It was an accident!" he shouted, tearing the strands from his face. "I'm a friend! I'm a weaver!"

But I'm not, he thought suddenly, with a cold shock of revelation. *Not anymore. I'm an unweaver. I'm the Unraveller. The Little Brothers make curses, and I unmake them. They're not my friends, they're my opposite.*

Kellen tried to take a step back and tumbled backward, hundreds of fine strands binding his legs together. He yelled and raked away fistfuls of threads from his chest until the countless flying strands pinned his arms to his torso.

Lying on the floor, he saw at last why it was so uneven. Under the shrouding web he could make out the hilt of a cutlass, the frame of a tambourine, a boot from which protruded a web-muffled skeletal leg . . .

He had blundered into a place not meant for humans, one that uninvited guests never left.

There were Little Brothers on his neck, his forehead. Fine strands settled on his face, gluing his eyelids shut and falling into his mouth, making him spit and gag. Soon he could do no more than wriggle in his new cocoon and give muffled screams in his throat. He could still feel the motion of tiny creatures against his skin. Every breath was harder than the last.

Perhaps he would rot in the floor of the web-castle, his skeleton a warning to other intruders.

When Kellen came round, he was retching and spitting out wads of dusty-tasting web. His eyelids wouldn't open, but at least there was a blessed feeling of air against his face.

“He can’t tell you anything if he can’t breathe!” someone was muttering.

Something damp dabbed at Kellen’s eyes, and eventually he was able to open them. He still seemed to be lying on the floor of the web-filled chamber, but now a man with a gaunt, worried-looking face was leaning over him. The stranger’s long hair was matted with cob-web. His expressive mouth twitched with concentration as he cleaned Kellen’s face with a wet cloth.

“Who are you?” demanded Kellen.

“Call me Cook.” The stranger cast a fearful glance over his shoulder, before leaning close to whisper. “You really shouldn’t have attacked the castle like that!”

“You have to help me!” spluttered Kellen. “The marsh horseman outside—he’s hurt! A rowan arrow! That’s why I’m here!”

“No, it isn’t,” Cook said promptly. “You’re here because the Little Brothers summoned you. They called on that marsh horse and its rider to bring you here, so you could explain yourself!”

“Explain? Explain what?”

“You have something that doesn’t belong to you!” Cook whispered urgently. “The power of unweaving! The loosing of thread from thread. It isn’t yours. It’s theirs. Where did you get it?”

“I’m not answering anything,” Kellen said through clenched teeth, “unless you help my friend!”

The breeze fluttered the gray-white swathes of gossamer. There were sounds faint as breath from all sides, soft as the sweep of a silk sleeve.

Brow furrowed, Cook twitched his head, looking this way and that as though hearing a multitude of voices. As he did so, Kellen glimpsed the man’s ears beneath his long hair. They were large, snow-white, and looked as though they had been fashioned from stiff linen. They swiveled slightly as he listened.

“Oh, now you’ve put them in a *very* bad mood,” the man mur-mured, standing up.

“Where are you going?” gasped Kellen.

"They want me to look at the arrow for them," the stranger whispered. "I'm not useful for much, but at least rowan doesn't bother me."

It was only when Cook had gone that Kellen understood the significance of these words. His strange new acquaintance was human.

Half an hour later, the stranger returned, rubbing his hands with cautious satisfaction.

"It's lucky that I'm such a good cook," he said, without preamble. "I can fillet any fish you name without leaving a single bone. I can paint an egg yolk without breaking it. You need a steady hand to take an arrow out of a man."

"Is he alive?" asked Kellen.

"For now." Cook grimaced ruefully. "The Little Brothers have staunched his wound, and his pact with the horse will hold off death for a while. But he will need a replacement heart. Do you have one?" He looked hopefully at Kellen, as if he might have a spare heart in his pocket.

"No." Kellen's blood ran cold. "No, just the one I'm using, and I need that. Where do we get one?"

"There are many things at the markets—" Cook began, then flinched and made little fluttering gestures with his hands. "Yes, yes!" he hissed, sounding harassed and alarmed. "I was coming back to that!" He looked at Kellen again, with a hint of entreaty in his eyes. "You *will* tell us why you have the power of unravelling, won't you?"

Kellen tried to quell his terror. How could he admit to a thousand Little Brothers that he had caused the death of one of their kind? He was too cold and miserable to lie, however. He was tired of secrets, including his own.

He told them the truth. He told them of the chance-met Little Brother who had unravelled calico with him. He told of the iron shackle, the bite, and the sad, dry debris that had fallen out of his sleeve.

From all sides came a low, dry, purring sound, like a hundred fingernails raking against the grain of velvet. The noise tingled in Kellen's ear and made his skin crawl.

"What are they saying?" he whispered, tensed for another attack.

"They're mourning," murmured Cook, his face twisted with sympathetic anguish. "That was one of their eldest, their wisest . . ."

"Are they angry?" asked Kellen, trying not to panic.

"No," said Cook, "but this . . . complicates things." As the purring yielded to barely audible sighs and rasps, Cook glanced this way and that, as if keeping pace with a conversation. "They were in favor of eating your hands to recover your gift, but now that they know that their elder passed its mission on to you—"

"Eating my hands?" erupted Kellen, before registering the rest of the sentence. "Mission? What mission?"

Cook looked furtive.

"You have to understand," he whispered, "that the Little Brothers have always meant well. The curse eggs . . . they're meant as gifts. A way for the powerless to hold their persecutors to account. So they find those who are filled with anger, pain, and a deep sense of grievance, and they give them the weapon they need to strike back. But four years ago, a poor cursed soul washed up on their doorstep in a little boat." He gave a wincing smile. "Me."

"You're cursed?" Kellen began, then felt stupid. "Oh. Your ears."

"Oh, no!" Cook tittered nervously. "No, no, the ears were a gift from the Little Brothers so that I could understand them! Specially woven with their own silk! No, my curse is that, during the darkest instant of each new moon, every human being within a mile dies."

Kellen gave a panicky yelp.

"Oh, don't worry!" Cook added hastily. "That won't happen for two weeks! Anyway, I'd fled into the Deep Wilds, hoping to find somewhere lonely enough that I wouldn't hurt anyone. When I told the Little Brothers my history they were . . . concerned. You see, my curse wasn't *fair*. My half-brother cursed me because he resented his father for marrying again and hated me for being born. My hosts started to realize that just because somebody *feels* wronged, that doesn't mean they are. So they woke up one of the oldest Little Brothers—one of the few with the power of unweaving—to ask its advice. It went out into the world of men to see for itself whether curses were being misused." Cook sighed. "But it sounds like it just couldn't resist joining in on the weavers' side when it saw them in a conflict!"

"But it didn't give me any mission!" Kellen said miserably. "It just bit me!"

"The fastest way to transfer its power," said Cook. "It must have decided it could trust you with it."

Kellen was too overwhelmed to answer. For years, the memory of that night had bruised him with guilt and regret. But perhaps the Little Brother hadn't seen him as a cruel betrayer after all. Perhaps it knew how hard he'd tried to save it and had viewed him as a friend to the end. He felt as though he had pulled a long barb out of his flesh and only then realized how deep it had been embedded.

It took the Little Brothers an hour to reach a decision, during which time Kellen peeled away his web cocoon and risked sitting up.

"Good news!" Cook said at last, giving Kellen a slightly panicky smile. "They're going to let you keep the gift of unweaving! But they . . . they don't feel you're the right *shape* for that power. If they take off your limbs, and weave you eight *better* ones . . ."

"I don't want to be a spider!" exclaimed Kellen. He looked down at his gloveless hands, and for a panicky moment he considered trying to unravel the castle after all.

No. Stay calm. If you attack now, you lose your only chance to talk to them.

"Listen!" he shouted. "I'm sorry about your friend. To be honest, I didn't know about his mission until today. But I've been carrying it out all the same, using the power he gave me. I've been finding unjust curses and unravelling them. And it's kept me busy, because *most* curses are unfair. Hatred is blind. Did you really only start to work that out four years ago?"

He could hear feather-soft seething in all directions. Perhaps the Little Brothers were annoyed now, but so was Kellen. His anger was rising, giving force to his words.

"Ever heard of Salvation? The criminal gang collecting cursers and using them as weapons? No? Didn't think so! That's because you're a swarm of stupid spiders living out in the swamp! You don't know anything!"

Calm. Calm! Kellen clenched his teeth and struggled to control his temper. Had it always been so unruly?

"You don't need a new Little Brother," he said. "You need a human to tell you what you've missed, because you've missed a lot. I can understand other humans, and you obviously can't. And right now, I need to be out there stopping Salvation! If you release me and help me save the marsh horseman, I'll show you what I can do." Kellen took a deep breath. "I'll stop Salvation."

The silence prickled all around him, and Kellen could not tell if it was the quiet of interest or animosity.

"If you succeed," said Cook, evidently translating, "they will accept you in your current shape. But if you fail . . ."

"Then I promise I'll come back here." Kellen swallowed. "I'll let the Little Brothers turn me into a man-spider."

"Are you *sure* you want to go to the Moonlit Market?" Cook asked for the third time.

"I need to find a heart soon, don't I?" said Kellen, with more bravado than he felt. "Or Gall will die." He looked down from the castle entrance at the solitary raft that bobbed next to the undulating plain of flotsam. Its single lantern cast a quivering blue light.

"Then you'd better wear this." Cook took off his own white marsh-silk jacket and handed it to Kellen. "You'll be safer at the Market if people think you're the Little Brothers' property."

Kellen accepted it reluctantly.

"So . . . I head seaward?" he asked. "How far is it?"

"Oh," said Cook with a tremble of fear in his voice, "you'll be there before you know it. So please keep your wits about you. Remember, don't eat or drink anything—"

"I know that!" Kellen interrupted scornfully.

"It will be hard to say no sometimes," Cook continued without any sign of offense. "Some creatures have tongues scaled in silver, whose every word chimes with sweetness. Whatever happens, if somebody asks you for something, don't give it to them. Even if you think it's worthless. *Especially* if you think it's worthless."

The Cook's tone of subdued panic started to infect Kellen too. The Moonlit Market was the stuff of whispered legend. That was where the People of the White Boats came to buy and sell treasures and treacheries, souls and seasons, lives and lands, dreams and destinies. Kellen shivered despite himself.

"Look for the Trappers," Cook went on. "A cluster of black boats laden with skulls, hides, and cages. They might have a heart your friend can use. They're not safe or kindly, mind. They'll trap and sell you too if you give them an excuse. But there's a lady in a boat with snakeskin sails who's a shade more honest than the rest."

"Thanks," muttered Kellen, then hesitated. There was one more question gnawing at his mind.

"Listen," he said, "can you ask the Little Brothers if . . ." He trailed off, then tried again. "My friend Nettle—she's about this tall, doesn't smile much, used to be a heron. Do any of them remember . . . I mean, did any of them ever give her a curse egg?"

There was an excruciatingly long pause, and Kellen wondered how his question was being passed along through the Little Brother colony. At last a single Little Brother descended on a thread onto Cook's shoulder. Cook's white ears twitched.

"This Little Brother *does* remember this Nettle. He says he is proud of the egg he gifted to her. A fine one—the finest he ever produced."

Kellen felt numb and empty. There it was. Gall had been right.

Nettle was a curser. A member of the enemy army. A whirlwind of hatred had walked quietly by Kellen's side, behind the mask of a friend . . .

The confusion made everything hurt more. He felt the betrayal would somehow be more bearable if he could only understand it.

"As a matter of fact," the Cook went on, "he's a bit offended. He wants to know why she hasn't used it. Doesn't she like it? What's wrong with it?"

Kellen blinked at the moon for a few seconds.

"What?" he said.

"Well, it's been over a year," said the Cook. "So he's quite upset. Doesn't she like his present?"

"A *year*?" Kellen's brain was full of moonlight and confusion. He'd never, ever heard of anyone housing a curse egg for more than a few weeks without cursing. "He's sure it's the same egg?"

"Oh, yes, yes, she's only ever had the one."

A year. Dizzied, Kellen thought his way back through a year's worth of Nettle's strange periods of quiet, her dark moods, her retreats into her shell, her grim and intense privacy, her ferocious self-control.

He didn't know what to think or how to feel. None of his memories made sense anymore.

Nettle didn't curse me. That at least he understood. He clung to the thought like a drowner.

Gall had been right, but not completely right. Nettle was housing a curse egg, but she had never cursed anyone at all.

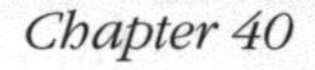

Chapter 40

THE TRAPPERS

You'll be there before you know it.

On a driftwood raft bound together with marsh silk, Kellen paddled for hours. There was nothing in any direction but the moon-glazed solitude of the water-filled woods. Black willows trailed their tresses in the water. Now and then, the *slip-slap* of a fish jump left a slowly spreading ripple.

As he struggled to keep his eyes open, his brain started to conjure new and stranger shapes.

A log bumped against the raft, and for a dreamy moment he imagined that it was a slim canoe of red wood. The white underwing of a passing bird seemed like a hand raised in greeting. A sudden wind stirred the trees to frenzy so that their leaves gleamed wild and white in the moonlight, and it seemed to him that on every bough hung lanterns that flickered with ice-pale light . . .

And then Kellen shook himself awake and found himself in the middle of the Market.

The little raft was surrounded by dozens of boats of different sizes, all strung with lanterns that blazed and guttered in the wind. He caught only glimpses of the figures aboard these vessels. Pond-dwelling eyes in a bleached face. A hand with long fingernails deftly counting coins of bone out of a bag of stitched skin. Shadowy shapes trimming feathered sails.

Kellen jumped as a garland of livid seaweed slapped down onto the raft next to him. An otter-faced girl grinned at him from the water, then spat fish-blood at him and dived down below the surface.

How long have I been here? he wondered, trying to keep his brain clear. *Have I made any mistakes already? Have I promised anything, or given anything away?* Nothing seemed to be missing from his pockets, but that didn't mean he was safe. *I hate the Wilds.*

In the distance, Kellen could see two great white boats with sails of shimmering white feathers and a jeweled bridge between them. There were figures walking on the bridge, as if on a rich man's balcony. Some held crystal goblets, though none seemed to have faces.

The White Boats. The heart of a hundred myths, the place where the greatest bargains were sealed and the biggest gambles taken . . .

Kellen's raft was suddenly jolted by a shunt from behind.

"Oh! I beg your pardon!" called a cheerful voice.

Looking back, Kellen was surprised to see a neat, pink-painted boat that would not have looked out of place in a sunny pleasure-lake. The two occupants were a man in clean striped linen and a woman in a frilly lace dress and bonnet. A picnic hamper sat between them.

Kellen opened his mouth to tell the pair not to worry but some instinct halted him. Instead, he smiled and gave the couple a friendly wave. The tiniest flicker of annoyance passed across the man's face.

I beg your pardon. Kellen had always thought of it as an apology, but it was actually a request. The man had asked for Kellen's pardon—his forgiveness—and Kellen had almost given it without thinking. What would have happened if he had? Would this man have taken his forgiveness away, leaving Kellen unable to forgive ever again?

"You're *new*, aren't you?" asked the man in the striped suit, leaning forward.

Kellen's unease sharpened. If you were in a dangerous place, admitting your own ignorance made you vulnerable. You were a feathered, clucking target in a wood full of foxes.

"Yes," murmured the lady beside him quietly, her open parasol shielding her face from the moonlight. "He *is* new. I don't believe there's a single little bone of him that's older than sixteen years. Except his *hands*. Something in them is very, very old."

"What's your *name*, fine sir?" asked the man, smiling a smile that stayed too wide even when he spoke. The lady's shadowy gaze still transfixed Kellen, and he was gripped by a fear that if he opened his mouth, the truth might leap out against his will.

The picnic hamper suddenly jerked and mewled. The couple gave it an annoyed look, and the man elbowed it hard. The distraction broke the spell, and Kellen took a deep breath.

"You've got good eyes," he told the lady. "But not good enough." He tapped the white marsh silk of his jacket. "Whatever you want, you'll have to take it up with the Little Brothers." It hurt his pride claiming protection like that, but he felt a wave of relief as the two strangers' expressions became disappointed and stony. Their boat receded swiftly backward into the darkness, without either of them making any pretense at rowing.

The shadowy figures on the other boats seemed to be paying Kellen no mind, but it was hard to be sure. Perhaps they could all smell a human in their midst, his warm emotions filling the air like the scent of baking bread.

At last he spotted a group of lean, black boats. The Trappers.

There's a lady in a boat with snakeskin sails who's a shade more honest than the rest, Cook had said.

One of the inky boats had sails that glittered as they billowed and rasped like an adder moving through undergrowth. Kellen paddled over and brought his raft alongside.

The boat was loaded down with cages. Most of them held luminous-eyed prankets, snarling and fluttering their insectile wings. The larger cages held other shadowy shapes, some hunched with their wings around them, others picking at their moss-covered fur.

The owner of the boat was a spindly woman with a red mask and a voice like ground glass. Her gloves had metal claws that she used to pick her teeth as she listened to Kellen's request.

"Hmm. A heart?" She tilted her head. "Tricky. I could sell you a human heart, freshly plucked, and sew it into your friend's chest, but it has to be the *right* heart if you want it to beat for him."

“Wait a minute!” Kellen didn’t like the sound of a *human heart, freshly plucked.*

“Does the patient have any children?” asked the woman. “If he has a child that loves him enough, their heart might do. When it is placed in his chest, it needs to feel that it is at home.”

“He doesn’t have children, and I don’t want to kill anybody!” protested Kellen.

“Really?” The woman seemed quite surprised. “Not even *one* child? If the man is young enough, surely he can make more?”

“Can’t you use an animal heart?” asked Kellen. “Or a magical one?”

“Oh, yes.” The woman smiled. “I could sell you a heart of chestnut wood, and your friend would never know hunger or grief. His toes would become roots, and he would feed on the sun and smile at the passing of the years. I could sell you the heart of a wolf, and he would never again be troubled by pity or remorse. Or the Little Brothers could weave him a new, white heart, and he would live in their castle and be thankful for their kindness. All those hearts would beat and keep him alive, but he would no longer be the man you know. Real hearts are nothing but trouble. They break and bleed and bring their owners torment. But without them, existence is hollow, only breath following breath.”

“But . . . isn’t there any way to give him a real heart without anybody dying?” asked Kellen.

The woman pondered for a moment, tapping her metal claw-tips to her cheek.

“Maybe,” she said after a moment. “One might do for both, but it would be dangerous. Do you know anyone with a small throat?”

“A what?” Kellen felt his eyebrows rise.

Before the woman could answer, Kellen heard a hoarse and deafening yell from one of the boats behind him.

“You!”

He flinched, but there was no reason to believe the cry had anything to do with him.

"You little scumrag!" The voice was almost incoherent with rage. "Hey! Don't ignore me, you weasel! Hey! KELLEN!"

Kellen froze. Names had power. You never gave yours away lightly in the Deep Wilds, and his had just been bellowed in the Moonlit Market. How many of those around him had heard it? A dozen nearby conversations had abruptly died.

He glanced over his shoulder. Behind him was a big black Trapper boat with a fox figurehead and square sails that glistened like oil. Like the others, it was loaded with traps, boxes, and cages. In one of the largest cages hunched a pallid, naked figure that looked mostly human apart from a hunched deformity in its shoulders. It had dark hair down to its shoulders and a silver collar around its neck.

"Look at me!" it yelled at him. "Are you happy?"

"You've made a mistake!" Kellen shouted back. "I don't know you!"

The stranger's face contorted with fury, and it threw back its head and screamed. The scream started out hoarsely human but then became the steely, deafening peal of a gull. The strangely hunched shoulders flared, gray-and-white wings thrashing and bruising their feathers against the bars of the cage.

"Yeah, you forget everyone soon enough, don't you?" shouted the youth in the cage. "*What have you done with Nettle?*"

Kellen stared at him, realizing who this angry youth must be.

"Yan—" Just in time, Kellen stopped himself from saying Yannick's name aloud. Hastily, he paddled the raft over to the side of the big black boat so that he was close enough to the big cage to talk more quietly. "What are you doing here? What happened to you?"

It was a shock seeing Yannick in mostly human form. Although Kellen had known that Yannick was sixteen, he'd grown used to thinking of him as Nettle's bratty little brother, sitting on her lap, making a fuss and begging food off her. He had never imagined this tall, gangly stranger, who had a sullen, Nettle-like slope to his eyebrows when he frowned.

"What *happened* to me?" To judge by Yannick's expression, this was also the wrong question. "I swear, Kellen—"

"Could you *please* stop giving everyone my name!" Kellen hissed through his teeth.

"Oh, did I give your name away?" said Yannick, opening his eyes mockingly wide. "That was careless of me! Oh, wait—you gave *me* away. Remember? 'Here you go, strange creatures from the Wilds, feel free to take everything in the broken carriage as a gift! It's not like there's anything important in there!' "

Kellen's jaw fell open. Little fragments of memory floated back into his head. Yes, he *had* told the Wilds folk that they could take everything inside the carriage. Perhaps the crash had happened while Yannick was in the carriage resting his wings and reporting to Nettle.

"Oh, hagfire," Kellen groaned. "Nettle's going to kill me."

"No, she isn't," said Yannick. "Because I'm going to kill you first, you useless, self-obsessed weasel."

Before Kellen could answer, he became aware that someone was leaning over the side of the boat not far away. He looked up and saw a man-shaped figure with dark red hair and a marsh-silk overcoat with a high collar. The stranger smiled widely, his teeth a little pointed, and Kellen thought of a chicken's neck gripped in a long muzzle.

"Interested in buying this one?" asked the red-haired man. "It's very special. When I bought it, it looked like a gull, but the binding collar shows its true nature. It's caught between two worlds, as you can see. Half ours, half theirs. Half-human, half-bird. You'll look a long time and never find anything so split-souled."

Kellen's mouth was dry. He wanted to turn on the stranger and demand that he set Yannick free at once. But this was the Moonlit Market. If he yelled about kidnapping and slavery, everyone would laugh. Everyone would notice the foolish, innocent human shouting in the market and would watch him with gazes like knives.

"How much are you asking?" he said instead.

"Make me an offer," said the red-haired man, flashing a grin.

Kellen ground his teeth. That was what traders said to wide-eyed, clueless idiots who had never left their village before. It made them panic, and guess, and give away how little they knew about what everything was worth.

What made Kellen most angry was the fact that the trapper was right. Kellen had no idea of the going rate for a cursed gull-boy. He pulled out the pouch of bone coins the Little Brothers had given him and furtively peered at them. Could he buy Yannick's freedom and still afford a heart for Gall?

"You'll need more than those coins," murmured the trader, echoing Kellen's thoughts. "I'm sure you have things you could trade that aren't in your hands or pockets. Maybe you'd even be glad once you were rid of them. Any memories that give you trouble? Tired of your shadow dragging in the mud behind you? Wouldn't you stride more spryly without your conscience? Of course you would! No? Then I suppose I'll sell to the Duchess. She wants the bird-boy for its excellent parts. Its plumage for a cloak of sky-walking, its organs for scrying, its tongue for an amulet . . ."

Kellen's face became hot. The trapper must have overheard him talking to Yannick and realized that they were friends. He knew Kellen couldn't let the older boy be dissected.

Do I really need a shadow? Couldn't I live without it? He glanced up and caught the trapper watching him with a long, speculative smile, his teeth gleaming a little too brightly in the moonlight. There was something familiar about that smile and the way shadows pooled in his hollowed cheeks. Kellen's hazy suspicions hardened into certainty.

"Half-humans are valuable, are they?" Kellen asked suddenly. "Does that include your son?"

The trapper lost his smile.

"Son?" He said the word uncertainly, as if he were tasting something new and hadn't made up his mind about the flavor. "What do you mean?"

"Didn't you know you had one?" asked Kellen, but he could already see the answer in the other man's face. "I met him the other day in a human village."

"Where?" asked the man. "When?"

"I think that sounds like valuable information," said Kellen, folding his arms.

"You're making up stories," said the trapper.

"Your son's about seventeen, with red hair like yours and the same way of smiling," said Kellen. "Oh, and trees talk to him and tell him where to find timber. Does that mean anything to you?"

Shadows deepened under the trapper's brows as he scowled in thought. Was he trying to think back seventeen years and work out which nocturnal dalliance had left him with a son? How many times had he slipped out of the forest into some lonely village?

"If it's true, I'll find him myself," he said, but didn't sound certain.

"Well, if you won't buy the information, I'm sure someone will be interested," said Kellen, trying to ignore the anxious banging of his heart. "What about that Duchess you mentioned? I bet she'd like to know where to find another half-human. I can even tell her his name—"

The trapper gave a low growl and grabbed Kellen by his collar.

"You better walk carefully after tonight," he hissed in Kellen's ear, "and hope your path never crosses mine." Then he pulled back, his narrow face looking more eerie without its smile. He pulled out a sheet of stitched parchment and began writing up a contract of sale.

With some qualms, Kellen told the trapper where to find Dog. He wasn't sure that Dog would thank him for the family reunion heading his way, but then again Dog could probably look after himself. The trapper unlocked Yannick's cage and tossed Kellen a small wooden key for the collar.

As Yannick clambered unsteadily onto Kellen's raft, spreading his wings for balance, Kellen could feel the weight of curious, predatory gazes. Others had doubtless noticed the valuable cargo on his raft.

I need to find a heart quickly, so we can get out of here . . .

But when Kellen turned to look for the boat with the snakeskin sails, he could not see it. He blinked, his vision darkening. Were those the other Trapper boats, their outlines blurring like ink droplets in water? Why were all the lanterns in the market dimming?

"What's happening?" he asked, feeling a thrill of panic.

"When the moon goes, so does the market." Yannick cast a pointed look at the bank of dark cloud creeping across the moon. A moment later, the moon was lost, like a silver coin in silt.

Everything became dark, and the noises of the market hushed and changed their texture. The hum of voices dwindled into the drone of insects. The flap of sails became the patter of breeze-ruffled foliage. All these little noises were lonely, cold, and clear. Even in the darkness, Kellen could sense that the market was gone.

"No! Not yet!" He had failed. He had no heart for Gall.

"So what the hell's happened to Nettle?" growled Yannick, cutting into Kellen's thoughts. "She's been in agony for days! I could feel it!"

Agony. That didn't sound good.

"Can you tell if it's hatching?" Kellen asked abruptly.

"What?"

"I know about her curse egg, Yannick!" snapped Kellen. "The Little Brothers told me!"

There was a long pause, then Yannick gave a small "huh" noise like air leaving a pair of bellows.

The moon floated clear and showed Kellen a lonely, tree-studded expanse of water, as empty as it had been before the market appeared around him. Yannick was staring into space, looking pale and shocked. Not incredulous, though. It was the look of someone who has finally seen a hundred fragments fall into place.

"You didn't know?" said Kellen. "But you two read each other's minds!"

"Yeah, but . . . it's Nettle." Yannick groaned quietly. "Everything's in code." He rubbed his chin against his wing absently, his eyes dark and haggard. Then he looked at Kellen sharply. "If you try to put her in the Red Hospital," he said hoarsely, "I'll peck your eyes out, then your brain—"

"Of course I won't! Don't be stupid!" yelled Kellen. But Yannick wasn't being stupid. What else could you do with a potential curser?

"I should have been there!" growled Yannick bitterly. "If you hadn't given me away, this wouldn't have happened!"

"It happened a long time ago," said Kellen softly. "She's had the egg for a year."

Yannick mouthed the words "a year" to himself, then slowly shook his head, looking thunderstruck. His shoulders slumped.

"I knew she was changing," he said quietly. "I knew something was wrong." He shook himself and gave a miserable, ugly, gull-like squawk. "I'm ridiculous," he said. "All this time I told myself I'd got the best of both worlds. Human mind, but the freedom of the skies. But really I'm *this*, aren't I?" He fluttered his wings, glaring at them with contempt. "Less than human, and not even a proper bird. Something you break down for parts. I should have been family. A brother who didn't fly away for months or poo on her windowsill."

"You're not that bad," Kellen muttered. "You always came when she needed you."

"I came back to her so I could think and feel properly," said Yannick. "And when thinking and feeling hurt too much, I flew away again."

It was a shock to hear Yannick talk that way. Of the surviving siblings, Kellen had always thought he was the happy-go-lucky one, who could take or leave anything in the world.

"I don't know where Nettle is," said Kellen. "But Gall thought he knew." Numbly, he gave a short, stark account of her disappearance and the ambush at the Throat.

"You think Nettle betrayed you to Salvation, don't you?" Yannick glared at him.

"She must have done!" Kellen said bitterly. "It's the only explanation that makes sense." His mind had circled and circled the question and always come back to the same answer. "And yet . . . gaaah!"

He stamped at the planks of the raft, glaring at the night sky as if it were to blame.

"I don't believe she'd do that!" he shouted. "It has to be true, and I *still* don't believe it! I just want to find her! I want to yell at her and force her to tell me what's going on, and . . . and make sure she's all right!" His words sounded weak and pathetic, and he flushed with embarrassed annoyance. "Can you find her?"

"If you take the collar off, I'll be a bird again." Yannick snapped at the air with the mouth that refused to be a beak. "Yes, maybe I can find her. But first, tell me everything."

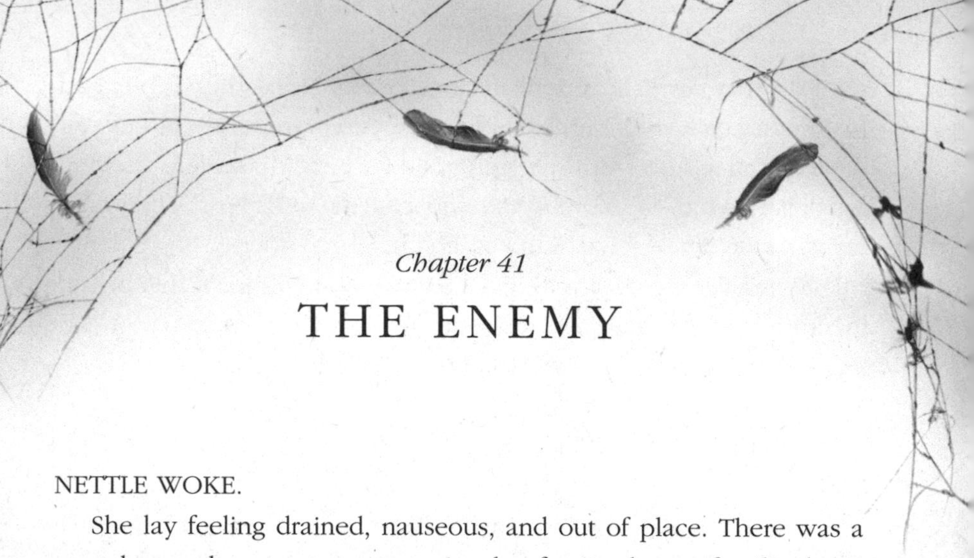

Chapter 41

THE ENEMY

NETTLE WOKE.

She lay feeling drained, nauseous, and out of place. There was a scratchy woolen counterpane against her face and an unfamiliar hammock curved beneath her back. Occasionally there were low creaks of groaning wood or thuds and clatters somewhere above.

There was no warmth against her back, nor sounds of another's breathing. Kellen wasn't there.

That's right. I left him behind. I left everything behind.

I found Salvation.

The thought made Nettle feel pure, cold, and empty, like a washed-out bottle. She didn't know who she was anymore. If she looked into a mirror, she thought she might see a girl of glass, unable to hold even color.

Nettle sat up groggily. In the dim light, she made out the little cabin in which she had spent the last day and two nights. The change of clothes she hadn't felt ready to touch, the green-clouded panes of the portholes, the door that she knew was locked.

Her memories of the last thirty-six hours were hazy. She remembered the Swan. She remembered encountering the scouts sent by Salvation. She remembered the long journey in the bottom of their boat with a blindfold around her eyes. She had thrashed, but not to escape. She had screamed, but not for help. She had been fighting only the thing inside her, no longer able to hide it.

Had she released it at last? No, she had forced it down yet again. She let out a long sigh of relief and exhaustion.

Nettle felt distant from her memories, as if they were a story she had been told about somebody else. She had been brought to this cabin. She had lost a day numbly counting the cracks in the ceiling and watching spiders scuttle furtively across its expanse. She had eaten without tasting anything. The words of others had fallen into her ears and sunk, like coins dropped into a well. She had answered a few of their questions, but only a few.

Run away! she had told them repeatedly. *You have to move everyone in Salvation! You're in danger!*

After that, Nettle had heard noises of motion outside—calls, the creak of oars, and the thump of footsteps on the deck above. Now and then, her hammock rocked slightly as the cabin gently tilted or bobbed. The boat she was in was on the move.

Nettle had allowed herself a little numb relief. Whatever happened to her now, she'd achieved her most important aim. If Salvation was moving their base, perhaps everyone was safe. Kellen and Gall wouldn't kill anyone, and nobody would kill them.

Later, there had been a muffled conversation beyond the door.

Yes, Nettle had heard someone whisper. *That's her.* After that, there had been no more visitors, no more food.

Remembering this, Nettle's blood ran cold. Had somebody recognized her, then? It was bound to happen sooner or later, she knew that. Jendy Pin could identify her, and Shay Ammet might also remember her.

Soon everyone here would know who she was. The Unraveller's friend. Salvation's foe. There would be new questions, asked with more force. If they asked her about Kellen and Gall, and she refused to answer, what would happen to her then?

I don't belong here either. Nettle hugged herself, feeling cold. *I'm everyone's enemy.*

A knock at the door made her jump.

"Are you dressed?" called a woman's voice. "Mr. Ammet wants to talk to you."

Nettle's stomach plummeted, but there was no point putting off the inevitable.

"Just a minute!" she called, struggling out of the hammock.

Dressed in borrowed shoes and a linen frock too long for her, Nettle stepped out into the light. It felt strange to be wearing woven cloth, a sign that she really wasn't Kellen's companion anymore.

Standing on the deck of a barge, Nettle blinked in the morning sunlight and looked out across Salvation. Her bewildered gaze drifted over boat after boat after boat, all nestling hull to hull. Twenty vessels, perhaps more, surrounded by dusty-pale reed-forest.

At first glance, it seemed that the boats had been reclaimed by the marsh-woods and overrun with green. On second glance, she realized that this was careful camouflage. Slabs of moss had been carefully laid on the barge roofs. The decks had been splotched and dappled with earth-colors. The "creepers" that festooned the sailing ships' masts were lengths of black cord bristling with green fabric leaves.

"This way," said the dark-haired woman at her side.

On the boats, people sat smoking pipes, eating breakfast, stitching sails, reading, or plucking wildfowl. Most were adults, though Nettle noticed a couple of teenagers not much older than herself. As she made her way from boat to boat, across planks and rope bridges, she felt the hairs on her neck rise.

The things she noticed were all small. A flash of something else before a smile. A distracted look, as if hearing a voice that would not be silent. Each was barely perceptible but a sign nonetheless—a dark speck hinting at the long splinter beneath the skin. Even now Nettle couldn't suppress a frisson of panic.

Cursers. They're all cursers.

But so am I.

.....

Shay Ammet's boat was larger than the rest, an ocean-worthy vessel with empty gunports.

"In the wheelhouse," said Nettle's guide.

Nettle climbed a ladder to the lower deck, feeling her legs and arms shake with nerves. She approached the wheelhouse, which was concealed beneath dead tree branches and bundles of reeds. The door was ajar.

Inside, a solitary man stood staring pensively into space. The light filtered through the smudged windows, and the bracken outside tiger-striped his face and lichen-smudged clothes, and for a moment he seemed an otherworldly creature in a private jungle.

The next moment, however, Shay Ammet looked round and smiled. It was the easy, confident smile of someone entirely at home. It made Nettle feel as if she had entered a private office, not a mangled boat in a lair of fugitives.

Shay Ammet had large, intelligent eyes and an air of gentle gravity. His gaze made Nettle feel that she was being weighed in the balance, calmly and without malice. She had felt that way on their first meeting, a little age ago.

"Hello again, Nettle," he said.

"You remember me." Nettle couldn't keep her voice from wobbling.

"Of course I do," said Ammet, his tone surprisingly gentle. "You needn't look so terrified! Did you think we'd drown you in the marshes once we knew who you were?"

"Something like that," whispered Nettle, her heart banging.

"This is Salvation," said Ammet. "We promise safety to every curser, whatever their past. You're one of us, Nettle. And you've found your way to us at last."

One of us.

Nettle could barely understand the words. Of course the Salvation scouts had worked out that she was a curser, that must have been obvious. But she hadn't dared hope for survival, let alone acceptance.

She didn't dare hope now. It was a trick, a trap. Her vision speckled and her chest felt tight.

Ammet walked round behind her, and then something nudged at the back of her knees. Looking back, she saw that he had brought a wicker chair and placed it just behind her.

"You look ready to faint away," he said.

He thinks he's a gentleman, Leona Tharl had said of Ammet. Nettle remembered that as she dropped down into the seat.

Ammet sat down on a second chair facing her, fixing her with a concerned gaze.

"I always remembered you," he said. "So young and slight, so determined to bear the weight of everything alone. I wanted to help you back then. I'd like to help you now. I know you've been hiding in plain sight for so long, surrounded by people who would turn on you if they really understood you." He gave a small sympathetic grimace. "Believe me, I know how lonely *that* can be. But you're safe now. The curse inside you isn't a crime, and we can help you control it. *You're not alone anymore.*"

Nettle heard this with a sensation like a warm, soft blow to the chest. It was a shock to realize how much she had needed to hear words like these from somebody.

"I wish I could give you more time to find your feet," continued Ammet, his gaze still clear and earnest. "But I need your help, urgently. We must find your friend Kellen. He came to the Wilds with you, didn't he?"

Nettle's heart gave a sickening lurch.

So that's it. He's handling me with kid gloves because he wants to capture Kellen.

She hadn't told anyone in Salvation that Kellen and Gall were in the Wilds, for fear of putting them in danger. Nettle felt the silence stretch, heavy with expectation. Ammet seemed kind now, but how long would he stay kind if she refused to answer?

Nettle hugged her ribcage and steeled her nerve.

"Mr. Ammet," she said, "I came here to warn you all that you were in danger, because I didn't want your blood on my hands. But I don't want anyone else's blood on them either. And Kellen's my friend. I can't betray him. I just can't."

"Nettle, I have no intention of hurting Kellen!" Shay Ammet seemed mildly appalled.

"Well, that's not what Kellen thinks!" said Nettle. "And you did send armed men and a Dancing Star after us." Somehow she seemed to be reliving her last quarrel with Kellen, but this time arguing the other side.

"Capturing you seemed like the only way to separate you from Leona Tharl's pet murderer so that we could have a proper talk!" said Ammet, his brow creasing with distaste as he mentioned the marsh horseman. "I always hoped we could recruit the pair of you. You both seemed likely to end up in Chancery chains. People fear powers they don't understand."

"Then why did one of you curse Kellen?" blurted out Nettle.

There was a flicker of annoyance in Ammet's face.

"One of my friends had a personal grudge against him," he said, frowning. "She regrets the curse now. If we can bring Kellen here, she'll talk to him and help him unravel the curse. Curses are a cruel weapon, but at least they're reversible, or they will be if Kellen joins us. Once Chancery meets our terms and guarantees our freedom, we'd like him to unravel all the curses we've cast during our long war with them. That's why we want him on our side!"

This sounded far too good to be true. But what if it *was* true? What if it was possible to save Kellen, Leona, and the little cloud-girl from their curses, without anybody dying or going to prison?

Ammet seemed to see the uncertainty in her face. He leaned forward so that his eyes were level with hers.

"Listen, Nettle," he said, in a tone of quiet urgency. "Kellen is in serious trouble. We need to find him quickly—if he's still alive."

"What?" The skin of Nettle's face tingled, and it was suddenly hard to breathe.

"Yesterday morning, Kellen and Cherrick Gall ran into some of my people," said Ammet. "There was a fight. My people tried their best to avoid hurting Kellen, but Mr. Gall grabbed him by the collar and disappeared under the water with him. We found no bodies, so Kellen may still be alive. He hasn't returned to the village where you were staying, and neither has the man Gall. Can you think of anywhere else they might have gone?"

It was a shock to learn that Ammet knew they had been staying in the village, but this surprise was soon lost in the anxious whirl of Nettle's thoughts. What if Ammet was telling the truth? What if Kellen really was in need of rescue—injured, half-drowned, or pursued by a feral marsh horseman?

"I don't know where they are!" she protested. "They didn't mention anywhere!"

"Then could Yannick find them?" asked Ammet. "He could search a wide area on the wing, couldn't he?"

Another blow, another revelation. How did Shay Ammet know about Yannick?

"You can draw your brother to you, can't you?" Ammet persisted. "I'm sure he's heard terrible stories about me, but together we can talk him round, can't we?"

Nettle tried to speak, but her throat tightened. Her eyes stung, then blurred, and a treacherous tear slid down her cheek.

"Yannick's not coming back anymore." Her voice came out sounding thick and choked. "He always found me before when I needed him, but . . . now he doesn't. He told me I was changing and that soon he wouldn't recognize me. I don't think he can find me now, because I'm too different. I'm no longer me."

She stared at her feet and tried to be glad. Yannick would never know what she had become. He could live the rest of his life freely on the wing alongside his gull-wife and gull-children, without her dragging him back to human misery.

"Please try again, for Kellen's sake," Ammet said quietly. "You're our best hope. Maybe our only hope."

. . . . .

Nettle climbed slowly back down the ladder to the lower deck, trying to clear her thoughts. Was Kellen really in trouble? Just for a moment, she felt a desperate longing for Yannick. Maybe she *could* still tug at him and draw him to her . . .

No! Nettle stifled the thought and forced her feelings down. *Think! You don't know if Ammet's telling the truth. You don't know if Kellen's really in danger. If you bring Yannick here, you might be luring him into a trap!*

Nettle realized that she wanted to trust Ammet. It had been such a relief to hear a kind, understanding voice. It had reminded her of their first conversation—the blessed feeling that someone was on her side, that an adult was going to take care of things. But Leona's word had not been enough for her, so Ammet's could not be either.

Instead, she gritted her teeth and focused on the flares of distrust that had flickered in her mind as they talked, the things that didn't quite make sense.

Ammet knows too much, she thought. *How did he know I was staying in the village with Kellen and Gall? How does he know about Yannick? He says he always wanted to recruit me—does that mean he knew about my curse before I came to the Wilds? How would he know that? I'm missing something . . .*

And he looked annoyed when I mentioned Kellen's curse. Is he angry with the curser, or was that a question he didn't want to answer?

Nettle sat down shakily on the damp deck and cast furtive glances around at the other boats. Nobody seemed to be watching her or waiting to manhandle her back to her cabin. Was she free and unguarded, then? Had she been accepted so easily as "one of us"? She doubted it. There would be discreet eyes on her even now and thin ice under her feet.

What was Salvation? Was it full of dangerous madmen trying to hold the whole nation to ransom, or desperate people who only wanted to protect themselves?

What was Shay Ammet? Was he a cold-blooded master criminal or a well-meaning man using ruthless measures to protect his community?

Everyone else seemed to find it easy to pick a side. Kellen, Gall, the Salvation cursers—all of them chose their army and picked up their weapons. Nettle felt like she was the only one with doubts, the only one who wanted to ask more questions.

Maybe Mr. Ammet is telling the truth. Maybe he never did mean me or Kellen harm. Maybe he didn't give the order for Kellen to be cursed. But maybe he did.

I need to know the truth. I need to find Jendy Pin.

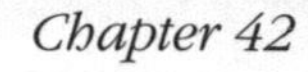

Chapter 42

WHERE YOU BELONG

NETTLE JUMPED AS A HAND SETTLED ON HER SHOULDER. SHE looked up to see the dark-haired, round-faced woman who had brought her to the boat.

"You haven't had breakfast, have you?" The woman's smile now seemed kindly enough. "Come with me! I'm Rue."

On the sunny deck of a sailing boat, Rue introduced Nettle to a willowy young woman with a narrow, nervous face and a boy of seventeen who flushed a lot, smiled obediently at everyone's jokes, and said almost nothing. The four of them sat cross-legged on the sunny deck of a sailing boat, sharing seed-covered flatbreads and crayfish soup.

Nettle felt tense and disorientated, as if she'd woken from a nightmare to find herself at a picnic. Why were these people being so friendly? Didn't they know who she was? It soon became clear that they did.

"Nobody will judge you for anything you did before, love," said Rue. "You were lost, that's all. Now you've found your way to us, and that's all that matters."

These people have probably been told to keep an eye on me, Nettle reminded herself.

Nettle's new friends were keen to know whether she had everything she needed. Within minutes, Nettle had been lent a comb, a reading candle, a handkerchief, and a boar-bristle toothbrush.

They seemed interested in her as well. Was it true she had been cursed once? Which part of the Shallow Wilds did she come from?

"Who do you hate?" asked Rue, with the matter-of-fact tone of one asking a commonplace question. *Where are you from? How old are you? Who do you hate?*

Nettle was about to say that she didn't hate anyone and close the conversation down. Then it hit her, with warm and sudden force, that she didn't have to lie. She could tell the truth to these people. This revelation was frightening and wonderful.

"I should have hated my father's wife," she said slowly. "But she died before I could. Everyone thought that would make me feel better, knowing she was gone, but I needed someone to be angry with! She wasn't there, so everything I felt had nowhere to go. I drown in it. I can't get away from it. So sometimes I hate the world. I hate everything."

There. She had said it. The words were out at last, and the sun still shone. Some invisible cord that had been strangling Nettle's soul loosened, making it easier to breathe.

"Is your curse still in the egg or flown free?" asked the willowy young woman.

"In the egg," said Nettle, but she was struck by the phrase "flown free." It made curses sound as natural and beautiful as birds.

"My curse is flown." The young woman held up a cowrie shell, which she wore on a string round her neck. "My husband," she whispered, as if afraid the shell might hear. "He was a brute, and I . . . I don't blame myself anymore. But I can't just dump him in the woods. I'm hoping I'll find a way to change him back so that I stop feeling this . . . *weight*."

She fingered the hole that the cord passed through.

"I made that hole while I still hated him," she said softly. "I hope it doesn't go through anything important."

"I cursed once two years ago," said Rue, "and now I've another in the egg. I probably would never have cursed again, if they hadn't locked me up and taken away my girls." She closed her eyes, pressed one hand hard against her heart. Her face spasmed, as if in pain.

"At least Mr. Ammet got you out of the Red Hospital before anything happened to you," said the teenage boy. "Do you know what they do to cursers there?" he asked Nettle.

"I went there once," said Nettle. "I saw the shackles and helms—"

"Oh, they won't have shown you the special rooms!" said the boy, his bashfulness replaced by a fierce animation. "They keep cursers there till they're sure their families don't care about them, then they cut into their skulls. They dig out the curse eggs and make amulets out of them. Do you see? That's why they lock us away! They're farming us!"

Nettle flushed, not sure whether to feel frightened or embarrassed. She couldn't imagine the kindly doctor at the Red Hospital carving cursers open, and in any case, she didn't think curse eggs were real, solid objects that you could cut out of people's heads.

"I haven't heard about anything like that," she said tactfully.

"Well, you wouldn't, would you?" he replied. His manner wasn't exactly contemptuous, but there was an edge of exasperation. "Chancery keeps it quiet, and everyone believes what Chancery tells them. We're the only ones who know the truth."

"Gently!" said Rue, and patted his hand reprovingly. "She's only just got here!" She tutted and gave Nettle a sympathetic glance. "I know it's a lot to take in at once," she said. Apparently Rue believed these claims too.

Nettle nodded mutely and let the others change the subject. She didn't *think* Chancery were cutting into cursers' skulls, but what did she really know? She couldn't be certain, and her new friends apparently were.

Rue had chores for the rest of the morning but invited Nettle to "come along and keep me company." Nettle immediately agreed. It would give her an excuse to move around the boat camp and keep an eye out for Jendy Pin. The inhabitants were surprisingly busy, mending nets, grinding flour, scrubbing decks, and plucking wildfowl.

As Nettle followed Rue from boat to boat, strangers greeted her with welcoming smiles and surprising warmth.

"So you're the new girl! Nice to see a bright young face around here!"

"If you find yourself tripping over that skirt, let me know and I'll take it up a few inches!"

Every greeting put a crack in Nettle's defenses, in spite of her wariness. How intoxicating it was, this feeling of being *liked*! Really liked, by people who knew what she was! For a year, there had been a poisonous undercurrent of doubt and self-hate every time someone smiled at Nettle or treated her kindly. *They wouldn't if they knew the truth*, a quiet little voice in her head had told her. She had felt like a fraud, a human-faced monster fooling people into offering their trust and affection.

But here she was, surrounded by people who knew her terrible secret and didn't hate her at all. If she lowered her guard, she knew she would be overwhelmed with gratitude to them all.

Amid all the smiling faces, however, Nettle saw no sign of Jendy Pin. Eventually she risked asking Rue if she knew the name.

"Oh, you don't want to talk to her." Rue's motherly face creased with disapproval, and she lowered her voice. "She's a drunk. No liquor stronger than small beer is allowed here, and she's lost without it. She even started buying gin from some woman in a nearby village and smuggling it into camp!"

"Really?" asked Nettle, as casually as she could. Evidently the secret trade with Linnet had been discovered.

"Yes—and she wasn't the only one buying things from that woman." Rue tutted. "They could have got us all killed! We only found out three days ago, and that's why we had to move the base. Our enemies had got wind of it, you see."

"What?" Nettle had assumed that Salvation's move was because of the warning she had given the day before. "Three days ago?"

"I think so," Rue said vaguely. "Yes, that's when Mr. Ammet told us enemy agents were on the way."

.....

At noon, everyone stopped for work as one and went to a central barge to collect their lunch. As she queued with a wooden plate, Nettle tried to make sense of what Rue had told her. Were Nettle, Kellen, and Gall the "enemy agents" Ammet had meant? If so, how had he known they were coming?

Just as Nettle was being handed her ration of bread, cheese, and fruit, she spotted a familiar-looking figure on a distant deck. It was a long-limbed woman with lank, dark hair and a sour mouth. When she noticed Nettle, she stopped dead before turning tail and hurrying away.

"Something wrong?" asked Rue, noticing Nettle's distraction.

"Back in a minute!" Nettle hurried off after the disappearing figure.

Nettle caught up with the woman just as the latter was sitting down on a crate and taking a swig of her small beer. Her hair was tied back from her long, angular face, her mouth a little open, showing the break in one of her front teeth.

There was no doubt. It was Jendy Pin.

Since the visit to the Red Hospital, the missing Jendy had loomed oppressively in Nettle's imagination. But here she was, a real live woman, with mosquito-bites on her neck and reddened calluses on her hands.

When Jendy noticed Nettle, her jaw fell open.

"You!" The woman stared at Nettle in horror, then glanced around and lowered her voice to a whisper. "I'm not meant to talk to you!"

"Why not?" demanded Nettle.

"They didn't trust me to play along! Everyone's supposed to make you feel welcome, and I . . . I can't forget what you and that boy did to me. You two broke my *heart*! That curse I cast four months ago—my blood and soul were in it. And you two just pulled it apart, like it was a game! How could I smile at you and say 'Welcome to Salvation'?"

"You got your revenge, though, didn't you?" Nettle whispered fiercely. "You cursed Kellen!"

"I didn't!" Jendy gave an angry sound like a sob. "I wish I had," she muttered, her eyes desperate. "If only I had! I *tried*. I tried for *months*. I did everything they said—the fasting, the drugs, the chanting—but it didn't work! And now I see the way everyone looks at me. If you buy a hen for the eggs and it doesn't lay, the hen gets the chop, doesn't it? I'm hanging on by a thread here! If I get in trouble again . . ."

"If you didn't curse him, who did?" Nettle was still trying to untangle Jendy's panicky sentences.

"One of the best cursers." Jendy cast a glance over her shoulder. "Ammet's favorite. She—"

"Nettle!" called a male voice. The teenage boy Nettle had met at breakfast was hurrying over. Jendy took advantage of the distraction to rush off, leaping from boat to boat without bothering about the plank-bridges. "Was that woman bothering you?"

"No!" Nettle said quickly. "We were just talking." Having seen Jendy's miserable terror, she felt an unexpected urge to defend her.

As she walked back to rejoin Rue, Nettle was still haunted by Jendy's fearful manner and gabbled words. One detail Nettle could not shake from her mind: When Jendy had started to talk of Kellen's curser, she had looked nervously over her shoulder . . . but not toward the rest of the boat-village. Jendy had glanced toward some unseen point in the depths of the shivering, shimmering reed-forest.

Later, while pounding a laundry bat into a tub full of soapy water and clothing, Nettle kept sneaking glances out at the reed-forest. Where had Jendy Pin's frightened glance been directed?

Beyond the clustered decks of the boat-village lay a margin of shimmering, gray-blond reeds, and from this rose a softly sloping ridge, shaggy with ferns, moss, and grasses. It loomed about fifteen feet above water level and seemed to curve in a horseshoe shape around the camp.

"What's that?" Nettle asked Rue.

"They say it's the outer edge of an ancient barrow," said Rue. "A hollow hill with tombs in it. But it caved in centuries ago, and the tide washed out its innards. Now there's just that wall left."

"Tombs?" Nettle didn't like the sound of that. "Isn't that dangerous?"

"Sometimes," admitted Rue. "An old barrow like this attracts things. Gallow Glimmers. White-Handed Ladies. And not all the eels in the water are eels."

"Then why did you come here?" asked Nettle. She was suddenly very aware that all around the little boat-village was mile upon mile of whispering reeds, shimmering water, and merciless, treacherous Wilds.

"The wall's a good defense and hides us from sight," answered Rue. "Besides, Mr. Ammet has some creatures contracted to him acting as lookouts and guards. If Chancery try to attack, they'll regret it." For the first time, Rue's voice had an edge.

She glanced at Nettle and smiled reassuringly.

"Don't worry, pet," she said. "You'll be fine if you're careful. Stay out of the water, and keep to your cabin after sundown, even if something calls you. Don't go outside that boundary wall. If you hear the alarm bell ringing, hide in your cabin until you hear it again."

Nettle shivered in spite of herself, and as she did so she noticed a hint of movement at the top of the ridge. The trees that sprouted from the slope quivered for a moment, then the ferns below it began to thrash, as if something bulky were making its way down the slope.

"What's that?" she asked.

The older woman peered at the slope, brow furrowed.

"What's what?" she said.

"There!" Nettle jabbed a desperate finger toward the distant, twitching foliage. "The undergrowth!"

"Hush, now!" Rue looked at her in dismay. "There's nothing there! What's wrong?"

Oh no. Oh, please no. If I can see it and Rue can't, then it's come back for me . . .

Nettle felt her chest tighten as the panic took hold. Any moment now the Swan would break free from the undergrowth, battle its way through the reeds, and fill the bright sky with its wailing as it came for her . . .

It was only when Rue grabbed her arm that Nettle was able to focus on what her companion was saying.

“I can see it now!” said Rue, and Nettle realized hazily that the woman had said this more than once. “It’s a deer! Look!”

Nettle looked back toward the ridge just in time to see a pale brown, antlered shape bound away up the slope. It was not the Swan after all. The panic drained out of Nettle, leaving her weak and shaky.

“You’re pale as chalk!” Rue put a concerned arm around her. “Come on, sit down.”

Nettle sank down onto Rue’s washing stool, feeling embarrassed but achingly grateful.

“I thought it was . . .” Nettle began, then trailed off.

“Your visitation?” Rue prompted gently. “The thing only you can see?”

Nettle nodded and took a deep breath. To her horror, all that came out was sob after pathetic sob, as if she were a small child. The world blurred, and then Rue’s arms closed tightly around her. It broke Nettle’s heart, because it made her feel young and warm and safe. It was like having a mother, and she had almost forgotten how that felt.

“It’s *stupid*,” she croaked angrily, hating the way her voice shook. “It’s a *swan*! Just a bird. But it’s . . .”

She frowned and took a moment to rub her stinging eyes hard with her knuckles.

“When I was cursed, I spent years as a heron, but now and then I remembered who I was. And once I remembered while I was killing some cygnets. Really young cygnets . . .”

She swallowed hard, trying not to retch.

“Ugly, blind, and wriggling, with just a few fuzzy black feathers. I watched myself doing it, thinking *Stop stop, somebody please stop this happening*, because I couldn’t bear it. Deep down, I couldn’t believe the universe would allow something so sick and horrible. But I couldn’t stop. I grabbed one by the neck with my beak and shook it, and shook it, until something broke and it stopped moving its stubby wings. There was another I dunked over and over till it drowned. The smallest ones were still alive when I swallowed them. And that was when I realized, deep in my soul, that nobody was going to save me.

After that, their mother kept following me. She didn't attack me, just shadowed me at a distance. I don't know why, and I don't think she did either. Not for revenge. Birds don't hate. Maybe she was staying close to what was left of her babies. Maybe I was all she had left. After a while, she wasn't there anymore—I think perhaps she starved and died. Eventually Kellen broke my curse, so I *was* saved. But it was too late. I'd already known with all my soul that I couldn't be. When I have visions of the Swan, she's huge and full of pain. She still doesn't hate me. She wants to give me a baby I haven't murdered yet. She wants me to eat that too, and I can't bear it. It's so *stupid*! Why am I haunted by this *bird*? Most of my family are dead, and the ones that aren't will never be the same! Why don't I have nightmares about that? Why do I keep seeing the Swan?"

"Pain has its own rules," Rue said simply. "We don't choose what breaks us. There's no wrong way to feel."

"When I see her, I remember what I really am." Nettle swallowed and wiped her face. "Just a gullet in ghoul-gray feathers who kills babies. I can't be saved, because I don't deserve to be."

"That's no way to talk!" Rue gave Nettle a slight shake. "You're one of us—gullet, feathers, and all. Here we save each other! So, you say that this Swan wants to give you a chick. And you won't let her?"

"No!" Nettle shuddered, her skin crawling. "No, I always run away!"

"Oh, love." Rue sighed and stroked Nettle's head. "You can't run away forever. Someday, when you're ready, you'll need to take that chick from her. Once you know what your curse is for, and where it's meant to go."

Nettle tensed up in Rue's hug.

"What if I don't want to curse anyone?" she asked.

"You don't have any choice in that, do you, love?" Rue gave Nettle a little squeeze. "It'll come out sometime, whether you like it or not. But maybe you can choose *where* it goes, so it won't hurt anyone who doesn't deserve it. We'll all help you when the time comes. We'll help you make sure the curse flies right and hits a mark where it'll do good instead of harm."

Nettle realized that she could hear a ringing sound that definitely wasn't in her ears. It was an insistent, metallic clanging from somewhere in the boat-village.

Rue released Nettle, eyes wide with dismay.

"That's the alarm bell!" she said. "Something's been spotted near the camp! We need to get belowdecks!" She grabbed Nettle's hand and pulled her to her feet. "Maybe it wasn't just a deer," she murmured under her breath.

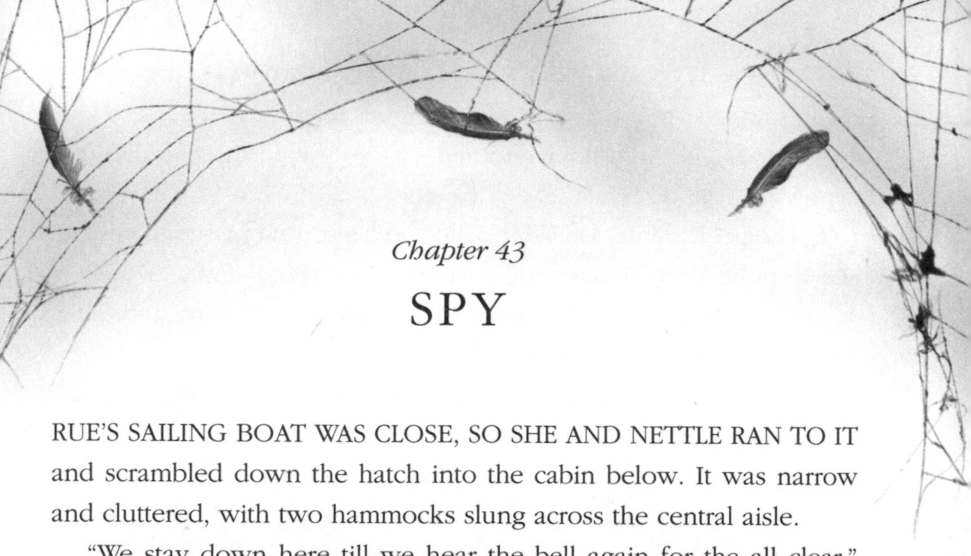

Chapter 43

SPY

RUE'S SAILING BOAT WAS CLOSE, SO SHE AND NETTLE RAN TO IT and scrambled down the hatch into the cabin below. It was narrow and cluttered, with two hammocks slung across the central aisle.

"We stay down here till we hear the bell again for the all clear," Rue told her, then smiled and patted one of the hammocks. "This'll be yours, once you're ready to move in!"

Nettle looked at it, unsure whether to feel touched or panicky. It sounded as though she had been assigned a home and a family. It was wonderful, but it was also too much, too strange, too soon.

Rue was watching Nettle tenderly, looking for a reaction. Perhaps Nettle was imagining the gleam of hope and need in the older woman's eyes.

"You have daughters, don't you?" Nettle asked. *Am I just a substitute for them?*

Rue hesitated, then seemed to come to a decision.

"Yes," she said. "Wait here—I'll show you."

Rue retrieved a battered wooden box from the far end of the cabin, and then the pair sat down cross-legged on the floor. Rue opened the box and very gently took out a picture.

"Here they are," she said. "My girls."

The damp-stained paper showed a faded sketch of two little girls, one smaller and plumper than the other. They were skillfully drawn, but creases now ran cracks through their faces.

"My cousin drew this two years ago, not long before I was arrested," Rue whispered. "Aren't they pretty? I try to imagine how they look now, but I can't." She stroked the picture. "I need to get back to them," she murmured. "Mr. Ammet says Chancery is ready to crack. Just a few more curses, and they'll have to make a treaty with us. And then . . . then we can all go home!"

Go home? Did Rue really think she could just walk back into her old life, without anybody throwing rocks at her or running in fear?

"My girls write to me," continued Rue. "Look—Mr. Ammet found a way to get their letters to me!"

A much-thumbed handful of papers were thrust into Nettle's hands. Rounded, clumsy writing filled the pages.

"Chancery put them in an orphanage," said Rue, and Nettle saw her soft, motherly face contort in anguish and rage. "I hear all about it! They're like prisoners there, forced to make baskets so the owner can sell them. Wearing their little fingers to the bone! You see this?" She pointed to a dark splotch on one of the letters. "My youngest bled onto the paper, because she was caned so hard it took the skin off her knuckles."

Nettle read some snatches of the letters, and her instincts tingled.

> . . . we miss you but we know that someday you will come and rescue us . . .

> . . . Lily cries every day but I tell her that soon we will all be a family again and everything will be happy like it was before . . .

Little kids don't write like that, even if they're miserable! thought Nettle. *They write things like: "The orphanage smells and the walls are spotty. Mr. Blue is always cross. I am getting good at spelling. Today I saw a white dog."*

It's not just the words either. If this is two years of letters, why doesn't their handwriting change over time? They're seven and nine now, but the handwriting in the letters hasn't got any better. Hasn't Rue noticed any of this?

Nettle looked into Rue's eyes and saw a darkness as wide and all-consuming as the sea. Love was there in the darkness, but love winged with rage.

I can't tell her, thought Nettle. *I can't tell her these letters might not be written by her daughters. She needs them to be real.*

Rue had pulled out more papers and now thrust a charcoal portrait of a man into Nettle's hands.

"This man," said Rue, her voice tense and knife-like. "He's the one doing that to them. He's the one who had them brought to his orphanage. He's the one making slaves of them. He's the one who I'll curse, when the time comes. I know all about him." Rue began leafing through the papers with frantic, trembling care. "I'm learning him like a tune. Look! This is his handwriting—that's a tuft of his hair folded in paper. I know where he was born, what scars he has, and what he likes to eat. And I know his name. He's called Creskin."

Nettle stared at the charcoal portrait in her hand. Even though it was badly smudged, she still recognized the shaven head, scar-flecked eyebrows, and expression of incredulous annoyance. The last time she had seen it had been on an island within sight of Mizzleport.

"I've met him," she said aloud. "He works for Perilous Contrivances."

"No!" said Rue with unexpected sharpness. "I told you—he runs an orphanage!" She looked at Nettle coldly and uncertainly, as if a stranger had suddenly appeared next to her.

Nettle swallowed, feeling a precipice beneath her toes. She had contradicted Rue's creed, the chant of her soul. If she said nothing, however, Rue might curse an innocent man.

"Rue," she said quietly, as if calming a dangerous animal, "I think someone's made a mistake. Perhaps it's the wrong Creskin—"

"NO!" Rue glared at her, as if Nettle had struck her. "Why would you say that? I *know* it's him! I . . . I can *feel* that it's him! When I close my eyes to sleep now, I can see him in the darkness. He's the one! It's all his fault!"

"Rue." Nettle could feel the ground giving. "He's not—"

"STOP IT!" Rue's motherly face contorted, and something changed in the atmosphere of the room. Her eyes became windows into an endless, turbulent night. And now those night-eyes no longer saw Nettle as a friend. Nettle was an enemy, a betrayer, a heretic.

Nettle leaped to her feet and scrambled up the ladder to the hatch. She flung it open and pulled herself out onto the deck, her hair whipping her face in the freshening wind. Behind her, she could hear Rue calling out to her, sounding panicky and uncertain.

"Nettle, love, pet, don't go! It's dangerous!"

Nettle slammed the hatch down behind her and ran.

The sky was gray now, and the boat-village deserted. Leaves danced jerkily on the eddies of the air, and lumps of moss tumbled slowly across the decks. Nettle jumped from boat to boat, until she reached a place where deck yielded to reeds and water. She stopped, gasped cold air, and stared out at the thrashing reeds and silver-smudged sky.

I'm alone, thought Nettle. *Everybody else is belowdecks*. The unexpected relief of that! It had been so hard to think clearly when she was surrounded by smiles. They had been like a drug fogging her mind.

Snap out of it, she told herself harshly. *Nobody here loves you. You know that, don't you? They're all "playing the game," like Jendy said. They're making you feel welcome because Mr. Ammet told them to.*

Her pockets were heavy with everything her new friends had lent her, binding her to them with invisible strands of gratitude and obligation. Sharing food, sharing chores, sharing secrets . . . Already Nettle could feel her bruised heart aching to open up to everyone around her. She was so very tired of being alone.

That's how you're supposed to feel. Maybe the kindness is real, but it's still a trap. A trap for sad, frightened, broken people, to make them feel like they've come home. People like you.

They want you to curse their enemies and find Kellen for them. That's all.

Beyond the rippling water and the reed-dance, Nettle saw something pale brown moving through the ferns and young trees. It was antlered like a deer, and she could just make out a silver collar around its neck. As it raised its head to look toward her, she could see holes of bottomless black where its eyes should be.

Nettle ducked down out of sight. When she next raised her head to peer, the stag was dragging something large up the slope. Even at this distance, Nettle could see that it was the sprawled body of a woman. Its head was missing, but it wore clothes that Nettle had last seen on frightened, desperate Jendy Pin.

She was right, thought Nettle. *This isn't home. This isn't salvation.*

She made up her mind, then opened it to the skies.

Yannick! she called out silently.

This time she almost seemed to feel the tug of a great painful cord between them. Then there was a scratchy sensation in her head, a jubilant, uncomfortable jostle of prickly thoughts and feelings. Yannick was close—closer than she had realized.

I'm here! she shouted in her head. *I need you!*

I'm coming! The yell was distant, and familiar as a blister, familiar as the smell of bread . . .

It's dangerous! she called back. *There's an evil stag!*

But already there was a new pale shape in the gray sky, soaring and circling in a way that only one gull did. Her gull, the *right* gull . . .

She raised her hands up, and the familiar shape swooped down and smacked unceremoniously into her neck before scrabbling a perch-place on her shoulder.

Nettle, Nettle, Nettle! Yannick's thoughts were almost gull-squawks. *Are you hurt, did they hurt you, if they hurt you I'll—*

No! She stroked the top of his chocolate-brown head and felt almost sick with joy at seeing him. *They've been kind—*

So are we with Salvation now? asked Yannick. *I don't care, just tell me which side we're on. I'm with you whatever. You know that, don't you?*

He knew about the curse egg. Nettle could feel that knowledge like a new wound in his mind.

I'm sorry I didn't tell you, she said.

So you should be! Yannick nipped her ear painfully. *I wouldn't care if you turned into a dragon and slept on a pile of a thousand skulls! I'd still fight for you till my feathers fell out.*

They spilled their thoughts into each other, urgently and chaotically. Yannick's thoughts tasted of cloud-cold and herring-scale. Nettle's spirits climbed giddily as she learned that Kellen was alive. In turn, she gabbled everything she had learned about Salvation. *You abandoned me, you abandoned me*, they told each other without meaning to, but that had been part of their mind-song for over a year. *I need you*, they told each other angrily, and for once they both managed to hear it.

We don't have long, Nettle said. *The others will come out of their cabins soon. We can't let them see you.*

So have you joined them or not? demanded Yannick.

They think I have, answered Nettle. As she said this, she knew with deep sorrow that she had not joined them and never would. She was a spy after all, a viper in the grass.

Yannick . . . Salvation could have been wonderful! Unhappy, frightened people helping each other and building a new life! Perhaps it was even like that once, I don't know. But there's something very wrong with it now, and I think it's because of Shay Ammet. I think he's manipulating everyone here, lying to them and using them as weapons. The rest aren't bad people. They're just desperate and wounded, putting their faith in the first person who told them they weren't monsters.

Ammet's clever, Yannick. Every moment I'm here I'm walking on eggshells—

Then let's get out of here! interrupted Yannick, flapping his wings as if he wanted to carry his sister away.

I can't! said Nettle. *If I try, I'll be eaten by eels or have my head bitten off by a stag. And there are things I can only find out here. Yannick, I need you to tell Kellen everything I've told you! He can change you half-human again with that collar, can't he?*

Yannick clicked his beak doubtfully. She could feel his pain at the thought of leaving her again.

There's one more thing, Nettle said. *Yannick, can you fly up and see if there's anything over there?* She pointed roughly in the direction that Jendy had glanced.

With only a slight grumble, her gull-brother pushed off, flapped upward some twenty feet, and circled.

Nothing! he called down to her. *Wait . . . There's a barge over there, all by itself!*

Nettle bit her lip hard, conflicted. All the things she had learned had been slowly easing together like raindrops on a window and forming a shape that she did not like.

There's somebody over there nobody wants me to see, she told Yannick. *It's the person who cursed Kellen. And I think I know who it is.*

A number of questions had been bothering her. How had Ammet known about Yannick? How had he known that Nettle and her friends were coming? How had he found out about the trade with Linnet? How had he discovered that Leona was his secret enemy? If Nettle was right, she had the answer to all those questions.

Who? asked Yannick.

She told him.

No, he said instantly.

Nettle became aware that the tinny sound of the alarm was ringing out again. The all clear was sounding. At any moment the people of Salvation would emerge . . .

Please, she begged him, *I need to go belowdecks! Keep watch from the sky, so you can see her when she comes out. We need to know if I'm right!*

She leaped from boat to boat, then hurried into the barge where she had been staying but left the door open so that she could see her brother's small, beloved shape in the sky.

Lots of people coming out on deck, he reported. *But nobody's come out of the lone barge yet. It's a big barge, with a green-painted door, lanterns on the deck—*

Don't get too close! Nettle begged him.

Wait! Yannick's thoughts sharpened into alertness. *The door's opening! Someone's coming out. A woman in a headscarf . . .*

There was a pause, then Nettle sensed Yannick's feelings of shock, disbelief, and pain.

You're right, he said.

Nettle closed her eyes tight, wishing with useless anguish that she had been wrong. Yannick's mind was bare and open with hurt. She could almost feel the wind beneath his wings, almost see through his eyes. The barge below surrounded by shivering reeds, the solitary woman on its deck, her dark auburn hair flickering around her face . . .

It's her, he said. *It's Tansy.*

He had liked Tansy, it seemed. He had liked her more than Nettle had ever realized.

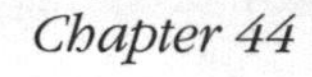

Chapter 44

STRATAGEMS

KELLEN'S JOURNEY BACK TO THE CASTLE HAD BEEN A DAMP AND difficult one. The silken threads holding the raft together had gradually come away, finally releasing the timbers so that he fell into the water with a splash. He spent the last part of the journey kicking his way through the water using a log as a float.

When he finally reached the castle just after dawn, the Little Brothers had refused to let him back inside.

"No offense, but you seem very upset," Cook had told him through the crack of the door. "They don't trust you not to unravel everything."

"I'm soaked and freezing!" yelled Kellen. "OF COURSE I'M UPSET!"

This didn't seem to reassure the Little Brothers at all. Eventually Kellen had calmed down enough to climb onto the platform of flotsam without it falling apart.

Cook had brought Kellen breakfast, dry clothes of marsh silk, and news of Gall. Life seemed to be seeping from the marsh horseman slowly, like light leaving the sky. The horse sprawled at the base of the castle shivering, all pretense abandoned, its hide frog-slick and its eyes silver-skinned.

"I need the Little Brothers to make me another raft!" Kellen insisted. "I need to go back to the Market and talk to that trapper again!"

"There won't be another Moonlit Market for three nights," Cook told him. "Be patient."

But Kellen could not be patient. He paced and fidgeted and fretted. He scanned the sky looking for Yannick. But the gulls that flew down were all the wrong sort—big, boisterous white ones that strutted and flung their heads up and down while shouting *keeee-kyark-kyark-kyark* at the world.

"Fine! I'll make my own raft!" Kellen tried to use twine and creepers to bind driftwood together. Again and again, he found that his own hands had pulled them apart and that his lap was full of splinters and frayed threads.

It was late afternoon when a black-headed gull swooped down toward Kellen, something large drooping from its beak. It landed clumsily on the flotsam platform a few yards from him, and a familiar puzzle bottle fell from its beak with a rattle.

"Yannick!" Kellen scrambled over and held out the silver collar. The black-headed gull hopped toward it, with an air of reluctance and much nervous wing-twitching, then ventured its dark head within the collar.

When people changed shape, it always turned Kellen's stomach. There was no good way for feathers to burrow back into skin, or for a beak to soften into flesh, or for joints that bent one way to start bending another.

Even after the collar had changed Yannick back to a winged boy, he spent half a minute lying on his side, making tiny keening noises in response to Kellen's urgent questions. At last Yannick blew his own salt-tangled hair out of his face and managed a human word.

"Food," he said.

After Kellen had managed to pour some fish stew down Yannick's eager throat, the winged boy's eyes took on a less foggy, animalistic expression.

"Nettle?" asked Kellen.

"Alive," said Yannick. "And spying on Salvation."

Kellen listened to Yannick's croaked explanation and was overwhelmed with relief. Nettle was alive and well. And she hadn't betrayed him or Gall. Nettle had taken her own headstrong, thorny path, but she was still the friend he knew—intractable, loyal, maddening, and courageous.

Of course, that meant he could get on with being properly annoyed with her.

"Idiot!" he muttered, trying to blink the mistiness out of his eyes. "What was she thinking? How are we going to get her out of there?"

"There's more." Yannick grimaced despondently. "You're not going to like this."

Yannick was right. When Kellen learned who his curser was, he did not like it at all.

Tansy.

"She knew everything," Kellen said faintly. "All our plans. We always contacted the Rescued through her. We let her read Leona's letter—that must be how Salvation found out that Leona was their secret enemy. And Tansy knew we were going to Amicable Affairs the next day. No wonder the Dancing Star was waiting for us. She knew that we were heading to the village with the red tower. She must have rushed from Mizzleport to warn Ammet. But that doesn't explain the ambush at the dead tree . . ."

He spent a moment thinking and tugging at his hair.

"Yes, it does," he said after a moment. "If Tansy told Ammet about the secret black market, he probably found out who was responsible and forced them to tell him where they'd been meeting Linnet. That's why there was a trap waiting at the Throat. He knew if we were investigating the secret trade, we'd turn up there sooner or later."

The truth explained a hundred things, and at the same time Kellen could make no sense of it at all.

Tansy. Warm, wise, confident Tansy. Everyone's big sister. Kellen's greatest success story.

Kellen didn't feel angry, sad, or betrayed, the way Yannick clearly did. The news was too strange for that. It was too surprising even to be a shock. A lightning strike would be a shock. This was like lightning that drew letters in the air or flew from flower to flower. It meant that Kellen was mistaken about about everything.

"I never understood her," he said, feeling empty and light-headed. "I thought I did. I thought I understood what she'd been through, what she felt. But I didn't. Cursers and the cursed . . . all the things I knew about them were wrong."

With sudden vividness, he remembered what he had shouted at the cursed merchant with the bleeding hands, a little age ago.

It doesn't even matter which of your victims cursed you. Because in this case, the problem is you.

"This is my doing," he said numbly. "I walked this path. That's why I'm cursed. That's why I'm here."

"What are you talking about?" asked Yannick.

"I ran away," Kellen said. "Over and over again. Unravelling's the easy part. The bit after that, when you've got all these loose threads, and people crying . . . I don't know how to do that part. Nettle's good at it. I just can't deal with it. I quit while I'm ahead, while I'm still the hero. Because if I stick around, I'll mess up. I always do. I'll get something really wrong, and then I'll be the bad guy. Then I'll have people chasing me out of town, so I might as well run away first. And the cursers I helped arrest . . . I just left them in chains and tried not to think about them."

"All right, so you're a mess," Yannick said, then sighed. "But your heart's always been in the right place. You didn't deserve to be cursed. Punched in the face, maybe, but not cursed."

"That doesn't matter," said Kellen earnestly. "My curse isn't just a puzzle to solve. I need to unpick everything. I need to unpick *me*. I need to find another path, and do something important to put things right . . . but I don't know what."

Following Nettle's instructions, Yannick had retrieved the puzzle bottle from where she had hidden it at the base of the red storage tower. He had managed to carry it by gripping its leather loop with his beak, but the effort had exhausted him.

When Kellen turned the screw to allow conversation, the Dancing Star was reluctant to speak.

Where is the girl? it asked eventually in its fire-crackle voice.

"She went to Salvation, using the directions you gave her," said Kellen. He couldn't help sounding accusatory. "You knew she had a curse egg, didn't you?"

There was no answer, only faint rasps and rustles.

"What's the point of talking to this thing?" Kellen said harshly. "It's on Shay Ammet's side! We should drop it in the marshes and let it lie in the mud forever!"

My contract binds me to obey that man, said the Dancing Star, after a moment. *He sent me to catch you in the cage made of my hands. He ordered me to bring you and the girl to Salvation.*

"I know," said Kellen bitterly.

That is why I could tell the girl the way to Salvation. The Dancing Star's voice curled slyly. *I was following his orders and bringing her to him. She was not an enemy, she was a curser who wanted to join Salvation. I was not disobeying him. Now she has joined them and met that man. She can talk to him and understand him. When she knows what manner of a man he is, she can curse him. Make him a fly or a toadstool or a hot cinder so that he can never give me orders again. Maybe he will die of it, and I will be free.*

"Is that what Nettle's planning?" asked Kellen, aghast.

I told her she might do these things, said the Dancing Star. *She said she would see what breed of man he was and decide what needed to be done.*

"I don't *think* she'll curse him," said Yannick, looking anxious. "Not unless it's a last resort."

"But she can't, can she?" asked Kellen, confused. "Cursers are immune to curses!"

That man leads a league of cursers, rustled the Dancing Star, *but he is not a curser.*

"That's it!" exclaimed Kellen, as revelation hit. "That's why Shay Ammet's been trying to capture me from the start! He needs me as insurance! Salvation deals in curses, and curses ruin lives, and people whose lives are ruined sometimes become cursers. The cursers of

Salvation can't be cursed in revenge, but Ammet can because he's not a curser! And now, thanks to us, everyone knows he's the leader of Salvation, so he's a target. He wants me under his control so I can cure him if he gets cursed. That's his weak point!"

"But I don't want Nettle cursing him!" said Yannick.

"No," agreed Kellen, "and it wouldn't help anyway. Even if he died or disappeared, the rest of Salvation would still believe his lies and keep cursing people. We need another plan . . . a way to bind them somehow, so they have to give up this war. A bargain they can't break . . ."

"A bargain for what?" demanded Yannick.

"Oh!" Kellen stared upward into the sky as his thoughts cleared. "I've got it! That'll lure him out! Wait—I should look at the wording of the contract of sale we signed with the trapper—Ow!"

"Don't do that," growled Yannick, who had just kicked Kellen. "Don't drop mysterious hints without explaining. Nettle puts up with it, but I *will* headbutt you."

"Shay Ammet needs me," said Kellen, "so if we use me as bait—"

"That worked so well with Pale Mallow," muttered Yannick. "I definitely don't remember you nearly drowning."

"It'll be different this time," said Kellen, feeling his spirits rising at last, his thoughts flurrying and gleaming like sand granules in sunlit water. "It'll be safer. Or . . . differently dangerous. I think I've got a plan."

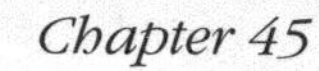

Chapter 45

A HURDY-GURDY WIND

IN THE CRISP PREDAWN MORNING, WHEN DEW WAS STILL dripping from the rigging, Yannick came back to Nettle's boat. He perched on the rim of a porthole and tapped on the glass. Nettle rested her cheek against her side of the window and they passed thoughts to each other like notes.

The plan's dangerous, she said, *for all of us*.

He sent her a wordless thought like a hug or the gentle smoothing of a loose feather. They both knew that they had accepted the plan.

"All right," she said aloud. She walked out onto the deck of the boat, and a black-headed gull flew out of the gray morning air and landed on her shoulder, his red feet cold against her neck.

Nettle walked boldly through the waking boat-village and heard urgent whispers on either side. She noticed a couple of people run off ahead of her. By the time she reached Shay Ammet's boat, he was waiting on the lower deck, ready to speak to her.

"I did what you said, Mr. Ammet!" Nettle's voice came out sounding quavery and frightened, just as she hoped. "I called my brother back and asked him to find Kellen. Mr. Ammet, Kellen does need your help! He's in terrible trouble!"

"Well done, Nettle!" Shay Ammet came forward and took her hands in his moleskin-gloved hands, chafing them as if to warm them. "You're a good friend to Kellen. Where is he?"

Nettle was very aware of the picture they made—a courtly gentleman in a velvet coat comforting a poor, shivering waif.

"He's a prisoner!" she said. "Some creatures captured him! He's on a big black boat near the sea's edge."

Shay Ammet's expression tightened with alarm and annoyance. Only a madman would try to raid a mysterious ship manned by things from the Wilds.

"Are you sure?" he asked.

"Yes!" Nettle didn't need to feign nerves. "They're going to put him up for sale, Mr. Ammet! At the Moonlit Market!"

A fierce little spark of hope dawned in Shay Ammet's face.

"When?" he asked, his grip on Nettle's hands now a little intense. "When is he being sold? This is very important, Nettle!"

"Two nights from now," she said.

"Two nights . . ." Shay released Nettle's hands. "There's time. I'll go there myself. I'll have my boat made ready. Wait there, both of you. I have more questions . . ."

Other Salvation members were called over, and Shay Ammet talked to them in quiet murmurs. Nettle stood with Yannick on her shoulder, her nerves prickling.

Suddenly she sensed a throb of alarm from her brother. The gull launched himself into the air, just as a fishing net was flung over both of them. Nettle flailed at it, pulling it off her face, just in time to see Yannick hit the deck, his wings thrashing in the threads.

"Calm him down, Nettle!" ordered Shay Ammet, as one of his underlings grabbed the tangled gull off the floor.

"The net's hurting him!" Nettle protested.

"It won't harm him if he holds still." Ammet fixed Nettle with his earnest, plausible eyes. "I'm sorry, but we know how unpredictable Yannick can be. We can't have him flying away and forgetting about us right now, can we? We need him to direct us to where Kellen is."

"You're taking my brother with you to the Market?"

"I'll need to bring both of you. You're the only one who can talk to your brother. And . . . if you're on hand, he's more likely to stay focused."

Ammet still sounded reasonable and sympathetic, but Nettle was getting better at seeing through his facade.

He doesn't trust us completely yet. He probably reckons that I'll be more obedient if he has Yannick captive, and Yannick will follow orders if he has me.

So we need to let Mr. Ammet think he's won.

Nettle did her best to look docile and cowed as everyone around her hurriedly made the boat ready. When Yannick was put in a birdcage, she had to force herself not to run to him.

I'm fine, he snapped, but she could feel his suppressed panic at the confined space, the bars too close for him to spread his wings. *We knew this could happen.*

Nettle watched helplessly as Yannick was carried belowdecks, out of her sight.

Before long, a green-stained foresail was raised on the mast of Ammet's boat. No other boats were being prepared. Presumably Ammet felt he could travel faster with just one craft.

Just as all seemed ready, three men boarded the boat. Two were cursers Nettle had seen around in the boat-village. The third man stumbled along between them, as if in a daze. He stared around him with puzzled, sky-clear eyes, which widened as they settled on Nettle. She saw recognition in his face, followed by exhausted confusion.

It was Harland, Cherrick Gall's husband.

Again, Nettle felt a dizzy sense of unreality. What was Harland doing in Salvation? He had seemed so earnest and straightforward, the very opposite of a curser. Had Nettle been fooled by him too? It was only as he was being led belowdecks that she observed the cords binding Harland's wrists.

Shay Ammet noticed her concern.

"Don't worry about him," he said. "He's just . . . insurance. A way of avoiding bloodshed if we meet our friend Mr. Gall."

So that was why Harland had disappeared so suddenly from his lodgings in Mizzleport! He hadn't given up on Gall at all. He'd been kidnapped by Salvation.

Somewhere the tinny chime of the alarm bell sounded, and Nettle could see everyone in the boat-village hurrying for cover. The two men who had taken Harland below reappeared and sprinted for another boat. Only Nettle and Shay Ammet remained on deck.

As the hatches on the other boats slammed shut, Ammet pulled an old, grimy hurdy-gurdy out of a box. He donned the shoulder-strap, rested its fiddle-like bulk against his torso, and began to turn the crank. As the turning wheel chafed its strings, the instrument gave out a mournful droning chord like three voices lost in desolation.

The wind freshened, and the sun slid nervously behind a cloud. All around, Nettle could hear the reeds whisper and hiss, as if exchanging some terrible news. The gray-green sail flapped and cracked loudly as it abruptly filled with air.

"You should go below, Nettle," said Ammet, his eyes scanning the reed-forest. "You might find the rest of our crew . . . unnerving."

Descending hastily belowdecks, Nettle found herself stooping in a cramped but well-furnished cabin. The flickering lantern-light gleamed on walls of oak and polished brass and on brightly woven rugs. It also shone upon the cabin's other occupant.

"Hello, Nettle," said Tansy. She was sitting on an embroidered chair in smart traveling clothes, a hip flask in one hand. She didn't smile, or sweep Nettle into a hug, or offer her a drink.

Nettle searched the familiar features for her friend and could not find her. The sunlit halo of warmth that had always surrounded Tansy was gone, dead as ash.

"Hello, Tansy," Nettle replied, and sat down on the nearest seat.

"No shock?" asked Tansy in the same flat tone. "No hysterics?"

"Not really my style," said Nettle.

The boat rocked slightly, then began to move. Nettle could hear it crunching and creaking its way through the reed-forest with increasing speed.

"If you're going to say something, say it," said Tansy, sounding tense for the first time.

"All right," said Nettle as calmly as she could. "How long have you been with Salvation?"

There was a pause while Tansy took a swig from her hip flask.

"It was your fault, actually," she said. "Shay helped your brother Cole get a place at the sanatorium, so he could keep an eye on him. He thought he might turn into a curser, you see—all that ranting and screaming. But he didn't. He got better. About six months ago, you stopped visiting Cole, and I started coming in your place. That's how Shay met me. He saw through me right away. He realized I was a curser and recruited me."

There had been a ulterior motive to Shay Ammet's apparent kindness, then. Cole had looked like another curser for his collection. Nettle also noticed Tansy's use of Ammet's first name and wondered how close she was to Salvation's leader.

"So you were already a curser when you met Mr. Ammet?" Nettle tried to ignore ominous sounds from above. Aside from the droning lament of the hurdy-gurdy, heavy footfalls shivered the wooden ceiling above Nettle, causing trickles of dust to fall. Evidently Ammet was not alone on deck.

"Yes," said Tansy, and this time there was an edge in her voice that Nettle had never heard before. "I told you—it was *your fault.*"

She turned the hip flask around in her hand so that the lamplight glinted on its metal.

"You don't know what I went through, pulling myself together after my curse," Tansy went on. "It was months before I could put a brave face on it, and even then I was crumbling in my shell. And then Kellen turned up with *you*. You'd been cursed for three years, and lost both your parents, and seen your brother murder your sister. And you seemed . . . *fine*. Calm. Controlled. Always looking after other people, as if nothing had happened to you. You made it look *easy*!"

"Easy?" Nettle echoed in disbelief. She had always felt like a mess, a bundle of broken parts held together with twine, painfully inferior to the flawless, radiant Tansy.

"I couldn't bear it," said Tansy, her voice shaking. "So I hated you. And I hated myself for hating you because I knew I wasn't being fair. But one day I realized that I didn't *need* to be fair. The world hadn't been fair to me, and it never would be. It was such a relief when I gave in and let the curse grow! My egg stopped being my secret agony. It started to feel like a secret power."

Nettle had forgotten what it was like being hated. Suddenly she felt as if she were back under her stepmother's gaze again, watching a veil slip.

"So why didn't you do it?" asked Nettle, trying to keep her voice steady. "Why didn't you curse me?"

Tansy gave a bitter laugh.

"I did," she said. "I cursed you nine months ago. And it didn't work. That's when I realized that you weren't calm, or whole, or perfect. You were a curser. A fraud, just like me. So, how many people have you cursed?" Tansy rolled her eyes as Nettle flushed and hesitated. "Oh, don't play the innocent. You were already a curser nine months ago, and you've got another curse egg now. How many?"

"I'd rather not say," said Nettle. *None* didn't seem like a safe answer.

"I'll bet." Tansy's tone had bite. "More than eight?"

"Not that many," said Nettle, still not looking up.

"I'm still ahead of you, then."

"And . . . one of your eight was Kellen." Nettle tried to keep her voice neutral. Anything she could find out might help Kellen unravel his curse. "Did Mr. Ammet order you to do that?"

"Not at first." Tansy gave an impatient sigh. "He went to the trouble of rescuing that awful Jendy Pin, because he thought she'd hate Kellen enough to curse him."

Nettle remembered the mysterious note that Gall had shown them on their first meeting.

A good choice. She has every reason to want revenge against the young unraveller of curses. After all, he's the one that put her behind bars.

"Why?" she asked. "Why did he want Kellen cursed?"

"It had to be the right sort of curse," said Tansy. "Something to show Kellen what it was like being a curser. Something to make him a trouble and danger to others. Everyone would reject him, Chancery would try to lock him up, and he'd have no choice but to run to us for protection. That was Shay's plan. But the stupid Pin woman couldn't muster the curse. Everyone says cursers keep on cursing for the rest of their lives, but we have quite a few duds in our camp. It's as if their hatred burned out after the first curse. So I took care of it instead." Tansy regarded Nettle through hooded eyes. "Is that a problem?"

Nettle took a deep breath.

"No," she lied. "If you hadn't cursed Kellen, I'd have done it myself sooner or later."

She felt the atmosphere in the cabin change. It didn't exactly thaw, but Tansy's face became less guarded, more animated.

"We were just puzzles to him, weren't we?" Tansy scowled at her reflection in the flask. "Puzzles that were supposed to go away once he'd solved us. He takes the credit and his fee, and he walks away while we're still shivering in hell!"

Nettle couldn't argue. The way Kellen lost interest in those he rescued *had* sometimes filled her with a deep and shameful rage.

"Everybody told me—*everybody!*—that I must be so very grateful to Kellen," Tansy continued. "How happy I must be to be free of that terrible curse! Every time I agreed with them, and smiled, I felt like I was swallowing poison. Slowly I realized that I would always be 'the harp girl.' That was all, that was the sum of me. I would always be the victim, a bit part in somebody else's story—Kellen's story. And my part of the story was over, because I was cured. I'd been solved. My job was to be happy and grateful forever. But what if I couldn't feel happy or grateful? What if I didn't even want to be? I couldn't ask anybody that, because I already knew the answer. It didn't matter what I wanted or felt. It has never, ever mattered. My story was things happening to me. I was cursed, then I was cured. The End. *I* didn't matter."

Tansy took another drink from her flask, then let out a long, jagged breath.

"When you're a curser," she said, "at least you matter. Your feelings smash a hole in the world. I don't have to be alone with my pain anymore. I can share it."

Nettle watched the shadows pass and flicker over Tansy's face. Perhaps the woman Nettle had admired and envied had never existed. But could the real Tansy, with all her darkness, have been turned to another path if her closest friend had not been Shay Ammet?

"I wish we'd talked properly a long time ago," Nettle said impulsively.

"I didn't want to *talk*, Nettle," Tansy said harshly. "I didn't want you to fix me or make me feel better. I'm tired of being somebody's else's success story."

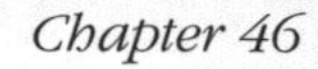

Chapter 46

THE SILKEN SNARE

HOUR FOLLOWED HOUR AS THE GRAY DAY WORE ITSELF OUT. In the low-ceilinged cabin, the lanterns swung, and Nettle felt vibrations through her feet.

She could still sense Yannick's mind somewhere on the boat. He was being kept in the dark, and his thoughts were queasy and ruffled with unease. She suspected that he was probably in Ammet's own cabin, which was off-limits to her. Nettle hadn't been allowed anywhere near the cargo hold at the stern either, and she guessed that this was where Harland was being kept.

All the while, Nettle heard the thunderous footsteps above amid the howl of the wind and the droning of the hurdy-gurdy. Occasionally a low, long scraping sound set her teeth on edge.

They must be creatures from the Wilds, she told Yannick silently. *Ammet has probably bound them to him, the way he bound the Dancing Star.*

This is bad! said Yannick in Nettle's head. *We thought Ammet might bring us along, but we didn't know he'd come with a monster bodyguard. We're going fast as well. At this rate, we'll get there before Kellen's traps are ready!*

Tansy was fractious and unpredictable company. Sometimes she stayed sullenly silent for hours. At other times she talked at length about her curses, watching Nettle with predatory keenness for any sign of shock or disapproval.

It's like she's testing my loyalty to Salvation and wants me to fail, thought Nettle. *But I don't think she really knows what she wants from me. She wants me to die in a fire. She wants to know I'm as bad as her, so she doesn't feel inferior. She wants a kindred spirit, so she's not alone.*

Nonetheless, Nettle struggled to seem calm when Tansy admitted to cursing the little cloud-girl.

"I was really supposed to curse the Head of Contracts." Tansy yawned. "I'd never met him, so I went and watched his house. He wasn't there, but . . . I saw his daughter. She went to the park with her nursemaids. I followed, and watched, and helped her call her dog out of a pond. She was so sweet and trusting." Tansy's voice hardened. "It's easy to be innocent and trusting when nothing bad has ever, *ever* happened to you. She was so loved. So safe. I hated her."

Nettle's heart stung with a complicated grief. For the first time, she wondered what her stepmother's early life had been like. Had she regarded her stepchildren with a similar agonizing envy?

A faint rustling sound issued from the depths of Tansy's coat. She tutted and pulled a red, lacquered box out of her pocket. When she opened it, a brief breeze seemed to erupt from it, fluttering her lapels and swaying the loose strands of her hair.

"What's that?" Nettle asked.

"A nuisance," said Tansy. She pulled a small handwritten note out of the box. "When you turned up in camp, I had to move my boat away from the others so you wouldn't see me. Shay gave me this so he could send me food and messages. He's got the other box—they're a pair. But now he keeps using this to send me orders."

She read the note with an air of malaise.

"Apparently we're passing a fang-shaped rock covered in carvings and kittiwake nests," she said. "Why don't you ask your brother where we go next?"

After directions had been passed on, Nettle stayed in silent conference with her brother.

Don't, said Yannick. He knew that Tansy's words were still swirling in Nettle's mind like ink in water.

I can't help it! Nettle said, miserably. *When I talk to Tansy, I feel like I'm looking into a dark mirror. Falling into it. The things she thinks and feels—I recognize them, Yannick!*

I know, said Yannick, his thoughts jagged with anger and love. *But you're nothing like her. Nothing at all.*

Nettle realized that he was right.

I've been fighting a losing battle against my rage, but I never stopped fighting. I never vented my anger on other people. I did *try to help the other members of the Rescued, and it wasn't an act. I wanted to save them from feeling what I feel.*

It was a strange sort of comfort, a glimmer of lost sun behind the black clouds that had filled her mind for so long.

I'm not calm or whole or perfect. I'm really not. But I'm not Tansy.

Late at night, when Nettle was dozing in her chair, the boat juddered. The hurdy-gurdy halted its disconsolate song abruptly, and there was an airy roar from above, like the wind howling through cold caves. Shay Ammet's voice could just be heard above the ruckus.

"Tansy!" he was shouting. "Bring lights!"

Nettle followed Tansy out onto the deck and peered upward as Tansy held her flickering lantern aloft.

The boat had clearly been passing beneath a huddle of great trees, some entwined so that trunk cleaved to trunk. By the light of the lantern, Nettle could see that all of the trees were draped with fine, freshly spun cobweb. It hung in pale, translucent canopies from the lowest boughs, hard to see in the low-hanging mist.

The mast and sail were trammeled with web, the greenish canvas wreathed in white. The wind still filled the sail, and the boat creaked and strained forward like a living thing, but the webs held it back, stretching without tearing. The lantern-light glittered on thousands of tiny forms in the silken canopies, spiders of every size.

"Don't touch the strands!" shouted Shay Ammet, who was staring upward in thinly disguised fury. "That's no ordinary web!" He glanced round, and noticed Nettle. "Your brother never mentioned this!"

"He flies over the trees!" Nettle protested quickly. "He probably didn't notice!"

At the prow, a single shadowy figure struggled in a tangle of strands. It roared, flailed dark claws, and flicked a long, tapering tail of bone. The web was clearly strong enough to hold even creatures of the Wilds.

Another indistinct figure was just visible at the stern, trying to cut away trailing strands with a long sword. Silver gleamed at its neck, and dark antlers crowned its head. With a shiver, Nettle wondered if it was the same creature she had seen dragging away the headless body of Jendy Pin.

"Tansy, fetch me another lantern!" called Shay Ammet. "And the two-handed saw! We'll take the mast down if we must!"

While everyone was busy on deck, Nettle seized her chance and edged down the narrow, unlit corridor that ran between the cabins. Ammet's cabin was locked, and she didn't dare try to force it. Instead, she continued toward the stern, then knelt down and tapped on the hatch that she suspected led down into the cargo hold.

"Mr. Melbrook?" she whispered, remembering Harland's surname from the letter she had seen in Gall's possession.

Beyond the hatch, there was a small creak and an intake of breath.

"Who's there?" As predicted, it was Harland's voice.

"Please—we have to be quiet!" Nettle glanced back down the corridor. "We can't let them hear us talking!" Even with the sound of sawing and shouting above, she didn't want to take too many chances. "It's Nettle—we met you at Amicable Affairs, and asked you about your husband—"

"Everyone has questions about Cherrick," Harland said quietly. "Sorry, I don't know where he is, and I wouldn't tell you if I did."

"I already know where he is," said Nettle bluntly, "and I'm not going to tell Mr. Ammet." As Harland started to ask an urgent question, she cut him off. "Please—just listen! I'm not really with Salvation! We're both hostages. Mr. Ammet wants to use me and my brother to talk my friend Kellen into joining him. And he's probably planning to hold you at knife-point if your husband turns up."

"I don't think that would do Mr. Ammet any good," Harland murmured sadly.

Nettle thought of Gall abandoning his mission to race across Mizzleport in search of his husband. She remembered him holding Harland's damp letter in the moonlight, looking blank-faced and bereft.

"No," she said. "It wouldn't do him any good in the end. Because if Mr. Ammet threatened you, I think your husband would chase him to the ends of the earth, even if it meant tearing the whole Wilds apart."

There was a pause.

"Oh," said Harland. He sounded worried and taken aback but perhaps not completely unhappy.

"Listen," said Nettle. "We're both in danger. Once we're no longer needed as hostages, we're expendable. I wouldn't trust Mr. Ammet not to kill us or trade us for something at the Market. We need to work together, because soon we need to escape."

There was a long creaking groan above, then a crash like falling timber. More shouts, then a turbulent chuckle of water. Slowly the boat began to move.

"Is there a plan?" asked Harland.

"Several," muttered Nettle. "But I don't think the first one worked."

Chapter 47

REVENGE

BY DUSK THE NEXT DAY, KELLEN HAD GNAWED ALL HIS fingernails to the quick.

There was no sign of Yannick, nor any word on the success of the web traps, and the lack of news gradually ate at Kellen's nerves. He was used to taking a leap with half a plan, but Nettle had always been there to point out the flaws in his suggestions. Checking his own plans for holes was exhausting.

The Little Brothers had been happy enough to weave the giant web trap, but they didn't like Kellen's main scheme at all. They didn't want to put Kellen up for sale and risk his precious spider-born skill falling into other hands.

"Tell them it's just a pretense!" Kellen begged Cook. "They pretend to sell me! They draw up a contract that's a trap for Shay Ammet! Can't they do that?"

Eventually the Little Brothers agreed, but with much uncertain chittering. The idea of putting something on sale at the Market *without* selling it seemed an alien idea, almost an unholy one.

As a buttery moon gleamed low in the sky, Kellen clambered aboard a freshly fashioned wood-and-cobweb raft. Unexpectedly, his impatience chilled to apprehension. The cramped, bronze-and-oak cage smelled of animals and old urine. His stomach clenched with panic as its door clicked shut behind him.

"There's a catch so you can open the door and escape if you need to," Cook told him, with a bright but terrified smile. He had been fluttering with nerves ever since it became clear that he would be accompanying Kellen.

"Hey!" shouted Kellen as a heavy cloth was thrown over his cage, plunging him into darkness.

"We need to hide you from sight," Cook told him, tugging the cloth slightly so that Kellen was allowed a narrow slit-view of the world outside. "We don't want other buyers taking an interest in you."

Kellen tried not to touch the cloth, for fear of unravelling it. There were Little Brothers concealed on the raft this time, and he sometimes felt them scuttle across his skin or hair. He didn't know whether to find their presence comforting or disquieting.

As Cook began to paddle the raft forward, Kellen found himself remembering all the stories where people ignored warnings.

. . . on waking, he soon forgot the prophecy of the dream woman and rode on toward the forest as planned . . .

. . . he laughed at the screaming coin, cast it down, and ground it beneath his heel . . .

. . . she was too busy talking to the fair youth to notice the warnings carved into the gate . . .

Now he thought about it, characters like these were seldom given names or happy endings. They became warnings themselves, rag-clad bones that crunched under the boots of the true hero later in the tale.

Even in the dark, Kellen felt the change, the shift from night noises to the stealthy but busy sounds of the Market. A smell seemed to suffuse everything, cold as moonlight and heady as wine.

His mind was fogging again, telling him that he was goods for sale. If he wasn't careful, he would forget his own plan.

"Where are we?" he whispered.

There were a few incoherent noises outside.

"So many crows," gasped Cook at last. Apparently he was struggling to keep his own head clear. "I think they can smell me."

"We were heading for the Trappers' boats, weren't we?" prompted Kellen. It had seemed the most natural place for the Little Brothers to sell an Unraveller.

"She looks like my mother," Cook breathed, in a frightened, entranced voice, "but so much younger . . ."

"Cook!" Kellen risked reaching out and punching at the man's ankle.

"Yes!" Cook sounded as if he had snapped to attention. "Yes," he added more sadly, and began to paddle again.

I remember this place now, thought Kellen. *Why did I think it would be a good idea to come back here?* Somehow in daylight he had forgotten the drug-like pull of the Market, or the way that the night air crackled with peril and uncertainty.

"Fine ears, well made," called out a voice that slithered coldly, like a raindrop down glass. "Are they for sale?"

"No!" squeaked Cook. "Respectfully, mistress, none of me is for sale. But we have a pocket sundial for a forgotten sun, a love song in a bottle . . ."

Cook trailed off and heaved an unsteady sigh of relief. Presumably his interrogator had lost interest and moved on.

"Can you see anyone else human around?" asked Kellen, fidgeting. "You're looking for someone tall, dark, and well-dressed."

"No," whispered Cook. "No, I . . . I really don't think anyone I can see is human."

For the first time, it crossed Kellen's mind that Shay Ammet might not take the bait. Even as he thought this, however, something hit the cage's cloth with a soft thump and a flutter of wings. There were some guttural, conversational *gheek* and *ghuk* noises, and then a small, dark-headed shape wriggled its way in through the slit in the cloth.

"Yannick!" whispered Kellen with a flood of relief. "Where the hell have you been!"

He fished the silver collar out of his pocket, and held it so that it surrounded the gull's neck. A moment later he regretted doing so. Suddenly he was sharing the cramped cage with someone bigger and bonier than him, and his face was full of rough, palpitating wing.

"Gaah!" he yelped, spitting to keep the feathers out of his mouth. "How many elbows do you have?"

"Careful!" whispered Yannick, banging his head on the cage roof. "Mind the plumes! I need those to fly!" The bigger boy's skin was clammily cold, presumably from his journey through the sky. "Listen! I can't stay long!"

"Not without suffocating me, you can't," muttered Kellen.

"Shut up and listen!" hissed Yannick.

Before either could say more, however, a raised voice nearby made them both jump.

"Good evening to you, silver ears! Do you know you have a bird on your raft? I just saw it swoop down among your wares."

Kellen winced. Yannick's descent had apparently drawn attention.

"What?" Cook sounded flustered. "Oh! That . . . that's just a gull. It . . . follows my raft sometimes, hoping for food."

"A bold gull," continued the other, sly as silk. "A singular gull. In fact, I think I've seen it before."

Kellen recognized the voice. It belonged to the red-haired trapper with the long foxy smile, the one who had sold him Yannick but hinted at a future reckoning. Of course, Cook had been paddling obediently toward the trappers' boats.

"What's in the cage?" asked the fox-smooth voice.

"Ahh . . . that is . . . a creature for a very specific buyer." Cook sounded panicky. "A sickly thing, but with selective appeal. For . . . um . . . a niche collector."

"How intriguing!" The sharp-toothed smile was almost audible in the trapper's tone. "I specialize in the uncommonplace and loved-by-few. How much are you asking for it?"

"I . . ." Cook's brain seemed to have run aground.

"Will you trade it for this braag-skull flask that holds more than a man can drink?" the man asked suavely. "Or this nightmare mask? Shall I throw in this soul-flower? No? Really? What is your buyer offering?"

Kellen was aware that the Little Brothers were scuttling feverishly around him. He hoped they weren't tempted by the trapper's offers.

"It must be quite a prize you have under there," continued the trapper. "A rare thing. A precious thing. Perhaps a monkey-faced thing that talks too much, and knows too much, and thinks it's very clever? Something like that?" There was no mistaking the smiling malice in the trapper's voice.

He knows it's us, thought Kellen, heart hammering. *Maybe he heard us talking*. Creatures of the Wilds never forgot a grudge. He didn't know how much the trapper would pay for a chance at petty revenge, but apparently quite a lot.

"What about a pair of good, simple human ears like the ones you once had?" suggested the trapper with dangerous gentleness. "Or a fine, seafaring boat that will take you to another shore where nobody knows you? Or a mirror with a reflection that talks back, so you are never lonely again?"

The raft creaked as Cook shifted his feet and gave a shivering sigh.

"I'm sorry," he said. "I . . . I can't."

"We'll see about that," said the trapper, his tone abruptly losing all softness.

There was a pause, punctuated only by the *splash-splash-splash* of Cook hastily paddling away.

"What's happening?" whispered Kellen, when the suspense became too much. "Is he following us? Can he hear us?"

"No," murmured Cook. "But he's leaning over his boat's rail and watching us leave. And . . . now he's calling over to someone in a rowing boat. He's talking and pointing at us."

"So much for avoiding attention," muttered Kellen.

"Can't be helped." Yannick shifted into a slightly less bone-crushing position. "Listen—Ammet sent me to scout ahead and find out where you were. His boat will be here in less than an hour."

"The webs didn't hold him, then," said Kellen. His hopes hadn't been high.

"They slowed him down," answered Yannick. "He had to leave behind his mast and sail and one of the creatures crewing the boat."

"Creatures?" said Kellen, gripped by foreboding.

His heart sank as Yannick told him about the ominous beings at Ammet's command and of Harland imprisoned in the cargo hold. It would be much harder for Nettle to escape if she had somebody else to rescue and man-eating monsters to evade.

"I don't know what those creatures are," said Kellen, getting out the puzzle bottle, "but I know someone who might." He twisted the spiral seashell so that the Dancing Star could hear Yannick's description of the creatures.

The horned one is a Gladelord, the Dancing Star said. *Dangerous and very proud. The musical machine contains the spirit of a stormwight. Its voice summons the wind.*

"And they're both bound by contract to Ammet?"

The Gladelord is contracted, said the Dancing Star. *It has sworn obedience before a Bookbearer, as I did. The stormwight is bound into the musical machine.*

"Wait a minute," said Kellen. "The stormwight isn't bound to Ammet? Does that mean that anybody can play that hurdy-gurdy and summon a wind?"

He wasn't quite sure how summoning a wind would help Nettle escape, but he suspected that if she summoned one big enough, she could at least cause chaos. In Kellen's experience, if your enemies were bigger, smarter, and more numerous than you, chaos was your friend.

They dared not talk for a long time. Soon Kellen removed the silver collar again, grimacing and closing his eyes as Yannick changed painfully back into a gull. Kellen leaned back as the bird flew out from under the cloth, and up into the warm and dangerous night.

"Did anyone see?" he asked Cook.

"Hard to tell," answered Cook. "I think a lot of people *are* watching us, though."

"That's not good," murmured Kellen.

"Oh." Cook gave a panicky little intake of breath. "We . . . we have company."

"Already?" Kellen's heart hammered as he considered his tightrope of a plan. A moment ago he had been fidgeting with impatience, but now he didn't feel ready. "Is it Shay Ammet?"

"No," said Cook. His tone was odd, filled with a mixture of awe and dread.

Kellen peered out through the slit and saw a woman walking across the water toward them.

Where the hem of her loose, silver dress met the water, it seemed to strike like rain, fretting the surface and sending out ripples. Even at a distance, Kellen could see her beautiful black eyes, which were very large and did not blink. Her mouth was wide open as if she were singing, but no sound came. Instead, he felt a tingle in his breastbone, as if some great bell were silently ringing and sending tremors through the world. Her arms stretched out in front of her, but her hands were tendrils of white mist that faded and formed, faded and formed.

His mind went blank. If she had reached out one of those smoky hands to him, he would have taken it like a little child and stepped out to walk the moon-gilded water with her. There was a painful thump, and Kellen guessed that Cook had fallen clumsily to his knees.

She put her head on one side, waiting for an answer. She had said something to them, Kellen realized. There was something they needed to do. They would do it, of course. The woman made her request again, and this time her meaning slid into his mind, like a cat nosing onto his lap.

It comes to our boat, she was saying. *It is sold in our auction. Come now.*

She gestured with her misty white hand, pointing past the black Trapper boats and the coracle traffic to where the great White Boats gleamed opalescent in the moonlight.

The most extraordinary and dangerous sales of the Market took place in the White Boats. Evidently the masters of the White Boats had heard a whisper of something wonderful and of great price and were demanding that it take its rightful place in their auction.

Kellen had little doubt that his fox-faced enemy had spread that rumor. Perhaps he wanted another chance to buy Kellen, or perhaps he just wanted to make mischief. Either way, the trapper had his revenge. There was now no way to lay a discreet trap for Shay Ammet. Unless Kellen could come up with another plan fast, he would be sold at auction and carried away a slave on some boat with night-colored sails.

He didn't ask Cook if they could say no to the woman in the silver dress. He knew that they could not, any more than they could breathe water or swim across the sky.

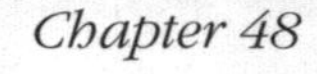

Chapter 48

HALF-CHANCE

NETTLE SENSED THE RETURN OF HER GULL-BROTHER A FEW minutes before Shay Ammet summoned her up to the deck. Emerging, she found that the reed-forest had been left behind. Nettle felt her heart catch as she saw an expanse of rippling, moonlit water on all sides, from which rose the twisted silhouettes of great trees.

"Nettle, is that Yannick?" Ammet pointed, and Nettle made out a gray-and-white, moonlit shape wheeling gracefully in the night air, vanishing and appearing as it moved between tree-shadow and moonlight.

"Yes, that's him." Nettle frowned, sensing Yannick's agitation.

"Has he found the Market?" said Ammet urgently. "Has he found Kellen?"

"Yes!" Nettle focused, trying to comprehend Yannick's jagged, urgent thoughts. "Yes, he says Kellen's on . . . one of the White Boats . . ." She trailed off, starting to understand why her brother was panicking.

What do you mean, one of the White Boats? she asked. *That wasn't the plan!*

That's what I'm trying to tell you! Yannick's pale wings sliced the darkness overhead. *The plan's gone wrong! Everything was fine when I left him, but I circled around the Market a couple of times to look for scraps, and the next time I saw his raft, some water sprite was leading it to the White Boats! So I swooped down and eavesdropped . . .*

Nettle gritted her teeth as Yannick continued, trying not to let her dismay show on her face.

"Kellen's going to be sold in an auction on a White Boat," she said at last. "Yannick heard people talking about it. He can lead us there."

Shay Ammet took some bone coins and talismans out of his pocket and frowned at them in a calculating fashion. He had probably hoped to buy Kellen quickly and quietly, before other buyers discovered that such a tempting prize was on offer. If Kellen was sold in open auction, there would be more buyers, and that would drive up the price.

He gave Nettle a reassuring smile, then led Tansy aside for a whispered conversation. Nettle couldn't help notice him darting glances at the siblings as he talked, and even on one occasion at the horned beast at the stern.

Kellen's plan is dead in the water! said Yannick. *Tricking Ammet into signing a dodgy contract won't work if half the Market's watching the sale. Even if Ammet doesn't notice it's a trap, somebody will!*

Yannick was right. At this rate, Kellen really would be sold to Ammet, or perhaps somebody weirder and worse.

Great, sighed Nettle. *Now we need to escape* and *rescue Kellen.*

Yannick didn't reply, but she sensed a burst of resentful worry, like a shower of sparks. He agreed but didn't agree. He wanted Nettle to save herself, instead of tangling with the Moonlit Market and the White Boats.

There's no point trying to escape till we reach the Market anyway, Nettle pointed out gently. *At the Market there might at least be distractions, or other boats for us to hide in. Out here, there's nowhere to go. You could fly away, but I'd have to swim, and so would Harland. Mr. Ammet's stag would catch us or kill us in seconds.*

Nettle had racked her brains until they hurt, coming up with escape plans and discarding them all as suicidal. Harland's presence made everything more complicated. If Nettle managed to sneak down to the cargo hold, she could unbolt the hatch quickly enough, but the rope around Harland's wrists would take longer to untie. Even if she managed to release Harland without the sharp-eyed Tansy noticing, there would still be the problem of getting past the murderous stag.

Well, said Yannick, sounding a little less miserable, *I know more about that stag now . . .*

As Yannick repeated the Dancing Star's account of Ammet's creatures, Nettle's gaze crept to the antlered shape at the stern. By daylight it had looked like a deer, but by night it was hard to make out, even when the moon shone fully on it. It appeared to stand on two legs, taller than a man, its silver collar bright. Somehow it was using a long pole to drive the boat forward, despite the depth of the water.

A Gladelord, Yannick called it. A proud creature, apparently. How had it come to be enslaved to a man like Ammet?

Shay Ammet was busy talking to Tansy. On impulse, Nettle risked giving the Gladelord a small, respectful bow. It was a silly gesture, she knew that, but she suddenly felt angry at the theft of the creature's dignity.

You won't win that thing round, said Yannick. *It's contracted to obey Ammet. The hurdy-gurdy's our best hope. Do you know where it is?*

It's probably in Mr. Ammet's cabin, answered Nettle. A stiff breeze didn't sound like much of a distraction, but they were short on options. *He hasn't brought it out since the boat lost its sail.*

Can you get into the cabin? Yannick skimmed low, then soared high.

It's locked, Nettle told him, *and I don't think I'm strong enough to break down the door.*

Nettle was realizing, very unwillingly, that sometimes there was no way to plan well. You just needed to know what you would do given half a chance, and then recognize your half-chance when it came.

Half an hour later, while a small cloud nuzzled against the moon like a cat, Shay Ammet's boat arrived in the Moonlit Market.

For Nettle, the arrival felt a lot like waking up. Suddenly her mind was diamond-clear. The previous days, weeks, and years felt flat and nonsensical, like the scrambled impressions of a dream.

Tansy stared around with distrust and unease. Nettle suspected that she had never been to the Moonlit Market before either and wondered what she was feeling and hearing.

Shay Ammet seemed at ease and was evidently known to some in the Moonlit Market. As a sloop with patched blue sails slid by, its occupant raised a clawed hand in greeting. Sitting on the half-submerged branch of a tree, two ragged figures called out to Ammet in guttural, cough-like barks, holding up silver amulets for his appreciation. He answered them only by inclining his head, and his boat continued to glide in the wake of Yannick's graceful arabesques.

Ahead, Nettle could see three boats larger than the rest, each appearing to glow with its own opalescent radiance. Yannick headed for the nearest, and as Nettle gazed upon the white ship, the rest of the Market faded from her thoughts. She saw only the dancing lanterns strung along its sides, the silver-rimmed portholes, and the figures walking its decks in bright-colored silks. They wore face-like masks, or perhaps mask-like faces. Smaller boats milled around the shining white ship, and she could see dark shapes scaling rope ladders to the decks above.

Her worries melted away. She couldn't remember what she was looking for, but she knew she would find everything she needed on the White Boat.

No, Nettle thought suddenly. *That's not the way I think. There's nothing you can buy that solves everything.* Perhaps her mind wasn't diamond-clear after all. Perhaps that feeling was just another trick of the Market.

"Nettle, I need you to call your brother down now," said Ammet, using his firm-but-gentle voice. He was holding the birdcage again.

Nettle's spirits sank at the thought of Yannick caged. She even opened her mouth to protest and then suddenly realized that this moment, this very moment, was her half-chance. This was what she had been waiting for.

She did not protest. She nodded obediently, and looked up toward Yannick.

Yannick, stay on the wing! she told her brother. *Don't land!*

Nettle then let her face crease with surprise and dismay.

"I'm sorry!" she said, turning back to Ammet. "Yannick won't come down. He says he doesn't want to go back in the birdcage!"

"It's for his own safety!" insisted Ammet. "This market's full of snares and dangers."

He was keeping his voice kindly, but he was clearly annoyed. He held all the cards and could force Yannick to land by threatening his sister. However, that would mean that he could no longer play the part of kindly protector. Nettle suspected Leona was right—Ammet *did* like to think he was a gentleman. He liked being gazed at with trust and admiration.

"I know!" said Nettle. "I'm sorry." She twisted her hands fretfully, then brightened. "Food! My brother can never resist food. I'll fetch some from the cabin!" She hurried down belowdecks before Ammet could react. To her relief, nobody followed her.

Two minutes later, she heard Tansy calling from the deck.

"Where are you? What are you doing down there?"

"Coming!" Nettle reappeared, gripping a bread roll. "Sorry I was so long, I . . . I broke a cup." This at least was true, but she didn't mention that she'd done it deliberately or that one shard was no longer with the rest. Nettle broke the bread and scattered it on the deck, as if trying to tempt Yannick down.

It's done, she told Yannick. *Now we just need to stall. Stay in the air . . .*

"Oh, this is ridiculous!" snapped Tansy impatiently, as Yannick continued to circle. She abruptly grabbed a handful of Nettle's hair, pulling her head back, and making her cry out. "Yannick, stop being contrary!" Her voice was warm and playful. "You don't want our friend with the horns to think your sister isn't being helpful, do you?"

She's bluffing! Nettle told her brother desperately, as the gull began to spiral slowly downward. *Fly away! I'll find you later, I promise!*

I can't let them hurt you, said Yannick. *I'm your big brother. Or at least I should try to be, just now and then.*

His red feet touched down on the deck, and Tansy threw a net over him.

Shay Ammet's boat had seemed large compared to the barges of Salvation, but as it drew up alongside the White Boat, it looked small and grubby. The great hull beside them was hypnotically white, making Nettle think of cherry blossoms and snow. A rope ladder dropped to them from above, unfurling as it fell.

"Take care of everything here," Ammet murmured to Tansy, then turned to the Gladelord. "Keep the prisoners safe," he told it, "but do not let them leave the boat. Do you understand?"

The great beast bowed its antlered head in acquiescence.

Birdcage in hand, Shay Ammet climbed the rope ladder toward the sound of muted voices and haunting, fragmentary music. He looked like a picture painted in moonlight and shadow, a dashing hero in velvet scaling the side of a phantom ship. Nettle thought of him letting Tansy do his threatening for him and despised him more than she had ever despised anyone.

I'll find you! Nettle mentally shouted to Yannick. She watched the swinging birdcage until it was swallowed by the shadows above. Her brother's thoughts grew thin with distance, and then she lost her grip on them entirely.

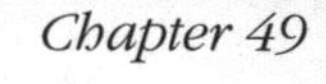

Chapter 49

DRAGONFLY

ABOARD THE WHITE BOAT, KELLEN CROUCHED IN HIS CLOAKED cage and tried not panic. He could see little, but all around he heard conversations he did not understand, in musical, lilting voices and guttural rumbles.

He wondered if he could curl up in a ball and play dead. Better still, perhaps he could play *ordinary*. Maybe if nobody was interested in him, he wouldn't be sold after all.

"If they ask," he hissed at Cook, "I'm just a weaver boy who wandered into the marshes, and you don't know what all the fuss is about."

"I . . . think it's a bit late to pretend that," whispered Cook. "The . . . the cloth . . ."

Kellen became aware that the fabric covering his cage was twitching and fraying. Countless threads wriggled, then fell away, crinkled with the memory of weft and warp.

Unraveller, he thought he heard a breeze-like voice whisper, and the word was taken up by others. *Unraveller*. Fame had escaped Kellen all his life, but apparently these slinking things of shadow had heard of him.

Figures approached, turning their heads this way and that, examining him with sibilant interest. He saw faces like reflections seen in rippled glass, twinned heads shrouded by a single crimson hood, empty eye-holes that poured smoke . . .

The last of the cloth fell away into heaped thread, and now Kellen could see his surroundings. The cage sat in the middle of the bone-pale deck, near to one of the masts. The ship itself seemed softly luminous, casting more light than the moon above. Kellen couldn't tell how many figures roamed the deck, whispering, dancing, and sipping from crystal goblets. They baffled his eye, seeming to ripple, merge, and multiply.

On one side of the cage, Cook hunched fearfully in a throne made of driftwood and living ivy. On the other side loomed a huge pair of brass weighing scales, some eight feet high.

The central strut of the scales was decorated with a three-foot-long jeweled dragonfly. Kellen thought it was a sculpture, until its wings buzzed abruptly into motion. They made a surprisingly deep sound, like rain on a metal sheet. All around, the murmurs of the crowd hushed obediently.

Staring at the dragonfly, Kellen could see its glittering turquoise scales, its veined wings, the many-jeweled mystery of its eyes. At the same time, he could see that it was a tiny and impossibly old woman, clinging to the top of the scales with skeletally thin arms, her long sequined dress dangling below her and starched folds of gauze protruding like wings.

The dragonfly-auctioneer pointed to Kellen's cage and gave a long, grating buzz, which somehow he understood.

The Unraveller, the buzz meant. *Spider-gifted, spider-cursed. Destroyer of curses, dismantler of mysteries, unpicker of souls. Who can offer treasures worthy of this prize?*

Despite himself, Kellen felt a tiny, irrational glow of pride at hearing himself described in such legendary terms. That glow faded fast, though, as he saw the indistinct figures draw nearer, like cats closing in on a trapped bird.

"You wouldn't want me!" he yelled. "I'll unravel every tether you put on me, every tie!"

Undeterred, some of the strangers were calling out to the auctioneer, in growls, whispers, and glass-clear trills of birdsong. The auctioneer ignored all these offers, until something else advanced through the crowd.

A magnificent gown of starlight and slug-silver was floating toward the cage, apparently unaided. Below it, dew-studded shoes walked softly, as if with the steps of invisible feet. Above, an oily black tiara hovered and dripped.

Duchess, was the whisper in the crowd, and Kellen remembered the fox-trader saying that someone of that name wanted to buy Yannick for parts. The Duchess glided over and examined Kellen facelessly. Then she turned to the auctioneer and held up an obsidian mirror across which faint images shimmered.

The dragonfly-woman nodded approval, and the Duchess placed the mirror in one bowl of the scales. The dish dropped a few inches, its counterpart rising.

"May I examine the goods?" asked a clear, well-spoken human voice. Through the phantasmagoria of half-seen shapes, a man in a blue velvet coat approached, his expression earnest and pleasant. In one hand he held a cloth-swaddled birdcage.

Receiving a nod from the auctioneer, the man drew close and looked down at Kellen with kindly, reassuring eyes.

"Hello, Kellen," he said quietly. "We've never met, but I'm a friend of Nettle and Yannick."

"I know who you are, Mr. Ammet," said Kellen, his voice coming out as a snarl.

"Nettle asked me to come and rescue you," said the Salvation leader, apparently unfazed by Kellen's tone. "And I'm afraid the only way to do that is to buy you. I'll need your help once the bargain is struck. There will be an oath for you to swear before the contract is sealed." He nodded toward two gray-robed figures standing on the far side of the deck, patiently holding closed books before them.

Bookbearers, thought Kellen, his heart sinking. If he swore allegiance to Ammet before a Bookbearer, no willpower, ingenuity, or clever contract would free him. He would be the Salvation leader's tool until one of them died.

"But people can be bought without anyone swearing an oath!" protested Kellen, remembering his purchase of Yannick.

"I'm afraid in this case it will be unavoidable," said Ammet, sadly but firmly. "I do hope I can persuade you, Kellen. It would be tragic if someone else bought you and had you stuffed, or ate you to gain your abilities. Nettle would be devastated. She misses you."

"Where is she, then?" A wild, impulsive anger was fizzing in Kellen's belly and tingling in his hands. "What have you done with her?"

"She's quite safe and well," Ammet said promptly.

"Prove it!" snapped Kellen. He wanted Shay Ammet to bring Nettle before him. He had the irrational feeling that if he and she were in the same place, even divided by bars, then somehow they would triumph. As a team, even a cornered, outnumbered team, they were unbeatable.

Ammet sighed.

"Very well," he said. He wrote something in a pocket book and tore out the leaf. Then he pulled out a flat, wooden box and opened it. Inside, Kellen glimpsed what looked like a bristling, bracelet-sized loop of woven stalks and stems. As Ammet lowered the note through the loop, the little slip of paper seemed to vanish.

Kellen couldn't take his eyes off the box. He was remembering the eerie, tense atmosphere at the tree-arch in the heart of the Wilds and near the walled-up hollow tree. He was feeling the same uneasy tingle now.

That's a Throat! he thought. *Half of one anyway. There must be a matching loop somewhere else, acting as the other end of the portal. That trader said I needed a "small throat," but I didn't know what she meant . . .*

Ammet was now pulling something small and brown out of the box. It was a loose, snipped lock of hair.

"Do you recognize the color?" asked Ammet, holding up the little twist of hair.

"That could be anyone's hair!" declared Kellen.

"What would convince you, then?" asked Ammet. "A finger?" His gaze was still kindly and humorous, but with those words the threat was laid bare, like a claw emerging from a cat's velvet paw. *We have your friend. Swear an oath when the time comes, or I'll reunite her with you, a piece at a time.*

Kellen's anger slipped its leash. He lunged between the bars and grabbed Ammet's arm.

The blue velvet of the sleeve flew apart under his grip, and the cotton below it convulsed and parted. Kellen felt his fingers bite into the warm skin of Ammet's arm before the man gave a loud yell and shook him off. Ammet stepped back, shakily pressing a handkerchief to five small, reddened wounds on his forearm.

There was a sound like a gong striking immediately to Kellen's left. Reflexively he turned toward the sound.

Something had appeared in the air directly in front of Cook. It looked like a naked, floating baby made of bright red stone. It had no nose or eyes, but its mouth smiled. It reached out and touched Cook's terrified face, then vanished. Cook flinched back violently with a whimper of pain. A tiny black mark had been seared into his cheek.

"Cook!" Kellen turned his attention to his companion as Ammet stalked away. "What was that?"

"My . . ." Cook swallowed uneasily, his ears swiveling while spiderlike shapes chittered and skittered through his hair. "My friends say that was a punishment. Bloodshed in the Market is a . . . a serious business. Since you're here as my property, our hosts punished me for your actions. Pl-please don't do that again." He began to shake uncontrollably. "Once I have three marks, they'll—"

"All right!" whispered Kellen hastily. "I won't!"

Ammet now approached the scales.

"My bid is this bird!" he declared, pulling the cloth from the birdcage. To Kellen's horror, it contained a familiar-looking black-headed gull. "This is a human boy transfigured, a creature of two worlds and none. Unique and valuable."

There was an appreciative susurration on all sides as Yannick's cage was placed in the empty bowl, which promptly descended two feet, hoisting the other dish aloft. With a sullen rasp, the owner of the obsidian mirror recovered it and stalked off through the crowd.

"He's not yours, Ammet!" yelled Kellen, and saw the Salvation leader flinch at the use of his own name. The sight filled Kellen with defiant hilarity. "His name's Shay Ammet!" he shouted, pointing. "Just in case any of you ever want to use that against him!" Kellen knew he was burning his bridges, but they were stupid, ugly bridges, and he hadn't been planning to use them anyway.

Meanwhile, the Duchess had pulled two screaming bone dice out of her reticule, and tossed them into her bowl of the scales, which promptly sank below its fellow. Kellen wished Ammet at the bottom of the sea, but didn't much like the idea of being dissected by the Duchess either.

Nettle, I really hope your plans are going better than mine . . .

Come on, thought Nettle. *Come on*.

She stood on the deck of Shay Ammet's boat next to Tansy, listening for any sound from below and trying not to fidget. If only Tansy had not called her back so quickly! If only Nettle had had time to cut Harland's bonds herself, instead of hastily giving him a shard of cup and a few whispers . . .

Tansy was watching her little wooden box like a hawk and occasionally pulling notes out of it. After reading one, she had insisted on cutting off a lock of Nettle's hair. In response to other notes, Tansy had fed various objects into the box—stone coins, a small book bound in yellow skin, and a chipped carnelian amulet.

Was it Nettle's imagination or was that a creaking sound from belowdecks? A faint thud and scrape? A sharp crack, perhaps of a levered door giving way?

"Oh, not again!" muttered Tansy, pulling out another note. Then she gave a start, staring at the door that led belowdecks.

Harland had just stepped out onto the deck, blinking in the brilliant moonlight. In one hand he held the hurdy-gurdy.

Tansy took a step back, pale with panic. Perhaps she was remembering that farmers need strength to till land and heft sacks of grain. Gentleness is often mistaken for weakness, but the two are not even close cousins.

She reached out to grab Nettle's arm, but Nettle was already running to Harland's side. Tansy glared at her, suspicion hardening into conviction.

"Gladelord, stop the prisoners!" she shouted. "They're trying to escape!"

The pale, antlered shape slowly turned its head and began to stalk toward Nettle and Harland in long, lean strides. There was no time to learn the art of playing the hurdy-gurdy and summoning a wind. No time to do anything but gamble.

Nettle grabbed the hurdy-gurdy out of Harland's hand and smashed it against the deck. The stem broke away from the belly with a twanged lament. When she stamped on the wooden casing, it cracked.

The broken instrument continued breaking, spitting shards of wood while spinning on the deck like an upturned ladybird. A thin wheezing moan became a wail, then a howl of savage joy, and a wind rose from nowhere, knocking Tansy off her feet. Even the Gladelord was forced back, shielding its face as it was buffeted by spray and debris.

The deck planks vibrated beneath Nettle's feet. All around, the air was laughing, with a sound like the sky tearing. The boat lolled and gave a long groan of tortured wood, its timbers buckling as if invisible hands were twisting it. The deck planks pushed out their wooden bolts and leaped from their sockets, one after another.

From below, Nettle heard a loud crack and the gurgling seethe of rushing water. The boat started tipping dangerously toward starboard. Harland grabbed Nettle's arm just in time to stop her tumbling down the unexpected slope.

Tansy screamed as water poured from the hold. She scrabbled against the deck for fingerholds, gradually sliding toward the waiting water.

"The ladder!" Nettle shouted over the howl of the wind. She and Harland scrambled on hands and knees up the sloping deck toward the rope ladder that hung over the side of the White Boat. Before they could reach it, however, a tall, antlered figure stalked into view between them and the white hull, its narrow hooves somehow finding purchase on the sloping, wet deck.

"I'll try to distract it," Harland said in Nettle's ear. "You run for the ladder."

"No!" said Nettle. "Listen, you need to get onto the White Boat and find Kellen before they sell him. He can tell you where to find your husband!" It was a ruthless bait to use, but Nettle didn't want the quiet man beside her to do something fatally rash. "Listen—I can distract the Gladelord! It . . . it won't hurt me." She wasn't at all sure this was true, but she managed to force conviction into her voice.

Nettle looked up into the Gladelord's blur of a face and found it had eyes after all, ink-dark and silver-sheened. In them she saw a spirit fierce as a winter frost and merciless as the slow throttle of the strangler vine. The creature knew no pity or tenderness, but in servitude it was learning regret and fear and felt them as a canker in its soul.

Struck by inspiration, she scrabbled at a protruding deck plank, pulling out two loose wooden bolts.

"Your Majesty!" she called out, over the howl of the wind. "We're not leaving the boat, Your Majesty!" She held up the two bolts, then passed one quickly to Harland. "We're taking it with us!"

The creature tilted its great head slightly to one side. She was giving the creature a way to twist the orders it had been given, but there was no guarantee that it would choose to do so. It owed her nothing, and she had nothing to offer it, except the chance for a small rebellion against its master.

What would Kellen do? Something stupid. Something rash. Something nobody would expect.

"You were ordered to protect us, weren't you, Your Majesty?" shouted Nettle. Unsteadily, she got to her feet and picked up a broken piece of plank. "Then protect me!"

With that, she turned and ran down the sloping deck, slithering and sliding. The edge approached and beyond it the water, churned white by the vengeful wind.

Hugging her plank tightly with both arms, Nettle leaped from the deck.

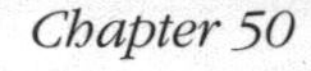

Chapter 50

HIGH STAKES

ABOARD THE WHITE BOAT, KELLEN HEARD THE WIND RISE TO A storm wail with eerie suddenness. The white sails above fluttered, then filled abruptly with a loud crack. The indistinct attendees clutched at their flapping cowls and capes and stared around in concern. Small, shadowy shapes in snow-white gloves could be seen running around the boat, fastening hatches, securing ropes, chasing chairs that had rolled away.

"What's happening?" Kellen asked Cook, but it was clear that nobody knew.

The blast rose to a deafening, jubilant screech. A violent gust bowled Shay Ammet off his feet. There were hisses and thin shrieks as others present flung themselves to the deck. One was borne up into the air, somersaulting, and spread lean blue wings to steady itself.

The wind dropped as quickly as it had risen, and the assembled company gradually rose to their feet again. There were mutters, though, and resentful hisses.

The mysterious gong sounded again.

Shay Ammet looked round in surprise and found the floating crimson baby inches from his face. As it reached out and touched his face, he gave a gargled noise of pain. The next moment it had gone, leaving a charred black mark on Ammet's cheek.

That wind must have been the stormwight, Kellen realized. Evidently the Moonlit Market considered Ammet responsible for the disruption it had caused. He was the one who had brought the stormwight to the Market.

For the first time in a while, Kellen felt a little fizz of hope. If Nettle had unleashed the spirit of the hurdy-gurdy, perhaps she had managed to escape.

As the crowd settled, Kellen became aware that he could hear a quiet, highlander voice drawing near.

"Excuse me . . . excuse me . . . is this the sale of a boy called Kellen?" Of all people, Harland Melbrook was picking his way across the deck, giving uncertain smiles to the slinking, silken figures around him. He looked like a strange joke in that setting, with his workaday clothes and two-day stubble.

"Over here!" called Kellen, and Harland hurried across to the cage. The farmer looked pale and out of breath, his clothes damp and spray-spattered. "What are you doing here?"

"Nettle told me to find you!" whispered Harland, kneeling down next to the cage. "What can I do? How can we get you out of here?"

"Is Nettle all right?" asked Kellen. "Did she escape too?" He listened with growing anxiety to Harland's hurried account of the stormwight's release.

"She's alive," Harland assured him. "I saw her swimming away from the boat, with one arm over a plank. And that stag-creature wasn't stopping her. It was walking along after her, jumping from plank to plank. Following. She said she had a plan."

Kellen didn't like the idea of Nettle being stalked by the Gladelord, but apparently it wasn't attacking her. For now she was at large, which was the best news he'd heard all night.

"She also said . . ." Harland hesitated. "She said you'd know where to find Cherrick. Is he in trouble too?"

"He's in a safe place," Kellen said bluntly, "but he's badly hurt." There was no time for tact. "He's going to die, unless we can find him a new heart."

Harland exhaled and stared into the distance, eyes wide and full of moonlight.

"A human heart?" he asked.

Yes, was the truthful answer. *A human heart. A heart that considers him home. A heart like yours.* Kellen knew what Harland was about to say.

The Wilds bred stories. Sometimes you found yourself in one, and not all of them had happy endings. Some were tales of tragedy, doomed love, or sacrifice. Perhaps for a long time some twisted string of destiny had been drawing Harland toward this moment so that he would be in the right place to offer his honest, loyal heart without hesitation.

"If that's all he needs—" began Harland.

"No!" snapped Kellen. "We're not ripping your heart out!"

He was remembering what the trapper had told him. *One might do for both, but it would be dangerous. Do you know anyone with a small throat?* Now that he knew what a "small throat" was, he had an inkling how Gall might be saved. But how could he get the throat-boxes away from Ammet?

Oh.

There was a way that he might deprive Ammet of his throat-boxes, and perhaps the creatures in his power as well. If he had no monsters, maybe Ammet would be unable to threaten Nettle, Yannick, or Harland. But there was a price, and the thought of it made Kellen feel sick.

"I've got a plan!" declared Kellen, before he could lose his nerve. "I just don't have time to explain! Right now I need you to bid on me. I can give you some valuables to offer. You need to push up the price and force Ammet to bid everything he's got!"

For years, Shay Ammet had taken a secret pride in his ability to navigate the Moonlit Market, without making ripples or falling prey to its dangers. The fanged and feathered things with which he traded sensed that he was another smiling predator, as clever and dangerous as they were.

It had always been like entering a dance. A dangerous dance involving rapid footwork, but one whose steps he knew. Now he felt as though the music of the dance were changing every few seconds while half the dance floor fell away into a chasm.

For the first time, he had been marked. He had been *chastised*. The indignity stung more than the pain.

And that farmer Harland Melbrook was at the auction, blundering around loose like a lost child. The sight should have been comical, but his appearance made Ammet feel as though he had fallen into a bad dream. How had the man escaped?

Ammet pulled out his portal-box to send a note to Tansy, but when he opened it, a deluge of marsh water poured out. He closed it again hastily.

"Excuse me," the farmer was asking people around him. "How do I bid? I . . . I have this." He was holding up a puzzle bottle, of the sort made by Amicable Affairs. "It has a Dancing Star in it. A *rare* Dancing Star. One that's walked the cobbles of the capital."

There was a hiss of interest all around. Appalled, Ammet watched as one bowl of the scales was cleared to make room for the bottle. As far as he knew, the only Dancing Star to have visited the capital was the one he himself had brought there.

"That creature's not yours to bid!" he snapped, unable to contain himself.

"This Dancing Star is mine by right of capture and possession," Harland Melbrook said carefully, as if reciting something he had been told.

"It belongs to me!" Ammet declared. "I can prove it! If you release it from that bottle, we'll soon see who it goes to and calls master!"

"What about that gull-boy?" asked the farmer, and his mild voice had an edge now. "If you let him go, would he fly to you? I don't think so. He's not yours to bid either."

While Ammet was still struggling to think of an answer, a whisper in his ear made him start.

"Shay!"

Tansy was standing next to him. She was soaked to the skin, her hair bedraggled. He suspected that she was shaking with rage rather than cold, however. He could see from her face that she had retreated into her dark place. Somebody would probably pay for that.

"The boat sank," she said, in a quiet, cold voice. "Nettle swam away, and your Gladelord chased her instead of rescuing me!"

Ammet had always made time for Tansy's grievances, but now he had not a second to spare.

"The contracts!" he hissed through gritted teeth. "The contracts I placed in your care! Give them to me!"

Ammet snatched a collection of very damp scrolls from his scowling companion and raised one over his head.

"A contract of sale for the Dancing Star!" he shouted.

"A contract of sale for the gull-boy," retaliated Harland Melbrook, drawing a parchment scroll out of his own pocket.

Again the ground gave under Ammet's feet. Nothing made sense. He was a child lost in the deepest woods, the darkness glittering with curious, hungry eyes.

The dragonfly-woman stuttered her wings pensively, then apparently came to a decision.

Both goods are claimed by right of capture and right of contract, she buzzed. *Both will be taken from here and released, to see which masters they seek.*

Enraged, Ammet watched as the puzzle bottle and the birdcage were taken away, the gull aflutter.

"I have another bid to make!" he declared quickly. He took out the twist of Nettle's hair and held it up. "A girl once cursed, who has become a curser. A circle completed. A snake biting its own tail." The poetry of it seemed to appeal to the gathering and auctioneer alike.

"But you don't have her either!" yelled Kellen, gripping the bars.

"You are mistaken," said Ammet loudly, and saw the boy's face fall.

It probably was not a lie, Ammet told himself. By now it was likely that the Gladelord had recovered the girl. However, it was important to make sure.

"Give me everything I left in your care!" he whispered to Tansy. "Then go and find out what's taking the Gladelord so long! Bring Nettle back here!"

Tansy gaped at him in shock. She was not used to him ordering her around so bluntly.

"I can't go out there by myself!" she protested.

"We have no time!" he whispered fiercely. "I have just promised to hand over a girl who was once cursed and who is now a curser. When the auction ends, I *must* be able to provide such a girl, one way or another!"

One way or another. Did Tansy understand the implied threat? Yes, she was hurriedly emptying her pockets and passing him everything he had entrusted to her, even the portal-box. He would reassure Tansy later and convince her that *of course* he hadn't really been threatening to hand her over in Nettle's place. But for now Tansy needed to be frightened enough not to argue.

As Tansy hurried away, still looking aghast and hurt, Shay Ammet placed the twist of Nettle's hair in the scales and watched them tilt in his favor.

When the door of the birdcage opened, Yannick erupted from it like a fish-scented arrow from a bow. Four swift beats of his wings, and the cold, sweet rightness of the air was his. He was king of the wind, the upturned world his plaything.

Below him was the luminous White Boat. There was little left of Ammet's vessel, except one half of the hull and a scattering of floating timbers. The boats of the Market were discolored blots against the glossy surface of the water, like tarnish-spots on an old mirror.

He circled tree-high, scanning the moonlit scene for Nettle. He could sense her, the prickly, contradictory cinders-and-milk feel of her mind. Yannick gave his screeching cry, rending the secretive quiet of the night.

Yannick! He could feel Nettle's relief at hearing his voice. He followed the tug of her thoughts, her voice in his mind.

He saw the Gladelord first. The tall antlered creature stood upon a floating timber, using a broken plank to paddle along and keep pace with a gray-sailed sloop. Two crow-faced men called to it from the rail of the boat, but it ignored them. Its pale, indistinct face was turned toward a third figure on the deck of the sloop, one that Yannick recognized at once.

Nettle! he called as he wheeled down to land on the rail beside her. Once again he felt the irreplaceable sense of wrong-rightness as their minds jarred into an embrace. Too much, always too much, and necessary as air.

The crow-faced sailors had eyes like chips of coal and dark purple rags that fluttered like feathers. In grindstone voices they called out to the Gladelord, wheedling and haggling, offering a string of stone coins from a drowned city if it would glide away and find trouble elsewhere.

These creatures . . . Yannick murmured.

They pulled me out of the water, answered Nettle, but Yannick could tell that she didn't trust them either. *I think they're afraid to do anything to me while the Gladelord's there.*

"Gladelord!" Another voice rang out across the water. "What are you doing?"

A flat-bottomed, yellowish-pale boat was approaching, with a single woman standing in it. She did not row or paddle, nor was there any sail, but still the boat glided steadily forward. As the boat drew closer, Yannick realized that its knobbly, ugly surface was made of bones of different sizes, glued together with something honey-dark.

The woman's clothes were dripping, her auburn hair clinging dankly to her face. It was Tansy, her expression cold and dull with malice. Yannick sensed that this was her true face, and something inside him tore a little, in a way that promised pain later. Tansy cast no reflection in the water, and Yannick guessed that she had haggled badly for her new boat.

"Don't just stare at Nettle!" Tansy shouted at the Gladelord. "Capture her! Bring her back to the White Boat!"

The stalemate shattered like glass. Both crow-sailors drew their curved knives as the Gladelord leaped onto the sloop's deck in one uncanny bound. Yannick launched himself into the air, ready to dive at anyone who came near his sister, and filled the air with his rent-metal screeches.

For Harland, it was like being caught in a fever dream. Nothing made sense, nothing stayed still, and he didn't fully understand the plan he was following. All he could do was trust his instincts and the frantic, muddy boy in the cage.

"Ammet has two special boxes!" the boy was saying. "You need to force him to bid them. It's your husband's only hope!"

They were interrupted by the sound of a gong, followed by a sharp cry. Shay Ammet, the man who had held Harland prisoner, was clutching at his own face in pain and outrage. Harland realized that there were now two small seared marks on Ammet's cheek instead of one.

"What was that for?" Ammet shouted at the surrounding night, giving up all pretense of calm.

One of your creatures has shed blood, buzzed the auctioneer.

Blood. Harland remembered the quiet girl who had freed him, and the stag-monster following her, and hoped that she was safe.

"Hey!" The caged boy had reached out through the bars and was tugging at Harland's trouser leg. "Wake up! The auction's about to end, and Ammet hasn't bid the boxes! You have to bid something! Anything! Quickly!"

Harland tried to focus and think, but it was not easy. There were silken murmurs in his ear. Other offers, other bargains, invitations to step aboard a low, forest-green boat, misty with pipe-smoke and incense . . .

"No, thank you kindly," he murmured.

If you meet a thing of the Wilds, be courteous, his mother had always told him. *But be careful too. Humans are walking treasure chests of precious things—dreams and memories and toes and teeth. All those things are worth more given than stolen, so they'll try to trick you into surrendering them.*

A treasure chest . . .

Harland pushed forward hastily toward the huge scales and the insect-woman that sat at its summit.

"My lady!" he began, hearing how desperate and clumsy he sounded. "Please—I need to bid again! I . . . know there are things humans can offer that have worth here. Thoughts, dreams, memories . . . things I can't put in the scales. I'm sorry, I don't know the worth of what I have. But I'm sure you do."

The great, insectile eyes settled upon Harland. In the myriad lenses, he saw his reflection shrunken and multiplied into a hundred identical, uncertain faces. What did she see? Two useless shortsighted eyes, hands calloused with work, a simple set of workaday wits, memories full of terrace-cutting and hay-gathering. A man reeking of ordinariness.

In spite of this, she did not banish him with a firmly shaken head. Her glittering gaze evidently saw something of value.

What are you willing to give? she buzzed.

"Anything but my heart," said Harland. "That's spoken for. I just need enough to beat the other bids."

All your memories before your fifteenth birthday, suggested the auctioneer. Harland had the feeling that, in her alien way, she was trying to help. *Your voice. And your daydreams.*

Harland felt an aching horror at the thought that he might lose all these things, but he nodded quickly before he could lose his nerve.

As the auctioneer declared the new bid, Harland watched the face of Shay Ammet, who looked frustrated and conflicted as he searched his now-empty pockets. There was nothing to stop Ammet throwing his own dreams or memories into the scales, but Harland didn't think he would. This sort of man would always find other people for the dirt, danger, and hard work. He would sacrifice anyone or anything but himself.

Ammet scowled for a long moment, then produced two matching wooden boxes, one of them very wet. With a set and angry expression, he dumped them into his bowl of the scales, which sank like lead with an audible clang.

For a moment, Harland felt nothing but relief. The boxes were in the scales, and Harland's own bid was overturned. He would not lose his voice, his daydreams, his childhood memories. The next moment, he was ashamed of himself. How could he stop bidding when a boy was about to be sold like a calf at market?

He glanced at the auctioneer, but she shook her head.

Nothing you have left is worth enough, she buzzed quietly.

Harland hurried to the boy named Kellen.

"I've nothing left to bid!" he said. "What do we do?"

"Nothing," said the boy, managing a shaky smile. "Ammet wins the bid. Which means he has to hand over the boxes, some of his monsters, and Nettle too, if he's caught her. That's what we wanted. *This was my plan*."

Hunched in his cage, Kellen watched the auctioneer raise a small staff and whirl it with a whistling sound. The answering patter of applause was like rain.

The auction was over.

It had to be this way, thought Kellen, hugging his knees.

The moon's glare was now softened by the thin cloud streaming across it like smoke. The gleam of the boat itself was becoming muted, sinking into dimness the way a mind slides into sleep. Shadowy shapes could be seen making the White Boat ready, skimming up the masts and riggings with the speed of lizards up a wall. On the far side the deck, Ammet and Cook were arguing with each other and an owl-eyed clerk.

Kellen sensed the Bookbearer's approach before he saw it. The gray-robed figure loomed over the cage, quietly and without malice, its smudged face turned attentively toward him.

"Getting ready to bind me into slavery?" Kellen's voice wobbled, but he could tell that the creature didn't really understand his meaning or his tone. It waited for the contract to be ready, and for him to agree to it, with the simple contentment of a plant anticipating rain. It had no notion that Kellen might be unwilling or unhappy. It was, he suddenly realized, an innocent.

"You'll witness anything if you're asked, won't you?" he asked.

You win, Ammet. I'll swear the oath you want. It's the only way to seal the bargain and keep everyone safe. Everyone but me.

Chapter 51

PROMISES

SHAY AMMET GLANCED NERVOUSLY AT THE MOON. HE WAS desperate to sign the contract and leave before the White Boat sailed, but the silk-eared man was still arguing details, until Ammet itched to throw him overboard.

"My masters will only sign a contract with Salvation!" the silk-eared man kept insisting. "Not with one man!"

"We do not have time for this!" Ammet said through his teeth.

"Nor do you have a boat," said the other man, with unexpected firmness. "If you agree that the boy is being sold to Salvation instead of you, my masters will make you a raft."

"Very well, but . . ." Ammet suddenly noticed that the owl-eyed clerk was already conjuring a contract, with a few wand-like waves of a quill. "Wait—let me see that!"

I tire of this, buzzed a voice as deep as thunder, sending a vibration through the timbers of the deck. Looking up, Ammet was startled to see two new shimmering moons filling the sky, each made up of hundreds of jeweled eyes. How had the dragonfly-auctioneer become so vast? Or had she just been masquerading as something three foot long, squinting her hugeness down into a jeweled effigy of her true self?

I do not like humans, she said. *Your hearts smell of earth and sweat. You miss notes when you sing. You bleed too easily. You walk in with stories tangled around you like briars and do not notice. You trip over everything and break it. You are too real, and it is wasted on you. I lose patience. Sign and begone.*

And so Shay Ammet and the white-eared man and Kellen the Unraveller all did as she bade and swore to the contract before the Bookbearers. Shay Ammet felt nothing, but he knew that the contract would be binding them all, strands of their souls shifting and hardening. Once payment was made, the Unraveller would be bound to servitude forever.

Shadowy ropes were hauled and a black anchor brought about, but the shouted orders sounded faint, like the distant cries of birds. A wind rose and the sails filled, the white deck tilting and tilting under Ammet's feet, and he reached out a hand to the rail to steady himself as the moon disappeared into a deep clot of cloud . . .

Then his hand found purchase on a smooth wooden surface, just in time to stop him falling. The moon sailed free again, and he realized that he was leaning against a slender mast, which supported a square sail of shimmering white spider-silk.

Ammet was standing on a raft of broken planks, webbed together with spider-silk. There was no sign of the White Boat or the Moonlit Market. All was still and quiet, except for the clouds racing over their silver-smudged reflections, the latter rippled by drips from the great, mossy trees.

On the raft beside Ammet was an oversized cage. Within it shivered Kellen the Unraveller, the boy who had put him to so much trouble and expense.

Shay Ammet gave a sigh of relief, feeling as if he were waking from a fever. The Moonlit Market had been a nightmare, in which it seemed that everything was slipping out of his control—that perhaps even *he* had been out of control. No matter; he had succeeded in his goal, and he was back in his right mind again.

"I'll need you to show a lot less initiative in the future, Kellen," he said, and was glad to hear himself sound so calm and in control. "Follow my orders, and only mine. Don't do anything to harm me or my interests. Don't try to escape or damage yourself. Don't talk unless I say you can. You can breathe, but don't do anything more without my permission."

It was important to give well-considered orders early. Right now, those would be twining their way into the fibers of Kellen's soul, becoming part of him and compelling him to obedience.

Nearby he heard a fish jump and land with a *schlop*. It made him jump, which embarrassed him. Where was he? Why hadn't Tansy come back? How was he supposed to propel this vessel without his storm-wight to fill the sails or his Gladelord to drive it forward?

"Time to make yourself useful, Kellen," he said. "Are you good at paddling?"

He glanced at the cage and froze, once again feeling that the dance floor had given way under his practiced steps. The cage door was open, and there was nobody within.

Perhaps the splash had not been a jumping fish. Ammet heard another quiet *splish* and scanned the water, spotting the head of a solitary swimmer some twenty yards away.

"Kellen! Come back!"

The boy did not obey. Why not? How could Kellen defy a contract witnessed by a Bookbearer?

Ammet snatched up a paddle and set off in pursuit. The boy made for a low, large, floating mass ahead. As Ammet drew closer, he realized that it was half of his own boat's hull.

Kellen hauled himself up onto the floating wreckage, gasping and spitting water.

"Kellen, stay exactly where you are!" Ammet tried again. "No more histrionics or heroics!"

"No, *you* stay where you are!" shouted Kellen. "That goes for you *and* your creature! Did you think I wouldn't notice?" The boy looked pointedly toward a tree ten yards from him, and Ammet realized that there was a figure standing in the shadow of the tree, hovering above the water. Its cowled shape was gray and indistinct, and there was something pale as bone where its hands should have been.

My Dancing Star. Ammet felt some of his confidence return. One by one, his possessions were returning to him.

"If either of you get any closer," yelled Kellen, "I'll drown myself! Or I'll cut my arm with this nail and jump in the water so the leeches and fish eat me!"

"I forbid you to do that!" called Ammet.

"You can't!" the boy retorted. He was shivering, but his expression was jubilantly defiant. "The contract isn't binding until you've paid! Until you've handed over Nettle, you can't order me to do anything!"

Nettle clung to her high branch, the moss soft and clammy under her touch.

How had she got here? Her memories were misty. She remembered a battle, crow-beaks agape with guttural threats, a flash of knives. She remembered dark blue blood on a moonlit deck. She remembered clambering out onto a bowsprit, grabbing at a low branch as it glided by, and dragging herself up onto it.

Beside her on the branch, something gave a faint *gluk* noise. It was Yannick, her beloved gull. He was hopping uncertainly, and one wing moved awkwardly when he fluttered it.

You're hurt, she said, feeling his pain. He had hurled himself at someone to protect her, she remembered that now.

"This is ridiculous." Tansy was staring up from her boat of bone. "Gladelord, bring her down!"

The tall, antlered being stepped out of the boat onto a half-submerged spiral of thick root, then began to swarm its way up the trunk, moonlight dappling its pale outline. Halfway up it halted, however, tentatively testing its weight on the next branch up, which creaked in protest.

The Gladelord's agility had made it seem feather-light, but Nettle now realized that it was heavier than she was. The slender branches farther up the tree could not bear its weight. It was still a foot too low to reach Nettle and would venture no further.

"You useless hat rack!" Tansy hitched her damp skirts, stepped out of the bone-boat, and began climbing the tree herself. Tansy was slender, and as she climbed past the Gladelord, the upper branches swayed under her weight but did not break. She hauled herself up onto Nettle's bough and glared at her.

Fly away, Nettle told Yannick silently, already knowing that he wouldn't leave her.

"I'm not going to wait for us both to die of cold," said Tansy, her face livid in the moonlight. "Either you climb down, or I shake the branch till you fall off."

"If I fall, I might break my neck or drown," said Nettle, heart hammering. "Mr. Ammet wants me alive, doesn't he?"

She saw a flicker of fear in Tansy's face.

"He'd forgive me," Tansy said, but she didn't sound certain.

"He doesn't care about you, or anyone else." Nettle was edging farther down the bough, feeling it bend dangerously beneath her. "He's using you. He uses everybody."

"Oh, so what?" snapped Tansy, her voice tight and unhappy. "Maybe he does. Maybe I use him too. Everyone uses everyone."

"No," said Nettle. "Not everyone. It doesn't have to be that way—"

"Stop it!" Tansy braced her back against the trunk, pushing her foot down hard against Nettle's branch. It dipped and wobbled, while Nettle clung on desperately. "Don't start the good girl act again! That's not what you are!"

"So we're cursers!" shouted Nettle. "We still have choices! We don't have to do what Mr. Ammet wants!"

"At least he accepts me!" said Tansy. "Do you want to know the truth? I'm *good* at cursing. I'm *good* at hate. I'm better at it than anything else I've ever done! This is the only power I've ever had!"

Tansy shoved at the branch again, and Nettle nearly lost her grip. Chunks of moss fell away below her, pattering on the black-and-silver leaves. Yannick flew at Tansy's face, but she knocked him aside, and the gull gave a squawk of pain, crashing lopsidedly downward through the foliage.

Yannick! Nettle sensed her brother collide with something awkwardly, his thoughts fogged with agony.

His pain filled Nettle with a blinding rage. A familiar storm rose in her head and heart, and it was hers to release if she chose.

I'm going to die here, she thought. *But I can strike back at the last. I can't curse Tansy. But I can curse Shay Ammet. I can make him wish he'd never heard my name—never wronged me, never caged my brother, never tried to use or trade me. I can cut the head from Salvation and leave it to bleed.*

Then Nettle looked up at Tansy's face. In the other curser's eyes she saw a place of blight, a dark desert where no tree grew.

"I won't do it," said Nettle. If reining in her own storm was her last and only victory, so be it. "I'm nobody's weapon. And I'm not hatred's plaything either. You can kill me, Tansy. *But you can't make me into you.*"

Tansy's face filled with rage and desolation. Too late, Nettle realized that Tansy had needed a sister in blight. Nettle had betrayed her by being less steeped in darkness. Tansy brought her foot down hard on the branch, which gave an agonized crack and groan.

"Stop!" shouted Nettle, as the branch split open near the trunk, baring strands of white wood. "Tansy, stop!"

Tansy stamped on the bough again, and Nettle felt a stomach-churning lurch as the branch broke. Nettle closed her eyes as she fell, flinching as something rushed up past her, raking her face. There was a jarring shock, and she lost her grip on the branch.

Kellen saw Ammet set down his paddle, spreading his hands in appeasement. The Salvation leader was obviously struggling to recover both his breath and his temper.

"You don't really want to die," Ammet said, "and the contract will be paid very soon. There's no point in getting off to a bad start, is there? If you're sensible, you'll find that serving me is not a bad life."

Kellen heard the unspoken threat. *If you keep causing trouble now, it'll mean trouble for you later.*

"Serving Salvation, you mean," Kellen corrected Ammet. "I'm sworn to serve them, not you."

"It's all the same," said Ammet. "I'm the leader of Salvation. I speak for them." Confident as Ammet's words were, there were cracks in his poise now, and beneath them Kellen sensed dangerous levels of anger. Perhaps Ammet wasn't used to seeing his plans fall so wildly awry.

"I know what you're planning," said Kellen. He felt that he'd never been so marrow-cold and bone-wet. When was the last time he had been properly warm and dry? "You're not going to stop ordering curses when Chancery offer you a bargain. You'll carry on using that threat to control everyone in Raddith forever. Anyone who defies you will get cursed. You'll be the secret king of Raddith, ruling by fear."

"You're wrong." Ammet looked saddened and taken aback. "All my friends want is to be granted freedom from imprisonment and persecution. If Chancery granted us that, we would happily lay down arms and live peaceably. The current war is of Chancery's making."

It all sounded so reasonable. Kellen gritted his teeth.

"So Salvation would stop cursing people if Chancery agreed to stop imprisoning cursers, is that it?"

He saw Ammet hesitate. Such a claim was a stretch even for this man, but the alternative was to admit that the cursers would continue cursing at will.

"Yes," Ammet said. "In essence. We'll stop hurting anyone if we're left alone. You must believe me."

"I do believe you." Kellen stood up, his stiff legs threatening to give under him. "Not because I trust you, but because you just said all of that in front of a Bookbearer." He turned to the shape lurking in the shadow of the tree. "You can come out now."

Ammet's face contorted in shock and rage as the gray cowled shape floated out into the moonlight. The pale object held against its chest was not a pair of bone hands but a spread book. It drifted across the water toward Ammet, its attention fixed on the oathmaker.

"Dancing Stars look a lot like Bookbearers," said Kellen, "and the other way around. So when the Bookbearer came to me on the White Boat to take my oath, I told it to meet me at this wreck after the market, to hear another oath. You're good at planning ahead. But I'm good at making lots of stupid plans really fast, and sometimes that's better."

The Bookbearer hovered in front of Shay Ammet, who stared back at it, white-faced. He was curiously rigid, as if this last shock had taken all power of motion from him.

"You speak for Salvation," said Kellen. "You said so. So now if Chancery offers the right bargain, Salvation has to accept it and stop cursing people."

"How are cursers supposed to do that?" demanded Ammet.

"We'll have to find a way together," said Kellen. "You and me and Salvation and the Little Brothers. You're clever. You can find a solution."

Shay Ammet continued staring at the Bookbearer, and Kellen wondered what he saw. His own defeat, perhaps. His intricate plans, laid over many years, unravelling before his eyes. His tight-jawed fury yielded to an unnerving calm.

"I have found a solution," Ammet said, and drew something from inside his pocket.

Kellen saw a glint of bronze as Ammet drove the blade into the indistinct face of the Bookbearer. The words that bound him were after all written in only one book, witnessed by only this Bookbearer . . .

Later, it was hard for Kellen to be sure what had happened next. There was a loud, long chime of a gong, and for a moment it seemed that the quiet air was crammed with tiny red figures. Baby-sized, eyeless yet smiling, all reaching tiny hands toward Shay Ammet. A blink later, they were all gone. The Bookbearer still floated unharmed.

The raft was empty. Shay Ammet was nowhere to be seen.

Sometime later, Kellen saw a solitary boat gliding toward him, without sail, oar, or paddle. A bedraggled female figure stood at its prow, striped with moonlight and shadow. It was an ugly, discolored boat of yellowing bones, but his spirits rose as he recognized its occupant and the black-headed gull perched on one of the thwarts.

"Over here!" he called. The bone-boat changed course and slid to a halt beside the wreck on which Kellen crouched. Nettle looked exhausted, muddy, and bruised, and there were dark stains on her clothes.

"Are you all right?" he called.

"Everything hurts," she admitted, one arm curled protectively around her ribs. "I fell from a high branch and hit another pretty hard. And I'm really wet and cold."

Kellen's own drenched clothing was miserably uncomfortable too, but that wasn't the most urgent consideration.

"Tansy's after you!" he said.

"No," said Nettle, looking rather unwell. "She isn't. You know everyone says you should never damage a tree in the Deep Wilds? Well . . . it turns out if you do, a Gladelord cuts your head off and hangs it on a branch."

"Oh." Kellen blinked, feeling shocked and saddened. Tansy had cursed him, but he hadn't wished a fate like that upon her. "And . . . the Gladelord?"

"It watched me for a while, and then it was gone. Only its silver collar left behind."

"Its contract with Shay Ammet came to an end," said Kellen. He winced. "He's, um, not here anymore. Attacking a Bookbearer seems to be a pretty bad idea too."

He hesitated.

"I tricked Ammet into saying some things in front of a Bookbearer," he went on. "He promised that Salvation wouldn't curse anymore, if Chancery agreed to stop persecuting them."

"Clever," said Nettle, and managed a small, subdued smile. "So Chancery can stop Salvation being a threat. We did it, then. We saved Raddith."

But that doesn't help the cursers in Salvation, Kellen thought. *Or Nettle*.

Kellen hadn't planned for this moment. They were no longer bickering, inseparable allies. They were the Unraveller and a lone curser, and their shared mission was over.

He didn't know what to say to her. Too much had happened, too many secrets had detonated like grenadoes. He didn't know what words to throw across the ravaged land between them. She looked rather embarrassed and uncertain too.

What do I say? I can't tell her everything's fine, because it isn't. I can't tell her nothing's changed, because it has.

"I couldn't tell you," said Nettle quietly.

It still stung that she hadn't, but Kellen could see why.

"I catch cursers," he said. "You thought I'd hand you in."

"I was too afraid to tell anyone, Kellen!" Nettle's eyes were bright with anguish. "Nobody would understand. And if I did tell someone, that would make it *real*. I just kept hoping it would go away. When the dark place in me started to grow, I told myself it wasn't happening. And if it was, then I would just make it better by force of will. I just *couldn't* be a curser. They were all monsters, weren't they? Everyone agreed on that. But then one day a giant black Swan came gliding toward me down a crowded street, and I ran. I told myself I'd outdistanced it. Isn't that stupid? I carried on as if nothing had happened. And sometimes I didn't see it for ages, and I started to hope that I'd got away. Of course I hadn't. The bad times got worse and happened more often. Do you know how frightening it is, when you can't trust yourself?"

Kellen thought of cloth unravelling and skin fraying from flesh.

"Yeah," he said. "I think I understand that better now."

"I don't know what happens now," said Nettle, sounding desolate and exhausted. "I can't see a way forward. Just black water all around."

Kellen racked his mind desperately.

"Listen," he said. "You could just . . . put your curse on me, couldn't you? Then I could unravel it, and you wouldn't have a curse egg anymore, and nobody else would ever have to know!"

"That's ridiculous!" Nettle looked utterly taken aback. "What if I turned you into a slug?"

"Well . . . then I'd be a brilliant slug," insisted Kellen. "An unravelling slug!"

"That's . . ." Nettle's face crumpled, her voice sounding unusually teary. "That's the most idiotic idea you've ever had. I don't want to curse anyone—definitely not you!"

"Sorry," Kellen said again, feeling that he was doing everything wrong, and then became aware that Nettle was helplessly laughing. He was caught off guard when she stepped off the boat onto his floating wreck and hugged him hard.

"Careful!" he said. "I don't want to unravel you—I'm still cursed!" But Nettle held on, and he tentatively hugged her back. It felt odd to be holding her small, tense, bony frame.

"You're such an idiot," she said.

"You're a fine one to talk, Miss I'll-Just-Run-off-into-a-Nest-of-Cursers-without-Explaining," he grumbled.

"If it helps with the unravelling, I can tell you why Tansy cursed you," Nettle said hesitantly, her arms still around him.

"I think I'm already starting to work that out," Kellen said slowly. "It's because I'm an idiot, isn't it?"

"Maybe a bit," said Nettle.

"I thought I understood curses because I could see their threads and pull them apart," said Kellen. "But I didn't. I'm sorry, I never understood what it was like being cursed. And I didn't understand cursers at all. I didn't even notice what was happening to my best friend."

He'd never called her that before. It was accurate but also sounded too weak somehow. Nettle was family and more than family.

"When I found out you were a curser," he continued, "the world turned upside down. I couldn't think straight. I tried to see you as my enemy . . . but I just kept remembering all the times you'd kept me alive. No, I *knew* you were my friend. Smart, brave, and probably the most sensible person I know. If you were a curser, that meant I was wrong about cursers. It means *everyone* is wrong about cursers."

Nettle had bottled up a curse for a year, but he no longer knew if that was exceptional. Maybe there were hundreds of Nettles out there, suffering in silence as they fought for control.

“Cursers are just people,” Nettle said. “The ones I met at Salvation—most of them were kind, loyal, or well-meaning. They’re not monsters. But nobody understands that.”

“Well, *I* do now,” Kellen said. “So it’s not enough to stop Salvation, is it? We have to save them as well.”

Nettle pulled back and examined his face. She was as inscrutable as ever, but he thought he saw a hint of hope.

“I have one more plan,” said Kellen. “It’s terrible and you’ll hate it. Do you want to hear it?”

EPILOGUE

IN THE DOVE-GRAY HOURS BEFORE DAWN, NETTLE STEPPED OFF her boat of bone and followed Kellen into the silk castle of the Little Brothers. She walked into a hall of trembling, milk-pale webs, where a thousand tiny eyes glistened like fractured glass. Nettle didn't like being the focus of so much attention, but there was no help for it.

"I'm Nettle," she called out. "I was promised to you by contract at the Moonlit Market. I'm a curser who was once cursed. A circle completed. A snake biting its own tail. I'm here to deliver myself to you in payment."

So now the contract from the Moonlit Market is paid and fulfilled. Nettle steeled herself and tried not to panic. *I belong to the Little Brothers, and Kellen is bound to Salvation. But this is the right path, thorny as it is. It's the only way to make a difference.*

"There's another reason I'm here," Nettle continued, raising her voice. "I'm here to tell you what it was like to be cursed and how it feels to have a curse living inside me, like a leech on my soul that I can't pull away. I'm here to tell you what your 'gifts' have done to me and to many others. You have already heard my friend Kellen. Will you listen to me?"

The nervous man that Kellen called Cook stayed very still for a time, his silken ears swiveling attentively. Then he looked her in the eye.

"My masters will hear you," he said.

So Nettle spoke with the Little Brothers for hours at a time over many days. She told them about the Rescued and Salvation, about Tansy and Ammet. She told them of Spike, Linnet, Pale Mallow, and Leona. She told them of Clover, Blask, Jendy, and Rue.

She told them of Yannick, Iris, and Cole. She told them of Nettle.

And the Little Brothers listened.

Kellen was relieved to find that Cherrick Gall was still alive. His horse was suffering from the strain of sustaining him, however. It lay sprawled outside the castle, its hide dank and dull, its eyes covered with white flakes like frost.

Harland had been brought back to the castle by Cook after the Moonlit Market. When Kellen emerged from a long conference with the Little Brothers, he was unsurprised to find Harland waiting for him with an expression of exhausted hope.

"The Little Brothers say they're willing to try," said Kellen, holding up Ammet's two throat-boxes. He had spent hours talking the web-sprites into cooperating with his idea, but now he felt apprehensive. Perhaps his plan would lead to the very tragedy he was trying to avoid. "You do know this is really risky, don't you?"

Harland tried to say something, then gave an embarrassed smile and a small shrug.

Yannick rode the air, feeling the temper and texture of it in every plume and nerve. For a while he flew with a cloud of gray gulls, who accepted him as almost-us, but then he pushed on for Mizzleport, the message-tube hanging round his neck.

When he brought Nettle's note to the Rescued, they learned of Tansy's betrayal with deep shock and dismay. The message was in Nettle's handwriting, however, so they believed it. Tansy had always been their sunshine, a warmth and light from above that gave them hope, but Nettle was something more. She was the quiet, accepting pool where they could drop their jagged feelings. She had listened to them properly and heard some of the things they could not say.

There was a second note for the Rescued to pass on to Chancery. This met with a less positive reception.

Why were two young vagabonds telling Raddith's elite diplomats and officials how to conduct their most important negotiation? One was a self-confessed curser, the other a fugitive from justice, and their story was clearly an absurd fabrication!

Human speech was always a little deep for Yannick's gull-ears, grating and churring unpleasantly, but he had no trouble eavesdropping on the officials. Soon he wanted to yell insults his beak could not shape.

The only notable who listened was Leona Tharl.

Though still cursed, she had intermittent periods of lucidity, and Yannick happened to deliver a copy of the letter to her house during one of these. Unfortunately, she no longer had power or influence in Chancery, since nobody wanted to trust anything important to an easily distracted bat.

She could, however, instruct her servants to bring a paper with the letters of the alphabet scrawled on it for Yannick to peck. It was a slow means of communication, but the two winged beings began to hatch plans of their own.

Kellen arrived at Salvation's boat-village in the flooded barrow not a moment too soon, and in some respects several days too late. The stronghold had been safe only because Shay Ammet's contracted creatures had been guarding the perimeter. With his death, the contracts expired. They all abandoned their posts, some of them claiming a life or two first, out of spite, after which the boat-village was undefended.

The members of Salvation retreated to the innermost boats of the village and burned torches at night to keep the worst of the dark beings at bay. Nonetheless, the Gallow Glimmers closed in, glossy as dead men's eyes. At twilight, the song of the White-Handed Ladies lured stragglers into the reed-forest, never to be seen again. Among the eels that were not eels swam a great marsh wyrm, its long snaking back blotched yellow and brown like a rotting apple. Nobody dared forage or hunt. Food ran low, and fuel ran out.

Kellen would not have been much help by himself, but he was not alone. Beside his borrowed boat of bone glided a glossily sleek marsh horse, shoulder-deep in the water. On its back rode a tall and ominous figure wearing a dark gray coat of clotted marsh silk and a red eye-patch.

Given previous bloody encounters, the last person anyone in Salvation wanted to see was Cherrick Gall. However, the sight of rider and horse tearing apart the giant marsh wyrm that had been attacking the boat-village helped diplomatic relations a lot.

While everyone in the camp was still staring aghast at the reddened water, Kellen climbed up onto a wheelhouse and rang the bell to get their attention. Seeing so many hostile faces, and a few dark flickers of curse rage, he tried to suppress his feelings of panic.

"You've probably heard of me," he said, "and I don't blame any of you who hate me. But I'm here to help you now. I won't betray you. I *can't* betray you. I've got a contract to prove it."

He told them of the death of Ammet and the bargain that had been sealed. There were panicky murmurs when the cursers heard of the last promises Ammet had made before a Bookbearer.

"So if we make a bargain with Chancery, none of us can ever cast a curse again?" asked one woman. "What about those of us who already have a curse egg? We can't hold it in forever! What are we supposed to do?"

"We'd have to leave Salvation if we felt the curse coming on," said the man next to her. "And then we'd be alone in the Deep Wilds, with nowhere to go. We'd die!"

This was the difficult part, the moment when Kellen might win or lose the hearts of his listeners. Their faces might darken with distrust as they reached for their weapons.

"I'm the Unraveller," he said. "I unravel curses. Until now, I've unravelled curses that had already been cast. I never even wondered if there was another way. But . . . I've been talking to the Little Brothers, and maybe there's a way to unravel a curse while it's still in the egg. It won't be easy, and . . . I can't do it without your help."

There were uncertain murmurs, and some exchanged dark glances.

"I'm not saying you have to give up your anger!" he went on quickly. "I think anger's all right, actually. Lots of you have been treated badly, and most of you never asked for any of this. But . . . hate's different. It eats you up and makes everything worse. You've all suffered enough already, haven't you?"

Ammet wanted me contracted to him alone, but I'm bound to serve Salvation. So I'll find a way to help them. I'll save them from shackles and the Red Hospital. I'll save them from being used by people like Shay Ammet. I'll help them find a way through their pain, if I can.

Cherrick Gall listened too, quietly recovering his breath. He had always been gray-faced, but now he looked haggard and ill in a much more human way. Sometimes Kellen caught him glancing around, as if the world were a stranger and brighter one than he was used to seeing. After his injury, he clearly had not expected to wake again, yet here he was.

Kellen was probably the only one to notice that Gall's fighting style had changed too. He was less reckless in his ferocity, a little more careful and hesitant. Kellen could guess why. Gall had more to lose now after all.

In Cherrick Gall's chest, where his old heart had been, the Little Brothers had placed a loop of woven stems, taken from one of Shay Ammet's boxes. The loop from the other box now enclosed the living heart of Harland Melbrook. Together the loops were a "throat," two places that were really one, so a phantom heart now beat in Gall's chest. It was still only one heart beating for two people, however, so the death of one of them would kill the other.

Gall now had to treat his own life as valuable, and he did not seem used to this at all.

Wearing his silver collar, Yannick shambled awkwardly into the silken castle, his gray-white wings folded.

"Chancery aren't listening to us," he told the Little Brothers bluntly. "We need a new plan. They might listen to *you*, but you'd need an envoy. Someone who can travel from here to there." He grinned.

"Someone with wings, maybe . . . Give my sister her freedom, and you can have a winged ambassador in exchange. Two, in fact. Two for the price of one."

Yannick knew that Nettle would be furious if she knew what he was proposing, but he had no intention of leaving her in the same castle as a silk-eared man whose curse might strike her dead at the wrong phase of the moon.

After listening to his chittering masters for a long time, Cook cleared his throat.

"You are split-souled," he said. "You chose your curse when you might have been freed from it, and that makes you . . . complicated. And perhaps useful. But if you are to serve my masters, you and your curse might benefit from some . . . modifications."

The new Head of Contracts liked to watch the sunrise from his roof garden while enjoying his first cup of tea. One morning, however, he reached his garden to find someone waiting for him in the gray light.

The lanky youth was dressed in clothes of white marsh silk. His hair was wild, his movements off kilter. Spiders crawled over his face and shoulders.

"How did you get up here?"

"The same way I plan to leave." There was something odd about the youth's smile. "You might say I'm an ambassador. And my masters are *very* keen that you give this letter your full attention." He perched a white envelope on a trellis.

The official shouted for his servants, who sprinted upstairs to protect their employer. Instead of showing any fear, the youth began to laugh.

As the first rays of the sun gleamed on the horizon, the laugh became a deafening scream. Bulges like gnat bites appeared on the boy's skin, then burst open to reveal tiny tufts of white down. The boy spread his arms, then seemed to warp and shrink, his screams becoming higher and more grating.

His clothes fell to the ground, and a winged thing erupted into the air. By the time it had vanished from sight, its scream was the thin, nerve-racking *khaaaah* of a black-headed gull.

After reading the letter from the Little Brothers, Chancery took the suggestions of the "two young vagabonds" a lot more seriously.

Word spread that the Little Brothers now had two ambassadors, a gull-boy and a bat-woman.

"It's perfect!" said Leona firmly, accepting a cup of broth from Cook. "I'm human by day, and a bat at night. Your brother"—she nodded at the gull on Nettle's shoulder—"will be a human at night and a gull by day. One of us will always be able to fly to the Little Brothers in an emergency." It was strange to see the Assessor full-sized and human. She made the Little Brothers' white clotted-silk jacket look smart and official.

"But you'll never lose your curses!" protested Nettle, who hadn't made her peace with the price of her freedom.

"A small price to pay to become an intermediary between the Wilds and mankind!" smirked Leona. "My old colleagues were livid with envy."

I suppose you get to live your two lives after all, Nettle told Yannick a little brusquely, but she couldn't be angry with him. Even now, she knew he was thinking of his nest, mate, and chicks.

"Does the Pact allow ambassadors?" asked Nettle. To her surprise, Leona laughed.

"Who knows?" said Leona. "There are good reasons why Chancery doesn't show people that document. It's an unbelievable *mess*. The humans negotiating it were all panic-drunk, and the great creatures of the Wilds don't think the way we do. Some pages are covered in paw prints or burned with golden tears. The two sides might as well have been trying to communicate by waving fish at each other from opposite shores. Everybody knows the bones of the agreement, and nobody is completely sure of the details. But the Pact works, because everyone wants it to work. Never underestimate the power of good intentions."

"I won't be able to protect you if you're flying to the Wilds, Assessor," said Gall, who appeared to be the only person other than Nettle with doubts about the new bargain.

"Of course you won't," said Leona. "Gall, I'm dispensing with your services."

Gall blinked his one eye and stared at his employer as if she had unexpectedly hit him with a rock.

"What?"

"You're useless to me now," Leona said cheerfully. "I can't send you into a fight without endangering a civilian, can I? And why should I waste money keeping a carriage when I can fly anywhere I like at night?"

"But . . . the contract was for life," said Gall slowly.

"Your pact with the horse is for life," Leona corrected him. "Your contract with me lasts as long as I want, and I'm releasing you from it. I think I've got my money's worth out of you. *Go home*, you stupid boy."

So he did.

The negotiations between Chancery and Salvation took many months, but at last a treaty was sealed before a Bookbearer. A base would be established for Salvation in the Shallow Wilds, somewhere safer than their boat-village in the flooded barrow. Chancery would not try to arrest them or interfere with their supplies, as long as Salvation kept the peace. Chancery would keep the location of the base secret so that no armed vigilantes went in search of them. Those carrying curse eggs, on the other hand, were allowed to flee to Salvation.

Any Salvation members whose curse eggs Kellen managed to unravel would be allowed to return inland. It was this prospect, more than anything else, that persuaded Salvation to agree.

It was not a perfect treaty, but such things never are. It was also clear that it would take far longer for the people of Raddith to regard cursers with anything but terror and stop recoiling from them.

"Sometimes you just have to annoy people," said Leona. "Changing a law is like digging a new field. You'll break ancient roots and blunt your spade on a lot of stones, but eventually plants will grow in your furrows, and your new hedge will thrive, and it'll be as though it was always that way."

When people heard that a girl from Salvation had talked the Little Brothers into being much more careful and infrequent with their curse eggs, attitudes toward the exiled cursers began to change. It helped that Kellen was now lifting curses with the cooperation of Salvation. Soon the little cloud-girl was safely back with her family, and the others cursed on Ammet's orders were returned to their rightful forms.

Gradually the idea of a "cure" for cursers took hold. When Kellen visited the Red Hospital to talk about the treatment of the cursers, the head physician, Dr. Lethenbark, was cautiously enthusiastic. They talked and talked, and in their minds a new Red Hospital began to take shape, one where shackles and helms were replaced by a long, slow path to understanding and finally freedom.

As Kellen had feared, unravelling a curse egg was difficult and painfully slow. He couldn't just solve a puzzle, free a victim, and walk away as he had done before. Instead, he had to spend long hours talking and listening. Sometimes he would unpick little threads of rage and grief, only to find that they grew back like weeds. The task did not suit his impatient nature, but like many things, patience can be learned.

The cursers of Salvation still sometimes frightened him, but he no longer felt the same instinctive recoil. He knew them all too well and understood the pain, loneliness, and fear that often lurked beneath their hate.

Watching Rue's face crumple as she handled new sketches of her daughters and real letters sent by them, Kellen could sense another few threads of darkness pulling loose and floating away. A little less haunted, and one step closer to seeing her children again. Such small victories were hard-won but filled him with pride.

"You'd be better at it than me!" he told Nettle when he visited her. "This sort of Unravelling doesn't feel like I'm using a magical gift.

Sometimes it's like I'm a ghost walking alongside somebody on a difficult journey. I can point out things they've missed, but I can't walk for them. I can't stop the briars tearing them or their feet aching. I've never done anything so *hard*."

"Trust me, it's harder for them!" said Nettle tartly, then blushed at her own outburst.

"I know." Kellen wasn't offended. He rather liked the fact that Nettle tended to voice her annoyance these days. While he was learning to rein in his temper, she was discovering how to show her anger instead of bottling it up.

Naturally, Nettle had been the first curser whose curse egg he had set out to unravel. It had been difficult for both of them. Nettle's habits of secrecy had been hard for her to overcome, but gradually she had become better at talking. Their mutual trust had helped.

Kellen's intuition had grown keener as the months passed. After a while he could sense her curse egg growing smaller and softer. It kept trying to pull itself back together, but eventually it became too weak to do even that. Nettle was now allowed inland on probation but had to wear a lot of iron in her clothes for the moment.

The Rescued needed Nettle more than ever, now that ex-cursers were joining their ranks as well as the ex-cursed. She had never thought of herself as the leader of the Rescued, but apparently everyone else had.

She lived at Tansy's eating house, which Leona Tharl had bought for the Rescued. It was haunted by memories of Tansy, but not all those memories were bad. Besides, one cannot throw away everything that is touched by pain.

Kellen had even more iron sewn into his clothes. The metal plates were heavy and clanked annoyingly, but Chancery insisted on it until his curse was lifted so that he was less likely to unravel anybody. Kellen was learning tricks of calm and suspected this helped more than the iron.

"How's the curse?" asked Nettle.

"Unravelling slowly," said Kellen, with a wry grimace. He felt squeamish untangling his own threads, as if he were operating on his own innards.

He had known that the only way to lift his curse was to do something big, change course, and atone as best he could. As it turned out, the long, slow salvation of Salvation was exactly what was needed.

But even if it wasn't, I'd be doing it anyway, he thought.

He rubbed at the spider-bite on his wrist and for the first time felt no regret. *If I hadn't been bitten, if I hadn't been thrown out of Kyttelswall, if I hadn't been cursed, I wouldn't be here right now. And this is where I need to be.*

Cole looked up from his book and saw the figure he had longed to see walking nervously toward him.

Nettle looks like Iris these days. The thought hurt, but it was now one that he could bear.

Her absence had been a daily ache. He could not help filling the empty space by imagining her resenting him, reproaching him, hating him. But still he had always hoped she would come back. Everyone else was kind, but nobody else understood.

He noticed her pallor and the iron in her clothes.

"I'm sorry I've not come for so long," she said. Apparently she was more nervous than he was. "I've been in a bad place. Several of them."

"Are you all right?"

"Better than I was." Nettle gave him a wary glance. "Can I tell you about it?"

They talked. And it hurt, the way opening a wound to clean it always hurts. And they agreed to talk again.

Tomorrow Nettle will wake up feeling lighter, as some burden eases. Tonight, however, she dreams of the Swan for the last time.

She is in the reed-forest of the Deep Wilds. It is the golden time before sunset, and something large is crashing through the reeds toward her. This time she does not flee, even as the sky darkens and

the wind wails with a human voice. She stands there on the quay outside a stilt hut and waits.

The Swan breaks from cover, its black feathers slick with blood, holding out the pale, wriggling thing in its unnatural hands.

Take it, the Swan begs her, in its sob of a voice.

"Hush!" Nettle reaches out and gently takes the cygnet from the Swan, wrapping it carefully in her shawl. It is not really ugly or horrible, she realizes, just very young, vulnerable, and cold. "Poor little thing. I'll look after you." She glances up and sees that the Swan's miserable, frantic eyes are her own. "I'll look after both of you."

She stoops, dips a cloth in the marsh water, and begins cleaning the blood from the Swan's feathers, leaving them glossy black. After a while, it stops wailing and quietly weeps instead.

"It'll be all right," Nettle says, and means it.

ACKNOWLEDGMENTS

I would like to thank everyone at Macmillan for being endlessly supportive and patient when my ability to write was swallowed by pandemic brain fog; Martin, for putting up with me when I was stir-crazy, squirrelly, and forcibly squeezing words out of my brain like toothpaste from a tube; my editor, Rachel Petty, for helping me wrestle a gargantuan word-monster into submission; Rhiannon, for wise, clear-sighted feedback; R and Jen, for taking me to the misty, mysterious, moss-covered forests of La Gomera; my agent, Nancy, for kindness and good sense; my sensitivity reader, Charlie; Mike Parker, for inspiring me with the gift of a small, perfect hag stone; the British Radical History Group's resources on the Spitalfield weavers; *The Gull Next Door* by Marianne Taylor; *The Herons Handbook* by James Hancock and James Kushlan; *Folklore of Lincolnshire* by Susanna O'Neill; *The Wild Swans* by Hans Christian Andersen; the legend of the Children of Lir; Scottish tales of the kelpie; and Northumbrian stories of braags and bargyests. Finally, I would like to thank the black-headed gulls who wheel exuberantly over the Thames, and the herons that grew bold during lockdown, watching me with ominous poise from walls and lampposts as I walked the quiet streets.

ABOUT THE AUTHOR

Frances Hardinge is the winner of the 2015 Costa Book of the Year for *The Lie Tree*, one of just two young adult novels to win this major UK literary prize. She is the author of several books for young people, including *Cuckoo Song*, *Fly By Night*, *Verdigris Deep*, and *A Face Like Glass*. She lives in England.